Praise for *Before Us Like a Land of Dreams*

"A narrative extravaganza that ponders the bristled roots of ancestry, unbroken by time or place, and the muddled truths and fallacies of family history that inform who we believe we are. This masterwork flouts expectations."

—*FOREWORD REVIEWS* (starred review)

"Anderson deploys voices from the American West as idiosyncratic as the southern voices that make up Faulkner's *As I Lay Dying*. The book's revelations and mysteries illuminate our own sketchy histories, the true stories we construct that are anything but whole but that help us survive. We all live in the Land of Dreams, which is to say in the land of our own and our ancestors' stories."

—SCOTT ABBOTT, author of *Wild Rides and Wildflowers*

"With this collection of imaginative, interlaced novellas based on the author's own family, Anderson explores the thorny entanglements of family, religion, and self, asking—with crisp, evocative prose—what portion of our lives do we direct, and what portion rests upon the 'dark hazards' of ancestral preordination?"

—JANA RICHMAN, author of *Finding Stillness in a Noisy World* and *The Ordinary Truth*

"Anderson's keen prose shreds the myths of American history . . . Previously erased, queers populate the small towns as well as the liminal spaces between settlements in the West and Midwest. If you prefer your American history whitewashed for purity, this book isn't for you. If you prefer [to] be cognizant, for example, of the indigenous genocide committed by heroes of the West, you will find, in Anderson's vision, a stark and tr̶ ̶ ̶ ̶ ̶ with white legacies."

—MICHAEL WALSH

BEFORE US
LIKE A LAND
OF DREAMS

BEFORE US
LIKE A LAND
OF DREAMS

a novel

Karin Anderson

TORREY HOUSE PRESS

SALT LAKE CITY • TORREY

This is a work of fiction. Any resemblance to actual events or persons, living or dead, is entirely coincidental.

"Invocation: Tooele Valley Threnody" was first published as "Tooele Valley Threnody" in *Nights Like These*, Fiddleblack Annual 2, 2014.

First Torrey House Press Edition, May 2019
Copyright © 2019 by Karin Anderson

Published by Torrey House Press
Salt Lake City, Utah
www.torreyhouse.org

International Standard Book Number: 978-1-948814-03-4
E-book ISBN: 978-1-948814-04-1
Library of Congress Control Number: 2018952003

Cover design by Kathleen Metcalf
Interior design by Rachel Davis
Distributed to the trade by Consortium Book Sales and Distribution

CONTENTS

My name is Legion: for we are many.

—Mark 5:9

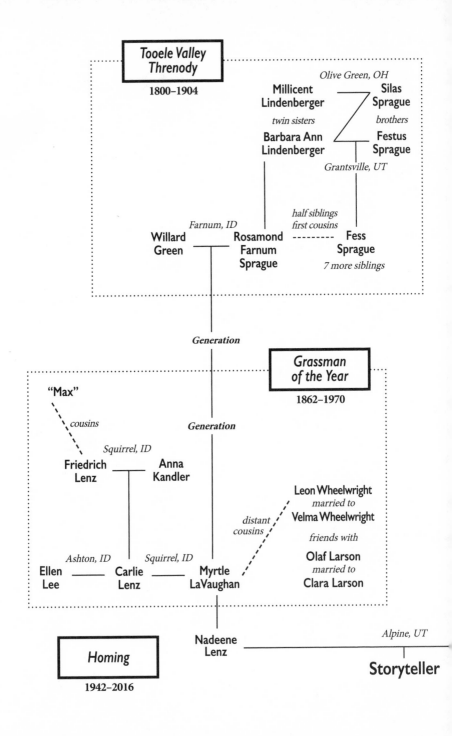

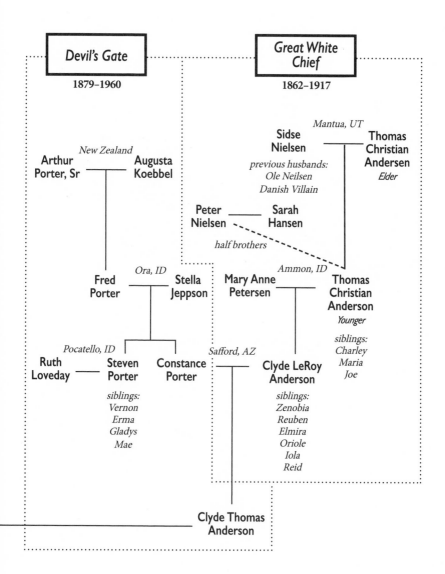

Devil's Gate

1879–1960

Great White Chief

1862–1917

Mantua, UT

Sidse Nielsen

previous husbands:
Ole Neilsen
Danish Villain

Thomas Christian Andersen

Elder

New Zealand

Arthur Porter, Sr —— **Augusta Koebbel**

Peter Nielsen —— **Sarah Hansen**

half brothers

Fred Porter

Ora, ID

Stella Jeppson

Mary Anne Petersen

Ammon, ID

Thomas Christian Anderson

Younger

siblings:
Charley
Maria
Joe

Pocatello, ID

Ruth Loveday —— **Steven Porter**

Constance Porter

Safford, AZ

Clyde LeRoy Anderson

siblings:
Vernon
Erma
Gladys
Mae

siblings:
Zenobia
Reuben
Elmira
Oriole
Iola
Reid

Clyde Thomas Anderson

HOMING

I get paid to call attention to the beautiful mysteries of life. Here's one: isn't it weird that I trade words for money? I've racked a slim retirement fund by making certain noises at certain hours. Certain marks on certain screens. But five years off the finish line I don't know that I have the stamina to collect. How many more earnest lies can I produce?

I tell my children so often they hear it as maternal white noise that every person who gets dropped onto this planet will trudge through sorrow. But not everybody gets to take in the goodness we've seen. And not many can keep hoping for more. We're not starving. We're not yet fleeing our homeland. We live in the remnants of a beautiful place. We love each other even as we drift in strange directions. Lies, maybe. Earnest, yes.

I used to believe the stories we told were more or less reliable maps of the universe. But the longer I look the weirder they get. A story is an incorporation of ghosts, morphing over the huge landscapes of our very small lives. I don't believe in ghosts but even so they interrupt when I wish to think about something else. Sometimes I fight my way through a crowd just to mutter Good Morning to the actual bodies at the kitchen counter.

A homeless guy at the Salt Lake Central station usually reaches the peak of dispute with his own legion just as I catch the commuter train for work: "Oh yeah? You have no idea what you're talking about you crazy fuck! Fuck you! Get the fuck away from me, you disgusting fucks!"

5

The train comes in. People get off. People get on. The train pulls out. Sometimes he's still there when I return, but by evening he's either beaten back the disgusting fucks or this is the hour they've overcome him. I believe he keeps the plaza safe for the rest of us and I'm grateful.

I used to watch my now-dead father walk around the house and yard quietly retorting to his personal ghosts. I smirked but now I answer to him in my own hours. He shows up in various ages and moods. He comes in settings and scenes. Although we come from Utah and Idaho, my early memories take shape in southern California. I was three when my parents rented a little pink house in Santa Ana, four when we moved to Canoga Park (a pomegranate tree from the yard behind ours draped its generous branches over the fence), and midway through kindergarten the year they bought a two-story house in Brea, in a brand-new subdivision shaved out of shady Steinbeck-era avocado groves.

In Canoga Park I went to school with children who were mostly as pale-faced as I was, but there were kids across the tonal spectrum. My just-older sister Marti had a friend named Allison Toyota, willowy and glamorous. Her shining black hair was sculpted into bangs and a clean pixie line at the back of her neck. Allison was smart like Marti. Allison spoke to me like a nice sister, petting my shoulders and smiling down from her slender height. I was enamored and wished for such a friend of my own. During playtime in the kindergarten yard, on the sunny edge of the kidney-shaped sandbox, Mrs. Updegraaf told us to reach for one another's hands and I obeyed, happy to make contact with a girl who resembled Allison Toyota. But she jerked her hand away and pushed me backward. She said, "You don't hold my hand! You're not my friend!" and turned to beckon a flowing princess with yellow ringlets who promptly sprang to. They giggled and turned in my direction and the girl with ringlets said, "We hate you! You think you're so smart!"

I learned nothing from any of this because my thinking was rudimentary and my emotions were as nuanced as the eight-color box of extra fat crayons allotted to my classroom desk.

Also in my class was my friend Sally, who lived down the street from us. We lived in a tossed-up tucked-back house. Sibling-less, Sally lived with her mother and father in an adjoining cul-de-sac. Their house was big and in my world deluxe. Sometimes Marti and I fantasized about being an only child with the whole run of a mansion, so we wistfully pictured ourselves in Sally's position. Sally looked enough like Corey on *Julia* that I understood my friend was black, but I could make no sense of this because her mother did not look at all like the nurse I loved on the TV series. My own mother wore a crisp white dress like Julia's to work, and a cap with a velvet stripe that I happily understood to signify the most important kind of nurse. Later I heard my parents mention that Sally was adopted, which explained why Sally's parents did not look how I had imagined. My parents also noted, in the kind of conversation parents don't believe children listen to, that Sally's family was Catholic. My Mormon blood congealed; I knew her family was doomed without the true gospel.

Sally was fun and diverting, and sometimes annoying and bossy and complicated just like the rest of my friends. I attended her birthday party, a large affair with art supplies and paintbrushes and a culminating show for our parents. We sat at a long table covered with butcher paper. I liked to draw and paint. I quickly became engrossed in whatever it was I was depicting, and every time I dipped the brush into the water cup I blew on it gently to stop the dripping. From across the table Sally told me to stop it because she was getting sprayed a little, but I kept it up because I meant no harm. And anyway I was one of the guests, so I was surprised when her mother scolded me for being stubborn and rude. It took me a long time to learn something from this: for one thing, my tribe clings fiercely to the intentional fallacy. No harm meant, no harm done. So don't tell us to stop it.

Later, after we moved to Brea, our mother sat Marti and me down for a little talk she must have been planning for a long time. She said, "Did you two know that your friend Sally was a little Negro child?"

I looked at my sister, who looked back at me with her eyebrows raised. We had a sister moment that would evolve into teenage eye rolling. It was as if our mother had set us down to explain, "Did you two realize that Tommy is your little brother?"

"Yeah," I said.

Marti said, "Uh-huh."

Our mother, who was gentle and smart and tough, always well meaning, looked peeved and said, "Oh, for heaven's sake. You did not!"

Marti and I had a sense at least that there were stories out there beyond our own. This was the United States of America, 1967. Our father came home from work to watch *The Huntley–Brinkley Report* (I thought it was Honey–Brinkley). Dad read a magazine called *Time* and sometimes we opened the old issues to scrutinize the photographs. Hippies were a ubiquity beyond the sidewalks of our shiny new suburbia. Although our parents refused to elaborate, we all pointed hippies out when we saw them. Once, driving out of the Malibu tunnel, my edgy-in-Utah, square-in-California parents, three little kids in the back seat, had been stopped still on the highway by a massive love-in. A churning sea of barely clad people surrounded our car. I perceived them as grownups. A skinny white guy wearing a furry kitchen rug as a vest seated himself on the hood of our little Ford Rambler. His long hair flowed like dirty water as he leaned in to wave at us kids. A creamy brown woman in a bikini top and enormous Afro strolled to the side windows and blew us all a warm kiss. Her teeth were white and her eyes dark liquid brown.

Our father flexed his square clean jaw.

Bodies milled and gyrated around us in a hot smear of humanity. Peace and love and sweating stink.

"What's happening?" my sister asked. "How do they know us?"

"Hippies!" our father said, staring straight forward, gripping the wheel as if he were still driving.

"What *are* hippies?" I had been wondering this for a long time.

"*Those* are hippies!" Dad said. "Right there! Take a look!"

Tommy gazed from his car seat and fell asleep in the heat.

That's all we got from our father.

Our dad spent two years as a Mormon missionary in the humid green maze of North Carolina. He'd already served time in the military, stationed in Japan during the Korean War. He'd lost his father a few years back to an exploding jet en route to Cairo. At twenty-three he was a bit older than the standard missionary. I don't know why he decided, late, on serving a mission. But then again I do. We resist and cling; he was answering to a dead, angry, exacting father.

Missionary dress code at the time required the white shirt and tie still characteristic of the young "Elders" who sift the streets of nearly every city on the planet. My dad didn't love the tie, especially in the Southern heat but he said he could live with it. Much worse, in 1958 the missionaries were compelled to wear Rat Pack fedoras well beyond their fashion wave. Once, Dad said, he and his companion stopped their bikes at a crosswalk in Raleigh, waiting for a green light beside a bouquet of campus girls on the sidewalk. My dad had an easy grin, perfect teeth, and a manly cleft chin. His current companion was long and lean, a scarecrow under a Bing Crosby hat. Elders and coeds eyed each other, everybody coy. Elder Anderson shot a grin toward a pretty brunette. The girl smiled wide and sang, "*M-I-C-K-E-Y . . .*"

Peals of high-pitched laughter. The light changed and the Mormons hit the pedals.

* * *

Grand entertainment in our home in 1967, Brea, California, consisted of watching our father wrangle a roll-up tripod screen while our mother closed the curtains against the suburban light. One of us kids was granted the honor of flipping the switch on the industrial-strength green projector. The hot little fan inside emitted a faintly chemical breeze. The sculptured avocado-hued carpet scratched our crisscrossed ankles but it didn't matter. This was a magic show in a way my own children, who carry telephones with tiny movie screens, who take pictures and post them to five hundred people in a couple of digital moves, will never appreciate.

I loved seeing the pictures of my sister Marti and me snug and adorable in snapwaist footie pajamas, or dolled up in Easter bonnets on Utah's Capitol Hill or running on tiny legs toward the receding California surf. In 1967 I turned five, so those photos were arrested fragments of a very recent past. For me they encompassed all the time there ever was. But for our parents they were vivid moments in the continuum of much longer lives.

I disliked the glowing images of my father in a tie and hat. What is now to me a charming photograph of a young man feeding pigeons in a deciduous park was vaguely ominous then. The fedora signified an intractable past. I strained to see beyond the boundaries of the screen, shifting sideways and craning my neck to perceive something more. It seemed my parents could float right into the scenes. Spurred by the visual prompts, they carried on with stories. They left us children behind in their murmurs and concurrings. They laughed at private jokes. In those moments they were people from another world and it frightened me. Maybe I caught some metaphorical whiff of nonbeing, the voids before and after a brief slideshow. It was a world in which I was not even a premonition. Nor my sister nor little brother. My youngest sister Teri is similarly unnerved by photographs of us before her time: she just doesn't exist.

It strikes me now that the brightly lit images held the sweet- est seasons of my mother's life. She sent the generous excess our way but her heart went to our father. Maybe I knew we were only a byproduct of the central show. "That's enough! Make a new one now!" I'd command, in 1967, back when I was five with my vivid young parents. And a new bright image would appear.

On a brief and overdue sabbatical I hit a writer's block I couldn't afford, anchored by a belated existential crisis that I had neither time nor resource to quell. Cause of crisis is typical fifty-four-year-old divorced white woman/working mother stuff: I can't deny I'm aging. I have not lived sensually enough and maybe it's too late. I love someone but am now too damaged to configure.

I broke my damn leg acting like a teenager and I'm not the right age to bounce back.

I'm packing too many postponements to ever relieve the pressure.

I want my mostly grown kids to get on with their own lovely ludicrous lives and leave me to salvage mine. And, God, I do not know how to let them go. I cannot perceive my own features on the other side of the gulf.

I no longer know who to be.

I can reason myself out of an absurdist impasse better than anyone. Not looking to chat about it but this one is potent and threatens to exterminate everything precious. Bills and to-do lists were not distracting enough so my stopgap response was to get in the car and drive, like any self-respecting scopophilic American. This in the season of the new Sagebrush Rebellion in which fringe Mormon cowboys are convinced that God has called them to lead civil war against the government. This in the season of freeway billboards that say "GIT SOME Guns and Ammo" and barn walls painted with "Civil War in the West! Call 1-800-KIL FEDS." This in the season of planning my strategy for easing as many students out of the classroom as I can before the one with the right mix of passionate intensity blasts me into a red smear on the whiteboard.

I've spent a lot of time, post-Emersonian that I am, trying to figure out why it is that living in beautiful scenery so often turns human beings into violent fanatics. It's not what Wordsworth predicted, or Thoreau or Whitman or Brigham Young. Hawthorne maybe. I believe we live in a season of peculiar and mounting hate. Still, I live here and I intend to gape.

February is cold where I live so the best direction for low-budget wandering was south. The southernmost city in the United States I had an alibi for driving toward was Safford, Arizona, where my father was born. I had never been there. Dad's memories of his very early years were vibrant as a magic lantern. He had a roster of little stories set in that town, all stocked with the charm of first consciousness.

Here's one: at the elementary school there were two lunch lines. One was for Anglo kids, the other for Mexican. Anglos got hamburgers or meat loaf, limpid spaghetti or macaroni and cheese. Mexican kids got tamales and tacos and tightly wrapped burritos with roasted chiles and refried frijoles. Little Tommy wanted lunch from the other side.

"No, you can't eat that," the teachers said, steering him firmly back to the Anglo line. "That food is too hot for kids like you."

Probably that's why we all crave Tabasco.

Here's another: the men and boys in the Safford Mormon ward went to pick beans at the Church Welfare Farm. Seven-year-old Tommy's job was to guard the stash of ripe watermelons cooling in the dammed-up stream until the picking was done.

"Don't let anybody make off with these," he was instructed. "Be a big boy and keep them safe."

Tommy picked up a stick. He patrolled the stream banks, vigilant and self-important. Soon enough he spotted a Mexican kid about his age, creeping through the tamarisk.

"Get out of here!" Tommy shouted. He waved his arms. He whacked the ground with the stick. He started to holler for reinforcements but the *muchacho* shot away like a cottontail.

Tommy reported his heroics when the big men came back.

"Aw," said the stake president, Spencer Kimball. "You should have let him have one."

As far as I know my father never went back to Safford after his family moved north to Salt Lake City, closer to home folks. I don't believe any of his siblings did. My grandmother Connie, who inhabits much of my own early memory, was troubled by the little grave where they'd left a newborn daughter. At one point she looked into having the tiny body exhumed and transported to the family plot in Idaho but the coroner in Safford recommended against it. Likely the wooden casket and its contents were reduced to dust. Maybe it was the stark gravesite that kept anyone from returning—a story too poignant to be disturbed.

Or maybe Safford was Eden for my father's original family. The place before the defining sorrows.

Could have been the formidable distance. I discovered on this long drive, seventy-four years after my grandparents loaded their young family of seven into the car and left that dead malformed baby behind, that it wasn't just the miles. The geography is staggering, only partly what I had come to expect from Arizona. Grand landscape reassures me that Why Be is an unanswerable question, and so I tend to stop asking for a while and feel better. Eighty or so years on a planet like this one is such a puny interval it usually seems reasonable—even sweet—to see it through.

I'm generally satisfied to believe we exist to watch sunlight strike Permian planes. But I was driving south in a chokehold of personal crisis so maybe I wasn't myself.

* * *

In the middle of my first grade year, Dad took a job writing contracts for Morton–Thiokol in northern Utah and we migrated toward home circumference. We lived for a year in Perry, a tiny orchard town just below Brigham City, a reasonable commuting distance from Thiokol set on the north shores of the Great Salt Lake. Since California schools taught children to read in kindergarten, I was the only kid in the class who could make out every word in the first grade reader. Again this generated accusations that I thought I was smarter than everyone else, but I feared the opposite. I was haunted by a singular terror that I was the only person who didn't understand what was going on. It was a language thing. I was endlessly quelling a notion that words meant one thing to me and something else to other people. I was afraid I had learned the language wrong, that I had linked intelligible sounds to the wrong objects and therefore assembled different meanings from everyone else. A whispering black line occluded each sentence I deciphered. I had begun to avoid television because I feared internalizing the wrong messages, pitching beyond communal human comprehension.

A freakish moment after I started school in Utah worsened my anxiety. The first day on the playground of Perry Elementary I heard a sickening noise. I didn't even register it as a sound. Hearing it felt like the time I had bitten into a brightly colored ornament at Christmas. I knew the candy red cherry wasn't real fruit but I had anticipated the sensation of smooth plastic resistance against my teeth. Instead the surface gave way to a hardened foam that shot a sharp chemical taste up through my sinuses, down my throat, and right on into my bloodstream. Queasy for hours, I believed I would die of poison but I was too ashamed of my childish misjudgment to report to an adult who could rescue me.

That is, I would rather die than reveal how stupid I was. And now on the playground I was seized by that same chemical revulsion at the sound of an electronic "bell," a tone I had never heard and could not process. All the other kids turned and ran to line up and our teacher, a very old woman named Mrs. Snow, shouted at me to get over here this minute like a good girl and I rushed to comply.

Mrs. Snow had a way with first graders. She was tough and unsentimental and walked with the authority of years of experience with six-year-olds. During reading time kids in the class would get up and walk over to my desk, pointing to the page. I read the hard words for them: "something," "marbles," "tricycle." But I feared I would get in trouble for doing someone else's work, or that I would incriminate a potential ally. Mrs. Snow paid no mind but it worried me and finally I asked her, "Is it okay if I tell them the words?"

"Don't you want to help your friends?"

Relieved of my righteous concern, I also convinced myself I was in league with a teacher who approved of my capacities, which was a good thing. But I also remember that year as a stream of "little n----- boy" stories and jokes from my beloved teacher. Mrs. Snow loved Kipling's *Just So Stories*, which makes even less racial sense now that I think about it than it did in the first place. Once Mrs. Snow brought us Rice Krispie treats, which she said were exactly the same treats a little n----- boy from some oft-read-to-us-story hid in his pockets for the friendly elephants. The word, I knew, was a very bad word and a mean one but her use didn't quite seem to be mean so much as something else I did not understand. It worried me, all the time, weighed upon my mind, but I did not know how to question or protest.

Wagging her finger like Shirley Temple, Mrs. Snow told us tales of a little boy named Georgie-Go-Wash-Your-Face, warning that we might ourselves be mistaken for little n----- children if we came to school without using soap and water the way we ought. I understand that this word is not appropriate for the twenty-first-century page, not even in blank form. Yet it was appropriate for first graders in Perry, Utah, a Mormon town so devoid of ethnic variation in the 1960s that I had to look up, in my fifties, which Native American tribe had coexisted with my Scandinavian ancestors in that vicinity only a century before.

Couched in caveats and qualifications, that word inflected our playground language, foyer talk at church, family reunion jeremiads, jokey asides by high school teachers. I recall my aunt, a strong, generous, hardworking woman unloading in the company of her sisters: she was *so damn tired of n----- women screaming at her in her own home, so sick of putting up with those banshee howls* every time her kids put a record on the player. Her kids—the same ones who listened to Aretha Franklin and Sly and the Family Stone and Ike and Tina Turner—our cool big cousins who dazzled us with their snark and sophistication, once asked Marti and me when we were visiting from California how we could stand to live in the same place as n-----s. My sister and I were stunned at the blunt force of their terms. But none of the adults, including our parents who probably didn't want to call out other people's children, balked at the usage and so we said thinly, "It's fine," although as I've said we didn't intersect much beyond backdrop.

Later that night before bed our mother reminded us that it really was not a nice word and we definitely should not use it, but our cousins didn't know better and it was none of our business what other people said. So we should leave it at that. And, she added, no matter what make sure you never use that word around an actual Negro.

Whatever else it did (plenty), that word iterated my early fear that language was more brick than window. I longed for, and feared, access beyond.

But if misinformation counts, that season in Perry was a soaker. In review: I learned that little elephants crave Rice Krispie treats. I internalized a Pavlovian response to electronic tones, laying the groundwork for a future relationship with smartphones. I learned that if I didn't wash my face I would become a little black child, which I knew wasn't true but sometimes, in that early season of wondering why I was this but not that, or that, or that—I wished it were.

Also I learned that there might be more to procuring babies than prayerfully asking Heavenly Father for one after marriage. Although I didn't learn exactly what that extra step was, I crossed one explanation firmly off the list, thanks to a kid named Rory.

On that sunny afternoon, late snow in patches on greening lawns, Marti and I streamed out of the church with all the other kids after Primary, a Tuesday after-school riot. Children stomped the tender lawn or convened on asphalt and sidewalks as we waited for our mothers to retrieve us.

The old church in Perry was a monument. Oldtime red brick, leaded windows, stone foundation. The white steeple lifted the building from the pioneer grove like a tall ship. Rory was climbing the huge ponderosa on the north lawn. A born professor, he shouted a new interesting item of information at each succeeding branch. Topping out near the steeple's height, Rory grabbed a slender branch with one hand and swung himself outward in a grand gesture.

"And I know something about moms and dads! I know how they make babies!"

Sister Pedersen steamed off the church steps where she had been doling out farewells. She huffed up the lawn to sight the boy in the foliage. Segments of Rory were lit up by the late afternoon sun.

She craned her neck. She cupped her hands to her mouth like a megaphone. "Rory! Shut your mouth and come down from there!"

Rory crowed like a bantam. "My sister told me what they do when all the kids are asleep!"

"Rory! Come down now! I'm going back inside to call your father! Do you want him to come here and take a belt to your behind?"

Rory beamed downward and posed a question to all but Sister Pedersen.

"Don't you want to hear how moms and dads make babies?"

The big boys, fifth and sixth graders, answered in chorus from the base of the tree. "Yessss!"

More Primary ladies materialized to stand in an urgent colorful row of blowing skirts.

"Rory!" they shouted in unison. "You hush and come down! Down! This minute!"

"Okay!" Rory called. "Here! It! Goes!"

The women flanked, traveling fast toward a gaggle of children, grabbing arms, trying to herd us back in the building before Rory could fill us in on the dirty secrets of reproduction. But it was too late.

"Here's what they do! They take off their clothes and then they rub their bums together. And that's how babies get inside moms!"

Sister Pedersen looked about to faint.

Sister Tibbets stood on a stump to address us, as if we were suddenly going to sit in neat rows and hearken. "That's not how it happens, boys and girls! Do you hear me! Rory is incorrect! Do not go home and tell your parents that this is how babies are made, because you will be one hundred percent incorrect!"

Another teacher, a very tall one, strode to the tree in her skirt and blouse, shoes off. She looked determined to climb up there herself to apprehend the criminal. I was more invested in what would happen to Rory once she grabbed him than in entertaining the bizarre vision he had invoked. Probably like every other kid in our baby-making community I had mulled over questions of small siblings. But Rory's explanation was so outlandish that I dismissed it outright. For once I was confident I was in on the true facts. My parents would never, ever do that—and yet anyway here we were, Marti and me, and Tommy at home, fully existing. So what now, Rory?

I did want to see whether that grown lady could climb a tree. But Marti tugged at my arm and pointed to our car, and there was our familiar (and pregnant with another brother) mother, beckoning.

My personal stereotype of Arizona hatched itself in a visit to my mother's parents when Marti, Tommy, and I were small. Our grandfather Carlie Lenz was an oldtime Idaho rancher. Born in the right skin, endowed with the right inclinations in a magic historical moment, he was the real thing if there ever was one. What John Wayne pretended to be. But by the time I knew Grandpa he only kept a few cattle. "A few" for him was a hundred. He smelled like Pendleton wool. He wore bolo ties and oval silver belt buckles. His voice was a hoarse rumble.

Grandma Ellen told us to call her "Gram" because "Grandma" made her sound old. Her hair was orange and she wore cat-eye glasses and red lipstick. Compared to our unadorned and methodical Grandma Anderson, Gram Lenz was exotic. Gram fashioned herself after Nancy Reagan and Jane Russell. She knew how to pose for photographs: turned to the side a bit, shoulders squared forward, one hand behind her back, feet in a handsome ballet stance. Later when we started to go bad my siblings and I entertained each other by trying to catch her off guard with a Polaroid camera, but it was a waste of precious film.

By the time my generation appeared, Grandma and Grandpa Lenz were in the habit of leaving the subzero winters of southeastern Idaho for the sunny climate of Arizona. They were, Gram explained, "Snowbirds": retired people who flocked to warm places during the cold northern months. My grandparents had picked up this pattern earlier than some of their contemporaries as their youngest daughter, my aunt Louisa, suffered from respiratory stress. Twenty degrees below zero in an Ashton January was in her case life threatening. Far more fascinating to Marti and me, however: Aunt Louisa had a glass eye. I imagined it was magic, like a crystal ball. I wished for one too.

I used to think I remembered the Christmas we spent in Mesa, but it's likely extrapolation from the square Kodak prints, 1965. Marti and I wear stripey jumpers of many colors and black Mary Janes with ankle socks. We're looking sharp in our white-rimmed sunglasses. Tommy is a baby in our mother's arms. Dad sports a crewcut and chinos. Mom is slender in a formfitting floral dress. Gram and Grandpa and mostly grown Aunt Louisa stand with us as tall two-armed saguaros surrender in the background. Later in Idaho summer, a picnic drive to the transparent plunging Mesa Falls in Island Park below Yellowstone caused me to believe that Arizona and Idaho were a single location. Same word. Same grandparents. Same long drive.

My mother's genetic people die sudden and easy. Their hearts quit and down they go. Her birth mother Myrtle died at thirty-three of cardiac arrest. Carlie lived much longer but still died early, barely seventy. He came home from church, answered a telephone call, and dropped mid-sentence, dead before he hit the floor. My mother's older sister Mary Ann made it to eighty, a good life of hard work, Republican politics, children and grandchildren, long Sunday drives with her husband Herb to Sun Valley or Bozeman or Salt Lake City. One night she cleaned up the kitchen after her grown daughter's birthday celebration. She walked out in the summer evening to tend flowers and fell as if the blooms had yanked her to the ground. I think about my mother, now past eighty herself. I think she's healthy. She awakens early every morning to walk around the local gym track with the senior citizens' Silver Sneakers club. But her folks' habit of sudden death always reminds me that this time might be Goodbye.

Thirteen years younger than he was, Gram spun into a funk after Grandpa Carlie died. Ellen was the kind of woman who knew how to be strong in the role of helpmeet. She worked herself and her children like a drover, inside and outside. She came from hardtack backwoods Mormons. When she was ten she maintained a small trapline for extra money—collected bounty on rabbits, a nickel a hide. Skinned them herself. Ellen worshipped her men with a rather obsequious ardor. Her husband. Her father and brothers. Her sole son. Maybe this was symptomatic of a strong girl raised to cover for family tendencies that stood out, even in a rural culture prone to protect ugly secrets.

Her first marriage was to a Mormon man who furnished her with a son and daughter. Then he delivered Ellen and the two toddlers to her parents' front porch. "Here. You can have her back," he said. That's all of the story I've ever gotten, possibly because she's not "really" my grandmother and despite the insistence that there were no divisions among the combined family, there are. Here's another: some of our cousins forget there was another grandmother and some of us do not. To some it doesn't mean a thing. To some of us, although not even our mother remembers her, she means a lot.

Once Ellen got herself paired with a good man she rose mightily. She had a lot to prove to the impeccable Lutherans who encircled Carlie like a national treasure. And she proved it. She was not a tender stepmother even by my mother's respectful account. But she took excellent physical care of Myrtle's daughters although her heart was not exactly maternal toward them. The family grew to six children, five girls and Jack, the boy who never could transcend the impact of early molestation and schoolyard bullies. When we all gathered, Gram used to quietly tell us girls, "You just stay close to me and I won't let anything happen to you."

My father was more blunt, widening a subtle and for my mother deeply painful family rift: "Jack, you come closer than twenty feet to my daughters and I'll kill you."

Eventually Aunt Louisa, her mother's darling, testified to convict Jack's predictably damaged son for molesting his younger cousins. Louisa paid a brutal emotional price, as such courage is prone to exact. Ellen, who had deflected the violent truths of her existence in ways that must have ravaged her, broke enough in public to say, "All this fuss over a little touching!" which can still drop my jaw. But it makes me wonder what she had been compelled to naturalize, early and immutably. I feel no great affection toward Ellen as I recollect her, but I admire her. Her life was a marathon of emotional discipline. "Well done" is her legacy. She taught my mother and therefore my sisters and me how to back out of a bathroom, for example, ticking off a scrupulous checklist: a visual run up and down the walls, floor to ceiling and back. Tiles in squared rosters of nine. Towels and washcloths bleached and folded into conformity, edges aligned. Mirror and faucets gleaming. Check again for smudges. Porcelain spotless and shined. Floor. Rugs. Curtains. Back up a step and repeat. That kind of housekeeping generates its own feminine capital— the right, nay duty, to check behind the dials of other women's ovens for neglected grime and purse one's superior lips. That kind of housekeeping is an editorial skill; I've learned to back my way out of a manuscript in the same way.

Well into her fifties Gram would don jeans and tall boots, stride out to a saddled horse, and sling up. If Grandpa hadn't died she might have kept it up another decade. She'd giddy-up Carlie's vicious biter and run him out, returning at a stately trot. Her lawn and flowered yard were tightly engineered. Her interior decoration was unsubtle: she troweled a vigorous layer of sharp-ridged plaster swirls up and down every wall of her living room to prevent kids from leaving fingerprints. But the farmhouse itself was gracious, tight against the brutal weather, and mostly she gave us the run of the upstairs, its beckoning attic stocked with vintage toys, dress-up gowns, and best of all an apple crate filled with oldtime stereoscope cards and two ornate viewers.

Ellen wilted like a belle without her husband. Once her man was gone I doubt she could discern her own form in a mirror.

Eventually she retrieved something of herself but for years after Carlie died, Gram was a wet mess. The spring before I turned eighteen she asked me to drive her all the way to Mesa. Her sister Pearl and Pearl's husband Dean were heading down from Portland. They had a room for her to stay all winter if she wanted. Ellen bucked up. That was the first time I navigated an interstate odyssey. I chauffeured the woman who had conquered thousand-acre-cattle-ranch wifehood to Old Folks' Trailer City in Grandpa's purple Cadillac. Gram played a repeating eight-track the whole damn trip because it reminded her of Grandpa: *Lay your head upon my pillow / Hold your warm and tender body close to mine / Hear the whisper of the raindrops flowing soft against the window . . .*

She tuned out the words beyond that line because it was a cheating song, not a "Your head isn't on my pillow anymore because you died of a heart attack and left me here alone" song. Between repetitions Gram mustered some emotion to explain a few things about my mother's dead mother: "Myrtle wasn't a great housekeeper, you know. Neglected the details." And, "She absolutely spoiled those little girls. They needed some real training by the time I took over the job." And, "Myrtle got all of the good parts. She got to be with Carlie when they were young, got to show off those little girls, but she left the hard work of raising them to me. Now she's in heaven enjoying him all to herself. This after I've done all the work!"

Also: "If you come live with me until I die I'll leave the house to you."

Gram died when I was forty-nine and she was ninety-eight.

None of this surreal experience seemed weird to me. At seventeen everything and nothing is strange. It's the same at fifty-four, come to think of it. The trip implanted my yearning for Western highways.

We made it to Phoenix, a big city but not the sprawl it is now. Reaching suburban Mesa required no negotiation of the metropolis. I floated that Cadillac through sunny trailer parks and striped cabanas, past unnatural green golf courses, dodging golf carts toting old white people wearing Bermuda shorts and jaunty fedoras and wide-brimmed sunhats. We pulled up to Pearl and Dean's place and they streamed out to greet us. Pearl and Dean were a matched pair, possibly attracted to one another by the jarring likeness of their rubbery pink faces. They were kind to me. They took me out to eat at a hamburger diner. They asked me about my career plans. I waxed eloquent over my intention to make my way through Europe as an itinerant artist. They all came along to the Phoenix airport to see me off to Salt Lake City.

The most traveled route from Salt Lake to Arizona drops through Flagstaff and Phoenix in a sequence of dodging highways. The road less taken falls more directly south and rides along the New Mexico line. Much of US-191 was, until recently, US-666, but that became too much for Bible-believing drivers. That may be one reason the road keeps a certain remoteness, although the crash rate can light it up like a battlefront. On the current map it is the most direct route to Safford from Idaho Falls, keeping east, but I doubt my father's parents drove to their Arizona home that way. Approximating 191 would have required a wide detour around the Navajo and Apache reservations, crisscrossed with double-track. I have no idea what my grandparents thought about Indians—likely something paternalistic but uninclined toward an encounter halfway through a sticky, crumb-ridden passage with squalling children.

Even so I took 191 south to trace my father's memory. Salt Lake City to Moab is so familiar that I should be tired of it, but I'm not. Most of Utah's population clusters along the Wasatch Front where the jobs are. But at the bottom of Utah Valley at Spanish Fork, the state rises toward the Colorado Plateau. Driving becomes an intermittence of high mountain ranges, rural towns, and long strange trips through jagged desert. At Crescent Junction where 191/666 picks up, the stark gray formations color up into red, yellow, orange, and purple sandstone: cliffs, canyons, mesas, violent chasms carved by tinsel streams.

Twenty-five years of teaching and mothering have depleted my conversational reserves. But in Moab I gathered enough nerve to text a high school friend, Maria Kee. I had another five hours of daylight. I hoped she would help sharpen my eyes to Navajo country.

"Stop to see Canyon de Chelly," she sent back. Unequivocal. "Plenty of places to look down. You only need a guide if you're hiking in."

I pecked out thanks but then my phone dialed her number out of its own perversity. I didn't notice until I heard a tiny voice on the passenger seat saying, "Hello? Hello, Karin?" I panicked and pushed the stop button. I texted a few minutes later with a flat-out lie that I had not realized my phone had made a call. I would have enjoyed talking to her. But I wasn't emotionally well, and even when I am I can't imagine why anyone would want to hear me yak unless they've paid tuition and have to.

When I knew Maria we attended American Fork Junior High in Whitepeople Central, Utah. Even so, several kids spoke Spanish and English interchangeably but at the time I poorly perceived such wonders. Also quite a few Navajo and Hopi kids came up to northern Mormon cities through the now-controversial "Indian Placement Program." My grandmother had taken in a boy named Murray. He was sixteen and a junior, the same as my Uncle Jerry. They lived to tease my sister and me to tears. I don't know what happened to Murray; most of those kids graduated from high school and went "home" to Utah, Arizona, or New Mexico reservations expected to—what? Transform their communities into chambers of commerce? Pose for postcards? Murray lived with my grandmother for nine months of the year for seven years. Nobody's been in touch.

Sarah Begay lived with my aunt and uncle. Uncle Glen had northwestern tribal blood so although she was much older than the other children, Sarah blended visually. She was two years older than I was and she and Marti and I drew together during family visits. At eleven, Sarah was broad shouldered and built solid, preternaturally maternal. When she came to our house we headed to the unfinished basement to cook up rubber butterflies in Marti's Thingmaker oven. I don't know what happened to Sarah, either. I don't know whether people who were taken from their homes for most of their childhoods would wish to be tracked down by relatives of the people who took them in. I'd guess it could be a bad dream to leave behind. Then again it seems odd that white families could say goodbye to "cousins" they've called their own and never see them again.

The internet, however, has wrought surprising returns. Well over thirty years beyond high school I've enjoyed casual communication with hometown accomplices. We're surprisingly various. Corresponding with Maria Kee has been one authentic reward of recalling a season of my life I acknowledge with caution.

Maria was smart and beautiful. Artistic. Her hair was long, very dark brown and wavy. Her vivid smile was only part of her charisma. Any time she was in one of my classes I knew I had a friend in the room. She had the same effect on everyone. I knew she called Travis Williams her brother and she said she was Navajo, so I assumed she came up from the reservation for the school year. In eighth grade Maria and I collaborated on a poster for Indian Appreciation Week. We drew a little Navajo boy looking all wistful and cute. Free-floating red buttes rose up behind him. An eagle hovered. Our masterpiece should have won the contest but we were robbed by a couple of cheating ninth-grade boys who used an overhead projector to render a bare-chested warrior, full headdress, spear, arms outstretched, sitting on a pony. My indignation knew no bounds. Those boys were not even Indians.

In high school I gained weight, and frizzed my hair to insinuate that I smoked weed, launching the first of several paradigmatic breakdowns that chuted me out of my ancestral faith. I was vaguely aware of Maria, among other friends coursing her own route, but I was too self-absorbed to attend to other people's stories. I drifted into a new world. Another strain of language in college drew me into a convoluted metamorphosis. Gradually I disintegrated into something I better recognize as myself.

Maria prodded me, from the distances of our grownup lives, to ponder the Navajo Long Walk as I gazed over the rim of Canyon de Chelly. I drove through the last remote red towns in southern Utah: Monticello, Blanding, Bluff. I recalled students over the years who came from each town, mostly amicable but recalcitrant white uberconservatives even though here the larger population was Native American. I neared the turnoff toward Hovenweep's exquisite towers but stayed my course, crossing the Arizona line into Mexican Water. The high mittened buttes of Monument Valley jutted beyond the southwest hills. Sandstone magnitudes contoured the curving road—smooth loaves, deep recesses, fins, pinnacled juts. Round Rock was patterned with little houses and barns, pickups and trailers and sheds and dogs. Mules and ponies. People in the distance getting on with whatever the twenty-first century requires of them. I passed a playground bouncing with black-haired children attending school in their own town, going home afterward to the people who made them.

A huge shapeshifting butte dominated my south view. A wind-carved arch gave a teapot handle to its western pitch. Thrusting orange fingers rose against blue sky. The road approached, passed, and then wound around the butte, granting me a near 360-degree view of its fluid contours.

* * *

During the month I spent in England with the precious Anglophile I had recently married, my grandmother Connie Anderson died in Utah. I had known it was coming but hoped she'd hold on until we returned. A stroke had knocked her off course before our departure and although she had regained speech—slurred but intelligible—and lost the deathly pallor, the truth of mortality was upon her. She was eighty-six.

Grandma had been anxious for me to embark and return. To England, I mean. She had assigned me to find the "family castle" in Essex. Bring back photographs, maybe a souvenir. "Something from the land itself," she said. "Bring me some dirt and leaves."

Not sharing the love of all things British that characterized my hometown, nearly everyone in my family and my husband's, and my peers in the English MA program at Brigham Young University, I did not know where Essex was. "London" and "England" were in my mind interchangeable terms. I did appreciate Matthew Arnold's "Dover Beach," and so in re: "Dover" I savored some concrete imagery of waves and the tiny sound of rolling pebbles. I had memorized the final lines almost by instinct:

> Ah, love, let us be true
> To one another! for the world, which seems
> To lie before us like a land of dreams,
> So various, so beautiful, so new,
> Hath really neither joy, nor love, nor light,
> Nor certitude, nor peace, nor help for pain;
> And we are here as on a darkling plain
> Swept with confused alarms of struggle and flight,
> Where ignorant armies clash by night.

Whatever made me ask awkward questions over the course of my erratic education was no wish to play renegade, although I was sometimes rebuked for that. It was not some fresh or original intelligence. In graduate school, just as in first grade, I did not know how to efface irrelevant complications. I had a sharp memory for facts and names; I could recall books and experiences in Technicolor, a party trick that had passed for smarts and sometimes smart-assery since I was a child. I had been warned to veer away from certain questions that would not evacuate my cluttered head, so I had honed a subconscious habit of holding discrete items of information apart from one another. But sometimes I forgot. And so in class I asked my lit professor why we would read a nihilistic poem like "Dover Beach" at Brigham Young University.

Understandably she misread my intent. I didn't comprehend it very well myself but I had been profoundly moved when I read "... Hath really neither joy, nor love, nor light, / Nor certitude, nor peace, nor help for pain ..." It wasn't a conscious reverberation. But even the relatively happy experiences I brought to poetry were tinged by an apprehension that joy, love, light, certitude, peace, and help for pain were tenuous. Consider my great-grandma Porter, who spent the fifteen years before her death frantic to return to a lost home, urgent to rectify tragedy she could no longer name. Consider Hannah Bastion, friend of my aunts, who grew up under the meanest despot in my hometown. She loved her children as irrationally as I love mine. She died of leukemia just as the world was opening to hard-earned joy. Consider my mother, made of early resounding loss. Consider—well, the list went on, and widened its circumference, all filed in my home philosophy under *All is well, all is well.*

I blurted the question awkwardly but it was sincere. I did not know how to harmonize the certitude of my home faith with the resonance of despair. I was beginning to sense that Emily Dickinson was the great American horror-master. I could not understand why Willa Cather or Walt Whitman, or Langston Hughes or Flannery O'Connor were as actual people One Hundred Percent Irrelevant to their earth-shattering language.

I had picked up Momaday and Erdrich and Hurston on my own time. I did not know what to do with that stuff but it wove bright ribbons through my foggy brain. Sherwood Anderson set an image in my mind that shook me in its hard compassion: that half-naked old woman in the snow, eaten by her own dogs.

"Fine examples of local color," I was notified, "but topicality cannot rise to the status of Great Literature."

"I'll say it again," my professor said again. "A truly literary story has nothing to do with you or your little life. Now excuse me while I bring us back to a more relevant graduate-level discussion. Here in graduate school."

And so the day my husband accompanied me to Paddington Station, put me on the bus toward Chelmsford, and circled back to the relevant cultural immersion of the London art museums, I found myself with an entire day to not ponder why in the hell I was sitting on a double-decker bus farting its way through the claustrophobic streets of a city I felt no communion with. I tried to absorb the ambience of the roundabouts and stacked-up flats and pubs and pharmacies. I wished to look pleasant, young, and adventurous, but not too conspicuous—a literate sort who knew how to deploy the Oxford comma. A futile performance: I was the only upper-deck passenger once the bus slugged into something like open country.

"What do you even want to go out there for?" my husband had queried. "If you want to go out to the country, go to Bath or Stratford-upon-Avon. You're an English major. Why don't you go see where Shakespeare was born?"

"I promised my grandma. You know that. There's that castle out there."

"England is a castle a minute. Like mountains in Utah. You have to pick the good ones, like Hampton Court or Tintagel. You're wasting a whole day. There's nothing important."

I pointed to the map. "Well, look. Maldon."

"What's that?"

"They cared not for battle?"

He furled his pretty lips.

I arrived in Chinle, Arizona, to a snarled late afternoon mess. Maria's intelligence notwithstanding, I nearly drove on through. I waited at the stoplight convinced that every vehicle would rush into the intersection at once, but the left turn arrow beckoned me through and then I swerved into the parking lot of an oversized Super 8. The lot was packed with Subarus and Toyota trucks. Tourists speedwalked toward the check-in to book the last rooms. I put a foot out but could not make myself go in. I retreated to search my phone for an alternative.

Holiday Inn. No.

Thunderbird Lodge. Fine.

I poked in a debit card number and hoped for the best. I followed the road east toward de Chelly itself, expecting to see some shoddy motel within a block or two. But beyond an early small sign and arrow there was no hint of safe bedding. I had a tent and sleeping bag to survive a twenty-five-degree night in the campground but the prospect was dismal.

Turns out Thunderbird Lodge was in the park itself, Navajo proprietors. Turns out I needed to follow the signs to Sacred Canyon Lodge, its former name. As I've aged I've become accustomed to linguistic mismatch. There was a charming 1940s look to the place: sturdy Craftsman stone and wood. Birds sang in the backlit trees. I took a deep breath and stepped out of the car to walk toward the office. A young man about the same age as my older son—mid-twenties—wafted from the shrubbery to show me a sinuous piece of carved cottonwood: an eagle atop a pueblo, crowning a twisting pathway.

My son is an artist. I like to think I have an eye.

"Not bad."

"Cheaper than the gift shop. Twenty-five bucks? I just want dinner."

I gave him three tens. He grinned and beelined for the quiet cafeteria.

I put the art in the car. I thought about my son. Serious and angry, slender and witty. Gay. Self-righteous, generous, fraught. An artist with an eye so potent it makes him in that one way superhuman. A youthful bitterness that may save, may annihilate him.

Loyal to his mother beyond practical justification.

I'd been thinking about men. Trying to understand them, to stop assuming things. Consider them one by one, as fellow humans with something in common. But particulars were too much to consider, for too many minutes, in my state of mind. I reapproached the office, checked in, and threw my bags into the room. I walked back out petitioning that eagle god for one more hour of sunlight. I wanted at least to see the White House Ruin but had no guess how far it was.

Not far. I turned left at the sign and drove another mile on a thread of pavement. The parking lot was empty. I got out, took a few steps, returned for a jacket, and walked out to the edge. I stood one easy step away from a leisurely freefall, but it was beautiful here and I remembered I had come to witness.

The sun lit the clifftops across the deep gulf of evening air, saturating the high flats. The bright blaze striped the tops of the imposing walls, illuminating juts and sculpted waterways waiting to cup the next flash flood. A hundred feet below the rim, the shadows cast purple across every Pantone shade of orange. Shallow snow stippled the larger scene, accentuating the river crescents, metering suspended angles of repose. The canyon is narrow. Maybe a big human shout could be heard from one bank to the other on a still evening like this, but it's grand and gracious in its sweep, and deep, compartmented by jutting walls, opened through narrow transits into sky-ceiled rooms.

The river meandered like a Chinese dragon between the silent cliffs.

I scanned the five-hundred-foot walls for the White House, afraid the sun had already dropped too darkly. But there it was, way down and to my right, neat and squared, tucked into an egress the shape of a human eye. Were I a child I would have believed I could cradle the tiny town in my palm. The front ledge was fortressed by an infantry of fitted stones, opening at key points to hoist allies or smash enemy fingers. Vermilion desert varnish striped the sheer wall above.

On the canyon floor just below it stood a complex of kivas and apartments, roofless and interconnected like the canyon it mimicked. Before Anglo marauding ran its course, structures of this kind still sheltered the everyday objects of ancient lives and deaths.

The verdant flow below these ancestral sites was the site of a Navajo ambush on Colonel John Washington in 1849. Navajo fighters had stalked Washington's troops from the east. The troops pushed cannons. Washington surely knew he was under surveillance but the ignorant army had no idea how many eyes were upon them, nor from which nooks or overlooks. Once the four hundred American soldiers reached the stretch I could see now, three hundred Navajo defenders attacked from above. Washington's men blazed away but the bullets struck sandstone. Washington resorted to blowing pointless cannonballs. Navajo fighters descended the sheer canyon walls, overpowered the cavalry, and then allowed survivors to flee to Chinle. A cheap paper treaty was signed soon after between Washington's army and a nonrepresentative handful of men they labeled as Navajo chiefs.

Of course the Navajo tribe had already agreed to peace with their own formalities a few years prior at Fort Canby. Over a hundred Navajo celebrants had been massacred by frightened US soldiers on that treaty day for displaying multitude and exuberance. Afterward Chief Manuelito advised his people to never again reveal themselves in numbers. Thousands of human beings lived in the sandstone heights and depths of their vast home territory, but beyond that early paranoid vision at Canby, the Anglos refused to comprehend.

The sun went down completely. The cliff walls turned deep blue and black. More than a thousand years ago the lights of the pueblo would have flickered up from the darkness like a jar of fireflies. I drove back to Thunderbird.

I did not care to see my drive to Safford as a second pilgrimage for Grandma Connie's sake, and I sure as hell didn't want to make it homage to my long-dead grandfather. My long walk in my twenties out to the red brick castle in Essex, England, seemed sentimental enough to cross grandma-pathos off my list. I had found the family castle after a three hour foodless and waterless trek, very pretty but meaningless beyond my grandma's romantics. I stood at the swan pond, gazing blithely across the water toward the gatehouse, a lovely crumbling structure now sectioned into three or four squalid flats. A matted rug hung from one of the upper windows. Broken toys littered the side yard. I strolled around the edge of the water to snap a few photographs of listless floating birds. Might as well have been decoys. The Real History stood in the background, the country estate of the sadistic toady Richard Rich. But at the time I didn't know that much about him or his sick political pastimes. I stood in that spot because my grandmother's grandfather had been born there. As a child he had nearly drowned in this very pond.

I put a few stones in my pocket. I picked a few tiny purple roadside flowers from the abundance, pressing them between the pages of my notebook. I knew it would matter to Grandma and I loved her.

My grandma Connie Anderson was broad shouldered and big boned. Oldest daughter of an overelegant mother, she spent much of her youth chafing against maternal admonitions about charming a future husband, which helps me comprehend, painfully, why Grandma kept her starry eyes for the capable but deeply flawed man who chose her and did seem to love her.

Grandma cared not for housekeeping. She was a lousy cook. Her heart was in her yard and garden, a stunning acre of oldtime horticultural glory: apricot, apple, and plum trees. Currants and raspberries. Long rows of carrots, peas, beets, potatoes, squash, tomatoes. Purple irises that she called "flags." Hollyhocks, orange daylilies, four o'clocks, daisies, primrose, lilac. A meticulous system of little ditches and headgates to maximize her weekly water turns. She laid red flagstone walkways in arcane routes from one section of vegetal design to the next. A massive locust tree in the backyard shaded the swing set.

She loved books. Grandma lined her house with them, although she was alert to the hazards of our mutual attraction to the page. "Leave the bad ones be," she admonished, more urgently as I grew. Her mind was sharp and hungry, her insights critical and astute, but she kept them curbed.

My family lived up the hill. We weren't direct neighbors but the far backs of our lots were nearly adjoined. My brothers and sisters and I would follow a path through our father's beloved apple trees, step over a couple of stiles, and emerge into Grandma's yard, picking and eating as we progressed. Usually I'd find Grandma in the garden, weeding or hoeing or fussing along the ditches. She'd reach a pitch before her water turn, calling my father hourly, then quarter-hourly, to make sure he was ready to help her pull the headgate up near Patterson's barn. She'd stand at the gate waving her watch. Dad and Grandma were snappy and irritable with one another, but also tender and close. They loved fruit trees. They loved the sucking sound of a shovel, scraping into the mud of an icewater ditch. They despised posers and grandiosers and tricktalkers. Both strode the planet with the cinematic recall of born storytellers.

* * *

In England I planned a lovely story to tell Grandma about the lush greenery of Essex as I plodded back toward town between hedgerows, past thatched cottages and crumbling estates. I stopped at the Church of St. John the Evangelist which the locals had told me to admire: twelfth century, and it truly was beautiful—surfaced with halved globes of slate, fist-sized and matte-textured like eggshell on the outside, glassy like gelled candy within. Even now similar stones lay about. I put a small one in my bag. I pressed my hand into mud and made a dirty print on a page of my notebook.

I walked into the curio shop/post office while I waited for the London bus. I bought a postcard, wrote something on it, and crossed to the far side of the counter to purchase a stamp from the same woman who had just rung up the card. I wanted Grandma to receive it with a Little Leigh's postmark.

"Post office isn't open yet, love."

"When will it open?"

"Ten more minutes."

I had a bus to catch in thirteen, across the street.

"I'm hoping to send this to my grandmother," I said. "In America."

"Well, you can do that. Just ten minutes now and the post office will open."

I could not tell whether I was dealing with a cultural gap or simply a peculiar person. "Is somebody coming in to open the post office?"

"Oh no. It's just me. But right now I'm working the store. At four o'clock I'll be taking on the additional responsibility."

What kind of post office opens at four? I could see a little cabinet with stamps. Right there awaiting commerce.

"Well, I really need to catch that bus back to London. My husband will be waiting for me. Could you possibly open the post office a few minutes early?"

She looked at me as though I didn't understand English.

"Post office opens at four o'clock. It is now seven minutes of four."

I stared. She stared back with arched eyebrows.

"How about," I suggested, "I lay down the money for a stamp. And then, maybe? At four o'clock you could take the money off the counter, fetch a stamp from that cabinet there, put it on this postcard for me, and slip it into that slot?"

The woman thought this over.

"Well, all right. That would be fine. Problem is, you have to buy international stamps in fours. You'll need to buy four stamps. I won't be able to break them apart until four o'clock."

"Fine."

Still the arched eyebrows.

I managed, "How much?"

I can't recall her answer but it required change. Which she would not be able to provide until the post office opened. At four o'clock.

"Keep it then!"

"Well, all right! But it sure seems like a lot of fuss for one little postcard."

I ran out to the street, waving my ticket at the red bus and it stopped for me.

"Don't seem all that difficult to get to the stop in time," the driver said. I wound myself up the spiral staircase to sit up top and admire This England all the way back to London.

Grandma was dead before I could carry my treasures home to her. She never received my postcard but we arrived in Utah in time for the funeral. I slipped the slate, pressed flowers, and Essex dirt handprint into the casket to accompany her on the four hour drive to the cemetery in Ammon, Idaho, where she was buried beside the man who had long ago fallen to the sea from a flaming jet.

* * *

Mormon Heaven is replete with rituals, arcana, hierarchies. I'm too irritable to explain in detail. But for the people I love who believe, the important parts are straightforward. The highest kingdom is saved for families "sealed" in Mormon temples, where certain men have the authority to link a woman and man together for eternity. People who go to the best heaven will produce infinite offspring and populate new planets. I may snark about this somewhere else but right now I'm holding to the dreamy version. I don't believe this stuff but my grandmother and father did, as do my mother and sister and other people I largely admire, who are themselves convinced I am educated beyond my intelligence. So although I assured myself I was not going to Safford, Arizona, to pay respect to the tiny grave of a one-day-old baby girl for my grandma's sake, I probably was. I lost a four-month pregnancy to miscarriage a long time ago. Helpful people say Oh Well and You'll Get Over It, but sensations recur. Elusive loss never quite fades. I'm in a mood to hover over little sorrows and I know for Grandma this one cut deep. Resurrection was her hope and solace.

On the first day of the big event, Mormon husbands will rise as the advance guard. Because they learned crucial signs in temple rituals they will awaken when called, answering with secret signals. The husbands will call up the wives. In most cases they won't need to travel far, but sometimes distance or decomposition or the fact of smithereened bodies must be surmounted. This worried me when I was a child, but I was reassured that the body and spirit are bound for reunification, and that this very planet I like to walk and drive upon will be the seat of celestial glory where faithful families will reside.

In Grandma Anderson's land of dreams, her husband springs forever young from the Idaho grave. He calls her up by her secret temple name and Connie comes forth. They'll collect themselves and crane about for the people they know. His parents, and his siblings with all their fancy names: Zenobia. Reuben.

Elmira. Oriole. Iola (whom I knew and loved) and Reid. Uncles and aunts, cousins and neighbors and friends, maybe enemies they'll have to reevaluate. A few surprisingly undisturbed plots. The risen count and assemble, take note of who's missing. Helpful ministering angels direct traffic, make maps and diagrams, check the rolls.

Most of my grandparents' children will rise too, called up in the same manner in their own locations, feeling out the lovely new flesh and bone. Sadly, down in Utah my parents will spot only one of their children, my very good sister Marti. Unless we go truly bad, the rest of us will make a showing on the second or third day, fairly happy to wake but too cynical, gay, enamored of the wrong kind of spirits, or overeducated to cash the whole check. I can't answer for that. I'm here in my grandma's vision as she takes her husband Clyde by the hand. They're calling up a stillborn baby boy buried right there beside them. He flies up into his mother's arms to be raised in a perfect world.

Connie and Clyde and baby boy now leave the grown revenants to their own pursuits and fly to deep Arizona. Grandma will stand beside her man, now cured of his temper I guess, as he calls the little girl up from the desert dirt. Just as it did for her brother, the ground will open and release a perfect child. The family will gaze at the old sleepy town with big Mount Graham above. They will recall the sweet taste of cold watermelon, the tang of roasted chiles in hand-rolled tamales. They will take in the desert valley spreading toward the mountain ranges. They'll say that it really was no time at all.

Here's what I command: also they will marvel at the thrall of ponies and Apache people, the Mexican *madres* and their own babes in arms, at gaunt Spanish knights in armor and Basque shepherds with their blue heelers. My Mormon grandparents will wonder how it is that these unendowed have also been called to rise on the First Day.

* * *

The Catholic saint Ignatius, founder of the Jesuits, was a practical guy. Although he worked to quell a youthful lust for fame, he wasn't prone to get carried away with intangibles. He came from a wealthy Basque family. Before he became a priest he was a soldier. Ignatius is a peculiar choice for a crabby twenty-first-century feminist looking for a temporary patron, but stay with me: he badly hurt his leg in battle which made him thoughtful. He came to Jesus but even in the zeal of burgeoning faith Ignatius did not limp around communing with ghosts. Even so, something profound happened at Loyola as he meditated upon New Testament scenes. Immediate reality gave way to the world of the stories and he discovered he could walk around in them. He tested the pattern and gradually systematized it for other seekers, thus transforming himself into the patron saint of retreating and thinking. Of course he also fostered the hard manly brand of Jesuit psychology necessary for conquering a New World; I guess that's another reason we crossed paths in Coronado country.

My colleague Rich McDonagh, my go-to Medievalist, said, "Ignatius? Oh yeah. You could almost call him a literary theorist. Hang around in a story. Imagine the stable where baby Jesus was born. Smell the manure. Pet the cows. Pick out a shepherd, a milkmaid, Joseph or Mary, the innkeeper, baby Jesus himself. Start up a conversation. Pretty sweet for a tough guy like that."

Enter and explore, detail by character by event, and it will become real. The concretes come from your own stratified experience, revealing weaknesses you won't acknowledge, hidden strengths, your complex relation to a simple anecdote.

"Stations of the Cross," Rich said. "Anchorite visions. All that stuff came from Ignatius. For him it was about taking the time—weeks and months, even years—to immerse yourself in sacred stories. Your personal relationship to the canon."

Good advice for our students even now but they usually know better. They aren't stupid; that kind of attention can render a story too much to contend with. Ignatius insisted that such a journey be undertaken only with a qualified guide. Revelations can be ambiguous. Compelling elements of a beloved narrative might be well-laid deceptions. Disturbing figures may carry the truest message.

I grew up with similar admonitions. Teachers, aunts and uncles, grandparents and parents taught me precise methods for discerning an evil spirit from a good one. I was raised among the speaking dead, the signifying yet-to-be-born, the throngs of Satan who would try anything to seduce me, and the hosts of Heaven who wished to guide me home.

In 1863 the Feds called up their golden boy Kit Carson to take out the only apparently placid Navajo people. In mainstream history Carson receives five-star reviews. He seemed to want an actual human life in the Southwest. Married twice before, at thirty-three he married Josefa Jaramillo, fifteen, daughter of a prominent Mexican family in Taos. In his time and place Carson shows up rather well. He loved his family and nurtured ties that wove through the complex cultural roots of New Mexico. He was faithful to Josefa. He witnessed nasty stuff on the desert frontier and came home decent. In general he was an advocate for fair treatment of native people, whatever that looked like in his eyes. He had a lot of kids and he brought them candy.

Carson didn't want the Navajo job. He'd tangled with his superiors over tactics and policy. He'd been dismissed for cowardice and reinstated—all that career stuff gets in the way of personal morality and I guess once he took on the Navajo cleanse he just said fuck it. Carson had some dark talents and he summoned them.

At first even Carson was in over his head. He could not locate the people he was supposed to fight. His troops killed fifty or so but due to Manuelito he had no statistics to help him measure progress. Navajo figures appeared and vanished like rabbits, always the same number no matter how many they shot.

Golden Boy got systematic. He ordered his men to destroy every source of Navajo sustenance: Wreck hogans. Strip the ground of firewood. Kill sheep. Carson cut a deal with the Utes, ancestral enemies of the Diné: keep what you plunder, come in for support and supplies. The Ute warriors were better at this than the American army and they also more clearly understood the magnitude. The People kept to themselves when unprovoked but they were no easy pickings. And they could hide anywhere—nooks and pockets, desert holes and high mesas. Must have seemed to Carson there were only a couple hundred more each new dawn.

Some nasty skirmishes. Escalation. As capable patriarchs are prone to do, Carson got fed up and then monstrous. Many Navajo families were secreted in the curtains of Canyon de Chelly but the food was dwindling. Carson ordered his men to burn grass and plug water holes with rocks and dirt. Winter slammed down but it was not until January that starvation and brutal cold brought The People in. They came in small bands, gradually gathering at Fort Canby, where once their tribe had danced in a celebration of peace and been shot down. Now Carson rewarded them with food and blankets but at this point Manuelito's admonition worked against the refugees. They just kept coming in and the Fort had no more provisions. Five to eight thousand people, depending on who's counting, at the brink of human endurance.

There were holdouts. Barboncito's band of men, women, and children were yet encamped at the top of Fortress Rock, which is like living on the roof of a skyscraper. They had climbed the monolith with rope ladders, pulling up as they ascended. Anglo and Ute soldiers guarded the base, believing the lunatics would come down for water. The People on the tower did in fact descend. They crept down at night as far as the cliff would support them and then made a hand-grip human chain down sheer wall to the water hole. Soldiers slept as the water they guarded flowed up in Navajo pots.

Later Barboncito called up dark magic, conjuring the right wind, and a warrior shot an arrow from the top of the butte, right through a Ute colluder. Utes read the signs, reconnoitered, and wisely hit the trail. The US soldiers watched them disappear. They arched their spines backward to reassess, then packed up and rode back to the fort.

Canby was a disaster. Navajo refugees everywhere, bereft. No food. Bitter wind. Snow on the ground. No sanitation, no shelter, no medicine. Thus began the Navajo Long Walk: four hundred miles of misery and death. An ancient nation driven on foot toward a bleak and foreign reservation. I heard the story of the Mormon migration so many times in my childhood it became simply a repeating trope, but I was never told this story of the Navajo removal—not in school, not in church, not by one single kid who came up to live among us.

It's not my story, but then again it is.

Those who survived the odyssey to Bosque Redondo, a flat barren piece of New Mexico desert where the government had already corralled mountain-loving Apache captives, were released into a landscape so alien it must have crushed their reason for surviving in the first place. People of the cliffs and mesas, sandstone nooks and hidden glens were abandoned, but for the resentful guards, on an unsheltered plain. The Navajo people dug holes to conceal themselves.

I drove hard south on old 666. By the time I neared St. Johns I felt confident I was driving on grandparent stomping grounds. Mormons keep track of each other, and old families abound in Apache County. Because I teach in a Mormon city I can recall students from several rural towns, fanned in from a pattern of old pioneer settlements.

St. Johns has been home to a handful of my students over the decades. As I approached I wondered again at how my profession has marked me. So many stories. I do read them, and beyond my dutiful marks they screw me up. Had I not read so many thousands of gut-wrenched student pages I would probably drive through towns like this and oversimplify.

Concrete examples?

A young mother from rural Utah, twenty-six, wrote about carrying the charred bodies of her two small children out of a machine-shed fire.

Blond, broad-shouldered Apollo, first counselor in a young-marrieds ward. Pretty wife, three cute children. Nearly finished with his degree in Computer Science but kept breaking down in his English classes, where caged words had a way of leaking out. He didn't know how to tell his wife he was aroused by men.

Local kid, slicked-up, rich, pomade-spiked hair. Brand-name sports clothes, impeccable high-top basketball shoes, superior simper. He spent his adolescence alert for the nights his otherwise passive father worked himself into an opioid rage. Nights like these the man promised to kill his wife and every last child. Nights like these the boy sat vigil at the top of the stairs, guarding his siblings with a butcher knife while their father tore up the rooms below.

A high school football player, one of seven brothers, all but one as robust as he was. His twin was born with cerebral palsy. The twin spent life in progressive stages of contortion. A twisted boy with a breathing machine was hard to transport but his brothers were big and had a system. They pushed the whole bed around the neighborhood. They brought him to every ballgame. The wracked twin brother was recently dead.

"People tell us it's a blessing. But it isn't. We miss him. He loved his life."

I can't stop: a nineteen-year-old woman up from a fringe town. Demure and doe-eyed, long hair pulled back. I suspected but didn't try to confirm that she came from a polygamous community. Her father was in prison for life, convicted for sexually abusing his grandchildren. Her mother was in a mental ward, for good. Her siblings had subsided to meth and so the state had assigned her permanent custody of five nieces and nephews, ages two through nine. Social Services had helped arrange time and funding for college.

What was I capable of at nineteen?

The distant view of St. Johns included a huge smokestacked factory to the east. Looked like it made rocks. The town itself was held down with scrap metal: Old cars—some picturesque, some not. Gearboxes, factory debris, rusted ovens, wrought-iron bedframes. "No wonder I'm such a badass," one of my favorite students ever, a bespectacled guy from this town, told me once. "I come from Mad Max country."

Yellow hills rose again on the other side. A Delft-blue mountain surfaced to the southeast like a whale. I figured I was headed for it and the highway confirmed with a swerve. I had been in the car for a very long time. I reached Springerville, an Americana town at the base of the mountain. Nothing was familiar. No point of reference but Safford, over the peaks, south and then a straight shot west. And Mexico.

The terrain from here looked like my piece of Utah: arable desert valley surrounded by high blue mountains. Pines and snow called attention to altitudes. I could see why early Mormons settled here and why the Apache people were livid. I was certain my grandparents, especially my grandfather, a deer hunter, had been drawn to these mountains back when Clyde was nothing but alive and young, destined to live on into old age which was forever. I tried to keep it light as I fielded memories of my own young motherhood in the house we lived in, the first one that felt like *us*. Little children magical in their awakenings, remarkable in every new word and skill and earnest question. Their father not fully set in a trajectory that later seemed inexorable. Me, optimistic that we could become the best of our parents, skirting their dark hazards. New trees, a garden, familiar mountains rising above us. Suddenly it was real: the dark cave of the garage, the bright sunlight of the backyard, kids in the sandpile chattering like chickadees.

I shook them out.

The road climbed quickly. Signs informed me I was driving the Coronado Trail. Much further, I stopped at a remote viewpoint to survey a shifting sea of mountaintops east and west. The mural stated that this had not been Coronado's trail, even though it was called the Coronado Trail. By then I had been ascending, dropping, ascending, dropping and twisting around hairpins for more than two hours. Maybe I had covered sixty miles. I hadn't seen another vehicle, nor a town or habitation past a couple of tourist hamlets early on. Old snow lined the roads, setting hundreds of acres of burned-black trees to high relief. Grass poked out of melting holes. I feared that the higher passes might be snowed over but the road stayed clear.

I was the only person on the planet.

Turns out that 191 through the White Mountains is the "Least Traveled Federal Highway" in the Lower Forty-Eight. It twists like tangled string and it just kept going. If there was anywhere in the world to commune with my dead grandfather, maybe it was here. This road made these same switchbacks in the 1930s. When I was a kid, Grandma drove her boatlike Dodge Dart with one foot on the gas, one on the brake, knuckles white and teeth clenched. She would never have insisted on her turn at the wheel while he appeased back seat whiners. Clyde would have driven, as I did now.

I did not feel akin. It's an old grudge. Lately I've discussed this again with my brother. None of us, singly or as a group, know how to settle with that man.

Tom says, "Just don't make him bigger than he was."

Well, how big *was* he? How small? I don't know how to measure. What sets me off is that he keeps interrupting my narrative. He shows up because once he was there in a lot of places among people that I believe are mine. We all agree he was a man of his time, but that's true of anyone. What's harder to gauge are the aberrations.

That's my Kit Carson question, too. He didn't like doing what he had to do, so—he was a good man? He wasn't a bad man? He wasn't as bad as someone who *enjoyed* starving Navajo children? Regardless, once he got going Carson could do it better than anyone. He had a talent for sheer unmaking, the kind that required him to summon intelligence and imagination. He had to plan it, and then make a clear decision to get on with the killing.

I doubt my grandfather particularly enjoyed beating the hell out of his sons. If the people who made us walk around in the people we are, then I guess Clyde had a temperamental threshold that broke like a cliff bank. Flat ground, good walking, and then a drop into a chasm that just kept widening. I don't think Clyde was a sadist. He doesn't strike me as a joker. I did see my father, a few times, take pleasure in punishing the slightest gesture of effeminacy in boys. Neighbors, nephews. His grandson. I wonder what he was reenacting but I'm not willing to cut slack. I'll simmer forever. Those moments convince me that everything my grandfather feared in himself got rolled up into a black knot and jammed by force into his son. When Clyde let loose with his disproportionately huge hands, he was brutalizing some apparition of himself. And once he got going the man couldn't stop.

Maybe the real danger is to make our grandfather smaller than he actually was; women in my family learn to diminish the men who stomp a leg into every single story. It's an "Okay, yes, but" move that we've honed to let us get on with the plot, so we can get on down that endless twist of 191, or 666, or the Coronado Trail that is not Coronado's trail.

I will now think of my father, five or six years old, kneeling on the seat, smudging the back window with peanut butter breath and greasy handprints as he wondered when they could stop and play in the trees. No doubt my grownup dad would have let loose a cascade of memories, gestures, speculations at the mention of the White Mountains. Maybe my aunt Mary, a year older than my father, could tell me something, but she's not chock full of tales from what she recalls as a bitterly unhappy childhood. But Dad remembered his father Clyde as a witty, generous, attentive and charismatic guy, a role model were the temper diminished enough. My father longed to be held in his father's circumference of warmth, and if he ever was it had to be very young. I know what stirred him. High mountains, long roads, neat campsites and frypan breakfasts, clearly rooted exactly here.

These were pleasant ruminations by now but that road wouldn't end. The high summits dusted eleven thousand feet. Once I crested, once the drop down the other side began in earnest, the pitch was garish. I swung my head from one side to the other and back just to take it in. The speed limit dropped to ten. By the time I reached the open-pit Morenci Copper Mine, alarming as Mordor, I had been driving the White Mountains for nearly four hours, a few gape stops included. I was unnerved and it was still an hour to Safford and getting dark.

What did I think I was doing here? At one time the prospect of becoming an eccentric old lady was appealing to me. I admire gutsy old broads willing to say fuck it all and take what's theirs after all those years of feminine responsibility and good behavior and maternal self-restraint. My fierce children are launching their own adventurous lives, just as I've always hoped for them. I ought to have parked my car as the valley dropped into the glimmering desert of my father's inception.

I should have stood on a jutting rock and howled like a wild coyote bitch.

I should have had myself a wanton epiphany.

Instead I gripped the wheel like a wan matron, fighting the panic that shrouded my vision with the twilight.

Four years of corralling the Navajo Nation inside a landscape made for itinerant wolves and crows convinced the Feds that they had made an egregious mistake. A Navajo record of the liberation entails a shooting wager. Somebody persuaded indolent soldiers to bet between a Ute and a Navajo marksman. A little leather target in a tree. Ute arrow close, but Diné arrow true. The People released. They performed a ceremony, calling the spirit of the coyote to lead them home. *Put the white beads in the coyote's mouth!*

Bernard DeVoto wrote that the Navajo people remain an unconquered American people: they live where they have been for centuries, in deep semblance of their ancestral lives. The landscape stands damaged but monumental. Their language is yet a living tongue. The tales of return, at least the stories accessible to someone like me, portray survivors dropping to the ground in joy at first sight of their own South Mountain. But the people were more than decimated. Homes, farms, livestock, seeds, and vegetation ravaged. Water stopped and putrid.

After they recovered, they were hit again: in a misguided twentieth-century campaign to curb overgrazing, the Bureau of Land Management slaughtered thousands of Navajo-Churros— rangy, long-haired sheep brought in by the Spanish, perfectly adapted to the desert. The sheep holocaust caused parents to send their children away to survive. My friend Maria, born near Monument Valley, actually wasn't a Placement Program kid. She was adopted outright by the Williams family in American Fork.

"I could never give my children away," she wrote. "But my mother was told I would have a better life."

When the Navajo kids our age went home to their families for the summer, Maria bid them farewell until they returned. "I had to go through some counseling because I felt like I was abandoned by my mom, and just met my birth father about six years ago. I remember visiting my parents on Thanksgiving and spent a couple of weeks with my mom after I graduated from high school. My Anglo parents treated me as their own, so I really don't know anything else. I got married while I was at BYU and all my kids were born in Utah Valley."

Maria and her husband moved their family to a town at the north boundary of the Navajo Nation for the sake of her husband's business. He had grown up on the reservation but lived with a Mormon family during his school years. Maria wrote, "Like I said, we had very good experiences living with our white families. My parents put me in their will and I will always consider them my parents."

Still. Old stuff tumbles down. Carson is a brutal fact of the Navajo narrative, in so many streaks and traces and blots it's hard to know how big or small to make him.

When my father was a missionary in South Carolina, he and his companion received a call from a middle-aged woman in the local ward.

Sister Caroline Hunnicutt said, "There's a man across the street from my house, just sitting in his car."

Dad waited for the point, but apparently she believed she'd made it.

"Um, okay. Does he seem dangerous?"

"No. I don't think so. But he's been there for a long time, and he's staring at my house."

"Have you called the police?"

"No. No, I don't believe that's necessary. Not yet, anyway."

Dad didn't understand what she was getting at.

"What does your husband say about it?"

"He's at work. I don't want to bother him. I thought maybe you and Elder Mendenhall could come over here and ask him what he's up to."

Dad wasn't crazy about that plan.

"Why us?"

"Well, he looks about your age. I thought maybe he'd confide in you. He doesn't look dangerous. It's just peculiar behavior."

Because he was the Zone Leader, Dad had spent this afternoon catching up with reports and bureaucracy. Elder Mendenhall was green and needed time to rehearse his parts should anyone ever let them in to preach. Dad was sorry they'd been home to answer the phone but he told Sister Hunnicutt they'd come in a few minutes. They put on their ties and stupid hats. They drove to the lady's house, passing by the guy in the car as they pulled in. Dad turned to give him a deliberate glare as they walked to the door, hoping he'd get the gist and pull out, but he didn't.

Sister Hunnicutt opened the door before they could knock. They murmured and hovered at the front window, peering through the curtains at the young man in the car. For the moment he was staring toward his hands, lost in thought.

"Are you sure he's watching your house?" Mendenhall asked.

"See for yourself."

Sure enough the kid raised his head and turned it in their direction, eyes fixed on the front window. They shrank back into the relative shadow.

"How long's he been there?"

"A few hours. But he was there yesterday too. Parked in that very same spot an hour or so before dark. I didn't think so much of it then. Winston didn't even notice, and maybe it wouldn't have struck me except he came back today and it doesn't appear he's fixing to go anyplace."

The elders crept back to the window. Dad stood to the side and peered out between the sill and curtain. The guy didn't look too big. He had dark brown hair. Full lips complemented a strong chin. Slender shoulders. Dad's best guess was that the stranger was about his own height or smaller.

"Well, elders," said Sister Hunnicutt. "Somebody's got to approach him. At the very least it's ugly behavior. A young man ought to have better manners."

It occurred to Dad that the guy might have a gun or a knife in his lap, but finally he said, "Okay, let's go talk to him."

The missionaries walked out through the screened porch. It was a gracious house in one of those old Southern neighborhoods that make Utah kids suspect they've been seriously cheated out of verdure. Oaks canopied the streets. Hunnicutts lived all over that county, an old family who had sheltered missionaries from suspicious townfolk a couple of generations back. To those old Southern Mormons, missionaries were standby helpers: young men at the ready to mow lawns for widows, carry hot-dish dinners, or approach strangers in cars staring at houses.

The stranger in the car saw them coming. He rolled up the window to all but an inch. Elder Mendenhall was a big guy, two hundred pounds of varsity muscle.

The stranger made no move to drive off.

Dad leaned down to speak to him through the window crack.

"Hi there. I'm Elder Anderson from The Church of Jesus Christ of Latter-Day Saints. This large man here is Elder Mendenhall."

The guy wrinkled his forehead. "I'm not interested in religion."

"Well, in this case, it's not why we're talking to you." Dad pointed his thumb back toward the Hunnicutts' place. "That nice lady in there says you've been parked here all afternoon."

"This street isn't private property, is it, now?"

"Well, no. But she says you've been staring at her house. It's made her uncomfortable."

The kid's eyes were dark. Dad said he thought then there might be some kind of Indian in him. Could have been Italian. Old Prussian. But he could see why Sister Hunnicutt had called the elders instead of the police or her husband. Put him in a shirt and tie and he could have passed as a Mormon missionary.

Which he did, a week or so later. But at the moment he looked like a bewildered boy in a cheap car. He lifted his eyes on up to the top of Elder Mendenhall's head, then back down to the name tag. He found his bravado. "That's funny. You're both named Elder?"

Mendenhall finally found a way to contribute. "No. My name's Stanley. Elder is a title. Like mister, I guess."

"Speaking of which, Mister . . . ?" Dad asked, and the guy said, "Bilson. But that's a foster name. I think I know my real name, though."

Dad couldn't think when he'd ever heard a statement like that.

"Yeah?" He and his companion both leaned in.

"What is it?" Mendenhall asked, surly.

The kid rolled the window all the way down before he replied. "Hunnicutt."

According to Dad, the Hunnicutts were pillars of the community—and within Mormon circles, the foundation too. They had a lot of money. The old kind. They downplayed their plantation roots, especially the tobacco, but even so their prestige in their home county went deep. For a moment Dad thought maybe this kid was some poor cousin, hoping to claim a minor position in the company or insinuate himself into an inheritance.

"Aw, come on," Dad said. "Those are nice people in there. If you want a job, go on down to the sawmill and find the foreman. Mrs. Hunnicutt in there doesn't run the business."

"I think she's my mother."

That shut Dad's mouth. Mendenhall could seem slow, but it was just a habit of measured reaction. After a solid one, two, three, four, five, he lit up like a roadside flare.

"Hey! That's a fine lady in there! Why don't you get out of the car and say that!"

Bilson said, "Stand back, then," and he pushed open the door and stepped out. He just kept standing up. He wasn't as thick as

Elder Mendenhall, but he was a good three inches taller, muscled and lean. Guess he'd been slouching in the car.

"I'm not here to make trouble," he said. "I just want to put
some questions to rest."

Dad pulled himself together. "So, you want us to go back in
there and ask a nice lady from church whether she had a baby—"

"Maybe it's not her. I don't know if my parents got married.
But I'm pretty damned certain that the old man is my father.
Hunnicutt. Magnolia Street. North Carolina. No town listed so
I've been trying out Magnolia Streets all over the place. Got a tip
from a clerk once I got free."

"Free? What did you get free from?"

"Orphanage. Raised by the Masons. They cut you loose at
seventeen."

Mendenhall took his hat off for that one. Spun it around in
his great big hands. Put it back on.

"How old are you now?" Dad managed.

"Twenty. I've also been doing other things, of course. Not
just combing through Magnolia Streets."

"Are you sure this is the right one?"

"No. It's just likely. I'm not doing this for fun. I don't want
to go knocking on doors asking people personal questions. Not
like you two."

That was fair. Dad glanced toward the Hunnicutts' house. He
saw a little stir in the window. He turned back to Bilson.

"Uh-oh," said Mendenhall, and they all started at the sound
of the front door, and then the porch screen opening and snapping shut. "Here she comes."

Sister Hunnicutt was a smart, straightforward woman, the
kind my father admired. He said he was a poor judge of a woman's
age in those days, but probably Sister Hunnicutt was forty, give
or take, which most likely all three young men at the car were
straining to calculate as she came forward. She had children, the
oldest fifteen. Sister Hunnicutt did not slow down until she was

upon them. The men pressed themselves against the car.

"What is it, boys?" she demanded. "What's everybody gabbing about that you've got to keep from the lady?"

None of them spoke.

Sister Hunnicutt eyed them up and down like she'd caught them smoking. She narrowed her eyes and pointed. "I know Elder Anderson, here. And I've made acquaintance with Elder Mendenhall." She craned her neck to address Bilson. "But I don't know who you are, young man. And I think I ought to, since you've been gazing at my house all afternoon."

Bilson was awful polite. He slid his back down the side of the car to make himself shorter. It still didn't suit his instincts so he bent his legs and squatted like a baseball catcher. Mendenhall folded his arms and leaned in like a delinquent. Dad stepped a little closer to Sister Hunnicutt in case he had to catch her in a Scarlett O'Hara faint.

He looked carefully but couldn't make out a resemblance. He could see a bit of the high councilman, though.

"Mrs. Hunnicutt," Bilson began. "My name is Homer Bilson. I grew up north of here. Up on the Virginia border. A town called Oxford."

He paused. The three of them watched her features for some sign of recognition.

"Never been there," Sister Hunnicutt replied. "What's that got to do with sitting in front of my house all day?"

"Well, you probably know the Masons have goings-on up there."

"I guess so. Mormons aren't Masonic, though. That's a misconception, young man. I'm happy in my religion."

"No—"

"You're saying otherwise?"

"No ma'am. I mean that's not what I'm up to."

"Then say it, for heaven's sake! What are you all gummed up about? Are you soliciting donations?"

They all stood now, everybody looking everybody else over and finally Bilson said, "Well, ma'am, I think you might be my mother."

Dad stepped back to take in her reaction.

Mrs. Hunnicutt looked completely blank. She didn't look angry, or mortified, or even distressed. The best he could say was she looked thoughtful.

They waited while she came to an understanding with herself.

"How old are you, Mr. Bilson?"

"I'm twenty. Twenty-one in November, ma'am."

"You say you grew up in Oxford?"

"Yes, ma'am."

"Isn't there an orphanage up there?"

"Yes, ma'am. Orphanage. Run by the Masons."

She reached her hand toward him. Very tenderly, she touched his shoulder.

"Stand up straight, Homer. Let me get a look at you."

Bilson obeyed, as tall as Dad remembered from a few minutes ago. Dad was embarrassed to stand here at a moment like this, just when a son had found his—

Sister Hunnicutt spoke, kind. "I'm not your mother."

Bilson said, "Please excuse me then. I won't bother you further."

"I never knew her. None of us did if we married into the family after you were conceived."

Bilson went pale. His leanness went soft and shapeless. He looked like a bullied kid, afraid to tell a teacher what he'd just been through.

"But you know who I am?"

Sister Hunnicutt smiled. "I think I do. That orphan upbringing didn't turn you criminal, did it?"

"No ma'am. We were treated kind, mostly. Like any kids, I guess."

"Then, come on in, boys. We have a lot to talk about."

* * *

If genetics alone make people anything at all, Homer Bilson was a Hunnicutt. Sister Caroline's husband Winston was Bilson's uncle. Winston's older brother, the Mormon stake president Montgomery Hunnicutt, was Bilson's father. Homer was the product of a youthful passion between a very young Montgomery and a striking Catawba girl. Nobody outside the immediate situation knew her name but they did know she was related to Chief Blue, who had in the 1800s led many in his tribe to Mormon conversion. Mormon Catawbas went as far back as Mormon Hunnicutts in the ancestral South, but even so the old planters informed their son it was the Indian girl or the inheritance.

Predictably, reputation and inheritance won. Every member of the Hunnicutt family had some inkling of this tale. But Caroline, an in-law, sitting here with her children's lost cousin, was taking deep risk in divulging it.

"What is it you want most?" she asked Bilson/Hunnicutt/Blue.

"I only want to know where I come from. I've lived my whole life without knowing who my people are. I think I can settle some things in my mind if I understand how I got made. I don't care if it's a mess."

"What you need is a story."

"Yes, ma'am."

"Do you think you can settle for that?"

"Yes. I have a girlfriend. We want to get married. I want to be able to tell my children a little bit about who they are. I do not intend to trouble anyone further."

My father watched a woman make a decision that could expel her forever from the favor of a powerful family.

She said, "All right then. There's a Hunnicutt reunion coming up next week. Everybody will be there. Everybody. You have some half brothers and sisters. They're nice children. One of them, Edgar, he's not much younger than you. Seventeen. Now I stare at you the resemblance grows. Then there's a couple of twin sisters. And two more little boys. Youngest is nine."

Bilson could not speak.

Sister Hunnicutt went on. "Your father Montgomery is an upright man. Now I'm looking at you I don't know if I can excuse what he did to your mama and you, but I'll bet he tosses and turns over it. I'm sure he wonders about your mother. I don't know that he deserves to know you're all right. But in any case, I don't believe he has it in him to claim you now."

Bilson was finding himself. "I don't need him to, Mrs. Hunnicutt. I just want to put things to order in my own mind. I'd just like to get a good look at him."

"His wife, you know. A good woman, but rigid. Old family. She probably knows you exist, but she'll never look the fact of it in the eye."

"I don't expect so."

Everyone sat amazed.

"Elders!" My father and Mendenhall jumped like busted candy bandits. "You two. You find this boy one of your silly hats."

She turned back to address Homer. "And you. Do you have a white shirt and tie? Dress shoes and gabardines? You don't look the size of either one of these jokers."

"Yes I do, ma'am. I work at Sears and Roebuck. I can look just like these clowns. However, my name is not Elder."

"Borrow this young man a name tag. And lend him a decent hat. This boy's got family to look upon. And *you*—" she said, looking at Homer, "For one day your name will be Elder. Elder Whatever-These-Boys-Can-Borrow-From-The-Ranks. You'd best rehearse."

Everybody stood to act.

"One more thing. This goes no further than us. Not ever. Mr. Bilson, please do not betray me."

* * *

Grandma Anderson said one of the best things about living in Safford was seeing a gaggle of Mexican kids making their way down the street, pulling a red wagon stacked full of homemade tamales, a nickel apiece. She'd step out and wave them over. So, once I calmed down, once I pulled off the diagonal strip of twenty-first-century traffic signals, franchises, and cheap motel chains, I thought to find a little takeout Mexican place. A few streets down I drove into a time warp. A gracious yellow-brick post office rose up, a clear landmark as I passed it on my right going south. And there was Main Street, nearly abandoned but preserved.

At the west end, a dignified city hall. But for the contemporary cars, my grandparents could have strolled onto the spot where I stood, engrossed in conversation, and walked the length before they realized something wasn't right. Suddenly they would notice how still the street had become, how many storefronts were empty or painted opaque or stacked with inconceivable objects. No billing on the movie marquee. They might wonder at the low roar of heavy traffic a few blocks north. But then they'd see the café was open just like it always was, with its shotgun floor plan and counter seats suspended over blue and white tiles. They might be surprised that it now served only Mexican food but they'd order tamales, just like I did, and probably have them wrapped to go, as I requested, and retreat to a safe spot in the outskirt hills to consider the strangeness.

As I did. I had already reserved a little camping cabin at the state park a few miles south of town. I was grateful for my own forethought and in defiance of my grandparents I bought a bottle of wine at the Circle K on my way out of town. I parked at Cabin 5, Roadrunner, opening the car door to a thicket of bird calls. Ducks, grebes, mourning doves, blackbirds. Other voices I could not name. It was too dark now to see the creatures but the shoreline of tiny Roper Lake was right there, screened by a tangle of willows and reeds. I unloaded my baggage. The cabin was cute. A playhouse. The front section had a double bed. Behind a half partition, two pine bunkbeds.

I couldn't help it: four little children. Irrational maternal reach. I don't expect that every woman is made to be a mother, but I was. One true thing. Small bodies tumbled past me, arguing as they chose their beds, settling in to arrange and elaborate and fall together into their private and compelling world. I hadn't heard from a single one of the grown versions in all this driving away, and I was glad because it meant they were each engrossed in their orbits. And so their small sudden return took me down.

I slept, or passed out, but at some point I walked back out to the car to fetch the yet-warm tamales, hoping they would help conjure ancestors rather than descendants. I carried the sack to the picnic table on the porch under the rising moon, relieved to be invisible to the quiet visitors from all their places. But I could not make myself eat. I left the wine unopened. I gathered everything and carried it across the dark lot to the trash bin. I walked to the lapping shore and stood in the dark. I stepped in a few feet, past my knees. Night birds called true to one another.

The next morning I took a walk around the lake, grateful for the new-knit tibia and fibula although they hurt. Another story, but it did make me recall Ignatius. I loaded the car. I intended to spend the morning walking through town taking notes, all writerly. I thought I'd cleared my head from yesterday's drive. I went north back to Safford, further than I recalled—about ten miles—and I reacted by swinging left toward town at the first intersection. I'd turned too soon, but the town wasn't huge and this looked like a perimeter, so I went forward.

A half mile more and I was passing gravestones to my right, and then I saw the arched entry sign. Safford Union Cemetery.

I yanked the wheel, squealing the tires. Crosses and Madonnas and glitter-foil buntings to my right and left told me I was not in the Mormon section. I pulled up to a tall community cross and veteran's memorial, queerly lavender. I parked and rolled the windows down. Birdsong struck like a chorale.

I stepped out and spun around to assess. The cemetery extended for several acres but it was easy to see I was in the old section. Tall cypress trees, filled-up plots. No grass in this desert bedding. Bouquets—some bright fabric or plastic, some real and wilted—and tinsel wreaths pulsed against the dull mineral background. Most of the plots had been walled into family rectangles. A weedy succulent provided random fist-sized blobs of green in the places nobody walked. Graves with Spanish names were colorful and highly attended. Saints and Madonnas, statues of Jesus. Buntings and streamers.

I surveyed the acreage to spot the uniform nonconformity, a section of headstones, flat and distinctively crossless, to locate my dead affiliates. I walked over to browse. Mormon epitaphs, line-carved images of hornblowing Moroni and spired temples. Still, there were many markers. Each family enclosure looked to be holding ten or twelve graves.

Diagonal from where I stood, just a few frames up, a barren plot. A small black headstone all alone. No flowers or bunting. No wall. Placed to keep cars at bay, a three-foot spigot pipe rose just behind. I walked over. There it was.

LORRAINE
Daughter of
Clyde LeRoy and Constance Porter
ANDERSON
Oct. 27, 1940
Oct. 28, 1940

I couldn't think what to do about it.

My single emotion was anger at myself for making foot-prints on top of the baby. In a climate like this the disturbance could last a decade. I backed up, sat on the low wall of the next plot over, and worked myself up about the footprints. I tried to distract myself by analyzing the site. One six-pound infant in a box that was, intact, maybe twenty-five inches long, fifteen wide. The rest of the plot was pristine. But for my footprints it was clear no boots had trammeled this spot for decades.

I believed I had committed an ugly trespass. I did not care to be a family representative. Most of my relatives would concur I'm the wrong person.

I took a few phone shots and sent them to my sisters. My pulse leaped in gratitude as they each answered.

I gazed up at big Mount Graham.

I've been clear with my children: cremate. Let fly the ashes. Do not enclose any remnant of me. No urn, no vials, no plaster or cement or dirt. Scatter. I don't believe in souls, and even if I did I don't see why they would hang around their own suffocated remains. I recalled the coroner's words to my grandmother: probably nothing to move. Dust. At this moment I hoped it was so, but then again I knew there had to be some forensic trace. Safford receives nine inches of rainfall per year. Perfect dry air, unsaturated ground. The southwest desert yields many artifacts, including well-preserved human remains, centuries old.

The first house I bought after my marriage collapsed like a sinkhole was a nondescript brick rambler with a glorious old-time yard. But the interior could have been a Museum of 1974, which can get to you if you didn't love 1974. The first month, the pipes under the kitchen sink ruptured. When the plumber came to tear it all out, the debris beneath the cabinets was archaeolog-ical. Mostly it was sawdust, with nails and cigarette butts stirred in. But laid out as if for admiration was a skeleton of a mouse, intact to the last vertebral tip of its tail, fitted like an intricate magical toy.

I should have been repulsed but I had to keep myself from caressing it, and now among all of that unsettled recollection I was picturing the exquisite bones of a human infant prone and pristine under my boot prints, the skin of her strange webbed fingers fallen away, the haunting caul that covered her face and neck dissolved, the deep structure of mystery revealed yet unresolved.

I sat longer and recalled a cold morning when I was fourteen and our parents were away on a weeklong trip. My brother and I walked in the morning chill, down that back line to Grandma's barn to feed the animals Dad was sheltering there until he returned. We knew the ewes were pregnant but they weren't yet due. Even before we cleared Grandma's stile we could see something was wrong. The horses stood away at the far end of the pasture. The sheep huddled against the barn, one a bloody mess.

We drew closer. A dead lamb lay in the open field, enclosed in its now-frozen sac. Another, a twin that may have taken a few steps before freezing, lay a few feet beyond.

A breath or two, a falter, all done.

This kind of thinking is why the many descendants of the parents marked on this baby's headstone would nominate anyone but me to trip to such a solemn site and eulogize. I tried to quit it. I worked to clear my mind and keep the space pure. I stood up to atone for the footprints. I knelt on my right knee and held the screwed-and-bolted left one out at an awkward angle. I smoothed the footprints with my palm, revealing soft fine dirt beneath the gravel. I made a circle. I eased up on the strength of my good knee and walked the larger plot to gather stones the size of peach pits.

The desert looks colorless until you pick it up: juniper green, terra cotta, cherts in black and blue, mustard yellow. I carried them back to the circle, careful about new footprints, and lined them into a spiral—"Spiral Jetty," my youngest would have called it, if she were here and still small; I recalled a good day with her, years ago, at the north shore of the Great Salt Lake. Now I stepped sideways to encircle the mini-jetty in footprint rays, hoping that at some point those nine annual inches of rain would neutralize them, and camouflage the stones. All of this business cleared my mind. I forgot myself and time dropped when I stood up. The air congealed above the little piece of ground that I knew for a fact my own people had stood upon, late October 1940.

I step in.

People mill about, printing this dirt with hundreds of tracks. The Mormon ward has come out, and the Catholic family that makes tamales as well. I am grateful for the crowd—not for my grand-parents' sake, as they're in no social mood, but for my own. The bodies allow me to acclimate.

Women huddle in little knots, all wearing hats, many holding babies. I wear jeans and boots, and because a Safford October feels a lot like a Safford February, a sleeveless cowboy shirt. My hair is straight and a little dirty. I make an effort to pull it into a civilized ponytail.

Children run about, shouting and tagging. Some settle a moment when rebuked but then light out again. Some are smart enough to stay out of reach. Men stand gazing outward, holding this hard domestic moment at arm's length.

Everyone here is emerging from a Depression. I compose a list of wonders and terrors these people have not yet seen. How much they do not know. I feel a superior tingle of prescience like air before lightning, but when it strikes up there on the high peaks, purpling the sunlight, I comprehend it's the flicker of my own unreadable future. Theirs has come and gone. I can see that, too, a black roiling mist fitting the harsh ridges.

I do not have a guide and now I realize why I should.

The people I hope to address are behind me but I am not prepared to turn.

I walk erratic to the north edge of October 1940. On the cinder road my boots sound like coins in a shaken box. The cemetery rests on a swell above the city. It's easy to trace every spot the channeled water touches below: neat family gardens, cypress rows, bright floral patches. Little houses beam up in stucco blue and green, butter yellow, tangerine.

I strain my vision northward over valley and range. I miss my children so sharply my chest feels scraped out. At this moment they feel more lost to me than the spectral noisemakers frolicking among the headstones.

They are not here. I am not anywhere.

Time cracks, bottomless and black and I drop down. Warm snow, powdered and deep. Salt water scouring my fine mouse bones.

I reach for the story. I turn to face the milling mourners. The extras are collecting their children and clearing out. I walk in a deliberate, counting pace, breathing to it, willing the last of them to drive off in their movie cars. The remainers are clearer now, figures I can sharpen the same way I focus a camera lens. Clyde and Connie stand together at the fresh-dug hole. It's larger than it needs to be to hold the tiny box, because first it had to contain a man with a shovel.

I halt to adjust the image, dialing back my grandmother's age. Her hair darkens. It's longer and pulled back in a careless roll. She came with a hat but it's on the ground. She moves more quickly than I remember. Her shoulders are strong and well defined but I recall she has recently delivered an infant, so her patterned dress smocks over a muddled waistline. Stockings black, sturdy shoes. I feel a surge of plain love at the distinctive way she nods her head, and how she stands, feet too far apart. She's the same height as her husband, maybe taller.

I am not ready to converse so I size up the man beside her. I know he is bald under his sharp felt hat, has been since his

early twenties. He's built small and tight. I see his masculine deft-
ness now, because my younger son is framed in likeness. My son
permits me to invent a man I never knew. Deep-voiced, soft-
spoken. Moves like lake water. He's made of dense bone and lean
muscle, stands in relaxed attention even here at the burial of his
baby daughter.

He's a compelling man, even with that fury—maybe, at this
point of my life, because of it. Still I cannot bring myself to speak.
I see my father, Tommy, and his brother Chris over there among
the trees, tired of this solemn not-Sunday afternoon. Tommy is
five since July. Chris is three, towheaded. He looks like a storybook angel but I know he's no such thing. Where's Lynne? She's
a toddler, barely a year older than this baby about to be buried. I
place her in her father's arms to test him. She squirms backward
and down, the way small walkers do when they want to explore.
He sets her down, but gently. She steps and tumbles, cries, then
discovers the dirt and colored stones.

I walk nearer, looking for a six-year-old. I know I can talk
to her. This one will play life hard and she'll be tough enough
to enjoy it. Right now she's a skinny line experimenting with
elegance. She's missing front teeth. She gives me a precocious
side-eye.

I say, "Hello, Mary."

She scowls, intrigued.

"You aren't supposed to be here," she says.

I spent a warm evening at Mary's place a few years ago.
Good wine and strong conversation. Sometimes I think Mary is
crazy. Sometimes I don't. Her daughters probably felt the same
about my father. I haven't seen Mary in a long time; she tends to
approach and retreat. Maybe this time, right here, will be the last.

"How do you know I don't belong?"

"You're wearing the wrong clothes."

I put my finger to my lips. "Don't tell anyone. No one else
will notice."

She's pleased to keep a secret. I point toward Tommy banging along the fence line. "Is that your brother?"

"Yes. Both. Stupid boys." She'll be surprised by how long she outlives her almost-twin. "Who are you?"

Another secret. "I'm a time traveler."

"You are not."

"Okay. I came down from Utah. I'm here to see your mother. She's very sad today."

"I know. The baby died." Mary is sympathetic but preoccupied with her own fierce thoughts. I want to prophesy while I have the advantage but I'm not here to dispense revelation.

I make a plan. One question per character. "Mary. What do you love?"

She thinks this over. "Nothing. I hate everything."

I veer from the plan. "Okay then. Who do you love?"

"I hate everyone."

That makes me laugh. "No you don't. You'll see."

"No, *you'll* see," she says and fades off as I walk toward her parents. Clyde sees me coming, nods as if he knows me but then double-takes.

I'm committed now. "I'm sorry for your loss, Brother Anderson."

He tilts his head. "Do I know you?"

"Parts of me."

"Where do you come from? You're made like my mother and sister."

"That's no revelation. My father told me that."

He is sifting evidence. This is the sort of day he might expect a visitation but I'm not the kind he's been watching for.

"Let me shake your hand," he says.

I know what he's up to. He intends to discern whether I am a good or a bad angel. I'm not certain I'm corporeal so I keep my hands to my sides. This means that I am a good messenger made of spirit; I will not offer a hand to deceive him. He waits me out. I slide my hands into my back pockets.

67

He appears to be satisfied, and he asks, "Do you know what happens to us?"

I know he will make his wife pregnant five more times. I know he'll soon move his family north to Salt Lake City. I know his definition of paternal discipline will escalate into what the law in my time would frankly call abuse. I know he'll buy a dairy farm in Alpine to try working his oldest son into compliance.

I know he'll die in a fiery explosion thirty thousand feet above the Mediterranean Sea, leaving one son at least to assemble himself in a house of broken mirrors.

He will have sixty grandchildren. He will not live to know a single one of us.

"Only a little," I say.

"What have you come to tell me?"

I haven't come to tell him anything. But here he is. Here he always is.

I've come to tell you to fuck off, you disgusting fuck.

I've come to tell you a whole family has filled in your absence with wishes, with justifications and incriminations, emulations, with a better ending to your story.

I've come to diminish you so I can get on with more relevant outrages.

I've come to tell you I understand it's plain infuriating to be alive and the gorgeous parts are only exacerbations.

I don't have it in me. These people are dead. He got what he had coming and probably more. Blown into black sky, lost in strange waters. Sent home rotting in a sealed box.

And so I fade.

"I came all this way, but the more I think about it, the less I have to tell you. The actual road is not like a line on the map. I just drove over that Coronado Trail. You've got to know what I mean."

He has my father's laugh. I like him. I fear him in all of us.

My grandfather and I glance together toward the little boys

throwing rocks at a post. Excellent aim. I pick up a smooth red stone and throw it clean in Tommy's direction.

Clyde says, "Oh. I see."

"Yes, but this is all you'll ever see of me. And I have a question for you."

He doesn't want to hear it but he attends.

"Are you better for them dead than you were alive?"

"How long do I have?"

"About a decade."

He is truly stunned. He takes stock of his little children. He reaches a hand toward his wife. He tilts his head, and straightens it to look me in the eye. I hold my bluff. I've played him with his own formula and so he squares himself to answer.

"You know, my father never relented at all. I've loved my own children better far than I received. I might have left him behind. I might have become better."

"Do you think you would have?"

"How can I know? I believe there's something of my mother in me."

He looks to the mountain. "A story of a man is not the man himself. My children will not wish me dead, no matter how much they wish me to be a better father."

I don't know. What children do not sometimes wish their parents dead?

Now he looks toward the sky, and then across the acres of the deceased.

I step a pattern of rays with my twenty-first-century boots. "How much is unforgivable? I saw you—the ghost of you—in my father's worst moments. I don't know how to forgive him. I don't know that I should."

He glints at me strangely, lifting his hand as if to touch mine. I don't know whether it's tenderness or an attempt to confirm his suspicion that somehow I am cheating the messenger formula. This man is not stupid. I jerk my hand away.

"How long are we responsible?" he asks. "When do we leave them to answer for their own good and evil?"

He flexes his jaw the way my father used to. He gestures downward, as if sweeping something behind him. "I've got to round up those boys. Please excuse me now."

My grandmother stands.

"We'd best go," she says. "They'll be coming in to close it up."

She knows the men with the shovels await.

I make them vanish another moment, and she relaxes. She meets my eyes.

"I'm sorry. I don't recall whether we've been introduced."

"Not yet and forever ago."

I conjure a bench and she consents to sit.

"I'm sorry about the baby."

"Well, I don't know what to say about that."

"Why aren't your parents here? Where's your family?"

"It's a long way. We had to take care of this. Some of them are driving down next week."

She thinks. She comes to a certain clarity and reaches to touch my knee. "How did *you* get here so soon?"

"Down the Devil's Highway. Don't ask to shake my hand."

She laughs at my joke, very gratifying, and she bobs her head as if to clear her mind. Neither of us can quite make out what time this is.

"How do things go with your husband?" she asks. "I only get to see the first part."

"Not so well. But the kids—wish you could know them. They'd worry you though. And I'll still do everything I'm gonna do."

She looks toward hers. Mary sashays in our direction. Clyde is bringing in the boys but allows them to meander. Baby Lynne is tasting rocks. The tiny coffin hovers over the abyss.

"Why aren't you acquainted with my husband?"

"He's only a story."

"No. Absolutely he is not."

"I watched you all those years, alone. I loved your house. You had people and solitude both. I must have come to believe that this is the way mothers go. A house empty and full at once. Books. A garden and trees, hours to be in them. But now I'm afraid."

"You ought to be. Did you imagine this would be easier than the seasons before it?"

She lifts her hand at the wrist, pointing a sideways finger into arid blue. "You spend your life trying to keep everything gathered. But when you succeed it's all about scatter. Children grow up and get on. As they must."

She gestures toward the grave. "You can't hold what must go."

She bumps her shoulder against mine. "And you can't let go what you must hold. This is a sin. The kind you still believe in."

We face west, tracing out the green and gray mountain, falling to silhouette. I wish to sit a little longer.

"Mount Graham looks a lot like Lone Peak. In Alpine. I mean in its general mood and conformation."

"We thought so, too."

The husband and children were very near.

"Grandma. Should I go home?"

"The day death comes for you, your life will seem briefer than this one in the box. No need to hurry it."

She stood in her time, urgent to greet the approaching men.

I lingered to catch a glimpse of Tommy, who gave me frank little-boy appraisal. A quick grin. He put his hand in his father's and waved me off.

Clyde: "Can you be so casually lost to them?"

Constance: "Go home."

I stood, sifting, and she said, "You can recite these words as well as I can. I will read them to you some time: 'There is a concatenation of events in this best of all possible worlds.'"

I read them again years later in a college French class. Concatenation.

Cela est bien dit, mais il faut cultiver notre jardin.

Something sat hard in my gut.

Mourning doves provided a two-note flute song as I walked back to my car. I kept driving south. I lost my bearings entirely. I could see Mexico, right there to my left, and I bounced along the ludicrous boundary wishing I could punch through to Patagonia.

At some point in the muddle I must have reached a turning point. A reluctant return.

Homer Bilson showed up to the Hunnicutt reunion with a name tag my father and Elder Mendenhall borrowed from another missionary. Bilson had trimmed up his dark hair, re-pressed his white shirt at Dad's apartment, donned a tie and hat. At the party, Sister Caroline took a liking to the extra elder. She took him by the hand and led him around to meet each member of her husband's family. Bilson calmly spoke to his half siblings and father, cousins, aunts and uncles, grandparents and even a great-grandmother, all of them inexplicably taken with the young man. They recited family stories, recalled legendary pranks, dished up more food. They reminded one another to never forget they were Hunnicutts, a proud name they must always live up to.

Sister Caroline made sure Elder So-and-So ate more than he could stand and then made him eat more. She packed biscuits and pastries, ripe figs and shelled pecans to last him another week. He could have stayed longer but abruptly he stood and graciously thanked the people around him. My father and his companion excused themselves too, saying they needed to get on now with the work, and the three young men took leave. Bilson said little during the drive back, but when they stopped he thanked them again, heartfelt and well-spoken.

Dad walked him to his car and shook his hand, wishing he could do more. Homer Bilson turned the ignition and pulled away.

* * *

That boy's story has stayed with me, of course, and it has meant different things in various seasons. When I was a child he meant ineffable sorrow, a first chilling comprehension that a family could throw a son or daughter away for the sake of reputation. As I got older, and relations became more complex, I sometimes envied a person who had every good reason to vanish into a new kind of being—no further tug of conscience or duty. The heft of family, and history, and of fixed and insistent meanings is no light load.

What is he now? The man himself is most likely dead or bent with age, recontoured by the future that beckoned from the other side of a turbulent gulf. His meaning to flat figures he has no reason to know he's touched, decade by decade?

For me, now, simply a foil. He drove away. I'm driving back.

IGNATIUS INSISTS
THAT I SUMMON A GUIDE

*Y*ou will become lost. Summon a form to signal your way.

Am I driving into vanishment? Maybe at the beginning I was.

You have turned toward home, nudges the crippled saint. *You may wend and witness. You may hear those willing to answer you. But recall your intentions, or every voice will speak malediction.*

I consider. But I am distracted by police trucks shrouded in the vegetation. I tap the brake, reading this as a peculiar speed trap. No. Border patrol. Large men with guns and uniforms—and dogs—step up to the sightline. I prepare persuasions. I reach for my wallet.

The men with guns and dogs perceive a small grimacing woman behind the dirty windshield. They wave me on.

I am not grateful.

Choose your guide.

And she's here, demure on the seat beside me. My father's best aunt. Beloved sender of birthday cards! President of the National Order of Does! Queen of the Idaho Lady Republicans! My grandfather Clyde's just-older sister, Iola.

Her orange hair is incandescent. Cat-eye glasses make her fierce although she weighs less than a hundred pounds. She sits, flickering but firm in the shotgun seat. She's a tiny ancient woman, and then a youthful girl, and then again the orange hair and glasses.

My brother has convinced himself that he saw me in the cemetery this morning.

"I've always wanted to tell you that your cousin Hazel gave me all your sweaters after you died. I was the only one who fit them."

I'm happy to hear it. I took pleasure in expensive knits.

"The black silk one—you know? With the silver threads. I still have it. My older daughter is made like you and me. I should give it to her."

Do.

I brake at the intersection: Buffalo Soldier Trail. She is preoccupied.

My mother. Made the same. That's how Clyde could rationalize you. He never could tolerate mystery. A pointless revelation.

She appears to enjoy the dry scenery. I wonder what she knows about me now, and how it might inform what she reveals.

I did not come to grant you visions. I am not come to love nor judge.

"Would you travel so far to someone you no longer love?"

I only mean that it is not my calling here. I have come to send you in.

I step on the gas. "I don't believe."

I am not come to help you believe. I send and receive.

"How?"

Limit your questions. Hold what's worth holding. No single form will tell you truth; no form lie.

I stop the car. I continue to drive.

This landscape belongs to the Apache people.

"Okay, here's my question: why are those Andersons so pissed off?"

Iola turns her head like a mechanical bird.

Because they are small.

Because they recall.

Because they are quick.

Because they are sick.

She opens the veil.

See as I speak:

My father was the first child of a miserable marriage. His mother Sidse Nielsen had come to Utah with a bastard son, my half uncle Peter, spawned by an old-world charlatan.

My grandfather was an inexplicable cuss. I know nothing of his childhood. I do know he married a proper wife and produced two children back in Denmark, but the man was not made for family relations. When he tired of domestic drudgeries he conjured heavenly visions to escape them. He joined the Mormons as pretense to move on.

They came in their own ways to Utah, but once they arrived, Sidse Nielsen and Thomas Christian Andersen married under Brigham Young's command. They helped settle a tiny town called Mantua. My father was born there. Those were dangerous years, Indians defeated and dire.

"Which Indians?"

Shoshone. That was the big violence. The small violence was Sidse and Chris. A matched pair of wildcats. Some things just get made in the body, far as I can tell. My father tried to exorcise the family temper. He admired his half brother Peter—wished to be, like him, a happy man. But mostly he boxed the rage intact and passed it directly to his sons.

The Mormons saw my grandmother Sidse as a fallen woman. Papa tried to take it in stride but he didn't have the constitution to brush off community censure. I think he married my exuberant mother to sweeten the harsh family strain, but he nearly broke her, too. I'd like to believe we girls became our mother. But you know we're all made after the men and women, both, who beget us.

You yourself have flung a vase or two. A stone. A plate. A cruel rejoinder. If you hit your mark—and I know you have—you've claimed the familial talent.

"I never aimed at a person, though."

You know what I mean. It's a talent, and this is where it came from. Don't get distracted. My brothers took the bruises. Our father enforced compliance in every slender detail—not rare in our generation but even then there was too much passion in it. Everyone saw it. You wonder how a son becomes his father? Don't be coy. You know the ways. My older brothers took it out on one another, and trained the younger ones to fight like bantam cocks. We were known in Ammon, Idaho—where our father and his brothers finally settled—as fiercely honest. Ramrod Mormons. Brutally hardworking sheepherders.

Behind our backs? We were known as a clan of småfolk, *chips on hard shoulders. Your grandpa—my brother Clyde—came at the far end. I was only a little older than him. He became what I might have, had I been born a boy. I loved my brothers. They were smart and gifted, and they longed for joy and levity and the kind of talk allowed to women. But their love was trained to strike.*

Look in.

Give them time.

Ask them to account for themselves.

Try to be gentle.

GREAT WHITE CHIEF

Peter Nielsen

Well, I saw some wonderments in my life. Wasn't short nor long, considering how the old toad who raised me steamed right on to eighty-seven. Thought I'd earned a couple decades to enjoy the continent without him, but only six years later down I went. Kidneys gave out—did their best after I took a hard fall from a new-broke gelding but there was only so much they could accomplish.

But what's fair? I got some thrills. Married a girl with a cork leg and I was damned lucky to love her. Ran sheep in the Idaho mountains. I raised good daughters and sons even though not a one would stoop to farm, and life granted me one last stretch of peace after all the fuss—a little more time to appreciate my grandbabies.

Life's a parade of visions. Plenty to see. If I had to rank, strangest thing I ever saw was twenty-two elephants tumbling like mountain boulders off a high bank of the Snake River. A man can't complain if he's granted life enough to see a herd of elephants plummet into the roil of his own home waters.

My mother Sidse had a long life, almost as long as the jack-ass she married when I was eight years old. Old cuss fathered my half brothers and sisters as well as a couple of Danish snobs none of us ever met. Mama's last years in my half brother Chris's house were peaceful. They made sure she had a nice room of her own with a door to shut, but by then her memory was so sedimented she could hardly loosen a piece for the sake of civil conversation. At least not without dredging up a whole bucket of sludge. My brother and his wife were a little ashamed of her, what with her divorces, so Chris and I veered off conversations about our mother. I'd like to say my half siblings were wound tight due to their father's blood but then again we all shared the same mama. The whole lot of us could ignite quick on a small spark. I'm willing to say though that my brother Chris did right by her. The boy spent his whole life trying to keep us linked together. He figured it would all work out once we were an eternal family in the Celestial Kingdom, if only he could keep herding us toward a magical destination where we could love one another in all the right ways. The whole lot of us, even those distant Danes.

Chris was a man to keep his pieced-up heart together by answering to God every jot and tittle, hoping the installments would build him into his own man beyond his father's namesake. Made him tense company though. He sent the old family temper right on down to his sons, all good boys but packed like gunpowder. Me, I think it might be heaven for us to go our own ways after the resurrection, if it ever materializes. We might look in on one another every few thousand years. That way maybe we'd exchange more pleasantries than blows. Eternity is one hell of a long time is what we'll all come to understand, wicked and righteous alike.

I learned something about that when I was a kid in the old man's house. Hunger is waiting, and waiting and thinking up ways to measure empty air to fill its own void. It's striking bargains with God that don't pan out the livelong day because you simply ain't the one with the influence. Hungry is part of it but I'm not just talking about an empty gut.

Once my mama married that abstemious ass I didn't eat but once a day, and that from a plate he doled out to his tally of my wage since before sunup. He worked me so hard I didn't achieve eighty pounds until I was fourteen years old. Mama said my real father was a slight man, too. Maybe that's how she worked her mind to let old Andersen starve me half to death, at least until she crossed a line of rage that marked her too deep to recover. She was a tough bird, never truly did buckle under to anyone's rule. Not even God's but that doesn't mean she didn't feel awful about it. Carried a dark sense she wasn't really a woman, she was so contrary, and I believe it frightened her. She gave good feminine behavior hard effort in seasons of remorse.

She was broke like a beaten filly the summer she descended Emigration Canyon into the Salt Lake Valley. I was seven but I can't say I remember it beyond a strange sensation of dreaming. I was one sickly excuse for a son. I walked the prairies but I'd been clinging to her back like a backwards joey since Rock Springs. All I recall from there is a long pulsing sensation. The world around me a blur of painful blue and pebbled light. I was her firstborn, bastard son of an insubstantial Dane who wouldn't claim us. Mama made that easier for him by traversing a cold ocean and two thousand miles of American continent.

Far as I'm concerned, Ole Nielsen was my true and only father. He saved my mama's reputation, marrying her just about the point she couldn't hide the signs of me back in the old country. I figure those Danes liked to say they knew I was no Nielsen, but at least they had to whisper it once she was married to a decent man. He was good to me in every way I can recollect, and happy at the birth of my brother and baby sister. Wish he could've seen America. But I guess that's just a way of wishing that an entire family had coursed along another path. My mother told me to quit that kind of wishing so many times that I was mostly trained off of it past our first year in Utah.

Of the five of us who had set out from Denmark, only my mother and I reached the Salt Lake Valley. She told me she was grateful I survived it but I can't help but think she wouldn't secretly wish me dead at some point or several, just to shed weight on that endless trek. I was the lone reason for her to keep on; she'd lost the other children and the only man who ever did right by her.

Once I was grown I traveled back to Denmark as a missionary, hearkening to the prophet's command, leaving my wife and children home. I sought to locate the scoundrel who conjured me in twenty minutes of spare heat. I kept trying to picture him, spent the whole time I was preaching on about the Angel Moroni half-gazing for a blond slender villain who looked like me. But in that country everyone resembles a lost bloodline. My reward for seeking a skulking progenitor was to lose my Sarah back in Utah. By the time I got the news and then made it home to Mantua, our children had already learned to care after one other. My mother had kept them in bread and stew but the woman had offered them not one word of sympathy nor gesture of tenderness. I doubt she remembered how.

Sidse Nielsen Andersen

Each time I was shameless enough to show my own sorrow I paid the cost. Nobody rolls out a tear they don't come to regret. Sooner or later we learn to hold it in.

By the time I blubbered in front of the general population of Salt Lake City I'd already seen a pretty Danish boy deny me and his son, swear he'd never touched me in his life even though the baby favored him from the day he crowned. And I'd seen my good husband Ole Nielsen rolled off a ship into the silver mirror of Atlantic water with the body of our little Niels in his stiff dead arms. The child was but four years old. The sailors wrapped them up in a canvas sheet and I sewed them in. The once-rosy baby girl cried in Peter's bony arms while I stitched slow and careful. Some of the sailors and many passengers also failed. After the first week of illness there was no canvas to spare, so bodies were dropped into the sea wrapped in family bedding or overcoats. Water so still, so long, must be a colony of parents and red-spotted children at the bottom.

When the wind finally came it blew no change of fortune. We idled in quarantine on Battery Island. Immigration nearly sent the whole boatload back where we came from, especially when they understood we were Mormons headed for Utah. I suppose they figured it would be near the same if we took what was left of us and the measles on to Salt Lake City. Those of us who recovered or never got sick to start with took the train to Nebraska to rendezvous with the Mormon teamsters, sent out to bring us and a swelling company across the prairies. And those cursed mountains. I held my fevered baby girl for a week in Florence while our company provisioned for the walk west. We buried her same day as several others, her body a tiny bundle amidst the mummies. I marked her place with a stone, size of a man's fist, and we turned our faces toward Deseret. Scrawny and water-eyed, Peter took my hand and strode out but he'd taken the measles too, back on the ship. He'd borne them out but his skin stretched into taut bird leather, drawing pale around his angled face and narrow shoulders.

Later I found myself grateful the boy had no recollection of the days he clung like a monkey to my back. We'd begun with a share of a wagon, teaming with a diminished clan from our sea voyage. By the time we emerged from the hot mouth of Emigration Canyon, a mob of valley Saints had gathered to greet their kin or prey on the destitute. Our wagon was empty of nearly all but ticking and sick babies. I set Peter down, claimed my cast-iron pot, and groped in my pocket to affirm that I yet had fifty cents. The coin was no reassurance. I staggered back, oddly light. I sat myself in the dirt beside my son and broke into public sobbing.

That day finished my habit of tears forever. It was not because I became stronger. Maybe we only have so much salt to spare.

"Sister," said a fat, smooth-lipped man in Swedish, "I perceive that you and your child are alone. The West, lo, even here in our miraculous city of God, is no place for a single woman and her orphan. I can offer you succor in your season of want. I only ask that you aid my dainty wife with her housework and we will care for your earthly needs in your season of anguish."

I understood his words, his slick Swedish turn on our rougher Danish tongue. I should have discerned the pompous diction of an opportunist but all I could register was hope for shelter for Peter. And so I spent my first season in Brigham's valley abject as a slave, attending our benefactors night and day. Peter and I froze near to death every night in a rotting wagon box behind the house while the apostolic children slept in down. We shat in the weeds and then the snow beyond the boundary of the ample yard, out on the edge of the howling desert.

I was so reduced by the time the Spring Conference came about, I fell for the lordly blessing of Brigham Young and the old goat he urged to propose to me. Prophecy must have seemed the only thing more real than misery.

Thomas Christian Andersen, the Father

Holy writ decrees that God tries whom he loves. I came early to the contention that he must love me dearly. I never got a fair hand in Zion. Though I grasped the Iron Rod looking neither to the right nor left, God rewarded my valiance with ungrateful wives and wanton children, particularly the useless fool I took in with his mother. I thought I would finally be granted the great joy promised to me when I sacrificed all for the Restored Gospel of Jesus Christ. But I was answered with spite and ingratitude.

Brigham Young himself pointed Sidse out to me at a gathering of the Saints in Salt Lake City. "Look there, Brother Andersen," he said. "See that lady with her young son, a widow among us right here in Zion. You're a single man with no warm breast to comfort you when the day's work is done. A righteous Elder in Zion must surely find joy in the company of such a handsome woman. And that boy clearly needs a father. I'll see you at the Endowment House before this month is finished."

I looked her over as she spoke to her son, a waif the size of a half-grown nanny goat. His blond hair fell past his shoulders like a girl's. Sidse stood straight legged, arms wrapped tight around her waist when she spoke. When she turned her head she gave us a hard stare that drew plenty in but yielded nothing in return. Her cheekbones rode high enough to slant her eyes, dark like some thread of Gypsy or Black Russian had once wove itself in. Her boy though was an urchin straight from the gutters of Copenhagen. Could have dropped him back in that city and he'd fade into the flock of pickpockets like they were all made of the same flaxen work shirt.

Suddenly I realized I already knew who the woman was: Sidse Nielsen, sharpened like a tomahawk over the years since I knew of her in the old country. Those of us who joined the Mormon faith back there, we stuck together. It was as if we'd branded our own foreheads with a hot iron. All of us had family that wanted nothing more to do with us. My own barbaric wife had seized our two innocent children once she saw I would not be dissuaded from the only true and living gospel. She returned to Aalborg to hide in shelter of her family, and even importuned my own for redress.

This Sidse was in Denmark harboring ugly secrets, passing as respectable under cover of a husband who claimed that girlish boy as his own. The child was the bastard of a man she would not name. For many converts, burning faith was mere alibi. Many tares in the Mormon wheat. I reckon they hoped to leave her reputation as far behind as they could, come to America where nobody would discern her dark history.

I protested to Brother Brigham. I already had a wife and children. I reminded him that my heart was rent over the children who refused to unite with me in this life or the next. I wrote to them regularly, toiling to convince them of the true gospel and to join me in Zion. I told them of the sweet visions of celestial glory that carried me through each day. I explained how the gifts of prophecy and personal revelation were theirs to partake of, would they only find in their hearts to be grateful to a father who sacrificed all he loved to mark the path to the Kingdom of God.

I did not care whether their mother ever darkened my threshold again. The scriptures ordain that a wife should cleave unto her husband. A man is the wife's broker with God. I'll stand and testify at the Judgment Bar and God will hold her to her defiance.

Brother Brigham said, "Well, even so, if your Danish family comes around to truth, they must convert to the principle of Celestial Marriage. You well know that I am the husband of many wives. I cannot rescue every woman in the valley. Brother Andersen, God knows you can manage two, especially since one of them presently wants nothing of you."

We gazed again across the square, facing the western mountains and the bleak salt desert beyond. In the foreground Sidse looked gaunt and haunted, a silhouette against the afternoon sky. I'll allow she was beautiful in her strange way. A woman's figure, a man's stance. Maybe it was abandon, a refusal to posey up. She stood alone, watching her son as he crept along the fence line tracking a rat, or a rabbit—some creature in the between of nature and civilization.

I told Brother Brigham I believed that woman was plain unmanageable. He retorted, "Are you a man? A woman's opinion matters no more to an Elder of Zion than a flyspeck on a windowpane. Make sure she comprehends this right from your first approach. Treat her like a spirited horse; don't let her get the better of you. She'll settle soon enough to her right temper. It's a relief to them, even the contrary ones, to answer to their nature."

I don't question the man's a prophet but it's apparent to me now, too late, that even a prophet cannot know every last thing. God himself would have a time of it with Sidse. Or then again maybe it goes to show that even He is more contrary than we comprehend.

Thomas Christian Anderson, the Son

Early as I can remember anything, I recall my mama and papa fighting. My childhood friends had folks who might shout once in a while but mostly it was just blowing steam in a heated moment. Little Valley was a fingerbowl in the hills, halfway up the canyon road toward Cache. My family's fury twisted through it like a dust devil.

I made it my task to defend my papa, to admonish all who got him riled and self-righteous. Which I came to understand was everybody, but especially Mama and Peter. My solution was to try to make every soul line up like curried horsehair with Papa's every edict. I was confounded at every turn. Eventually it made me understand that the necessary way the civilized world gets on is by shedding great shards of its own heart. We must learn to make everything smaller than it truly is.

A meeker wife might have kept my father in a condition of greater mental peace. Could have kept him muttering to his own internal apparitions rather than shouting indignations from the rooftops. Problem with Mama was that she was fully capable of looking out for herself, and I guess by the time she married my papa she was beyond all wish for patronage. The woman could not say sorry. My mama would never forget old harms.

I think now about the women who played their right roles in our times. Probably every single one sometimes wished herself to be a widow, my own wife included. I wish it were not so.

Peter Nielsen

My mother carried me over the mountains and into the Salt Lake Valley the same year the United States busted into Civil War. It seemed no business of ours. We hardly felt like Americans. We spoke Danish for years amongst ourselves. We had been registered on the East Coast and sent on to a place that most of the nation viewed as Gadsden's Mexico.

Yet we felt concussions. Past those first hellish months slaving for Salt Lake royalty, and after Brigham Young had inspired old Andersen to marry my mother, we moved up north, past Brigham City and beyond Hell's Gate to Little Valley—a beautiful spot four months of the year, a frigid impression the other eight. We'd been sent up with nine other Danish families. Long after the apostle Lorenzo Snow pet-named the place Mantua, the rest of us kept right on calling it Little Copenhagen. Andersen staked a decent plot, but with such a brief growing season all we planted was overtough flax after the Church's orders. Mama coerced enough beets and potatoes out of the ground to stock the cellar. Livestock did well up there but that meant we had to follow the herds about, protecting them from their own natural stupidity. And hungry Indians.

First year we went up there, 1863, Shoshones were in the straits of desolation. Feds under Connor had trooped up from California, itching for harm. The soldiers were resentful, as they were missing their opportunity to split up and kill one another in the war of North and South. January they had slaughtered three, four hundred half-froze Shoshones holed up above the Bear River all in a single morning. Plenty of braves were killed, but once Connor's men tasted blood they kept right on at the women and children. Mormons all across the valley tried to say they had nothing to do with it, that they too were victims of federal wrath. But Mormons traded with the Indians in daylight and then quartered Connor's men that ungodly cold night before the raid. Some even joined up. I fear that blood runs deeper than faith. Mormons were white people, no matter how they set themselves apart. Wanted no more trouble on the land they stole.

The land *we* stole. Clearly I didn't feel so wrong about it that I hightailed back to Scandinavia. The West in all its turmoil was my home. Little Valley had long been a stopping place on the trail to Bear Lake for whites and Indians both. When they'd felt friendly or just too uninspired to threaten immigrants, Indians saw the pretty vale as a place to trade furs and handiwork for flour and calico. They viewed themselves as permitting passage. For a while they didn't even mind the Mormons running cattle up that way. No objection to a little stolen beef.

But once we Danes pushed up there, digging and erecting to demonstrate our intentions, we helped to turn a desperate population of Indians murderous. Webers marauded from the east and south—light and fast in their home range. Shoshones came up frequently over the trail from Cache Valley, now in no temper to pass without a brutal satisfaction. We'd heard stories. Children forced to walk in the snow on legs chopped to the knee, just for the entertainment. Women hung by their long braided hair, roasted alive over Indian flames. The ruddy straw-haired Danes hunkered down, ten families in plain view from every slope, a full circumference of ridgelines above us. Nobody strayed far. Some men kept watch while others took shifts building a rude fort. Women huddled together, tight grips on children, wide-eyed like frightened deer.

All but my mother. She said she might as well argue with a hungry Indian as a cantankerous pigeon of a husband, but now I look back it's clear she was nervous, too. She kept the baby wrapped against her. She would not lay him down even while he slept. I told her once I'd keep an eye on him while she walked for clean water. She seemed relieved and started off. I looked the kid over, just grown enough to sit on the quilt and gaze, wet lips and wide eyes. His little gown bunched over his fat legs. Looked like badger bait to me. Mama got twenty yards off without looking back, then about-faced without even breaking stride. Trying to look casual and incidental, she shook the bucket and thrust it toward me. Then she bent down and scooped up little Chris, swung him to her hip and set off again, expecting me to run after.

By midsummer the cattle had eaten everything near the settlement and the old man figured I'd be no sacrifice if I caught Shoshone caliber between my ribs. He volunteered me as herdsman. An eight-year-old my size had no business up there in the hills alone but Bishop Jensen said he'd send a horseman up every hour or two. He said keep the cattle visible from down below, just push them up high enough to find some new sweet grass, and they'd all keep an eye in my direction. At that time old Stepdaddy was attempting to pose as the sort of man to provide some lucky orphan with a kindly father and protector. Yet two or three times already he'd taken a belt to my bare behind and sure did savor it. Although everyone was hungry that season, I was especially so. My new father figure saw to it that I earned every bite I put in my mouth, and the pay was spare.

I guess that's why even Mama consented to send me up that day. She was simmering a barley stew and wanted to put some food in me without Andersen laying down the law. Bishop Jensen and other men and boys made an elaborate show of coming up the mountain with me, some on horses, some walking, everyone shouting and joking like it was some grand parade. Forty head of longhorns ambled up the slopes, snatching at tufts and moaning about the exertion. Once they contented on a rolling hillock, Henning Sorensen said, broad and loud, "Well, boy, not a Injun in sight. Perhaps they all slunk on down to Brigham City to beg bread."

Bishop Jensen said to me, "See there, how clear we can see the settlement? We'll be able to see you just as brightly so don't you worry. I'll send a horseman up regular. No Shoshone wants trouble with a herd like this. They know better than to steal the truly valuables."

Old man just glowered, hoping I'd put up a fuss so he wouldn't have to portion the stew, and they all rode on down the hills, vanishing and reappearing behind the switchbacks. I could hear their voices bouncing off the valley walls, gaining a rolling run and coming back up sometimes so clear I could make out every word, sometimes muffled and meaningless. I saw them reenter the settlement and heard the men take up their tools.

I stood squinting. The cattle were content in the grass. Not one hardly murmured, just kept ripping up bunches of green and nudging one another for the best bites. I was scared of Indians, but right then I was too hungry to think beyond what to put into my own stomach. I got busy walking the edge of the herd, not so much to keep perfectly contented beasts from straying as to scout out a humanly edible root. Maybe a berry bush. But I wasn't the only one footing it through those hills looking for sustenance. If it could be eaten, it was eaten, as I recalled upon suddenly finding myself face to face with a breechless Shoshone boy about my age, and then his whole family and probably every surviving relative coming up a deer path from the other direction. Maybe they were coming after our cattle. More likely they were just as surprised as I was.

I knew better than to run or shout, or throw a stone.

Shoshones first looked startled by a towheaded boy up so high alone.

Then they fell into a loose circle, a human fortress around their children, and took a gander for more of my kind.

Then they realized I was the whole army, standing post on a number of healthy cattle.

The men drew together in spontaneous council. They were restrained at first, never getting louder but certainly more animated. Whatever they were saying made the boy I'd first come up on tense up and relax a little, both, and he sidled closer to me, partly to make sure I didn't make a run for it. But I think also to look me over. The boy was a sight: long dusty hair in a Shoshone pompadour. Buckskin shirt just long enough to make him decent, bare scratched brown legs down to the beat-up moccasins. I must have looked just as sorry. My hair was cropped shaggy after my stepfather's impulse to make me "presentable." Some hung down in hanks and other parts were shorn near to the skull. My canvas trousers were caked in dust and I wore a double-pink calico shirt cut down from a larger one, patched and worn so thin at the shoulders the bones nearly shone through. I guessed that under his shirt, his ribcage stuck out like mine, caverning over a stomach so underfed it hardly knew how to digest a bite of decent food. I figured he slept all night clutching his gut, like me.

"What do they say there?" I asked the boy, guessing he spoke at least as much English as I did.

He eyed me, wary but also superior as if he'd like to show he could beat me at jacks or wrestling. He took long enough to answer, I thought he wasn't going to. But then he said, "This is very much cows."

We stood side by side, inspecting the beasts. One of those longhorns could make this whole band feel downright hearty for at least a week—more if they rationed smart.

I said, because even hungry I liked to brag: "Not so many. More in the valleys."

"Bigger herdsmen in valleys." He had a point there.

A couple of women had by now joined the Shoshone conference. One of them pointed my way, murmuring and adamant, but unlike my folks in agitation, none raised an arm nor voice. I shifted, suddenly very frightened, and with the fear came a wave of rage at the men who thought my life might be worth trading for a bunch of damn cattle, especially at that son of a bitch Andersen who preened like some hero I should thank for starving me under the hospitality of his dugout roof. I looked toward the valley, obscured from this spot by a stand of oak, thinking how much I wanted everyone down there to watch this herd scattered like angry ants. The boy misread and tensed up, ready to throw himself on me if I set to hollering. He signaled the men. They nodded. One held up an arm, adjourned the council, and turned to consider me.

The boy said, "Only listen. Stay stand. No scare."

The man strode fast but stopped just short of running me over. He dropped to a knee to talk to me straight. The boy leaned in, too.

"Hungry," the man said to me. I interpreted this as a statement of his condition and his family's. But the man shoved me gently with a couple of fingers at the sternum. He ran the side of his hand up and down my ribs like a piano trill.

"Hungry," he said again. I nodded, comprehending, now also hungry for sympathy like a pathetic child. The Shoshone man waved over a couple more of his compadres. They came and stood, bending their heads down toward me. One, a fellow with a white man's hat and long Indian leggings, light blanket about his sinuous shoulders and waist, put out his hand to shake. I reached out and he held my hand firmly, gave it a single pump and dropped it. He said, "Please to meet you, Great White Chief," and they all laughed quietly, and I caught on to the joke and grinned a little.

The first man remained on his knee. He assessed me up and down. He signaled the women and one of them brought three sego roots, still covered in dirt, and a pocket of parched pine nuts. She held them out to me and the man said, "Eat," and the boy looked like he wanted to grab some and bolt. But he stayed still. I reached out and took the roots, stuffing them in my pocket. I held both hands, cupped, for the nuts, and she filled them. I licked a couple of kernels direct, then crunched them in my teeth, marveling at how good they tasted. I held out my hands to the boy. His eyes went up to the elders and they let him decide. He reached with a finger and thumb and picked out one fat kernel, put it in his mouth, and sucked to make it last.

The man in the hat said to me, "Great White Chief. We need cows. Understand?"

I nodded.

"Trouble for you," he said.

I stood as tall as I could. "It don't matter," I said. "Trouble for me all the time."

"Shoshone once friends. With Mormons."

I didn't know what to say, so I answered, foolish, "I'm terribly sorry."

The man said, "You kill Shoshone at Bear River?"

"No! I didn't even live here then!" I answered, but again I realized the Indians were teasing a pint-sized fool with jutting ribs and a haymow haircut, not worth scalping. But they were nervous, too. A clutch of adults walked out to the periphery, peering from the edge of the oak. In my tension I had lost track of time, but it occurred to me that the bishop ought to be keeping his promise about now.

The lookers signaled, not yet ready to retreat, but they could see something afoot in the half-made settlement. If men were starting up on horseback, the Shoshones had half an hour at most to hightail. They should have cut the herd and lit out that minute, but instead the man with the hat took time to set up a situation.

He held out his hand to me. Like a father. I took it with trepidation but also an uncanny gratitude. I walked with him to the edge of the meadow. We stood between the cattle and the settlement in full view of the Danish dugouts. The boy hung back with the others. I saw them cut two steers and a cow out of the far edge of the herd and set out fast. I would have hell to pay but I knew they'd catch it worse. I hoped with all my heart they knew where to vanish and lie low.

Hat Man still held my hand, holding a finger to his lips to keep me quiet. He turned his head to watch the cattle disappear over the crest, stood and waited another minute, and then he let loose with a terrific Indian shout. I perceived the sudden scurry below. Women were crying out and pointing, kids gathering up to see. The man picked me up and gave me a shake. He set me down again, scooped up a handful of grass and dirt and rubbed it into my hair, gave me a cuff on one side of the head and then the other. He yanked my shirt and the fabric tore in his hand, baring my bony shoulder.

He said, "Also I am terribly sorry," and gave me a light punch in the chest that surprised me so much I hit the ground on my butt and hands. He leaned over in a way that must have looked menacing from below and ran a couple of dirty streaks down the length of my trousers. I watched in a sort of trance. He lifted my chin with a finger to make me look him in the eye. A long scar marked a bowie cut down his cheekbone, traveling over the lips and nicking his chin.

He said, "You got to cry a little, Yellowhair."

Finally I understood, and I let out a wail they might have heard all the way down to Brigham City. Hat Man took off running. I stood up, walked careful so as not to shake off too much dirt, and checked the remaining cattle. They were placid and undistressed. I settled on a rock to await my rescuers. Up they thundered. First it was the youngbeards, then the elders and bishop, and then mean old Stepdaddy, holding back to give the Shoshones one more chance to make an example of a scarecrow boy. Everyone crowded around. I worked up some tears and snot and for a while pretended to be so shaken up by the Indian abuse I plumb forgot to tell them about the three missing longhorns.

Soon enough they got to counting and so I had to recollect. The bishop sent a posse after the Shoshones but they must have slipped into pure atmosphere. Old man looked mad enough to take his fists to me but Bishop Jensen said, "Chris, the child's been through enough. Leave him be. We should have known better than to leave a scrawny boy up here to fend for himself."

I contorted my face to a martyr's countenance, snuffled some more, and turned my back on my stepfather. I knew he'd put me to bed with no supper, but I shoved my hands deep in my pockets to feel the pine nuts and sego root, fervently wishing the Indians Godspeed.

Sidse Nielsen Andersen

Why did I let the men of our community put my son at risk? Has the world been so transformed in your time? Do you stand before me here, with hindsight so clear—you cannot interpret the bargains of so many mothers before you?

Peter Nielsen

As far as I know, the whole band got away. But over the next decade the Shoshone presence diminished in overall defeat. Chief Sagwitch called in what was left of his people and they came all at once to a grand Mormon conversion, which I have to say by that point was sharp strategy. Eventually Brigham Young ordered a stretch of land west of the river to be spared up for the converted Lamanites. Some say he fixed it so Indians could stake homesteads just like white folks. He named it Washakie after the dead good chief in Wyoming. He set the still-damp Mormons to farming, first in one spot and then another until white folks got used to the permanence. Shoshones and Bannocks that didn't line up at the baptismal river—same as the battle river—signed on to the new federal reservation at Fort Hall, some of what's now Pocatello.

Meantime there were periodic scares, enough to make all us white Mormons justify stories of our own courage and virtue. The Indian tales became alibi for holding our own kind to a brutal standard: *We used to fight Indians and here you are complaining about hoeing ten acres of beets!* My stepfather was the high priest of all that. He wasn't much kinder to the children he personally produced than he was to me. But I was oldest by eight years, just right to be held up as example to the younger ones. Andersen made me a daily demonstration.

One of his better methods of keeping me busy was to send me down to Brigham City, carrying a mysterious muslin-wrapped parcel to a young man named Julius. Obviously it was a letter—in fact, often the neighbors caught me on my way out and handed me one or two of their own, usually bound for family in Denmark. What Andersen's correspondence had to do with Julius I had no notion. Once the mail coach got regular I'd trudge down once a week, weather permitting. I asked no questions, but even so Andersen declared he'd tan my hide and tack it up if I didn't keep my nose in my own business. Mama just pursed her lips, shedding no light on the mystery.

In a way I didn't mind the job. It was four miles down the canyon, only some of it steep, a reasonable walk for a kid with nothing better to do in a livelong day. Hell of a lot better than cleaning a hog sty. The walk back up was a chore, but sometimes I'd hitch a ride behind some traveler's saddle or hop on back of a lurching wagon.

Mostly I'd make my way down, gaze about at the general sights of a slightly bigger town, beg horehound or peppermint from the mercantile, and wend slow as I could justify toward Julius's place. At the beginning it was actually his mother and father's place, but I was instructed to ask after Julius. He was a lank, thoughtful type, unusually dark hair for a Dane. Seemed a little absent. Usually he'd just take the bundle and blink his dawn-blue eyes. Every so often he'd give me a penny, or as the plantings came of age, a peach. Once he walked back out to the street with me and asked questions: my memories of Copenhagen. The journey to Utah. My mother's history.

At times Julius would take the bundle into the back of the house and then return it to me all tied up again. "Tell your papa to look inside."

I always corrected him: "Step-papa." And once he answered, "I know that better than you do, little step-cousin."

That was the clue I needed to account for all this. Took some time to reason it through, but after a while I figured out the old man had a family still in Aalborg, a wife and a daughter and son, who I'd wager were delighted to send him off to the American hinterlands in the name of his new salvation. Andersen wrote copious epistles to his Danish offspring. Judging from our experience in America, I'm convinced the missives were rambling tirades about ingratitude, which is the reason the family stayed distant and immune in the old country. Julius was first cousin to Andersen's Danish daughter and son. They had all played together as children. I couldn't help but imagine the boy in Denmark as Julius, and the girl as spare-limbed Julius in a Danish frock.

Andersen never said a word about them to the rest of us. Not until we were mostly grown and he took to declaring which would be the privileged and which the unlucky heavenly family. Eventually he made my mama stand proxy in the Endowment House. He made her speak the words of eternal sealing on behalf of a woman in Aalborg who wanted no truck with us, neither in this life nor in any distant Mormon heaven. It takes a certain genius to mortify two women in a single holy rite.

Later in my life I came across Julius, a chance passing in Malad. When I knew him in Brigham City I thought he was a grown man, but now I realized he was not so many years older than me. We sat down to a trailside supper and he asked, "Anyhow, how old were you when Uncle Chris threw you out of that house?"

I snorted. "Sixteen. That was nearly nine years under his roof. It was a good thing he sent me packing. That was all either one of us could stand."

Julius sat, quizzical but restrained. I waited to make sure he wanted more and then I said, "And I didn't steal no ox. I told him he better give me something to help me make my way. Told him for all the work I'd done he could at least send me off with a start on livestock."

Julius said, "He should have sent you with a hell of a lot more than that."

When I left Mantua I was thinking I could sell the ox or even put it to work, but mostly I'd just wanted to make that miser yield something up. We'd been boiling for weeks. The old man said, "You'd better get on out of this place for good, you gutter rat," and I answered, "I can't do it fast enough, but not until you give me one of the oxen."

My mother said, "Chris, you give this boy a good one, or so help me I'll make sure you never sleep easy in this house," and he barked, "You shut your mouth, woman."

But the kids were crying and he was afraid of her, so he picked out the second best, a broad gentle blue named Sigurd. Andersen saw me off with the ox and a Danish curse. Mama didn't cry but she clamped her jaw and kept her face toward busy hands while she packed me brown bread and yellow cheese and ham, wrapped in a piece of old quilting. And set near the top, delicate, half a rhubarb pie.

"Don't you touch that pie," she snarled at the old man, who was grieving over the remainder. He shriveled and slunk out the back door. I went out the front, took Sigurd's halter, and down the valley we went. I was thinking to head toward California but to tell the truth I had no idea where it was. I was so young and lonely and scared, I simply wandered the Bear River Valley for a few bewildering weeks. I slept in the bluffs or edges of green lucerne fields or new-planted orchards, hunkering against the beast for comfort.

I was up near Tremonton one night, crazy from the mosquitoes, mad at the universe, hungry still and thinking I could pick or herd or hoe—or, damn, shovel manure—tomorrow for some farmer. Sigurd settled himself in greenery just outside town, tired after the day's drifting and lazy grazing on the river flats. He made it clear he was going nowhere. I could have gone on wandering a few more hours, could have knocked on some doors asking for work for the next morning, but Sigurd was a big ox, healthy and well trained, gentle despite his life under Andersen's whip. Bait for a thief, and just as I was thinking about all this a slicked-up pirate with a big mustache, overneat kerchief, leather vest with a star, hat brim not quite covering a red scar across his forehead as if he'd been recently plastered with a rock, pulled up with a mule team and said, "Where'd you steal that ox from, boy?"

Next thing I knew, Sheriff Lafitte had Sigurd locked tight in a stall in a clean Tremonton barn and me in a filthy shed built off the stack of adobe he called the city hall. Three other bodies in there already, and as I got used to the murky light I could see they were all boys like me. Each was asleep or pretending to be, two in cleared corners and one on a narrow workbench, facing away. I sat spine to the wall. I was not in my right mind. For a spell I felt strangely calm to have been relieved of the burden of choice. Didn't have to figure out where to go or where to sleep. It vaguely occurred to me I might get something to eat. I imagined someone might recognize me in the morning, connect me to Julius and his people, and find a way to notify my mother.

I think I fell asleep in that half manner we maintain when there's nothing to do but worry and wait. In any case I dreamed or maybe even had a vision in which I was clinging to my mother's shoulders as she walked. The mountain ahead of us was at once inviting and forbidding. She herself was soft and comfortable, yet also dry boned and very sharp. At first I believed I was a small boy, so light she hardly felt my weight, but then again I would comprehend with a shock that I was a full-grown man, bigger than I had ever been in actual life. I felt her stagger, catch control of faltering knees and hips as she nearly went down at the upturns, but she always recovered, shifting her strength and weight to navigate each segment of the steep stony trail.

It wasn't so much a dream as an unbroken place. I don't mean everything whole. Just unmeasured, but for step, step. Falter, assess, step, step. An immortal condition. I believe I've returned to that place, here, as I await.

It's not precisely anticipation.

It's not precisely anything, in those moments that are not moments at all. And, inside the jail, once I became myself again there on my mother's strong but frail back, clinging to her hard-forgiving shoulders, time returned and I came to in a rage so blind and feral I sprang up like a cougar, howling and clawing at my bug-bitten arms and neck, kicking at the walls. I screamed at those defeated sleeping boys to awaken.

"Where's my ox?" I howled, banging at the sorry excuse for a window. "Let me out of here! Sigurd! Sigurd! I'm right here! Sigurd, come on, boy! We have to get out of here!"

One of the boys, hair a filthy sorrel thicket, leaped up and started into a loony guttural chant, as far as I could tell summoning the vengeance of every Irish soul taken by the Blight. The gaunt drunk in the corner stood and stared about, then heaved and vomited against the wall. Clearly it improved his condition. He set up a racket along with us.

The boy on the bench did not move at all.

"Sigurd!" I called to my ox, and Famine howled, "Open this door! We're hungry!" and Vomit cried, "You sons of bitches! You'll pay for this!" and suddenly the door opened, stunning us with the blinding light, and we fell back. Sheriff Lafitte said, "Shut your sniveling traps! Pray down an angel to save yourselves, you scrawny turds!"

He tossed something in to us, tied in a vile handkerchief. He slammed the door. We heard the bolt shove true, the key in the padlock, and we settled in the suddenly silent murk, breathing hard and straining to get a better look at one another.

Famine said, "Who's that on the plank, there?"

Vomit gave the corpse a shove. The body fell to the floor and sat up. Shoshone. Cleaner than any of us, cropped hair shining even in the dimness. Decent shirt, canvas pants, and a good pair of work boots, still tied neat and tight.

"Stinks in here," the Indian said.

"What's in the kerchief?" Vomit inquired, and we opened it up.

"Smells like what you just tossed up," said Famine to Vomit. We all sniggered.

We leaned in to look it over. Foul moldy goat curd. Danes love their blue cheese but this was another phenomenon. Runny in the cracks, pocked with green mossy fur, crusted like a rotten egg. It made me feel dizzy and sick well beyond the smell and mold. Suddenly I remembered a thousand nights in my stepfather's house, giddy with hunger and hopeful after another day of endless backbreaking work, leaning in for my share.

My brain gave way to pure white heat. I don't personally remember how it went from there, but Vomit, who grew up to be a pretty evenhanded Mormon bishop, son of a local self-righteous bigshot whom I will not name here, recalled every detail. He told the story a little better every time we chanced upon each other over the decades.

He said I pulled a flint from my deep trouser pocket. I churned up a thin, then healthy flame in a pile of oily rags collected from the clutter. I scared the daylights out of my companions in the shed, all of us locked in there like lambs awaiting slaughter, coaxing the flame to light. The shed brightened like the noonday sun when I added the cheese, which sputtered, then melted, then fed itself into a greasy flame.

Indian caught on, took the whole bundle in a shovel to the back wall of the shed where it connected to the city hall. We set again to howling, all four of us in the same savage tongue. The flames shot up the wall, either to burn us alive or free us. Lafitte opened the door and we burst out, scattering like the Sons of Israel.

Next thing I remember, Indian and I were seated contrite on a bench in the Box Elder Courthouse. We weren't exactly on trial. We'd already been sentenced. Timbimboo—as many of them in Washakie as Andersens in the white towns—was going back to the Indian farm with his folks. It was not exactly a prison, but in the minds of certain citizens a good place to keep Shoshones out of sight. The boy's only crime was being an Indian at cross-trails with the wrong zealous lawman. Until I burned down the shed and almost the Tremonton City Hall, my only crime had been trying to find a vagrant spot to sleep with a healthy ox named Sigurd.

Igniting a cheese fire had complicated the matter. I soon realized that what all of us stray boys, Elders of Zion, Shoshone Mormons, amateur deputies, and a few curious onlookers were waiting for was the arrival of someone to formally recognize me. Julius showed up first, heralding the imminent arrival of a committee of Little Valley Danes. I heard the fuss out in the courtyard, and the old man's hot rasping voice demanding entry, declaring his intentions to show me a thing or two. But miraculously it was only my mama who entered the building. She looked mad as a dunked cat but held her composure. She walked straight toward me. Timbimboo said, "You got it coming now."

Julius went out to calm the old man.

Mama reached a hand to me but stopped short, redirecting it to adjust a hat string.

She turned to the judges.

"This boy has seen enough."

The magistrate said, "Sister Andersen, we're here to help him. The boy needs sustenance. Plenty of folks know your son.

No one's told us he's a bad boy. Plenty say he works hard and—"

"Where's my ox?" I howled. "What did you do with Sigurd? That's my ox and that damned sheriff took him away!"

Several men stepped toward me. Timbimboo whispered, "You want to go to real jail? Keep your teeth together."

Mama put her hand up and I knew to be silent. She asked the magistrate, "What are you suggesting?"

His voice was calm, the regular and soothing tones of a fairly reasonable man accustomed to his own authority. "Sister Andersen, we want to call your Peter on a mission."

Mama recoiled, about to let loose a torrent. But the magistrate, who was also a bishop's counselor, continued unperturbed. "Don't worry, now. He's too young to be sent abroad. We're not assigning him to proselyte. We're calling him to work for the season on the church farm up on the river. The ox can go along if it truly belongs to Peter. They'll both receive board and care in exchange for solid work. We can all supervise his progress. You can visit, affirm he's safe and well fed. You can bring him comforts and clothing."

My mother stood, dark and piercing. She directed a long assessing glare at the magistrate and then moved her eyes across the whole committee. One by one by one. No one spoke another word until she had memorized every face.

She said, "Sounds like a detention, not a mission."

"If he shows us he can do well, within a month or two he'll be free to come and go after the work hours are through. After the harvest he can, if he chooses, move on to a more independent life."

"What if I protest?"

The men looked uneasy but another stuffed shirt said, "Sister Andersen, your husband is the head of the household. In the eyes of the law, your protest means little if he demurs. In the eyes of the law, in fact, your son is a dangerous criminal. He could be charged with possession of a stolen ox—"

I felt an effusive squall coming on, but the boy beside me jabbed hard to my ribs and I shut it down. My mother said, icy and helpless, "That ox belongs to Peter. We gave it to him before he left home."

"You and the boy say so, but your husband suggests otherwise. His is the legal testimony if it comes to that."

My mother made no motion or expression. The stuffed shirt continued: "Your son, Sister Andersen, dang near burned down a public building. He endangered the lives of his cellmates. In the eyes of the law—"

"Enough with the eyes of the law, Hiram," the magistrate interrupted, irritable and by this time wanting to get on with his own pursuits. He turned to my mother. "Sister Andersen, this is unquestionably the best course of action for you and your son. Let's keep your husband at a distance a bit longer if we can. If you'll consent to your son's mission call here and now, we'll take him out to the farm this very evening. He'll eat a hearty dinner, meet the good folks who oversee the operation, and you can trust every night for the next many months that your boy is sleeping nourished and sound. We'll make an edict before any other party—" he gestured toward the outside door, "—is granted opportunity for further influence."

So I went, not quite willing and yet relieved, to work at the Stake Farm at Bear River City. And Timbimboo walked out free as an Indian could be in that time, to join his arriving Shoshone clan. In those years they were still a sight to behold, some still faithful to the old leggings and blankets, some with high pompadours and feathers, some with cut hair and wide-brim hats and nearly naturalized into chambray shirts and denim trousers. Some wore moccasins. Some wore work boots. They all stood facing the same direction to claim their son, and all of a sudden I realized who he was. Who they were.

They knew me, too.

"Great White Chief," one said, not loudly but clear.

"Hungry," said another.

The rest of them laughed softly as I walked past in the custody of my kind.

Thomas Christian Anderson, the Son

After my mother and father returned from Brigham City, after they sent Peter to the farm, our familiar life fell apart fast. I was too young to grasp details. Even so I had become so long accustomed to a certain atmosphere that I had learned to feel almost familial in a room shored up with tension. It lined the shelves like food in the pantry. I had a way of looking forward to the relief of an eruption because it brought on a sort of exhausted truce, the most peaceful quality of our turbulent lives. Sometimes it could last a week or more.

The evening our parents came up from the lower city in the wagon, tired and angry, Charley and I gathered the little ones and herded them toward the house. I figured we could keep them quiet with a game or story while Mama made dinner and Papa fumed about or stormed toward the barnyard to take it out on the hogs. I hoped we could settle in to sleep before hell found opportunity to ignite, but our parents were at one another before they hit the ground. I clutched the baby in my arms and sang him an anxious rhyme and peered out the window. Papa was shouting about ingratitude, his most eloquent topic, and Mama was bracing stiff as a weathervane, holding off till the wind blew hard enough to turn her about.

I only caught snatches but I knew the gist. He wanted her to say, *Thank you, Husband*, for providing her with daily food and sustenance here in a hard land. *Thank you, Husband*, for furnishing a respectable name after bringing shame upon her own shoulders in Denmark. *Tak for det, min mand! Takke!* for keeping her filthy secrets a family matter. *Tak!* for children healthy and upright, disciplined in the right ways of God. *Tak!* for saving her from a life of servitude in Salt Lake City. *Tak, min mand!* for the prime garden spot to bury their own child, *tak for det*, for the noble restraint he'd shown so many years now despite that whining bastard son she'd bothered to carry across, who still wanted carrying—

And there it was. The wind rose and the vane swiveled. Our mother exploded in a storm of Danish I never as a child gained the will to interpret. She reached up with a strong practiced arm and released the horse from the wagon, slapping the haunch to make it bolt. Papa whistled after it but the horse kept running, and after a halfhearted league of pursuit Papa strode back, grabbing her arm and shouting now in Danish too.

Mama yanked herself from his grip and started for the house. I ducked into the back room with baby Joe, and Charley held tight to Maria's fat little hand. We leaned toward the doorway, straining for a safe glimpse of the next scene. Mama came in to throw anything she could pick up with one hand back out the door at him, thwarting his pursuit. She had a pelting arm on her, could have thrown discus and outpitched most of the men in Little Valley. Pots and pans clattered from the stovetop. Mama reached down and hove a skillet into the big atmosphere beyond the front door. *Tak, min ægtemand! Tak for det! Tak!*

She threw a cast-iron ladle. *Tak!*

A poker. *Tak!*

She pulled up a bucket of coal, picked clod-sized black missiles, and flung five or six like a Gatling gun: *Tak! Tak! Tak skal du have! Tak for det min mand!* Papa dodged and shielded his way around to the side of the house. We saw him running fast by the side window. He came up the stairs to the back door. He yanked it open and parted us like the Red Sea, taking her from behind just as she stepped out front to pursue him. He was past any rage I'd witnessed. He spun her around, took her to the wall, and slammed her hard against it. I could hear the rafters strain. She kicked at him but her skirts softened the impact, which only made both more livid. He held her with one hand gripped around her upper arm and pulled her toward the washstand. The razor strop.

Charley and I went wild. We'd felt the strop plenty but the thought of him taking it to Mama seemed some kind of swift-slow nightmare. Charley let Maria wail on the floor and lunged for Papa, grabbing him by the leg. Papa dragged him along the floor with each staggering step. I went in for Mama, holding her other hand, petting her arm, crying. "Mama! You have to stop! You're making him angry! Please, Mama! Just give him some peace and all will be well!"

When she shook me off I spun around and faced her, echoing the man she despised: "Just tell him thank you! *Takke! Tak!* Just make it stop, Mama! Show him some gratitude! It's the right way!"

Papa kicked us both away, throwing me against the doorway and dropping Charley on the floor, wind whisked out of his lungs. Papa hauled Mama right on out the front door again. He pushed her up against the wagon and held the strop aloft, all of us crying now like heeler pups. Our father's body was small and lithe, but uncanny strong in moments of intensity. He quivered, ready to strike as he shouted for the whole world to hear, pitching higher and hoarser about the proper line of authority, the humiliation of being kept outside while she bargained for the ingrate, putting her husband's own word to public doubt. Now the four of us stood still as spotted fawns, wondering if our father would bring the leather down but before we could find out Bishop Jensen and neighbors all came running. The biggest man in Little Copenhagen, Brother Holst strode to my father and clenched his enormous fist around the strop arm. Holst threw our father to the ground.

Papa sat, pale and shallowed out, legs splayed in front of him. He rubbed his eyes like a child and gazed up at the big man, uncomprehending.

"Stand up, Papa!" I cried and he reacted. He didn't stand but he writhed around and lunged at me on all fours, snarling like a wounded cat. Holst stooped again to grab and slam him down.

"Don't you move, Chris," Holst said, very soft and everything went quiet.

My papa did not move. Nor any of us. The bishop and his men stood in counsel like the ancient burghers. Papa sat stunned on the unyielding valley dirt. Mama stood all alone against the wagon, facing her townspeople, her pride forged and hollowed to brittle armor. As Charley and I huddled together the names I knew for all I saw simply dropped away. I witnessed the blue sky tinged with yellow sun and cloudless. Sound diminished but for a meadowlark, trilling each note, penetrating clean through the endless air. I heard it so clear. I knew its melody: I had heard it all my life but had not understood. Now I apprehended its whole meaning. I hold it now more perfect than any other memory, and know what it signifies.

But I cannot convey it.

And then the wail of little Maria, three years old. Her cries rent the blue, returning us to motion and passing time.

Sidse Nielsen Andersen

If the whole town had not come running in time to see me there in mortification, I wouldn't have stirred the mildest sympathy in a jury of my peers. Had I gone to the bishop in confidence to recount our family sorrows, he would have told me to go home and pray, to answer better and more contritely to my husband and all would be well. Should I then be grateful I could show the world my abjection? Should I thank God for granting my whole community a true glimpse of our misery? Even after this pageant, Bishop Jensen pleaded with me to serve my family better, to become an agent of peace.

"It takes two to quarrel, Sister Andersen," he said, a desperate note in his voice.

Such admonition used to cut right through to my heart, back when I yet had one to be cut. I still do not know how to answer. In my experience it takes one to get his way, and it takes the other one to say yes yes yes and still yes—whatever you need, *min mand*, every whim and counter whim.

Unto this last.

For a short season I was crazed enough to imagine I could step beyond the circumference. The Indians lived somewhere else—somehow other—did they not? The mountains beckoned in my long sleepless nights. Portrayed, in my desperate mind, an unmarked world. A place before the story.

But there is no place before the story. The wild Shoshones came in to be baptized. I came in broken beyond return.

Thomas Christian Anderson, the Son

Mama was implacable. She told Papa she was finished with him. One day while Papa went to the lower valley she wrapped us each a knapsack. She walked us out to the far southern nook of Little Valley, toward Devil's Gate, and before long a large man pulled up with a four-mule team and sturdy wagon. I wondered whether he was some lost uncle. Jovial, he hoisted me up beside him on the buckboard. Mama sat back with the children.

I found myself friendly and confidential. The man drove us up to the high wildflower meadows toward Monte Cristo, and we set up in the miner's shack during that first summer Peter spent on the mission farm. Mama renamed us all Nielsen, after Peter's best father. She told us that in heaven we would all be children of the same man: Ole Nielsen, a good man taken too soon. Another brother and sister awaited us in heaven, longing to be eternally sealed to us for time and all eternity. In the meantime they were preparing our happy family mansion on a beautiful street paved with gold, in a kingdom flowing with blue water and no winter in it.

In the mortal interim Mama called herself wife to this prospector with no history we were equipped to discern. A miner who was, until drink transformed him, benign and indulgent. He said he was un-drunk for good, sorry for the sins of his former life. Contrite as a pup. He said Mama kept him on the straight and narrow. He was no Mormon, which was fine because Mama saw all this as only a between time until we would be united with the dead Dane in the ocean. The prospector had been a railroad man in Corinne, now turned goldmine hermit in the high mountains. He wore a rosary around his thick muscled neck. He was dark and swarthy, handsome like a conquistador. In an uncomfortable way we liked him more than we liked our slight and pale angry father.

The prospector liked our mother very well. Beyond a joke with us boys or a high-armed swirl for Maria, he left us children alone. Paid no mind to baby Joe whether or not he cried. We climbed the high hills on every side of the shack. We ran barefoot in the mountain meadows. We chased squirrels and caught fish and for a while we were the innocent children of Eve. Whole weeks passed and we'd never see but one another, not even a Weber Ute, not a miner nor a Mormon traveler. We did not yearn for contact. Mama kept house and made little repairs and hummed tunes we'd never heard. When the prospector came home, once in a few days, they would vanish into the woods and we'd wait them out and then cook something over the fire—sometimes meat, sometimes bread, waving sticks over the embers. We'd sit well into starlight, warmed by the flames. We invented fables and sang half-learned songs from Mama's childhood. Sometimes we mimicked measures from the prospector's old-world language, a tongue I never identified.

One night after the mountains turned colder, the leaves gone orange and yellow, he came home slurring beyond any language at all. Redstagger drunk. He called us the names of other children. He tried to pick up quarrels we never knew, accusing us of lies, pretense, bitter betrayal. He took our mother out and locked us in. No one returned for us that night, nor the next day and another night and then we lost the thread of time entirely. With no fuel to keep the fire, the dark nights were bitter. We ate bread till it was gone, then foraged for scraps and drank from the bucket our mother kept by the stove. We pissed and shat through the floorboards. Charley and I kept the babies clean as we could. Too frightened to panic, too bewildered to do anything but wait in silence, we wrapped ourselves together in a blanket on the pine straw bed and fell into a lurid murmuring hibernation.

We awoke to a man's footsteps and the creaking door. A slender silhouette stood in the dappled slant of autumn light. We rubbed our eyes clear to perceive our big brother Peter in the rough frame. We arose and lurched toward him.

He said, "Put on your shoes and coats. We have walking to do."

Peter had cheese and jerky, and bread and apples, but he would only dole to us small portions to accustom our shrunken stomachs. He lifted little Joseph like a doll and settled the lad on his shoulders. Peter told me to take Maria's hand. He said, "Come on, Charley, scout us a trail."

We ate, morsel by morsel, making our way down the steep mountain trails toward Little Valley. Our mother awaited us in Sister Jensen's kitchen. Mother's eyes were opaque. She walked careful and tentative. The house was empty of its own people—no Jensen children, no mother or father, no forgetful grandmother. Only us. The whole town, even our father's house, was deserted. Mama took stock of each of us, set us in tubs of hot water and said to scrub ourselves till we had bright new skin. She issued each of us a miraculous set of new clothes. She carried the old ones out back to burn, where a fire was already set as if it had been lit there forever.

No one ever told us what happened during the days we were locked in the prospector's house. No one inquired further about our imprisonment. The bad man was gone for good and it was best we forgot it all. For a season we moved to a small frame house in Brigham City, closer to the mission farm where Peter worked. Papa sometimes came down from Little Valley. He would send Julius to fetch us and we'd spend a miserable day working at Julius's family's place under Papa's supervision, re-earning our right to our father's decent name, atoning for our outrages toward our upright forbear.

It wasn't so long before he found himself another wife. Plenty of willing brides. The new one, not quite a girl but nigh twenty years younger than Papa, was a widow sealed to her first husband in the Logan Temple. Both of them viewed it as satisfactory until they proceeded to the Celestial Kingdom. She moved into the house in Little Valley and set her modern hand to the decoration. Papa went on about how glorious and proper it was. Had to call himself happy just to prove the misery was Mama's fault at the foundation, and he made a point to keep recalling it to us. I don't know what their lives were like behind those walls once we left them to each other, and after a while I quit wondering. Gradually I learned the world was not mine to remedy, although I never did understand how to comfort myself with that knowledge.

I set to making certain that my name, which was also my father's, called up two very different men in the minds of those who knew us. We took back our father's surname as he demanded but we took to spelling it the Swedish way, Anderson instead of Andersen. The defiance reamed his heart to his dying day.

It was a meager renunciation. I spent my life too much made by him. My mother was not like other women, which caused us disquiet, but finally she was a woman and I did not comprehend her well enough to feel her in me. Papa's constitution was the founder of mine. My father's devotion to the Iron Rod galvanized the nerves in my back and arms and legs in moments of pure instinct. His legacy caused me to lunge in blind righteous fury toward misbehaving sons. I had a way of plunging into a dark agitation of mind and heart with no evident circumstance to account for it. I deeply loved my children but to my sorrow I passed an intemperate rage to my sons, high guard to my daughters.

I yearned for the easy nature that carried my half brother Peter through worldly exasperations. I tried to emulate his rolling laugh. My voice had the same timbre, and unless Julius stood between us our likeness made Peter and me seem like whole brothers. I prayed fervently for Peter's forgiving quality. He was the kind of man who frankly forgot affront. He disliked Papa for good reason but he learned to diminish his provocations. Peter joked and confided with his wife. His little children ran to greet him when he came in from the fields. They tumbled and frolicked, heedless to false dignities. Peter encountered more grief in his lifetime than I ever did but he culled vitality from the very conditions that sapped my own.

Instead of loving her freely, I portioned and patronized my capable wife. She was a beautiful woman, young in heart and bearing. She was made like a sparrow: fine and compact, bright-eyed and ever-moving. She was properly grateful to the blessings my hard work afforded. I believe she loved me well as I would allow. Annie was beloved of our children. She lent me an air of credibility as bishop of the Ammon Ward. She came smiling when I beckoned. Only I could feel the stiff withholding under her lightness when I said she could leave her work, and come to sit a spell on my lap.

Peter Nielsen

Despite my resentment, that season on the church farm opened my eyes to a world I was willing to inhabit. Plenty of grief was to come my way, and an ample share of plain absurdity. But after the farm, I learned through every season to improve the shining moments. Somehow it came to me fully that sorrow and sweetness both would slip from our grasp, and so I'd best gaze toward the stars as they dimmed.

The Shoshones had seen a whole world fall away from them. I swore I would pay heed to mine in my time. I didn't manage it continual but what I did I owe to Sarah Hansen. Her folks supervised the church farm. She ran wild on it like a pony, hair long and only sometimes braided. She moved easy like a boy in her gait. Of course I took notice, but girls as a category stopped my mind and tongue. This one in particular. One day I watched her climb a hay barn the size of a foothill, inching her way up the steep roof by clinging to the shingles that overhung the gables. She grabbed the lightning rod at the top and then swung a leg over the high beam line, hanging her feet forward on either side. She hollered and waved but I could see myself in her eyes, a tiny spider like to be crushed. I turned my back.

That night before supper I was grating potatoes for the work crew. Sarah sauntered my way. "Afraid of heights? Is that why you couldn't even take a look?"

I kept at the potatoes, taking each one down to a little white knob. She watched, amused. When she leaned in closer I grated my knuckle. Blood trickled into the bowl. I reached in with the other hand, clean, to scoop it out but made no other sign.

She said, "A little meat goes well with potatoes, anyhow."

After that she'd come by and tease as I hoed beans. She'd help me yoke big Sigurd and follow me through the long rows. She'd chatter on but she always kept me listening. She knew the names of rocks. I knew the plants but I was too timid to teach her. She traced the watermark that snaked along the mountain slopes above us, and on hot days we imagined we were gardening in the depths of a secret sea. We watched gigantic fish swim over our heads, ocean rays and sharp-toothed sturgeon and formations of glittering trout.

That girl could walk the whole length of a rail fence, smooth and straight as if it were flat pavestones. Her folks weren't saints, entirely, or they would have lost my interest a long way back. But they didn't mind a half-made rogue like me. They harbored no indignation that we were young and that the world and its glories gaped before us. Beyond the Hansens I never met anyone over thirty who never resented that latecomers might get the same pay as the first.

We didn't marry right off. She was young and I wasn't all grown myself. But like I said it was Sarah taught me to quit arguing with what can't be helped. She had a talent for it, but she proved it deeper as life presented itself. The summer she turned sixteen, Sarah caught a colt for its first shoes. She tied the halter rope to the fence, meaning to move away but the farrier came up the other side too quick. The colt shied and fought the rope. It gave Sarah a kick to the high shin so violent it tore right through her dress and stockings, peeling a long strip of skin and muscle to the ivory bone.

To our children this was an old tale that happened so long ago I had to explain to our youngest, named for her mother, that Sarah's girlhood climb up that barn roof and her easy stride along the thin line of a rail fence occurred with two human feet, not one and a cork.

The leg swelled and shone black. The elders arrived to anoint her with consecrated olive oil. They placed their hands on her head and promised a full recovery, but truth be told I don't know if anyone had faith to cast out the specter of death. I helped her parents pad a wagon. We softened it with ticking and blankets to make a bed and I rode with them, slow and anxious, to the hospital in Ogden. The doctor sawed through muscle and sinew and bone well above the knee to save Sarah from the poison of her own limb. Week after week she recovered, and lapsed, and then slowly returned. Everybody in Bear River City and many from Tremonton and Brigham and Mantua traveled down to the hospital at some point to sit vigil. But I was there most. After a while everyone, even Sarah, came to expect that I'd be there, sitting and waiting, firming up my courage as she returned to life.

She was laid up for weeks after she came home to the farm. She sat in a pillowed chair on the porch, or come winter lay on the bed they moved down to the parlor so she could feel a part of things. I came in and out, inventing errands—volunteering to beat rugs and wash windows just to be near. I secretly saved my money and then made myself brave enough to confer with the deep-voiced nurse in private.

Later Sarah accused me: "You taking up with Nurse Poulos?"

"I guess she'd be a good cook. And she looks tough enough to fight off a cougar. I might catch on to her."

Sarah's eyes opened wide. She flushed, almost showed me tears, and then looked fiercely away. She turned back composed. "Well, I'll see what she can do about a grizzly then, if you keep after her."

Nurse Poulos slipped me the word a few weeks later. I saddled a horse and mostly galloped to Ogden to meet the train and a crate. Inside was a leg for Sarah, light and strong, made of fine-grained Mediterranean cork.

It fit her fine. Soon Sarah walked almost the same way she'd strode before, just a bit of extra swing at the hip. It lent her an air of insouciance that would have strained another woman, but only enhanced the charm of my wife.

We made four children. The older three would have thought their mother diminished had she walked on regular legs. Little Sarah could only picture it all through story, because the evil returned in the hours after her birth. As I said earlier, I was away on a mission in Denmark, also keeping an eye out for the peckerwood who fathered me. By the time I got word from America, my beloved wife had been dead near three months. I found a ship, crossed the Atlantic, took a train to Nebraska, and bought a fast horse to ride hard to Mantua. My mother had settled the children, bringing them to daily clarity and material routine. She fed them well. They were clean and well kept, sorrowful but getting on. Mama had already taught them how to bear down and endure.

I do understand that enduring is a way to get from one point to a better. But seems folks get used to it—enduring, I mean—and then it has a way of turning into a virtue only of itself. It must yield satisfactions because a lot of people make no effort to go beyond.

I doubt my mother was capable of much beyond endurance by the time she had a chance to get on to something else. Strangely, the older I got, the more I remembered the sensation of that long walk to Salt Lake City. Seems I could never fall to sleep without at some point waking into a dream of myself clinging to my mother. My mother walking. Mostly I'd come to in my own bed and then get on to the real slumber. But sometimes I kept falling hour after hour into the dream. Nothing else happened in it. Just clinging and walking. Grind of footsteps on the hard trail. Sometimes a sensation of heat on my back.

Mama must have recalled in her own dreams the details I could not locate. And she must have relived, day or night in different states, that day the old man took after her with the strop. She may have absorbed the actual pain of a strike better than the public humiliation of rescue. The whole population of Little Copenhagen running maybe to intervene, but mostly to see the spectacle. That day made her a story in every household forever. And although she never spoke of it nor altered her countenance at the slightest remembrance, she must have stewed about that season she took the children up Monte Cristo. She swore me to silence and I kept it, but we're all gone now so I'll say this: somewhere there's a dead prospector in his own deep shaft. Would have made a good story but it's best he stays there to plug the hole.

Mama got to dreading all those old stories so much she generally shut her mouth for good once she settled with Chris and Annie, near my place in Idaho. We ran sheep in the mountains, Chris and me, Charley and Joe. Chris and Annie made Mama a nice room of her own, furnishing it with the best things left from a lifetime of losses. They were good to her. Annie was cheerful and quick-tongued, so much she could even make Mama laugh. Mama kept her door open, welcomed the grandchildren to come sit when all was well. But she shut it tight when the old tales came up. Even the happy ones.

Thomas Christian Andersen, the Father

It was Peter got the notion to abandon Little Valley. Lorenzo Snow himself called us up to that place and it was where we belonged. I wouldn't have give a damn if it was just the one—the worst one. But Peter influenced his brothers for evil, once he scouted Idaho territory cleared of the murderous Indians. By then the Utah Railway shot from Logan to Taylor's Crossing and beyond. Peter and his second wife, the one with two good legs, not the cork, and his children settled up there. He got to bragging it up to the others and soon it was an exodus. Their sister Maria was already married and off to the west mountains, out by that dead salted lake. Chris told his mother he'd build her a room in their new house. From what I hear she went directly to packing.

Peter rode down to Cache Valley on the train to help drive the wagons.

"Charley," I said, "you're the only one worth a bag of salt anyhow. Stay here and help me with the farm, the one God ordained for us. Here we have it, straight from the mouth of prophets. Mantua is your birthright. Angels surround our Little Copenhagen. You can inherit it all. Once I'm dead, the whole Andersen spread. Work it until I die and it's yours."

Charley gave it all one last look. He assessed me as if confirming I'd never die anyhow and swung himself up to the high wagon seat. "Come with us if you want to, Papa, but we're all going. You can sell here. You can stake a claim just like the rest of us."

They knew I wouldn't do it. An upright man will not be persuaded from his calling.

Chris said, "Well, Papa, why don't you just ride on up with us, give it a look? Help us drive the caravan."

"We'll send you back on the train. It's only a day's return."

Peter was checking harness. It made me so mad to see him I said, "Fine. I'll ride along. You fools are likely to run on up to Canada if I ain't there to say stop."

Children, big and small, darted around the wagons and beasts.

"We've been up there. You know that, Papa. It's already staked," Charley said. "Adjoining plots. Every one of us that could, already registered a piece."

"Well, you didn't drive the road. You paid your tickets and got off at the railroad stop like city folk. Anyhow I got my land. Mantua is my home, as decreed by an apostle of the Lord."

"Mighty mosquito-bit, from my experience," said Peter. "Can't them apostles do something about the mosquitoes?"

"You shut your irreverent mouth, boy."

"Do what you want, Papa," Charley said. "But we're nigh to depart for Snake River country. You'd best decide if you're up for some touristing."

The bishop said he'd send his sons to tend the livestock, which weren't much right then beyond pigs and a coop of chickens. Planting was finished. The boys had made sure of it. Plenty of rain coming. I could be back in a fortnight. Anna Marie, my one good wife, helped me gather clothing. I packed my scriptures and a book of holy Latter-Day discourses. Chris said everything else was provided. I set up to drive Chris's extra rig, two good mules. I helped lay down ticking and a tarpaulin, and even before I could hoist myself up to the driving seat a couple of grandchildren were deposited in the box.

For small children they were quite clean and attractive.

"What's your name again?" I asked the girl, who had already reminded me she was six.

She looked me over. "You're my grandpapa. You're supposed to know my name."

"Well, I probably do, but you ought to tell me so we can make sure of it."

She thought about this, and then said, "My name is Zenobia."

"That's a fancy name for a *lille pige* like you. Can you live up to a name like that?"

She eyed me up and down. "My papa put me in your wagon because I *am* a good girl. I don't cry."

"I guess he should have put you in with your grandmama, then. You must be made after her own hard heart."

"I wanted to ride with Grandma. Papa said I could if I put up with you the first day."

That stung me. I shot an eye toward Chris, who was securing his team. His wife Annie, showing now clearly that another child was on the way, waved to encourage me. That harpy Sidse sat in Peter's canopied cart, settled on a low chair lashed to the floor. Might as well been sitting in the comfort of her own parlor. Peter's boys and some of Charley's hovered around her. She conversed among them, affectionate, but she never once acknowledged my coming. She looked at everything and everyone but me.

I determined to win this child over.

I pointed to the other child in my wagon. "Is that your brother?"

"His name is Reuben. I know how to take care of him. My sister is Elmira. She gets to ride with Grandma today."

"I know your names. Your mama always did have fancy likings. But Chris could have done worse. She's a tough little hummingbird."

Zenobia said, "She's not a hummingbird. She's my mama."

"Idaho-*Ho!*" Peter called out, and the children thought it was very funny. We set off, up the old Indian Road and down into Cache Valley, and then on through Red Rock Pass into rolling Idaho. Most of the road skirted the reservation or passed right through it. I kept my eye out for Shoshone.

As we traveled it became evident to me that little Zenobia was as good as her folks declared. I took to her company and was determined to keep her in my wagon. I could see her, first day, eyeing Peter's cart, desiring to sit with her grandmama. I said, "You don't want to sit over there. Look how crowded that wagon is. Your old grandma just sitting like a stone. This is the good spot. I'll tell you some stories if you're a good girl."

"I told you. I am good. Mama says don't let you tell me different."

"What? What?"

She regarded me like a little falcon. I remembered something all the way back from my days in Denmark. I was a young father sitting with Julia, my firstborn, in the endless dark of winter. She was much the same as this one here. That night in the old country it was myself and the child, waiting for the distant return of sunlight. Julia's mother busy with the infant.

"Look here, Zenobia. I'll make you a baby doll."

She leaned toward me, interested and earnest. She asked me in a doubtful whisper: "How can you make a baby doll, Grandpapa?"

"I'll carve it from a willow branch. It won't be big, but it will be just right to live in your apron pocket. I'll show you. I've made one before, you know, for another little girl."

She found this impressive. "What little girl?"

"All grown up now. She lives in Denmark. She may by now have a child of her own."

Zenobia kept her gaze steady, eyes narrowed. But I could see I was winning her over.

I whistled up the line. Peter was in the lead but I called, "Chris! Stop the wagons! Give me a few minutes of pause!" and Peter called back, "What do you say, Chris? Give me the order!"

Chris shouted, "Just as well I suppose! Shade up here by the creek," and they turned off the trail, halting the teams where the stream opened up cool and quiet.

"You need to see a man about a horse, is that what?" Charley said to me, and I said, "Well, I don't mind while I'm over there, but I want to cut willow."

"He's going to make me a baby doll. To live in my apron pocket," Zenobia declared, and I said, "That's exactly right. So how about you boys come help me seek the right form over there at the creek?"

It was an excursion. All of us but sour old Sidse marched over to the thickets. The boys and I had a time of it, debating just the right branch—thick in the middle, two arms reaching like a child raising its arms to be lifted up. Charley unsheathed his bowie and cut it clean, trimming to a sturdy enough body, cutting the extending arms to the right length. He kept a long neck above them for attaching a carven head. We took the opportunity to rest a short spell. Zenobia stayed close to me, anxious to see me transform a stick into a baby. I stripped the bark from the smooth green wood and told Joe to take a hatchet to a dry fallen pine. He chopped out a block small enough to carve into a head the size of a green apple. Then as we resumed the journey I whittled and joined on the road's smoother stretches as the mules kept in line. Zenobia leaned against me on the buckboard, fascinated as I carved the trunk into legs and torso. I tapered the arms into wrists and rude hands, then carved the head round and worked ears and features. In camp, Charley took a brush and India ink and sharpened the eyes. The thing came to a kind of life.

But it was buck naked and indiscernible. Zenobia found this worrisome and wrapped it in a piece of muslin. That settled the matter for a quarter hour but as we rode she wrapped and unwrapped, worked the cloth into a kind of frock and then a blanket, and then a cape. She put it back in her pocket, then pulled it out, and then at breakfast she came to me and said, "Grandpapa, is this baby a girl or a boy?"

I hardly knew how to answer such a thing. "Child, why can't you just leave it be? It's a stick carved to illusion. Isn't that enough? Stop your questions. You told me you were a good girl!"

The girl burst into tears and ran to her mother, who shot me a quizzical glance and held out her hand for the toy. Annie held it up for examination. I could see the mother and daughter in conference and then Annie gestured toward Sidse, sending the child on to her grandmother. More talking then and presently I was overwhelmed by the sense that right before my eyes, three generations of females were showing me exactly how it stands in this degenerate world. Here in truth are men charged with right authority, direct from Jesus Christ to Joseph Smith the Prophet, and on to those of us worthy of the Melchizedek Priesthood. But since Eve's first sin, women in their secrets and connivance usurp the true power. I testify unto you that this is the cause of every mortal grief and the sorrows beyond. Women hold the power of destruction and damnation—even the little ones, because they hearken to their grandmothers in dark knowing.

I observed that whole afternoon as the child sat in Peter's wagon, compelled by her grandma's clever needle. Sidse stitched the muslin into a close-fitting cover for the doll's body. She softened the effigy into plumpness, stuffing the fabric with bits of wool. Now only the head and hands and feet were naked wood.

The mother and grandmother and girl child laughed as they

passed the doll from hand to hand. They spoke amongst themselves with animation and Sidse set to work again. She cut and stitched scraps of calico and chambray as the low dry hills passed behind us. She tied bits of yarn and soon enough the poppet was transformed into a tiny female like Zenobia. Calico apron and yellow braids. The child took it from her grandmother's hands and stood up in the wagon to wave the doll baby in my direction.

I turned away, feigning not to notice. But when we stopped for the night she ran again to show the poppet to me. I recalled the commandment against graven images. It occurred to me that I may have set in motion a portentous sin, that I had propelled the child across a threshold toward that place women go in the shadows of witchcraft and discontent. Although she was only a child, I sensed that the dark wiles of femininity were nigh to overcome me and so I said, "That's just fine. Now you can ride with your grandmama in the women's wagon, like you told me you wanted. Now get along."

I cannot say whether the child looked pleased or aggrieved. I was never able to interpret excess emotion as I myself was inclined to clean reason and masculine intellect. Chris said, "Papa! What's the matter with you?"

Peter laughed. "That's right, little one. You come ride all the way to Eagle Rock with your old Uncle Peter here in the women's wagon. You can sit right up front on the buckboard with me. You can help me drive if you want."

Her mother said, "Go on, Miss Zenobia. Ride with your uncle and grandmama, but make sure you wave back to us from time to time."

The rest of the journey was a misery to me. A dark veil fell over my soul. I witnessed my family moved with their conniving mother to a gentile territory. As I boarded the train toward Utah I understood this to foreshadow the Resurrection Day—in which I, a faithful man all my life, would be transported home to the Celestial Kingdom even as my descendants were assigned to inferior glory. I found bitter satisfaction in this on my return to the place the prophets had decreed as my domain. My sons traded their birthright to cling to rank maternity.

I got to brooding, sinking into despair as the train rattled southward. I turned to scripture for comfort. I carried some sermons of Brigham Young and began to read from these holy speeches. But I only found myself in darkness even as the dry sun of the Portneuf hills illuminated my window.

Before, reading sermons by the great apostles of the only true and living church upon the face of the earth had ever increased my holy contemplations. The Lord granted unto me the gift of discernment. I liked to look upon many souls: some who would be redeemed by saving principles, some destined to minister unto us transformed by celestial glory. But now the Lord showed me some, like my unfaithful wife Sidse, who were bound for Outer Darkness.

Traveling away from her I felt sorry for the woman. In the tenderness of my heart, her sure damnation seemed a sharp chastising. I have ever been a compassionate man. I would not believe it was the Holy Spirit testifying such awful things to me. I put it out of my mind as much as I might, but the Spirit testified that my sorrow was weakness. The Spirit bade me believe that it was the Father's mercy to bless me with such private counsel. He said to my mind, *My son, thou must as well hear of the damned as well as the saved.* Yet I gave no credence to the Holy Ghost's promptings, convincing myself that it was an evil spirit come to deceive.

Then for my unbelief the Lord drew from me all dalliance with angelic figures. He suffered me to have many evil thoughts. Beforehand, I had enjoyed sweet anticipations of prophetic fulfillment in the mornings as I performed my chores (always keeping after the lazy children). But suddenly I was filled with foul mindfulness of lechery. I came to believe the Devil held me in the palm of his hand, boring into me with cursed thoughts. Before, I had partaken of visions of gold plates and strong angels, men of the mountains and vales of Utah calling forth the new Kingdom of God in the Great Basin with the power of the Holy Melchizedek Priesthood. But now I partook of abominable sights no matter how I resisted.

It seemed as though I was beholding women's hidden filth. I saw diverse women of the Kingdom: old and young, wives and virgins. I saw Indian women and gentile, Mormon and apostate and demure and craven. I could not put them out of my sight, each revealing their audacious woman-parts unto me. And the Devil bade me in my mind to choose which I would have. Despite myself, I liked better some of them than the others.

Upon my homecoming my wife withdrew from me in fear. Still my thought was that every woman deserved my wrath. When I partook of the Sacrament, when I took to my prayers, or when I performed any good deed, cursedness crowded my mind. I took counsel from President Snow and asked him for a blessing. I did all that I might but found no release. I went to my fields and cried to God. "Alas Lord, thou hast said that thou wouldst never forsake me. Where now is the fastness of thy word?"

I fell to the ground. The hot sky was transparent. I could see straight through it into nothing. I despaired and cried out again.

Soon after, a good angel came unto me. He offered his hand and I took it and felt firm flesh and bone, so I knew the angel was a glorified man who spoke truth: "God hath not forsaken thee. Nor never shall he ever forsake thee. But because thou didst not believe that it was the Spirit of God that showed thee that you shall be saved and Sidse be damned, God chastised thee."

I said to the angel, "Persuade the Lord to speak to me as he did before, and I shall believe that it is also Him that spoke to me about damnation."

"Man, Jesus will not take this away until thou hast suffered one more day for each apostle of the Latter Days. The Lord is not wroth with you, but in His wisdom He gives you this trial to show you your calling and election made sure."

Verily I did suffer that pain until twelve days had passed, and then, as if a great weight was suddenly lifted, I had holy thoughts, as holy as ever before.

I was filled with joy. I cried unto the opening sky, "I shall believe that every good thought is the speech of God. I thought I was in hell! Lord, now will I lie still and be intimate to thy will."

Peter Nielsen

Leave the old man to his fever dreams. I'll show you a vision. A real one. I wish I could have told my mother about the elephants. She would have enjoyed the account but it happened in 1917, well after she was released from the old man's mortal hell.

The new century seemed a world beyond the one we inhabited as children. Now even my own children were grown, and although I never quit missing Sarah I did all right with Eliza, too. She was good to the children and it had been a long time and we felt like a family. I could have kept right on enjoying my old age, but as I said, I didn't get so many years as I would have chosen for myself.

But in 1917 I was youthful for my years and I knew my way in the world. I'd been to Denmark and California and a lot of places between. I felt at home in Ammon, the little town my brothers and I pretty near founded. I was old enough to recall the old tribes and recount the striking changes in the Shoshone and now Mormon country that defined our time. I liked my Mormon family and neighbors, mostly kept the faith myself but enjoyed the company of other types just as well. I took a liking to folks my family saw as decadent. Barkeeps in Idaho Falls. Women who brought in the business with their easy talk. I liked the Indians down to Blackfoot and Pocatello: a certain wit, their peculiar way of gazing at folks who believed they themselves were the spectators.

Everyone in Ammon and Blackfoot and Idaho Falls knew the circus was coming. Not one soul of any tribe or philosophy intended to miss it. People found reason to be in town the day the train came in. I had business at the hardware but I'd be lying if I said I didn't time it to take a long gander at the arrival. I hoped to make conversation with the circus folks, usually characters with rough histories and the good will to relate them. The day was windy even for an Idaho spring. Cold gusts rushed up from the western flatland, settling and then flaring up again to strike houses and wagons, a few fancy new automobiles, and train cars and folks on horses. The circus men were straining to set up the rudiments of the big top. Some of them walked into the city proper asking for volunteers to help drive stakes. I was delighted to lend a hand.

The Snake River is named right, coiling and turning as it finds descent toward the Columbia. At some points the bed gives way and the water plunges. The circus folks chose the lush parkway to the east of the river, where the water smooths itself like blue-green glass. The city was built where the river bends and straightens and bends again, but at the lower turn the flow breaks and tumbles across a wide arc of volcanic stone. Sound of it so resonant, you think you've gone sublimely deaf.

I felt right at home among the hardworking circus toughs. I made note of their tattoos. This work was just like fencing and I could see other local men just as happy as I was, turning our skills to a novel purpose. We watched the real hands place the king pole, and then we saw the handlers open the elephant cars to lead the beautiful lumbering creatures out. We knew they were headed our way because the elephants were the only force strong enough to raise the inside poles vertical. I thought I'd get to watch up close but suddenly the gale picked up again. Everything not tied or weighed down reacted, flying or rolling or slamming. A long flap from a small tent pulled loose and snapped loud as a shotgun blast.

Beyond the bank, just off the train car, twenty-two head of elephants went berserk. For a moment they spun and collided, but then found common direction. I'd seen cattle stampede. Even buffalo. But hell. This was something else. The wind was blowing, people running, elephants trumpeting Armageddon. Cars veered off the roads to make way. Horses scattered like mice before cats. The trainers tried helplessly to hold the elephants back by pulling the chains around their feet. The creatures thundered down narrow streets and around buildings, trailing flying chains behind them with such force that they tore bricks and siding off the corners. Then they pulled away entirely. The pursuers stood agape as the elephants made a mad charge for the river. Some were crazed enough to jump in of their own accord, a thirty-foot drop. Others shied off but the weight and frenzy broke the bank and every last pachyderm plummeted into the churning torrent below the falls.

By now everyone within a square mile was working their way toward the river, trying to get close enough to enter the scene without getting killed by it. I always loved a spirited horse so I was part of the action. After all the stampeding chaos and that dusty avalanche of elephants and rocks and dirt and even a couple of trees, suddenly it was all quiet. Just the roaring of the falls and a gathering crowd of circus people, Blackfeet, townfolk, and bumpkins like me peering over the broken bank into the whitewater. We believed the elephants were drowned and I expected to see corpses pop up southward where the roil slowed and the bed rose to shallow the water. That is, if the pressure of the falls didn't hold them down there forever.

But then somebody shouted, "Look there!" and we moved as a whole community, shoulder to shoulder on down the river at the current's pace, wondering. We all saw together the most astounding thing. By instinct, every elephant had put its trunk up to the surface for air. Twenty-two periscope noses, visible above the water like alien sea creatures peering back at us. The noses left little wakes behind them as they traveled toward the Broadway Bridge. Under the bridge they floated, and on beyond the bridge where the water calmed. The noses all shifted direction together, heading toward shore. The broad crowns of the elephant heads surfaced like buoyant boulders, and then their shoulders. Each mountainous beautiful dripping creature rose up like the sixth day of creation.

We gasped in wonder at each emergence. The wind settled and the elephants went tamely to their keepers. Those of us with herding skills flanked up and we drove them slowly back toward the circus site. Horses, mules, the elephants themselves, and cowboys, sheep men, Indians, and circus hands brought the herd in. Women and children and city men in their suits brought up the rear, keeping a distance from the dust and heft, some fearing another breakout yet compelled to follow.

As we arrived, the elephants caught whiff of that mist coming off the falls. We should have been more ready for it this time but we were surprised once more as some broke east toward the bank to jump in again. I guess they just enjoyed the sensation of freedom and water, of doing whatever they damn well pleased just like any of us. But this time we could better anticipate the outcome, so some of us rode down past the bridge to wait and pretty soon the renegades came up. We brought them safely back, and at least for the time being they were content.

Moroni Timbimboo, July 25, 1967, Washakie, Utah

Well, the farm here, it was settled along in about 1885, I think; and then the Indians were first—they farm first at Elwood. They homesteaded down there and then they, anyway, they—Brigham Young—wanted to locate them more again up this way, so they move from Elwood up here where they call Washakie now. They were all under United Order. You understand that, United Order?

They were all under United Order, the Lamanites are then. They all work together, you see, in a group and support themselves that way. When they first come here, they homesteaded—some of them homesteaded here and there, and then they worked to help each other. They first come in, had an oxen team to work with, to plow with; and they had some horses, too, but they plow with oxen. My father used to say they used to—you know how the Indians are; they wear a blanket like them, you know, had to wrap around on them all the time. They had—they just only had a breech cloth, you know, and then no trouser of any kind, but they had a moccasin. They go out there in the field and plow the way they are, you see. Them Indians, they dressed in the Indian custom then, long hair, and so it went on. They farm here and there, but there—a lot of this farming—a lot of this ground over here now been—they sold out. Them oldtimers, they sold out before they died, their homestead—to some of the white people around here. Then they finally, then the church bought them white people out again after that. Now the church had the whole farm down here, now, what the Indians used to have, but some of the white people, they still got the land homesteaded, but they still got their land around here now, but they were in there. I don't know how many year back, there were my grandfather named Sagwitch, and his cousin named John Moembugie. They were two chiefs of the band that was around here. I understood before they took a homestead down here in Elwood, they had—they were farming over in Franklin, too, besides; and they moved them over here then, and then at last they move—settled down here.

Frank Timbimboo, Son of Moroni, July 25, 1967

. . . as time went on, some of this land was owned by the church. A lot of it was owned by the Indians, and as they—as I remember, my grandfather's brother—and I think there were cases just like his—where he grew older, to getting along in years, too old to farm the ground, and then the church allotted them so much money every month and made provisions so that when they died, the church would inherit their property.

I think that possibly it was this religious aspect that made them settle down and do this. When a person has a conviction and starts to believe, I think it changes his life. It can turn a drunk into a pretty faithful man if he's convinced what he'd started to believe is right . . . the Indians seem like they were taught in Indian, but they accepted the Gospel, and they were quite faithful and real strong in their belief. Possibly this is the thing that changed them from the way that they roamed into— all of a sudden into people that started to agriculture.

My great-grandfather, Chief Sagwitch, which had a lot of dealings with the white people in this valley, had two names. His one name was Sagwitch, and his other name was Timbimboo, so we—when we joined the church and records had to be kept, then he took one of his names and used it for a surname.

Does it have an Indian meaning?

Yes, it means "writing on a rock," I guess is what it means. It probably—possible was a hieroglyphic writing on rocks that we see.

Peter Nielsen

In my older age when I got to dreaming about that walk to Utah, I'd stay in it, clinging to my mother's shoulders. Sometimes I was small and sick, sometimes too big and perfectly strong yet unable to release my grip. Then the dream gave way to that day on the mountain above Little Valley. I would be only that small ragged boy, no memory of having grown, facing that Shoshone Indian in the white man's hat.

He offers me his hand. He leans down gentle to my ear. He whispers, "You got to cry a little, Great White Chief." In the dream he reaches forever like a father. He wraps his arm tenderly around my shoulder just as I see his other hand raise a long blade to my chicken throat.

IGNATIUS INSISTS THAT...

Yes, I know. A guide. At least to the threshold.

Here we are: Fremont County, Idaho. Opened to homesteading in the late 1800s, "mostly cleared" of native "hostiles."

No guide I can conjure seems to know their actual way around this place. They keep pointing out the Tetons and the amber waves of grain. Won't show me what I want to see. Mind-numbing insistences. Trickle-down Manifest Destiny.

If you like to eat, thank a farmer!

Can't tear their starry eyes away from the golden cowboys and radiant housewives. The plows and harrows and combines. The uprightness of it all.

Welfare loafers, libtards, queers, tree huggers: move along. No place for you here. This is Real America.

Who's left to guide me then?

The saint intervenes. *Settle down. Listen better. Look. You've learned to see.*

And I do see something approaching. And I know what it is, precisely because I can't make it out. Here's a true story: the only ghost I can't explain away inhabited a section of stairs between the main and upper floors of my grandparents' Idaho farmhouse. Still does, according to the people who live there now. The stairway was steep, and in my memory thickly carpeted. It made a right-angle turn to the left at the very top. The three stairs just below the turn were multidimensional: you walked through the ghost, or its peculiar vertical space—unmistakably entering and exiting a sort of humid column. You could put your hand in and feel the difference—or stand halfway in, halfway out, at least if you could control the mildly electrified terror. Each of my siblings will back me up on this.

Of course we've wondered who it was, and why it would anchor itself exactly there. We've speculated but it's unsatisfactory. I've even come to wonder if the trace is animal. And so it doesn't exactly "speak" to me now, but here it is—or I'm back there in its spot—and it's setting the scene.

My mother's German grandparents, Anna Kandler and Friedrich Lenz, emigrated to Nebraska in the 1870s from what was then Prussia. They had children in America, and when the Snake River Valley below Yellowstone opened at the turn of the century for homesteading, they moved west again.

The Idaho landscape was breathtaking, both in its beauty and its winter cold, and—I feel sharply now—in the vestigial trails and camps of other peoples, very recently expelled. Friedrich and Anna produced one more boy—Carl Ludwig, the only child born in Idaho.

Carlie shocked his family beyond full recovery when he married a Mormon girl from the larger town of Ashton. Myrtle LaVaughan came out to live in the homestead house with him and they had two little girls. The younger one was my mother, Nadeene. She was four when her mother Myrtle died of heart failure on a frigid December night in 1939.

Carlie then married Ellen Lee—"Gram" to me—the woman I drove to Arizona when I was seventeen. She was Mormon, too, which doubly jolted the old Lutherans. She was divorced, and had two small children of her own. Carlie and Ellen made yet two more. The youngest, Louisa, really ought to be my guide here because she's the undisputed family queen of genealogy.

But I'm looking for the people she's not.

The artists. The apostates. The peculiars.

The ones who reproduced themselves in us, in other ways. This ghost should know, but it's only here to nudge. It gestures me on up the turning stairs and toward the attic. I don't even have to open the door to understand: the stereographs. As a child I spent hours in their three-dimensional thrall.

The sinister presence retreats. And now, Ellen Lenz—who always saw more than she let on, I imagine—shows up to set us straight.

Ellen Lee Lenz

Olaf Larson called himself a stereoscopist. The contraption used to view early photos was called a stereoscope and some of the pioneers who could afford it owned one. It provided hours of entertainment. Some of the early settlers took pride in acquiring an extensive collection of this type of photograph, with shots from all parts of the world.

Olaf also occupied and farmed a parcel of land in Squirrel, Idaho, in the early 1900s.

People living now who remember Mr. Larson say he was slight in stature, and a striking individual in appearance. He helped his neighbors thresh grain but his own farming ability lacked management. He stood out as a little different, perhaps miscast for his role. He received education at Moscow, Idaho. He could have been a professor.

Olaf had a project to improve the wild huckleberry, according to Nick Nichols, who as a boy often rode his horse by Olaf's place. Nick says his father and Olaf often debated the domestication of the mountain huckleberry. Nick's father told him, "Olaf, every huckleberry has to have its face washed every morning by the pure mountain dew, and it won't grow on an open south slope. It needs its feet planted in the rotting needles of the conifers and it doesn't grow well among aspen trees."

Olaf tried to move and grow the berry but was unsuccessful.

He was, however, respected for his knowledge of horticulture. Olaf told friends that prior to coming to this country his own father worked for the king of Norway as a gardener.

Leon and Velma Wheelwright knew Olaf quite well. They were well educated, and he was no farmer. In winter, Olaf would use four horses to pull a small covered sleigh to Squirrel or Ashton. His horses were thin and he fed them mostly straw. The Larsons would ski or snowshoe to school or community gatherings.

Olaf composed poems and on one occasion at a grange dinner and program, he wrote a poem about Leon. Leon was dressed as a woman and introduced as Mrs. Farnsworth, a state official of the Idaho Grange Association. Olaf fell for the "lady." His wife had passed away a few years previous and I think he was a lonely man. After finding out who Mrs. Farnsworth really was, he wrote a poem.

Anna Morre tells of the time she and another close neighbor were acting as sitters for the corpse of Olaf's wife the night before the funeral. Olaf told them to go to the cupboard and eat if they got hungry. When they opened the cupboard the only thing in it was a quart glass jar of pickled onions. They ate the onions.

Glan Sharp said, "I would often go up to Larson's place. He had a Victrola as tall as I was. He had many records and the stories that went with the music. His knowledge of history, literature, and music was remarkable to his neighbors. Olaf's father was a feeble man and as a boy I helped him haul his hay. My mother was with Olaf's wife at the time of her death. Olaf's heart was broken. His house had many handmade features. One was a knotted wood doorknob. He also used a wooden yoke to carry water from the creek."

He will probably be remembered most, this fellow Olaf who has come and gone, for his stereoscopic pictures. He photographed many of his neighbors. His prints will be viewed for many years and kept in museums. He enjoyed capturing the sight of the great productivity of the virgin soil and its hardy pioneers at Squirrel, Idaho.

GRASSMAN OF THE YEAR

My heart is simply melting
at the thought of Julian Eltinge . . .

—Dorothy Parker, 1916

Olaf Larson:

Those old Prussian homesteaders. Those people would not open their mouths to reveal an infernal thing. Public talking was plain against their constitution. What in the world did those *Deutsche* need to hide? If their souls matched their farms there was nowhere to hide a fingerbone, let alone a skeleton. Funny how they'd let me take my camera to them though. They were proud of their clean white houses and gracious barns, pleased to pose with their wagons and horses and their ruddy tidy children. They scrubbed their walls to starkness, then whitewashed and scrubbed again. They arranged plows and harrows and tractor parts in careful rows. Repainted barns and sheds at first hint of weatherworn. They shoveled shit into neat piles, organized I suspect by what kind of animal had produced it.

Folks like that either have nothing or everything to hide.

Me, on the other hand. I guarded a midden of secrets. That's not poetic flourish. My father collected oddities like a magpie. He had a plan to someday open a grand museum but as it proved out his talents were limited to preposterous accumulation. As a boy I'd kill time kicking rocks or staring into space as he haggled over the contents of somebody's attic, or waved his arms among impoverished Indians for "artifacts," or hailed down hucksters for the kind of outlandish treasures only cherished by squinty-eyed hoarders. Because I had watched him over the years I knew enough about the contents of his cellars and sheds, crates and lofts and old box wagons and basement and attic to forestall excavation for a very long time. After he died I lived resentfully under the material heft of too much history, unnaturally compressed. But I had coexisted with it all for such a long time I may have feared my own dissolution in disturbing it.

I guess my own secrets were visible enough to foster speculation. The old biddies of our culture-bare clutch of towns thought they knew all about me. Maybe some. They knew me as the eccentric local bachelor, even though I'd had a wife. My place, inherited from my father, displayed no generational talent for farming. Folks gossiped about my odd preoccupations: huckleberries. Fat music records and a grand Victrola, the only object in my house I cared to polish. My friendship with Leon and Velma Wheelwright, an odd couple in their own way and a whole lot younger than me. The poems I once wrote for a fascinating widow.

A full crock spills over. And in a place like Squirrel, Idaho, folks pretend to keep strictly to their own business but that's only because they don't. Busybodies love to cluck. I know what they said. Ah, the wit.

Friedrich Lenz

Back in Pomerania, in the 1870s, I had a cousin. Max. He was a young Siegfried, handsome and strong in a way that made other boys picture themselves as him. We all clamored for friendship and he gave it like candy. Max and I had grown up together, within three months the same age. Neither of us had a memory that didn't encompass the other but I looked to him for guidance as if he were older. It seemed in his presence there were visions I could not perceive. He took them in by frankly gazing.

Yet he was young, and youth is foolish. On a day he should have been perceptive he was blind. But before I saw him again, years later in the American Dakotas, it did flicker through my mind that he knew more of himself than any of us wanted to believe.

The summer after we turned eleven, Max went with his father on errands to the Dischenhagen piers. We lived a few miles from the waterfront, our fathers always working at this or that. I wanted to ride with Max and my uncle but my papa, hired to trench and lay footings, kept me home to help. I was resentful as I pictured happy Max strolling the wharves. In my mind I could see him catching the eyes of the younger boys or batting his lashes at pretty girls, shrugging a shoulder, grinning, offering witty speculation about the ships and their wares. Max could make our sober fathers laugh outright.

I breathed grit and stone dust all day, smelling pungent hod as I longed for the scents of the port: silver fish half buried in ice. The dizzying burnt smoke of sugar melting on cast iron to brown caramel. Pastries and bratwurst. Potato pancakes with sweet onion, smothered under soft cinnamon apples and sour cream. I was small and made of wire but I could keep all day to a task. I liked hard work but on this day I shored up a list of grievances against my good papa. Early afternoon I blackened a fingernail despite his admonition to pull my hands quicker from the piling blocks. It hurt and bled and we yet had hours to work. I went about with a great deal of muttering.

Entrenched as I was in self-pity, I scarcely registered the sudden commotion above. Suddenly I realized I was the sole figure below the sod. I heard shouts and my father angry but advocating calm, and then an anguished wail I could not grasp in its alien pitch. And yet I knew my uncle's voice. I hunkered into the masonry. The men cried out above me and then I saw my father's silhouette against the delft-blue sky.

"Friedrich! Come!"

I leaped up quick and monstrous, mind fogged by dread. I perceived my uncle, wide-eyed and wild. He pointed at me, shaking his forearm as if to rid it of leeches. He whined like a werewolf. Papa took my arm and yanked me toward home. A full two miles I was dragged like a marionette. We reached our door and he shoved it open.

"*Elisabet!*"

My youthful mother sprang to.

My father cried, "They've taken the boy! The sailors! The kaiser has the child!"

Mother grabbed my shoulders to shake me hard. "But he's here! How did you retrieve him?"

We all stood apart, staring each at another. My younger brother and sister crowded among us clinging, and after a moment of rare and perfect household silence my father said, "Not ours! Not our Friedrich!"

Bewilderment, before my mother understood. Then her cry rose to the roof and rained down. "Max? Our nephew Max? My sister's son?"

Finally I comprehended. My vision darkened under the magnitude. I had heard of this thing. Every boy had been warned of the conscript: young men taken and marched like prisoners of their own state, dragged from their labors and very doorways and shipped to faraway posts where they could not dream of escape. For their families they were lost forever, dead or so changed if they returned that they might as well be. We all knew of the conscript but Max and I were young enough to believe it was small threat.

But Max was newly tall and lean, a radiant pup stretching toward his destined frame. Even now I can see him turning at the sailors' approach, glancing up to meet blue eyes and flashing grins.

My cousin's smile. His easy heart. A wish to be recognized among this brotherhood. Those men a few years older, likely dragged into service themselves, suave and hard in their navy tunics. Max unsuspecting, then recoiling but more suddenly seized.

Over the rest of my life I imagined that scene ten thousand times over, never twice the same but for that grin I loved so well. My cousin's fate mortared in a swift motion of desire.

My mother ordered the children to the attic and they obeyed in a fear they felt more than understood. Mother swept bread and cheese, hard pickles, and the morning's boiled eggs into a rough sack. Father bundled my shirt and trousers and his own woolen socks into a tight bedroll. He stood at the window. My mother held my shoulder and fixed her sea-colored eyes on mine. I was just reaching a height to meet her gaze directly. My father said, "Come," and I followed him into the back dooryard, through a maze of alleyways and past the darkening fields to deep spruce forest.

"You're a big boy, Friedrich," he said. "No need to fear the woods. Solitude can be good for the soul in the right portions."

I stared around myself. Solemn evergreens, moss and stone, a gurgling branch of water. I had been there before but only in my father's company—small hunting parties and rare retreats from wives and smaller children. The soldiers kept to the garrisons and connecting roads. The woods still sheltered folk and faeries. I knew where I was but was not convinced I could find my way home.

My father continued. "You know how to make shelter. Your mother packed flint. Trap a hare if you can. Keep the fire very small and put it out if you sense approach. Stay quiet until I come for you."

"But, Papa . . ."

"If I don't go back now my absence will call attention. Soldiers are likely combing our town for recruits. I'll return soon to bring you news."

Some things are best forgotten. What cannot be addressed should be shut from the mind for what can. But those nights in the forest mourning my beloved cousin, fearing for my family, starting at every noise in the dense vegetation marked my mind forever. The more I labored to erase them the more they shaded my dreams, contoured every waking notion. Nothing seemed ever safe again. All I loved seemed bound to be drawn too soon away.

The next winter Mama died. Her lungs filled to drown her in bed. My father, after burying now his second wife, hardened to granite and spoke nearly nothing from that day forward.

I turned fourteen and wished to acquire a trade. My half sister spoke as my advocate and Papa roused himself to write a letter to relatives in Mecklenburg. Upon their reply he helped me gather all I had and found more. He packed the wagon and drove me ninety miles to Woldegk to learn blacksmithing. I promised to do well. He turned back to combine his remaining household with my sister and her husband. I watched him return toward my past. I turned to face the future.

Olaf Larson

Before I was born my father tended the royal gardens for the king of Norway. He was not patriotic so much as enamored of any strange or beautiful bloom that could break dirt near the Arctic Circle. I never saw Oslo; I grew up on the western side. *Nordfjordeid*: a word I pronounced rarely once my tongue accustomed to English. The place was all angles and water. Seeing opportunity to live free of a fanatic husband, my mother refused to emigrate with us. She was exhausted, I was half grown, it was time to part. I never saw her again. The Grand Tetons imposed across the eastern horizon from our Idaho homestead, recalling my origins. When I thought of the old country, sea and snow and mountain, I should have got all misty-eyed I suppose. For a long time I imagined I'd return with my camera to capture those old villages, ships in the fjords and goats on the hills. But each time I convinced myself to do it I packed up and headed the other direction. After too many broken threads in Idaho I left for Arizona, photographing Indians in their hogans and pueblos along the way.

Over my life I kept going deeper into the last traces of the New World, taking stereographs as I went. I never felt quite home anywhere, which caused me to pay attention to people who did, and the places and objects that made it so. A stereoscope could capture a distinct experience of depth. It required a special camera: two lenses to take a double view of a scene in a single shot. The doubled image was printed and mounted onto a rectangular card the size of a folded letter. To be seen correctly the card had to be set at the midline and then slid along a little plank extending from a binocular viewer. At a certain point the two images converged, leaping into a magical illusion of depth.

It seemed I could see more in the stereoscope than in the original scene. I could perceive nuance and intimation invisible in the fleeting moment of capture. I meant to become one of the world's great stereoscopists, and I did make a name for myself. But like vaudeville, stereoscope photography was lost in the wake of motion pictures. Still, in my time it meant an awful lot to me. An obsession I hope was healthier than my father's to hold what's lost: the round satisfaction of an Indian pot. Indolent figures of a defeated cause. The sensual folding of fabric, a farmer's hat, thrust of a thresher. A copper pit, a haystack, wooden shoes beneath a child's pinafore. A pony parade.

I lived a long time. In the fifties I went on to San Francisco and set up a studio. I lived another couple of decades as an artist in a city too queer to compare to anyplace but itself. In San Francisco I was simply another citizen. At some late point I realized how happy I was to call it something, at least, like home.

Myrtle LaVaughan Lenz

Because I vanished so early, I appoint myself here to be the voice of Olaf's pictures. I knew him. Everyone knew everyone some way or another. He lived out in Squirrel but his wife sometimes taught school in Ashton. Many of us children had learned to read under her careful tutelage. Clara was some sort of specialist, traveling from school to school providing extracurricular enrichment. Once, she brought Olaf in to talk to us about "visual composition." Mostly went over our heads but at least it was novel. He showed us many of his stereographs and we took turns gazing through the special viewers, amazed. He talked about "foreground" and "background," and for some reason that stuck with me, not necessarily in an artistic way but more in terms of memory. Something vaguely philosophical.

Folks in small communities pay attention to the ways of their neighbors. The population was growing but there weren't so many people that anyone got to pass invisible, especially if there was something peculiar. The Upper Teton Valley was a sprawl of sections we liked to call "towns" but beyond Ashton and Marysville that word was a stretch. Only those of us who lived there could tell one town from the next, but there was Drummond, and Squirrel, Warm River. Farnum, which my mother's folks first settled. Sarilda and Ora, Mormon towns. Conant Creek, LaMont, and Chester. Ashton was established to support the Butte and Yellowstone rail lines. I grew up there among boxcars and tourists, potatoes, cattle, and wheat. The clamor of coupling and switch-tracks.

Best thing about Ashton in the twenties was the Dog Derby. Every year on February 22nd the whole Northwest came to Fremont County. Didn't matter that week who was Mormon, who was Lutheran or Catholic or Pagan, who was Blackfoot, outlaw, or politician. Town drunk or stake president. Hundreds of people donned fur hats and woolen socks, warm boots and mittens to line our streets and watch the dogsleds run. Races all day, dancing all night, food and skating and music and whooping it up. At ten, twenty below zero the community converged.

Every other season was grueling work. Planting in the earliest weeks of spring. Machinery in perpetual maintenance. Everyone bargaining with their version of God for rain. Calving, feeding, herding, cutting, branding. Watching the fields of grain and potatoes rise to harvest. Well into October we pulled spuds from the near-frozen ground. Men in the fields, women in the kitchens and gardens, threshing season cooking for hungry workers. I lived long enough to establish myself as one of the best cooks in the region, which was a real accomplishment for a wife as young as I was. My husband Carlie never had trouble hiring because he paid on time and I fed them like kings.

But dead winter was an interval of leisure. We didn't care at all that the frigid temperatures would drive a polar bear into hibernation. We came out for the derby, standing at the bonfires, recognizing the unmistakable gestures of neighbors under winter layers. We heard the laughter and curses we knew from threshing, slaughtering, and birthing, church dances and winter pinochle. We admired and kept our distance from the wolflike teams that drew the sleds. Some of our own competed but the real handlers came down from Canada and Alaska.

Olaf Larson was always there, his two-lens camera hanging heavy from a neck strap. He wore jaunty black high-laced boots and a varsity scarf flowing from a groomed bearskin coat, but even with the extra bulk he was a sylph. We took merry note of his eccentricities but clamored to see his printed images. Everyone bought the cards when they came out. We gazed through the lenses, searching the scenes for ourselves and our friends. Mabel Towby once found herself in a scrape because somebody pointed out to her parents that there she was, right there in the photograph of the six-dog qualifiers when she should have been in school. She'd slipped out to watch her beau compete. An hour of hooky goes where it may in the age of mechanical reproduction.

I wonder whether Olaf ever experienced a moment in its original presence, or postponed every thrill until its photographic return. I wonder because I can't measure how well I learned to live either. It's hard to account for the person you are at seventeen or twenty or twenty-five, or even thirty-three on the bleak December day you didn't anticipate would be your last. I can't fairly describe the person I may have become, had I lived to raise my daughters. Had I baked enough lemon meringue pies and pot roasts and hot rolls for Carlie's hired men. Had I time to convince the formidable Mr. and Mrs. Friedrich Lenz I was more than the Mormon girl who lured their son from the Lutheran stronghold. At seventeen at the Dog Derby I was simply an exuberant kid. I was young and vivacious enough to run till dawn. My parents, aggrieved over the recent death of my sister Mary, mustered no supervision.

I could be silly but I was a painfully good girl—rigid in my Mormon conviction that I would see my sister again only if I followed exacting doctrines. I missed Mary so sharply that until I passed twenty-five I could not picture her face, even in my dreams. The one bald sin I committed was to marry a Lutheran. I convinced myself he would convert and we'd remarry the proper way once he was immersed, not sprinkled, in baptism. We would go to Idaho Falls to be sealed for time and all eternity in God's temple. But I think I loved Carlie Lenz enough to cling regardless. Pressed, I might have surrendered heaven with my sister to live in a lower realm with him.

Still, true to my faith I never touched alcohol. I shut my ears to profanity and never cursed. I prayed in my mind and on my knees, pleading with the God who would reunite me with Mary. My parents had estranged themselves from the gospel over some old slight. Their resentment simmered like a Yellowstone paint pot. Not even Mary's death had got them to repent; in fact they hardened further, isolating themselves from family and community. Fierce churchgoing may have been my way of rebelling. I woke up every Sunday while my wayward family feigned warm sleep.

I attended every meeting, every Mormon event, with my best friend Wanda. I drew closer to her family than I could at the time to my own. With her my levity was bright and real, but also a compulsion once light and friends and music overcame me. Had I lived longer I may have grown as somber as my mother and father. But I hope my joy in my daughters and their cowboy father would have kept me chasing life a good many years.

As it is I'm the void that drew the contours of my last living child, herself now gray and bending. I held her. I sewed dresses on the treadle machine for my two little girls. I curled their fine hair. I taught Nadeene nearly every word she knew, answering her every bright question, even rehearsing German phrases she must yet recall, inaudible echoes of her father's folks.

And this links us to Olaf, because he proves we were here. Traces of me line and dot the old stereoscopic cards. If I could point myself out you'd see I'm right there with my back to the lens, under Ott's neon sign. I'm the dot at the top among the ring of children at recess. I'm submerged under that woolen hat, in the crowd cheering the fierce huskies. That's my hand holding the casserole, Friday night at the social hall.

Olaf was an odd man but indispensable to us. I thought him old, but when I knew him he was likely only in his thirties. His odd manner made him timeless. He wax-curled a dandy mustache that defied the squalor of the homestead where he lived, first with his sickly and inconceivable father, then with his wife Clara, another woman who died too young. I lived to hold and love my daughters a little while but Clara faded in pregnancy, died an hour after her first and stillborn child.

Carlie remarried in 1940, the year after my death. But Olaf, not the fathering kind, remained a lonely bachelor once and for all after he was made wifeless and childless in a single night. Beyond unkind speculations about his carnal capacities, we all knew that Olaf was a man bereft. In Clara's dying weeks the women of the town, including my own mother, had come out to sit with her. Rarely a thing in the house to eat unless they brought it. The women always left food but Olaf never ate a bite that anyone saw.

Vigilants returned with accounts of locked doors, rotting sheds nailed shut, hingeless or no doors at all. Cellars obscured by overgrowth or rusting machines. In the house, figurines— children and fanciful creatures, miniature porcelain buildings from grand cities on shelves and windowsills. Furred by dust. A closet of coverlets beautifully made, folded neatly and furled for decades, moth-gnawed. In life Clara Larson faded into a quiet house filled with useless but oddly beautiful objects. In death she dissipated into the squalid property. A short silent affair of carpentry and shovels, no marker.

Olaf subsided into his singular preoccupations. He tramped the country gathering specimens. He held his camera between himself and the world. He insisted that he was not a photographer but a *stereoscopist*. My guess is that even among his kind Olaf was an eccentric man, but the Germans were convinced it was because he was Norwegian. But, truly, all those immigrants were enigmatic. They bore sorrows from a place of old forests and fairy tales. My husband Carlie loved and hated that old heritage. He was raised for this country. German as he may have seemed in town, Carlie was American born and made. I believe his father was proud but also it meant that his youngest son signified all that would never return. Whatever that was.

Friedrich Lenz

I took pride in blacksmithing, which might seem odd as I was the kind of man who took care to keep clean. I loved a tailored suit and spotless fingernails, smooth-combed hair fragrantly oiled. I was not tall, and all my life slender. My sons all took on a stature better aligned with the American farmers and cattlemen they became.

As my apprenticeship drew toward finish, the kaiser's Prussian kingdom teemed with young men like me. By 1875, the conscript was only a small threat; a new national solution was simply to bribe young men to emigrate. The government cleared our papers and passports, paid our passage, and sent us on to seek our fortunes in America's new-cleared Indian territories.

My mother was dead. My father was passionless and wan. My half sister's family had grown beyond a gaggle of little children. My sweetheart Anna Kandler was the daughter of a successful man who approved of me. I felt urgent to answer to all of this.

I had heard intimations from boyhood friends that my cousin Max had sailed nearly around the world, on ships that would never dock too close to home shores. Then I heard he had landed at New York, industriously unloading and restocking the vessel that had imprisoned him. Compliance and charisma had long fooled his mates and officers. Yet on his final descent to the wharf, ever-charming, this trustworthy mascot of the Prussian cause dropped cargo and ran like an impala. He must have shed his German sailor cap, jacket, tunic, trousers, even regulation underwear and stockings as he ran, naked and barefoot, keeping to the hedgerows and alleys, grabbing a shirt here off a clothesline, a jacket there, begging a long pair of American canvas jeans, playing dice and cards (or who can guess) for stockings and shoes.

He kept running so deep into America there was no possibility of recapture.

I did not know whether it was truth or lie, hope or legend, but the tales stirred something in me. I knew I too must change my life. I let my mother country exile me to America.

Olaf Larson

For God's sake. You've got me fuming now. *He will probably be remembered most, this fellow Olaf, who has come and gone, for his stereoscopic pictures.* And it was all for the glory of those hard-working farmers, *the productivity of the virgin soil and its hardy pioneers.* Yes, I did it all for Manifest Destiny.

Did any one of those overhealthy lady historians peruse my photographs of the Blackfoot beggars in Saint Anthony? Black-feet chose starvation over capitulation, never conceded a square foot of that virginity. I took photos of their powwows and the annual war dance, although by then it was mere parading. I stopped in the streets, sat down before them with my camera. They never spoke to me, rarely gestured. They gazed directly back or turned away as they pleased when I snapped the shutters. They were beautiful people even in penury. In better times their conical leather lodges were unmistakable, sewn tight and weatherproof, painted with patterned circles and botanicals. In high ceremony their clothing was hung at the neckline with ermine pelts and sometimes human hair. Their beadwork, especially the animal embroidery, was abstract and literal at once.

I went on to Bisbee, Arizona, for a spell after my years in Idaho. I'd had enough cold to last the rest of my life. I hoped to photograph other tribes who lived in some manner like their ancestors, but mostly they hung about the copper boom-towns like everyone else, looking for something to eat. Even the Apaches. In Arizona the land was a parched virgin. No pioneer felt inclined to make a stab at greening it up, at least not till the wetter climates were homesteaded to the farthest edges. Down near Tombstone it was still Wild West.

I shot an archive of photos there, all after I "disappeared" from Idaho, after my hardy neighbors shrugged their shoulders and picked over my desolated property, wrote a paragraph or two in memory of "this fellow Olaf Larson," the poetic fool who fell for Leon Wheelwright's antics at the Grange Dinner. I know damn well what "professor" means in Ashton Ladies' Society talk. Everyone believed I was a homosexual. Well, I loved my Clara and she loved me back. Conveniently she was no more invested in what women want from men than I was. We never did get beyond a lackluster carnality. But we took pleasure in one another's company, in the solitude of our own place. We would have loved our child, or children, and sent them to fine universities, on to unusual but valuable lives.

The Ladies' Society called Clara "plain" but I can say with an artistic eye that she was a beautiful woman. She wore her hair long when short and curled was the rage, pulling it back into a bun like women had for centuries. Longer I lived with her the more satisfying she was to look at. Her lips were rich and expressive and her eyes intelligent, even when guarded. I loved to watch her at the river. For a hefty woman she was graceful and athletic. She'd hop from stone to stone like a water nymph. She could stand barefoot on a rock the size of a dinner plate and cast across the water without a falter. She could hook a big one, reel it in, and take it off the line easy as if she were standing on a church plaza.

I credit the local ladies for coming out to sit with her as she diminished but it sure seemed like their central business was to report on the state of the house and farm. We were down to nothing. I had cared for Clara through the harvest and bottling season. I'll admit I was no farmer but I'd been out on the threshing teams and could put in a hard day's help—real help—for any neighbor in need, even while Clara was fatally ill. But what goes down in history? Society ladies show up to sit with Clara's body the night before the funeral. Dead baby wrapped snug in the cradle I made myself. I offer all I have in that moment and back they go to report that the only food in the cupboard was a bottle of pickled onions. Which they ate. Every last one.

In life neither Clara nor I were avid to eat. Sometimes we would pass an entire day before it occurred to us to make supper, which often turned out to be bread and butter and milk. Summers we'd eat huckleberries, wild asparagus, sweetened choke-cherries in season, beets and young potatoes from the garden. We picked purslane and dandelion and like I said, sometimes we'd walk out to the river to angle trout. Clara stored fat and I shed it; we ate the same portions and got on with other things. We both had a lot on our minds. Hers was bright and peculiar, and she lived contented within it.

And that huckleberry thing. Do the research. Botanists have tried to tame that little tyrant since white people came to these parts. My father was convinced he could figure it out. In the royal gardens he had made the coyest and most retiring of Norwegian flora germinate in just the right places and conditions. Huckle-berry was the only plant to defeat him. He kept records, drew diagrams and botanical breakdowns, and left them to me. Some people are made to play at questions. They slake their odd energy on crosswords, or chess, or magical boxes and contraptions. At least in this way my father made me in his image.

A huckleberry bush is a perfect production of wildness. It's always a trek to a huckleberry patch, deep in the pines and forest mulch. Each berry is smaller than a currant, richer than purple butter. Each grows singly spaced among piercing thorns. A skilled picker might collect half a bucket in a day along with bloodied fingers and a scratched face. The only other creature with the patience to savor one lush tiny globe at a time, all day long if it wants to, is a bear. Luckily it's usually in a good mood with something better to eat than a fellow picker.

Folks were always taking a cutting home to start roots in a bucket or streambed, and then easing it into the ground among a stand of windbreak pines. One out of a hundred would grow into a bush but yield no berries. One out of two hundred might make berries that tasted nearly as good as the wild ones. But it just couldn't be reduced to a set of principles. I wasn't the only one stabbing at the mystery. Indebted to my father's records, the university in Moscow was at it for decades. But somehow my huckleberry preoccupations chalked up as more antics of Crazy Olaf.

And then there's the matter of the delectable "Widow Farnsworth." In the end that's what I, Olaf Larson, was remembered for in Fremont County, Idaho. Not the last jar of pickled onions at my dead wife's sitting, not the lousy farming nor even the huckleberries or the Victrola. Not even for the hundreds of stereoscopic images of a brief world loved and lost. It was my love for Leon Wheelwright.

Myrtle LaVaughan Lenz

My family were townspeople, my father a merchant. Leon Wheelwright out in Squirrel was my father's younger cousin. Something in the family leaned toward the cosmopolitan. Leon was flamboyant and irrepressible. My mother said he would never, not even in grade school, grant the teacher a straightforward answer to the simplest question. Always found the circular route to an outlandish response. Leon went on to college and studied subjects most folks saw as frivolous, except Olaf and his wife which is why they all became friends. Philosophy and art history. Literature and music and drama. One reason Leon and Olaf were so close was that big old Victrola and Olaf's record collection. Classical and jazz, blues, folk tunes from the old countries, even records of Indian tribal songs. Neither Olaf nor Leon liked farming. Both were odd ducks but Leon's charisma, his flair for renegade innovation, made him a local celebrity. Olaf, with his strange preoccupations, his tendency to see only and always through his camera, his slight and effeminate gestures, was the butt of perpetual innuendo.

Leon took his time graduating, worked odd jobs and traveled some to delay his homecoming. Once he came home for good he sold off a piece of his dead father's homestead to buy a bi-wing airplane of all things, and he founded the first chapter of the Idaho Flying Farmers. Often we'd stand in our fields to gaze up at Leon's personal flight show. Sometimes the whole club would come flying in formation, landing one after the other on the runway Leon had bladed through his alfalfa field. Leon played at farming, did alright, and married an up-for-anything girl named Velma. She was only eighteen and I hear Leon was pushing thirty, but they seemed made for each other in the same peculiar way as Olaf and Clara.

Pretty soon whole airplane shows came in, loop-de-looping above the rest of us hard at work in our fields and landing in formation to settle in for a week of what was, for all us regular types, unimaginable leisure. You'd think they would spark resentment but no one begrudges a circus. Leon wore goggles and a leather helmet, and a long apricot-colored scarf waving behind like a banner. He'd fly low enough to tip his wings to any of us standing at the well or plow, anyone pinning laundry or shooing chickens. Schoolchildren ran and waved at recess. It seemed like some wild happy trickster god was acknowledging us simple mortals.

Friedrich Lenz

The closer I got to America the more I understood this was what God had planned for me. I did not know what to expect from this impending continent, but every day that ship drew me further from the Old World I felt my former life had been only a singular dream.

Thoughts of Anna reminded me that my old world was yet real. I knew she woke each morning to stir the fire for her mother, mourning her recently dead father. My half siblings had put great stock in my emigration, intending to follow. I knew my younger brother and sister encouraged our father, daily assuring him we were all bound for a new life. I felt this as great responsibility.

155

The American Lutheran Synod in Concordia, Missouri, was my Mecca. I said the strange word to myself over and over, standing at the ship's rail: "Missouri. Missouri. Concordia. Missouri . . ."

I asked the sailors to help me say it perfectly. They laughed, cheerful and rough.

"Mizooooouri," they said.

One tried to lead me astray. "Misery," he grinned. "*Mis*ery." But I could see he was joking by the reactions of the other men. Later I asked, "What means *Misery*?" and a Bohemian woman on the deck answered, "Poor, lost, sick, broken."

Missouri was promise. *Misery* was not.

What we accomplish as hopeful young men seems beyond belief once we grow old. I made my way through Ellis Island. I had some dollars in my pockets thanks to my family and the kaiser. I said, "Missouri, Missouri. Please direct me to Missouri," at train stations, crossroads, river ports. I walked and walked, asking for Missouri and then when I found it, I asked, "Concordia?" The closer I came, the more I heard my own tongue. Concordia was a college, a seminary, but also the beating American heart of Luther's Reformation. The synod took in every wandering German, gave us food and shelter, and showed us the Lutheranized map of America. The pastors saw I was young and devout.

"Nebraska," they said to me. "We know of a community in Hoskins. They need a hearty young believer like you. Have you considered the clergy? We will direct new families with daughters."

"I have my Anna. I intend to bring her out. With her mother. What is Nebraska?"

"An American place. Like Missouri. Fertile farmland. The Indians have been contained. Many settlements, mostly farmers, some dairy. Winters are cold, but what is cold to a Prussian?"

What they did not describe was the eye-watering flatness of Nebraska. Nor did I discover it right away because I took my time arriving. I was unprepared for the magnitude and amazed that this was all one country. I walked, took on odd jobs as I traveled, listened to stories of immigration and hardship, mad American success. Indians. Backwoods perversions. Strains of zealotry. I encountered immigrating Mormons who said the American continent would be refined to pure and prophesying glass, that the Indians were children of Israel. Christ's return would occur nigh I reached Nebraska. To the Mormons I said fare thee well, and to all and sundry I imparted the most recent news I knew.

All rumors of my cousin Max had contained the word "Dakota." As I traveled I pored over maps—hand-drawn, official, promotional, fanciful. I internalized distances, markers, routes. I kept north, surpassing Nebraska to slip across the Minnesota line. I veered westward toward the Dakota prairies. The territory was in an eerie state of natural silence, broken by birdsong or rumors of violence. Although they were mostly defeated I learned to avoid the single-file trails of the Sioux and Crow and Cheyenne. Travelers were inclined to keep within easy distance of the forts and squalid trading posts.

I was disconcerted by the Sioux. Many were distanced in the new reservations but mixed families, old allies, and scouts stood about the new brick squares. The sting of recent battles was sharp. The Sioux people were tall and I was not. I heard names of other tribes: Cheyenne and Crow, elusive Ojibwe.

The landscape was so monotonous as to engulf a pilgrim. A bluff or stand of trees, or a glittering blue lake, could misroute anyone but an Indian for days. Many navigated the distances more like ocean than land; stars and the position of the sun, sextant and compass. Despite the flow, human traffic was generally compressed. One Prussian cousin looking for another, asking about, might not be delusional in repeating a name, telling a story of kidnapping and conscript, beauty and harm. Such a query could leap from mouth to ear. Eventually, cousins once so inseparable as to be nearly a single boy were bound to find one another.

Olaf Larson

My friend Leon Wheelwright had a way of becoming purely enamored of something. Or another or another. The man was no dilettante. He put his whole smarts into whatever struck his fancy, which is why only he and a hell of a good-natured wife like Velma could have transformed an outback Idaho dry farm into an attraction where people would pay to play an old Scottish game in the boondocks, to bring their fancy rigs and pricey fishing outfits. Their goggles and airplanes. Who can think like that? I could I guess, but my best ideas were driven by compulsion. For Leon it was the joy of cunning and conniving. He was a grownup Peter Pan.

I admired Leon's easy love for people. He could make the craziest notion seem so rational that bankers would chase him down to give him money. Leon was lithe and handsome. He flashed strong white teeth under shapely lips. He wore his hair long like Errol Flynn and he pushed it back behind his ears when he leaned down to concentrate.

We both loved music and by golly did I have Leon beat in that category. He frankly admired my knowledge, mostly autodidactic but I do credit a personally attentive professor from my university days. I knew composers, their influences and epistemologies. One winter afternoon not long after Clara's death, Leon and Velma sat with me in what passed as my parlor listening to record after record on that Victrola. Bourbon, conversation and coffee, music. We settled into a modern mood: Berlin and Kern, and Salt Lake City's native son Otto Hauerbach, which led us to Julian Eltinge's recordings from *The Fascinating Widow*. We sang and danced, passing Velma between us and sometimes Velma and me passing Leon:

Don't take your beau to the seashore,
When bathing, don't take your beau to the shore—
For bathing suits reveal what petticoats conceal,
And if there's a slight defection,
You will never stand inspection . . .

We kept drinking. Singing and laughing. The conversation came back to Eltinge. Leon claimed to know him through a friend of a friend. He said Eltinge's mother dressed her son like a girl and sent him to perform at the classiest whorehouses in Butte. The jacket cover stated that Eltinge had graduated from Harvard—pure propaganda designed to class up an alley rat who had a strange talent for imitating girls. Leon said, "Shit, everyone who ever gulped in the sights of Rich Hill knew about that kid. His mama had a goldmine in that boy. What's the word? *Berdache.* But I think Eltinge might be a real gal, lost behind an ambassador. Seems to me he works a lot harder offstage on the man act."

Leon, who might have been double although two forms might not be enough, belted out Hauerbach's song with a couple of dirty little twists:

Mother often said to me: acting the part of a beauty fair
Will make us lots of money, honey, but in every case
    beware—
Beside a fellow's side, a gown your parts will hide,
But he'll drown you in a minute when he sees how you
    stick out
Girl if you go, but you've got something that shows
Don't take your beau along.

We giggled like twelve-year-olds and drank more. I wished Clara were with us. She would have stayed in her chair, frothed out a skein of bright knitting and quick remarks. Velma, still

159

so young, was the alter ego of my wife in public temperament. Velma had a wild wit that sometimes outran Leon's. She wasn't beautiful but she was petite and handsome, loud when it pleased her. She cropped her hair. Her voice was deep. Sometimes I doubted she'd ever been a child.

Clara had always hearkened toward shadow; except in a classroom her light was obscured among people who ought to have perceived her better. But Clara and Velma had deep affinities. They were upright but fearless, unafraid to be smart like men. They liked what they liked. Clara inexplicably liked *me*, and our mostly platonic relation suited us. We enjoyed our quiet hours but when Leon and Velma showed up, Clara took pleasure in the rumpus. Her degree was in literature. She read deeply and well, knew authors and titles no one, not even Leon, had heard of.

The Victrola moved to a more haunting song named for the Fascinating Widow herself. Eltinge's voice was pure but reverberant. Even the high notes retained a masculine depth, almost as if it truly were two sexes singing from the same throat. Eltinge seemed to comprehend that femininity always obscured something more direct. He seemed to relish it. My wife Clara, not so much. Velma, only when it was convenient.

Because he was a man, Julian Eltinge had a certain license to speak for the women of our time. He spoke eloquently for women's suffrage. He had his own magazine advising women how to choose the perfect gown. How to dip the eyelashes and make just the right turn of the hand. He had his own line of cosmetics: cold cream to soften and naturalize feminine skin, lipstick for every mood. Eltinge taught the work-tough females of America how to reinvent themselves as a whole new kind of woman. Velma Wheelwright didn't need much instruction. Turns out it was Leon paying attention.

Eltinge made explicit what everybody knows, deep down: women have to make themselves into women, day after day. Years later, after Carlie Lenz had lost his first wife and gone on to marry Ellen Lee, I saw that woman reach into the back seat of her car in Ashton to extricate a squalling child. A smaller one already anchored a hip. Ellen just leaned in sideways, reached one arm over the front seat and hauled a forty-pounder over and out. It wasn't even an effort—just one smooth athletic demonstration. I watched her plant the kid on the ground, straighten him up, shift the baby on her hip, and pull her feet together. Patted her hair, firmed up the posture, pasted on a pleasant helpful mask.

This very same woman was ever so fascinated by my moment with "Mrs. Farnsworth." She wasn't even there, but she had to put it in the history book. She knew some things. Ellen Lee Lenz could have punched Julian Eltinge out cold in one of his notorious offstage bar fights. She could work like ten men, inside and outside the house all day and every day. She'd drive her kids to exhaustion and then show up with Carlie at the social-hall dances, overdone with rouge and lipstick, giggling like a debutante.

Clara Larson

Olaf believed it was pregnancy that sapped me. It didn't help but truth is I just wore out on life early. I liked the world, loved a beautiful scene as much as anyone else. I was often charmed by the kids at the schools and I may have been a good mother. But always that old fatigue set in, a sense of separation as if I were already spectral in my own mortality. I lurked in an aquarium while everyone else breathed and walked easy in the air. As years went on I had to strain a little more, and the effort was tiring and finally unsatisfying even while part of me savored the fine threads of life. Olaf was happy in his preoccupations; he did not crave a hovering wife and he took joy in the friends who understood his peculiar insights.

Surely those tight-lipped Germans muttered amongst themselves about the state of our farm and house. I suppose there is no defense for my negligent housekeeping. It wasn't squalid; it's just that to me each object had its own relation to its place, its own communions with other things. I knew the little figurines weren't people. I wasn't crazy. It was about the material itself: porcelain and paint drawn from the earth, various places and contacts far away in time and place. An undiscoverable history of making and transporting, intention and touch, propinquity and trajectory. Too much to interfere with. So I left things alone.

Olaf liked to work wood. He carved that pretty hardwood door handle and it took on a life of its own after he installed it. The figurines that came from his mother's house in Norway were transformed. At one point or another every object in the house told me to leave it be. I understood. Time, moving through us like a soft relentless current, showed me the beauty of attending to its miniscule changes. Day by day. Minute by minute.

Of course the objects in the house stood in for more disturbing and hidden artifacts in the sheds and cellars. Mostly Olaf could put them out of his mind, he'd lived with them so long enclosed. But sometimes he'd roll and turn and mutter at night, cursing his father and pleading in Norwegian. And sometimes Olaf would come straight out with it: "Clara. The time will come. I'll have to dismantle it all. I don't know the right thing to do. I don't know how to rebury what's been so long interred."

My death was the only possible catalyst. It still took years but before he left Squirrel, hurt and bitter, every picture of its life worth taking taken, he went out. Day and dark night he purged his father's estate. Retrieved, reassigned, catalogued, buried proper. Broke, burned, and drowned.

Friedrich Lenz

I hopped place to place awhile in Dakota country, gravitating around Yankton. Mostly I enjoyed the adventure but my instincts were for settling. People in my home country were counting on me. The Lutheran movement needed stable families and church-building communities. I longed for Anna and I intended to provide her mother and her a comfortable living. I wished to do right by her late father's trust.

My first action was to find a blacksmith who looked busy enough to need a hand.

"Get along out of here," he said when I inquired. "You think I'm seeking competition? I got a good thing going. Got no family and I enjoy the heat."

I stood politely at the boundary of what the Papist O'Halloran saw as his own. I took care to remain just outside the shelter of the open-walled forge.

"I'm just finished with apprenticeship. No danger at all of competition. Just some help for you. Any work you assign."

He stepped a little closer. The man was enormous, barrel-chested. He looked at the moment like *Der Schwarze Mann* although I could see the Celtic copper in his hair and eyebrows as he approached the sunlight.

"German, are you, boy?"

"Prussian, sir."

"All the same," he answered. I did not demur.

"Most you types pretty industrious," he said. "But sometimes overcareful if you know what I mean."

"Are you concerned I won't work fast enough?"

"Maybe. I'm just saying, here you've been trudging the mud and heat of this godforsaken country and you appear to have bathed and shaved this very morning."

"Mr. O'Halloran, I promise you I can sweat and gather dirt and ash and if you'll let me, I'll work a month for free. Just let me sleep in the back. When you stop to eat, share enough to keep me walking through the day."

He stood closer, to reiterate his stature.

"I'll ponder it. Come back first thing tomorrow, and if I'm in the mood I'll put you to the bellows."

I did. He let me work. I learned from him and increased his business. A moral man, he began to pay me after two weeks of proving. After four months he extended his sign, "O'Halloran, Blacksmith," to "and C. F. Lenz" in tiny letters beneath. We were well matched. He liked to talk. I liked to work and didn't mind listening, so long as I was not expected to parley. Plenty of customers: a train of regulars and a daily mob of travelers. I usually paused to speak to the Germans, and the Austrians and Poles. Sometimes I heard news of my own town or people. O'Halloran conversed with the Irish, Scottish, and Welsh, even some English.

I kept word out that I was searching for a cousin. Tall, I said, but I don't know how tall. Blond. Beautiful, I tried to say, in the right kinds of words. A boy so striking that people were drawn to him; probably yet now as a man. "Max," I reiterated. "Stolen by the conscript. Taken to a ship. I have heard he fled this way from New York."

"Maybe he changed his name," I said to others. "I don't know whether I would know him on sight. But keep out an eye?"

And then one afternoon late, after a long sweating spring day at the forge and anvil, I watched an enormous man approach the shop. He meant to speak to me. I had not seen my cousin in many years but this was not him. This man had black curly hair, short at the sides, longer on top. Hair sprouted up from his chest, nearly adjoining his beard. He looked Russian or dark Slavic but he spoke clean German.

"Carl Friedrich Lenz? Did you come from Dischenhagen?"

I put down my hammer to face him. The top of my head did not reach his shoulders. My leather belt might not have buckled around his biceps. But he spoke softly, unthreatening. Feminine. His eyes were such dark green that the color was only evident in certain encounters with light. His face sprouted nearly a full beard, although I guessed it was only a day's growth.

I stepped back so as to look him in the eye. He stood heavy as bronze.

I said, "I am Carl Friedrich. Born very near Dischenhagen."

"You seek a man long lost?"

My heart stopped, and then began again in a rhythm forever altered beyond that moment.

I spoke very softly, not to be secretive but because it seemed unnecessary to project actual sound. "Do you have knowledge of my cousin Max?"

O'Halloran sensed the import and stepped behind the shop.

The huge man answered, "Come tonight after you close the forge. Come to the edge of the river under the bridge. Nothing to be afraid of now."

Somehow this made me angry. In German I said, "What would you mean by this? What kind of man do you think I am?"

He smiled and answered in English. "Your cousin loves and remembers you. He has suffered. To you he may seem greatly transformed. He wishes to speak nostalgically with the man he once considered closer than a brother."

He turned his back and walked toward the river as if to show me a path. I glanced down at my dirty hands.

O'Halloran wandered back nonchalant, blinking at me for a tale or explanation but I had none. We muffled the fire, set the tools in their places, and clamped the padlock. I walked into the cool air, intending first to bathe in my rented room but instead in the twilight I simply walked toward the river's edge. I walked the bridge road until a half mile from the water, then veered and took a well-trod path to the underside where transients and fugitives, the poor and indolent, and even sometimes women of ill repute made camp. Firelight shifted the shadows. Strange musics wafted and collided. I passed one group in a bestial frenzy. A toothless woman on all fours rocked on a makeshift communal table. "Do it like a dog!" she bayed, and the degenerates around her roared and cheered but none seemed willing to act.

I shuddered but walked on toward the river, passing a

group of indigent Indians, and then a squalid camp of women whose human communion halted beyond the exchange of lust for money, and then on beyond a group of wretched families so reduced as to slip through city to city by way of theft and begging. I wondered at the eerie silence of the children among them, even the infants. I wondered what places beyond this might offer them redemption. I considered what breed of humans could be so incapable that vagrancy was their only future in this land of staggering promise.

I passed the deliberate pause of a community of Negroes, clearly making their way west, probably hoping for a place beyond the old partitions of North and South. Finally, right at the river's edge I approached a neat and striking camp of canvas tents, a bright and solitary bonfire, an arrangement of logs and community seating and a harmonized brotherhood of song. The Missouri River glowed in the light of the stars and orange flame and the music rose, a men's chorus worthy of Wagner. Something stirred in me, deep memory and ancient longing and I knew without a doubt that my cousin Max was singing among them. As I tarried I watched a very tall slender man rise against the fire. He swiveled like a compass needle to face me directly. He stepped over the log, beyond the wholly masculine congregation and strode through the dark to greet me.

My God he was tall. Six foot six, maybe seven. His boyhood features had strengthened into something Olympian. Yet he seemed almost frail in the contrast between his boyish hips, slender waist and broad muscled shoulders. His hair hung long and lank, yellow-white glowing in the darkness. He was my lost cousin, beloved companion of my childhood.

"Max!"

"Friedrich," was all he said before he picked me up and swung me like a child. He set me down. He gave me a broad grin and I saw he was missing a couple of lower teeth.

I groped for words.

"Max. Cousin! I cannot believe you stand before me."

He stood half smiling, but also guarded and somehow foreboding.

So familiar yet estranged. I strained for access. "Your friend? Who is it that spoke to me?"

"Dmitri." He gestured toward the chorus and fire.

I glinted in that direction. Max stepped to block my view.

"My man. His name is Dmitri."

We stood facing in the dark and firelight. I could smell the food and refuse, sweat and perfumes of what seemed every tribe of humankind surrounding us. I could hear the lapping water amplified, the echo effect of the bridge's underside.

"Max. I do not understand your meaning."

He folded his arms. He spread his stance.

"Yes, Friedrich. You do."

And I did. I had always known a frightening truth about my beloved Max.

But I could not accept it.

He said, "The sailors. Yes, it was a crime. A terrible thing to tear a boy away from his home and family. But I knew my kind. I said no but also yes. I went with them, in a way willing, *needing* to be among them."

I staggered back but Max stood like marble.

"Then why did you flee the ship? Why did you run?"

He looked about to slap me into darkness.

"Friedrich. I do not ever wish to be a slave! I was a boy. They were men. I suffered great brutality. I grew to defend myself. I nearly lost my humanity. For a while I believed I had no heart remaining. You will never, ever understand what I have been forced to know. What capacity for love that remains? Well, it is a gift from the sea because I could not have preserved it of my own volition."

I drew the night into my lungs, threads of fresh air among the many human stinks. I studied the man who was without a doubt the most beautiful culmination of all my kin. How could God, creator of all order and beauty, allow this? Where was His hand in this tale of depravity?

I opened my mouth to speak but shut it again. And so Max opened his own and poured forth.

"Or I guess the grass is itself a child . . . the produced babe of the vegetation."

"*Was sagst du?*"

"Or I guess it must be the handkerchief of the Lord."

"*Was sagst . . . ?*"

"Or I guess it is a uniform hieroglyphic, and it means, sprouting alive in broad zones and narrow zones, growing among black folks as among white, Kanuck, Tuckahoe, Congressman, Cuff, I give them the same, I receive them the same."

He stopped, apparently expecting answer. I had none, and so he continued.

"And now it seems to me the beautiful uncut hair of graves."

"Max, my cousin, my brother, my blood. You have been deranged by this tragic separation."

"Tenderly will I use you curling grass. It may be that you transpire from the breasts of young men. It may be if I had known them I would have loved them."

"Max—"

"It may be you are from old people and from women, and from offspring taken soon out of their mother's laps, and here you are the mother's laps. This grass is very dark to be from the white heads of old mothers."

I saw the massive and virile Dmitri stand against the prehistoric fire and turn again in our direction. Max spoke on as Dmitri strode: "What do you think has become of the young and old men? What do you think has become of the women and children? They are alive and well somewhere; the smallest sprout shows there is really no death, and if ever there was it led forward life, and does not wait at the end to arrest it, and ceased the moment life appeared."

"Max!" I howled, almost like the squalid woman I had passed on the pathway. Suddenly I feared myself. Dmitri drew near and I snarled, ugly and wretched, "Sodomites? Buggery? Max! My God! Are you a man? Will you return?"

Dmitri said, "We have never been among you. There is no return."

Max was transported, speaking now only to himself or to all the world: "All goes onward and outward . . . and nothing collapses, and to die is different from what anyone supposed, and luckier—"

"How can you forsake all that can now be restored?" I meant only to touch him, but it was a shove and Max came to. He grabbed my shoulders and shook me hard. "Friedrich, it is I who found you! Dmitri approached you at great risk. How is this forsaking?"

We stood in the rhythm of the lapping waterline, the milling unsettled camps, bodies huddled together and drifting apart. I faced my golden cousin and his swarthy courtesan. In the darkness of my regard they drew toward one another. Dmitri put a gentle hand to Max's shoulder, a brief but potent touch. I was suddenly terribly conscious of my own parts. With great effort of mind and the fiercest shame I quelled myself.

Max said, "Friedrich, it is you who has forsaken. You left our home willingly but I was taken by force. You came to America yet you will not stand here among fellow Americans. Look around you! Here they are. This is not the dream of America. This is America. You see us now but in daylight this truth is invisible to you."

"This is not the truth! I see them perfectly, now and in broad light. I know what they are. These vagrants are not the makings of America's greatness."

"You see nothing at all, yet we will always be among you. Some will recede and many will rise but always we will be this nation."

I searched the darkness for God and did not feel him there. Nor the devil. It was as if there was no north or south. I could not discern a single constellation in the muted sky; the cosmos itself was deranged. I started at Max's voice.

"Friedrich, this is the meaning of forsake."

Dmitri spoke. This man could have cuffed me hard as a bear. "Where are the people you call your own, brother? You have left them behind. You are alone on this alien continent."

"Not long! I am working to settle, to make a homestead and send for the woman who will be my wife. I am preparing as well for my father, and Anna's mother. Your dear uncle, Max! I have forsaken no one! I am a pioneer!"

"As we are!"

My cousin spoke once more: "Go find and take what you believe is yours. Call up your kindred. Make your America in your image. But remember all who come to you will surely be taken. You know it is the way of this world. So many gone already. My mother and father. Your mother Elisabet. Three among our brothers and sisters. Time will take its due. The beautiful uncut hair of graves about to be cut."

"Max, I do not understand you . . ."

"No, my cousin, you do not. You have ears but you will not hear."

Max turned away and Dmitri paused. The man reached to shake my hand but I would not extend my arm. The Russian turned then to follow my cousin toward the night and flowing water.

I turned below the sudden apparition of Orion and fled from that river. I never saw, nor heard from, nor could bear to ponder my cousin Max ever again, although in a way he was with me to my final hour. I cannot relate his destiny. He stood at the margin of my dreams, never speaking, neither in love nor accusation.

* * *

I went back to the forge next morning and hammered like Vulcan. I worked so hard for O'Halloran, half a year, that he said, "It is clear, you crazy son of Bismarck, there is business enough for two forges side by side. I give you my blessing to hang your own shingle. I'll share my resources until you can stock your own."

I loved this man O'Halloran, which would never have troubled me nor caused consternation. It was a manly companionship, the warmth of difference and likeness in masculine brotherhood, but now I was haunted by the motion of Dmitri's hand brushing my cousin's shoulder. And so even in my gratitude I distanced myself, accumulating my own tools and working doubly hard to found my own forge on a clean lot. I kept my conversation within the boundaries of formal demonstration. I mortared a new structure of reserve in all my relations and prepared to move south to where I was first directed by the synod: Hoskins, Nebraska, a clean and decent Lutheran town. I sent for Anna and her mother. I saved passage money for my sober father, who died in Hoskins, whose grave stands even now as testament to our decent family order.

My family and friends continued to arrive. In Nebraska and then in Idaho we saw it our responsibility, having been so blessed, to sponsor new arrivals. We kept our home open to travelers and immigrants, and Anna's kind nature made it ever warm.

Our first child died the week she was born. Four more arrived soon and hale. I continued smithing and did well but the soot lined my lungs. I kept Anna awake with my coughing. News of homestead lands opening in Idaho caused us to imagine fresh air, and fresh beginning. First year of the new century I traveled by train with my oldest son and my brothers-in-law to sight the new country. The north spur of the Union Pacific ended abruptly in Pocatello; we hired horses and a guide to lead us on beyond reserved Shoshone lands, through thriving settlements like

171

Eagle Rock and Saint Anthony, then northwest toward what my daughter Martha later exclaimed to be "nothing but quakies and cowboys." The Grand Teton Range to the east.

We brought the whole family that next spring: now five children, baby Ida only six weeks old. Anna and her mother staked claims of 160 acres, as did I. My son Fred was of age to claim another parcel. I smithed at first, as the cowboys paid or traded well for fine work. But my lungs were giving out. My half siblings and their families arrived within a year to claim nearby sections. We built little cabins on each segment as required. We met our crop quotas. I was surprised to see how much Anna's aging mother took joy in her own place. Anna or one of the girls would ride the quarter mile on a mule to spend nights with her. We'd set up a soft chair in the wagon, tie it down, and bring her in for Sundays.

We worked very hard at farming. I was able to quit the forge. We built a tall, strong plank house facing the road just a notch from the quiet intersection. I bought five acres and rights to the Fall River current, had a great millstone brought up from Eagle Rock, much to the interest of our neighbors. Concordia commissioned us a pastor. We liked him well enough to pitch together and build a church with an adjoining parsonage.

Somehow in Nebraska we had all remained German. We spoke the old language. We answered to a pastor straight from Pomerania who never attempted to learn English. We were among our own kind, and beyond the strange flatness of that landscape I suppose we imagined we were Prussians in an uncanny segment of Prussia. Even Ida's first words were German although she learned to speak in the land of cowboys and quakies.

But this new country at the foot of the Tetons, this country that resembled our homeland, called us to be Americans. I found myself at the heart of a quiet community tumult. I became a reluctant dissenter. My youngest son, Carlie, was the pivot, our littlest boy who saw only America in that Teton skyline. Our son whose first words were English, who only ever dimly understood the talk of his uncles and aunts, who gazed uncomprehending as his old grandmother sang him to sleep in a foreign tongue.

Olaf Larson

In 1919, Dame Julian Eltinge, the male Sarah Bernhardt, graced us with a tour of the western United States. He had just returned from performing for the king and queen of England. Acclaimed in Europe, he now wished to pay homage to his frontier boyhood, returning a gift to the good plain folks who gave him his start. Eltinge promised songs from *The Fascinating Widow* as well as special numbers for his hometown audience. The premier show was scheduled in Butte, home of the grand female impersonator's first venues.

Eltinge acquired his stage name in Butte. His birth name was William Julian Dalton. A boy named Billy Eltinge had been the star's close boyhood friend. Rumor had it that Dalton watched his pal die in a freak accident when they were twelve. But who knows? So many tales.

Billy Dalton's father eventually figured out how his wife and son were living so well, and it sure wasn't thrifty use of his lousy pay. Billy was singing his heart out, in petticoats, on the local brothel circuit. The father beat his girl-boy nearly to death. So, maybe Lady Bill just left his best pal behind when his mama sent him East to the safety of relatives. Maybe the borrowed name simply marked remembrance of an early and unforgettable crush.

This tour was traveling through Butte to Idaho Falls, Twin Falls, then on to Ogden and Salt Lake City before leaping to the West Coast. Naturally, Leon intended to see the show. He wouldn't settle for Idaho Falls.

"Butte," Leon said. "It's Rich Hill or bust. We're going to pay the Widow to fascinate us in his own hometown."

And so when the day came we took the early train to Montana. Leon, Velma, and me. We played out the day wandering the pitching streets and narrow alleys, admiring the copper baron opulence and stately houses of ill repute. So many soaring churches and cathedrals, as if every denomination meant to prove their God was the richest. We sat down for lunch on the grass at the reservoir. We freshened up again in the railroad station, then hiked up the steep streets sedate as we could, trying not to sweat, along with a thousand other folks. At seven-thirty the crowd filtered through the pillared facade of Butte's grand Broadway Theatre. We dropped our lips, popping our eyes like goldfish, swimming in velvet and crystal. Every seat in the auditorium was sold. Folks looked mighty fine, as if every last person in the room had spent the day laying out each item of clothing, choosing and refusing, inside to out.

Men strained to look bored and uncomfortable, conveying to no one and everyone that they were merely here to please their wives. But it was clear they were also compelled by some other force. It made them twitchy and irritable. Women giggled and swooned and outdid each other in the balconies, which made me frankly wonder why it was that females were so openly titillated by a man in a corset. It was a puzzle I couldn't lay out clearly before the lights went down and the crowd broke into wild, almost bawdy cheers. Leon and Velma leaned forward in their seats, twinned in their frank curiosity.

I lived many decades beyond that night in Butte watching Dame Julian Eltinge exhaust herself, and return: costume after costume, act after act, song after song. Like a phoenix. I lived to see a very different breed of queer young men riot in front of television cameras at Stonewall in New York. In my waning years I saw drag queens strut the streets of San Francisco, a city of hills steeper than Butte's. Families have their affinities, yes, but just like a stereoscopist Eltinge was a phenomenon of his own time. He has no clear label beyond it. He died in obscurity, however wealthy that obscurity was. He lived a solitary life with his mother on a lonely sumptuous California ranch where he didn't have to make a public offstage spectacle of his masculinity. Away from the ranch, he picked bar fights. He smoked huge cigars. He got engaged to women, lit up the proto-tabloids, and always canceled at the last minute.

Maybe Eltinge was simply what he insisted he was—a man with a rare talent for mimicking women. Maybe we are all simply what we insist we are. He was something we recognized as a generation: we were immigrants striving to be Americans. But American was still a thing to come. We had to teach each other how.

On this night, every woman in the building strained to learn woman-ness from Julian Eltinge. Every man iterated a precise sequence of suppressions. All but Leon, who sucked it in like the personable vacuum he was. Velma enjoyed the show but for her it seemed little more than a bemusing recognition. I was transported at several points, and although I never really understood nor felt connected to the militant gay men of the sixties, that evening I did come to a truce with my own inclinations. I found myself grateful to Clara all over again, and at that point Eltinge lit into the title song of his great Broadway hit:

> My life as a widow to me has showed
> That Romeos want a girl that knows.
> The widow seems to have experience
> To gain love's confidence.
> The fascinating widow, the captivating widow,
> Her eyes just seem to spell the love her lips won't tell:
> Concealing yet revealing affection so appealing—

The crowd went wild. Eltinge vanished for half a minute as the orchestra soared, and then he was back in a wholly different frock and wig to sing a ditty just for us: "The Cute Little Beaut from Butte, Montana."

We hooted and stomped for an encore and Eltinge came back out in yet one more grandly tailored gown, but this time he didn't sing or dance. Instead he swept the Gibson Girl wig from his head, loosened the collar of the dress and shook out his shoulders, manning up to address the crowd.

The transformation was astonishing. We rose to our feet and applauded again, and Eltinge answered some questions until they took on a bawdy tone, causing the curtain to go down for good. Soon we were making our way out to the streets of one of the wildest mining towns of the West. It was past midnight and the streets were lit up, bars were open and inviting, knives and guns hung at the ready, cops and brawlers and women in get-ups nearly as lavish as Lady Bill's bumped against each other on the sidewalks. Alcohol flowed like springtime runoff. Velma took off her mincey shoes for the steep walk down to the station. She whistled a little tune from the show as she walked, but none of us spoke until we were back on the platform ready to catch the very late (or very early) train back to dead-quiet Ashton. We stood with a few folks but mostly it was us. The whistle blew from the northwest, approaching.

Leon said, "I'm pretty sure I could pull off an act like that."

Friedrich Lenz

Soon after we settled in Idaho I received a long letter from an old homeland acquaintance. I had apprenticed along with Saul Tuchel in Woldegk, and his brother Levi later joined us. They were talented craftsmen, industrious and humane. Their lives had improved under Bismarck, but, knowing the past, they feared the national future. Saul had been corresponding with Concordia. He had arranged for Lutheran baptism upon arrival in Missouri. He asked about homesteads in Idaho.

I spent a night considering Tuchel's words. I thought of our young local pastor, an enthusiastic believer set hard in old ways, as were many in this new place.

This was my first true new-world departure. I sent word to Saul to come to Idaho and bring his brother and any family who wished to settle. I wrote that the land was fertile, the winters very cold, the landscape so beautiful as to be inconceivable in moments of repose. I told him there were fine parcels available here among us in Squirrel.

I explained to him the meaning of "Squirrel," a ridiculous English word for a rodent that had lent its name first to the creek, and then to our town.

I assured him our town was not ridiculous.

I hoped they would come. Such conversions were rare in the old country but when the brothers arrived the next year they were American Lutherans and it made me glad, although I perceived the weight that marks a history obscured.

The night after my son Fred married Tuchel's oldest daughter, I dreamed my cousin Max. He stood in the portal of the Squirrel Lutheran Church, relishing the congeniality. As always I was taken by his guileless features. I wondered how no one else had sensed his remarkable presence. I took Anna's hand and turned my face in Max's direction, intending for once to meet his eye. I looked about for Carlie, thinking to gesture that he was my little son. But I could not locate my American child, lost among the food and frolic, and when I looked back toward Max the portal was dark.

Carlie Lenz

My father was an unreadable man. One thing I can say about him and know it's the truth: he liked to work. He was not unkind but he was strict. My brothers said he was soft on me, the little boy, but I can't think of an instance but one that maybe it was true.

Some contention had come up among the congregation about old ways and new. Could have started the year my father donated an acre at the crossroads for a nondenominational cemetery. Pastor Johann had refused to bury the dead infant of a transient Russian couple. Pastor said, "Yes, it is a tragedy, and my Christian heart is moved for those poor young parents. But this is a Lutheran graveyard. We must protect our standards."

My papa went out and mowed the corner acre. He called us out to dig, even my sisters and mother, and then he conducted the baby's funeral himself. That same week he fenced the lot. He went out with my brothers Fred and Otto and a couple of big Tuchel boys to unbury my mother's mother from the churchyard. They carted coffin and stone to the new cemetery, replanted my oma near the Russian baby, and afterward we buried kin and affiliates there. And so the dead marked our differences. Somehow in all of this my father convinced himself that I should become the young *Deustch* ambassador. The year I turned thirteen he informed me that I would be attending the public high school in Ashton, nine miles west, along with all the other regular American children.

I was horrified. I never loved school but at least in Squirrel I took my lessons with Ida and Otto, with the Tuchel kids and the Warsanys and Garz boys, all the children I knew and understood. We went to the church for reading and writing and catechism, fought among ourselves, took sides and then took other sides. We played in the fields during recess and told haunt-stories in the pastor's graveyard. Already I was American. I could not understand why my father's imperative was so sudden, and why it had so much to do with me. I knew no one in Ashton. The school was enormous. I had seen two hundred kids or more stream out of those doors at the end of a school day, when I went with my father or brothers on errands for the farm or mill. And there were Mormons, which my parents had always warned me against, and big boys who could beat me up if they didn't know my brothers, and girls in bows and frocks who terrified me.

"Papa, please. I'll be good. I'll learn everything the pastor teaches. I'm good at numbers—I just don't know how to explain them. I'll read better, I promise. Papa, please let me stay here with Ida and Otto."

He would not be moved. "You belong to something greater than only this congregation. You have been taught the right truths and you know who you are with God. We must be the best of the old ways and the most promising of the new."

"Papa!"

"This is the end of your protest," he said and put his hand on my shoulder. He turned and walked toward the quakies and the deep river.

Myrtle LaVaughan Lenz

Carlie's mother was kind, and in the right mood witty and almost silly. But she never surrendered a confidence, communal or personal. Whatever they brought from old Prussia was exclusive communion. I don't think they meant to be that way. If they had, it would have cracked. Carlie was one of his kind, no doubt about it, but even so he was altered by the Teton air, or the family drift from a fading world.

His father Friedrich made an unprecedented decision to send Carlie to public school in Ashton. Carlie had always disliked school but in Ashton he simply could not bear it. Years later, when I met him among friends at a CCC Camp dance at Warm River, I suddenly recalled the wordless boy who had slumped at his desk, sullen as a stone for half a year before he faded back to his homestead people. At Warm River, grown up and easy in his own element, he entertained us with an animated finish to that story: he went home in early spring declaring to his father that he'd never go back. He didn't care how anyone tried to make him. He announced he was going to be a cattleman.

Carlie proved he meant it by skipping school the next morning and starting up his father's kerosene-fueled John Deere before breakfast. But Carlie's legs were still too short to hold the clutch. The shifter jerked back, snapping his radius like a dry twig. The bigger ulna telescoped so deeply the surgeon had to cut the already broken muscle and pry the bone back out of itself with pliers and a flathead screwdriver. Then he wired and drilled, plated and rigged, and everyone hoped for the best. Our daughters liked to feel the hard heads of the old screws under their father's muscled forearm. He told them it was the only time he deliberately disobeyed his father. See what happened?

Yet the painful victory ultimately went to the boy. His miserable classroom days were finished once and for all at eighth grade. He grew up to be a smart and practical man, one of Idaho's noted ranchers but with no use for what he saw as the pretensions of formal education. His numerical mind made him quicker than any of the other bidders at the old Caldwell auctions. He always knew precisely how many cattle stood in his fields. He could estimate their weight and value within a half dollar. He kept accounts in his head better than any written ledger but could never explain how.

Although the Lutherans were a tight crowd, of course the Mormons were separatists too. With some distance I came to see how they created their own world—their own dances, their own picnics, even their own scriptures—then stayed happy and safe in the diorama they called Everything. The Lutherans kept their differences entirely among themselves. Mormons were more inclined to shut out the people who were once their own. In fact they tended to make a show of it. But I would have perceived nothing but taciturn unity among those Germans had I not married Carlie and moved out among his inscrutable people.

We married quietly at the Saint Anthony courthouse to soften the religious shock, then settled into Carlie's old family home. His folks had moved in with their daughter Martha Tuchel. His father's lungs were failing due to his years at the forge, but the man still carried himself with a formidable dignity.

Carlie had already purchased his first few head of Herefords, preparing to transform the old dry farm into a modern ranch. My parents, puzzled by my defection to the Lutherans after so many years of demonstrative Mormonism, approved of my husband but both of them died too soon to know him well. I was nervous but I convinced myself that Carlie would soon see the truth of the restored gospel. It was the single wedge between my husband and me and I can't guess where it would have ended—well or bitter—had we been given further years.

The longer I knew them the more I perceived what blasphemy my people's ways were to his. As a Mormon child I had grown up reciting, "We are saved by grace, after all that we can do." Such doctrine was rank heresy to Carlie's folks. And the suggestion of separate Father, Son, and Holy Ghost with all their parts was plain repulsive. More than once Carlie's father had to stand up from the dinner table and walk a mile toward the river to calm himself; we learned quickly to speak nothing about religion in his parents' presence.

They never took it out on me, even though all of Carlie's siblings had married proper German Lutherans. Two of Carlie's sisters married Tuchel brothers, and his two brothers married Tuchel sisters, which was beginning to produce a lot of double cousins. Carlie's sister Ida, plumb out of marriageable Tuchels, married another Carl Lenz, no relation at all. Folks called him Kels to distinguish him from my husband Carl, always called "Carlie" partly because he was the baby, but partly too because those people just couldn't stop giving their kids the same names. The point is, I married into a tight ball of yarn.

After Anna's ancient mother died, the men had hoisted the tiny homestead cabin from its foundation on her old claim. They towed it in on a flatbed wagon with a team of Percherons, closer to the barns and ample homes clustered around the Lutheran heart of Squirrel. They used the cabin as a toolshed, it was so small, and when I passed it I always thought of the old woman from an old world. Such change, so fast, between four overlapping generations. No wonder so much slipped away forever.

I speak here as if I know. I've been gone so long I'm an indistinguishable dot in the panoramic sweep of Olaf's doubled images of old Squirrel. But again I must insist I'm present, inside the framing or just beyond, among the machines and people and horses pulling sleighs through trenches of snow higher than their manes. Herefords and bison. Big-horned elk. Yellowstone bears. Moose in the river. Among the harvest spreads and hot-dish dinners, waves of tall grain and Tetons and Blackfoot parades, schoolchildren on long wooden skis.

Nearly my whole family died early of some congenital flaw of the heart, undiagnosable in our time. Mary was only the first. Carlie hitched the team in the middle of a frozen night of 1939 to drive my body to the Ashton undertaker, bundled in a covered sled across nine miles of snow so deep he could glide right over the fences and corrals. Wolves must have sung him into town. After that night everything rushed forward beyond me. My siblings were all dead before forty; our parents went down among us. All of us but my brother Raymond, who went on to misrepresent us well into his eighties. Beyond him, my daughters never knew my people at all, sixth-generation Americans by the time my grandparents came to Idaho.

Olaf Larson

A good while after our trip to Butte, after I forgot Leon's declaration that he too could play a woman, most of the local families got themselves out of their cold houses for the annual Grange Association dinner and variety show. The Association was a ranchers' and farmers' social club passing as a coalition. It did lobby a bit in Washington but it best functioned as a reason to fraternize across religious divides. Farming was its own religion—our truest. I was a member only through toleration.

The Grange Dinner was a big event, scheduled in early spring so everyone was busy but not yet lost in the throes of planting. Plowed snow lined the streets and empty lots like model mountain ranges. The roads were muddy and potholed and the evening chill could send even the toughest Idahoans running back for heavy coats. Still, the air had shifted, wafting a fragrance that hinted of soil and trout and awakening pine sap and so we were exuberant. Two-fifty, maybe three hundred people came in to the Ashton High School gymnasium from all over. I rode a horse but walked in with Anna and Friedrich Lenz, who had long ago helped my father settle. They remained kind to me when I passed their place on the way to town, always inviting me in for food. Their three youngest were with them, Otto and Ida and Carlie, all remarkably grown. Those kids were solemn by nature and training, but among one another playful. The Lenzes greeted their married children as they arrived with accompanying outback Lutherans. Mrs. Lenz said, "Olaf, I don't see Leon and Velma, but if we do we'll bring them over. Why don't you sit down here among the folks?"

People settled in and shot the breeze. We all waved to people we knew the best. I was fidgety as I had left my camera at home, rightly thinking it would be rude to wander and snap. Pretty soon Velma Wheelwright came in with some young men I didn't know. She introduced them as cousins, and it wasn't hard to believe as they were all as handsome and composed as she was. Three other women were among them too, hanging on Velma's cousins' arms. One, a bit older yet more striking than the debutantes, stood a bit apart. Velma made introductions. "Folks, this is Mrs. Farnsworth, member of the Northwestern States Grange Board. And this is the Lenz family, at least a good portion of them, some of the finest dry farmers in this area. Have you seen the flourmill at Fall River? That also is one of Mr. Lenz's enterprises."

"Ah, yes. I've heard that mill has made all the difference for the families out this way. And of course I have heard of the

Lenz family. Prestigious and upright people." Mrs. Farnsworth smiled, cordial but aloof. Those of us already seated at the table stirred, disconcerted. I studied the woman. Her beauty was disarming. Her strong cheekbones and clear features were perfectly highlighted with careful but unextravagant cosmetics. Her almond-shaped green eyes were direct yet demure. She wore a hat, shapely and well-chosen with a few arranged feathers. Mrs. Farnsworth sensed my eyes upon her and addressed me.

"I think I know you from somewhere. Can you think how we might have met?"

I had no notion. Whatsoever.

"No. I can't imagine how." That sounded rude, so I choked out, "Where is it you're from originally, ma'am?"

"Well, I grew up in Butte, but after I married we traveled a bit and then settled in Boise. I took on Grange Board responsibilities after my husband died. Maybe we've simply run across one another in passing?"

Mrs. Lenz spoke kindly. "Mrs. Farnsworth, I am sorry to hear this about your husband." She paused, emphasizing her sincerity, then took my hand. "This is our old friend Olaf Larson. His father settled here soon after we did. Olaf was a faithful son. He keeps his father's place. Mr. Larson also lost his spouse far too early. He is an accomplished photographer so you may have noticed him with his camera at events you attend in your Grange duties."

I nearly got up and bolted into the night but I worked up an expression of gratitude to Mrs. Lenz. I lifted my eyes to meet the widow's and then dropped them to my plate.

"Stereoscopist," I murmured, but no one heard. Carlie, Otto, and Ida were staring at Velma's visitor too. Mr. Lenz took notice and shot them a severe paternal glare. They got up to distract themselves but then had to return straight away as the announcer called the dinner to order.

"Where's Leon tonight?" Mrs. Lenz inquired. "Is he coming in late?"

"Oh, he's out with the Flying Farmers," Velma said. "They're doing a bi-wing show in Nevada tomorrow if the weather holds up. He left me to fend for myself with these bullies."

"Sit them down at the table next to us," Mr. Lenz instructed. "Then come settle yourself and Mrs. Farnsworth here among us civilized folks." He stood, ever and perfectly polite, to pull out two chairs for the women. It's what I should have done. Velma and Mrs. Farnsworth seated themselves just as Ned Hess, an easy talker and Mormon bishop, said at the podium, "Folks! Everyone settle down—find a seat among your friends and associates and let's get this nice evening begun."

We obeyed in subsiding waves. The chatter died down and Bishop Hess said, "That's right. So good to see you all out. It's been a long winter, ain't it? I know you're all stirring in your houses and barns, checking your tack and machinery, getting ready to put those seeds in the ground, getting all set for the calving and hatching. So it's awful nice we have an opportunity like this to get together and enjoy ourselves before we all turn to the many tasks of farming."

Hess paused and stood back on his boot heels. It occurred to us to give him and each other a tepid round of applause. The bishop looked satisfied. "Well, we have quite a lineup for you tonight. We ain't just farmers, you know. We have a nice dinner and then a variety show to keep you entertained. It's just like you're sitting in a fine dinner theater in New York, but without the snobbery. We've got talent right here and we're neighborly too, so you all can sit back on your hams and enjoy."

Dinner rotation had fallen to the Marysville Mormons, so all us Lutherans had it easy, although the Lutheran brethren had made sure a couple of cold kegs were delivered from Ott's. Kids from the Mormon Mutual Improvement Association were emulating fancy waiters, wearing straight black aprons at the waist and white towels over their arms. We said, "Why thank you, sir," or, *"Danke fräulein,"* as they brought our plates of prime rib and mashed potatoes dripping in butter and sour cream. They tried not to blush and bolt. Someone had managed a crop of very early greenhouse carrots, tiny and cooked just right and the winter-starved crowd blinked at the miraculous color. Later it was pies and cakes with whipped cream. Soda for the Mormons and coffee for everyone else.

We managed conversation such as those old Germans were capable of. Mrs. Farnsworth warmed up fast, enlivening the talk with tales of traveling through Europe and the fine theaters and excellent restaurants her husband had accustomed her to. She reported on the unhappy state of ruin after the war and expressed her concern for the German homelands. The Lenzes listened with guarded interest but offered little more. It was clear they considered their former lives a closed chapter, but they opened up some when Mrs. Farnsworth inquired about the new strains of alfalfa. They discussed the right conditions for growing hops, and young Carlie brightened when the discussion came to the matter of cattle.

"If you come to Boise, young man, I'll introduce you to the best practitioners in the state. The auction houses there have brought in new breeds and become a venue for lively exchange among modern ranchers. I'm convinced you'll find your place among them."

Carlie blushed and stammered, "Thank you," just as Bishop Hess stood up to announce the show. Like all emcee types, Ned Hess thought he was the prime attraction. Eventually he got down to the lineup and we were all surprised that after the usual high school glee club numbers, the Drummond school orchestra's cacophony, the outback family bands and a modern dance by the Ashton Girls' Charm School, we would be hearing a few numbers from Mrs. Farnsworth herself.

I lifted my eyes in her direction amazed, and too late I realized she was already looking at me and smiling in a most purposeful and personal way. Velma, too, fixed her eyes on mine and gave me a little squint but I could make no sense of it. I should have. Every cue was in place. Leon and Velma thought I would attune to the fabulous ruse but it just didn't come together in my mind. My emotions were strange and overwhelming; several times I thought I should excuse myself and go home early but it had been a lonely winter. I was grateful to be among kind people. I wished Leon were with us. He always put me at ease and tonight Velma was preoccupied, moving from our table to her cousins' and back, straining uncharacteristically to please the Germans and entertain the dappers.

I stilled my nervous hands and tried to converse. I kept trying to slip out from under Mrs. Farnsworth's increasingly direct attentions. I felt strangely aroused. Shocked at myself, I worked to put my mind elsewhere—to the sealed sheds on my father's stake and the increasingly urgent tasks of disposal ahead of me—just to slow my heartbeat. I even thought about that night in Butte with Leon and Velma. Reconstructing its revelations caused me even more surprise now. Because here I was, unmistakably fascinated by this stunning widow from Boise. The whole table noticed it. They all knew I was a solitary man. I felt the mood shift toward that ancient human instinct for matchmaking.

At some point Velma really should have pulled me aside for a little talk. She said later she truly believed I knew. It may be that we were all, even the most daring and modern of us, in over our heads. Old Mr. Lenz was distracted during the standard numbers. Otto couldn't stop staring at Mrs. Farnsworth. Carlie and Ida kept leaning in to pick up and drop some private sibling conveyance, glancing in the lady's direction and sometimes mine. I couldn't read their expressions and neither could their father, so after the next item in what was becoming an endless train of amateur numbers he barked, "Otto. Ida. Carl. Go sit with your cousins." They leaped up as a single force and scattered to other tables.

And now it was time for the final act. Vaguely I told myself that this would be the end of my frenzy. Bishop Hess's promise of a first-class show had so far fallen so short that Mrs. Farnsworth must also be an amateur sham. But she stood up from her chair like a queen, every motion a vision of grace and precision. Every woman in the room was shocked into deference. Every man tried to tear his eyes away from certain parts as the woman swept her way to the stage. Hess backed off like a schoolboy and the lady delivered a brief oration on the admirable modernization of Idaho agriculture, every syllable intact, each gesture an affirmation of our fine state, a tribute to its hardy pioneers and illustrious future generations.

And then Velma's boys stood up. Together they stepped out to one of the back rooms, returning with brass and a clarinet. One seated himself at the piano. The others settled in chairs behind Mrs. Farnsworth and gave each other a moment for tuning. My God they were handsome; I still don't know where Leon and Velma found them. They certainly were not her cousins. She was a local girl; in my right mind I could have listed every one of her country relations.

The whole Upper Teton Grange Association sat erect.

"I must say I so appreciate your kindness in allowing me to overstep my standard duties and perform for you tonight," Mrs. Farnsworth cooed. "You are all so generous to indulge me. My mother raised me with a conviction that I was bound for the stage, but after I met my late husband my heart was divided. I really am a Western gal at heart. I love the wild beauty of our expanses. I am captivated by the epic motions of building a nation. Yes, I do love the culture and accomplishments of the East. But my heart is also caught in the throes of the American seasons, the rhythms of planting and harvest, new life and the turning generations. I suppose I'll always be divided between nature and culture. I gave up my aspirations for performing in the great theaters but I could never entirely abandon my musical passions."

Velma's boys lifted their instruments. One of them said, "One . . . two . . . three . . . four," and they struck, opening with a flawless jazz prelude. The piano picked up, and Mrs. Farnsworth opened her exquisite throat for the first measures of "Sweet Georgia Brown."

It was a visitation from a superior race. She was, move for move, note for note, almost too perfect, and toward the end of the song something in the back of my mind began to assemble. The Widow Farnsworth and the boys transitioned to Hammerstein's "Bambalina." One of the musicians stood up to dance with her. The trombonist traded his brass for a hand drum and the pulse was lascivious. Every note, every step, Mrs. Farnsworth moved in a sinuous rhythm not too scandalous but with just the right flair, always adding that one subtle move that true genius brings to improvisation. The Mormons and Lutherans squirmed after the fashion of their own religions but no one found the necessary virtue to get up and stride out.

Now of course I can appreciate that my friend Leon—I told you he was no dilettante—had been practicing these moves since we saw Dame Julian in Butte. But at the dinner I was still straining to emerge from a certain fog. After the last notes of "Bambalina," Mrs. Farnsworth faced her audience of country kids and immigrant farmers, winter-dazed folks emerging from their various enclaves.

Dead silence. Not a squeak or cough. No scraping of chairs.

Bishop Hess cleared his throat. He made a small motion to get up but Mrs. Farnsworth held up a commanding but delicate kid-gloved hand. Hess planted himself back down. Mrs. Farnsworth placed kid-gloved hand on her hip. She rolled her shoulders, petulant.

"Why, didn't you enjoy our music? Can't you people even manage a round of applause for my boys here, who traveled so far tonight to entertain you?"

The cowboys and farmers, their wives and children, the Mormons and Lutherans and stray photographers and atheists sat paralyzed another ten slow seconds and the lady said, "Well?

Can't you show my boys some Fremont County hospitality?"
and Bishop Hess leaped to his feet and held out his hands to
the crowd and showed them how to applaud. The place went
berserk. Everybody got to their feet, hooting and exclaiming,
and the brass boys picked up again, played a loud interlude until
the piano took over to calm us, evolving toward some familiar
chords. Mrs. Farnsworth stepped up, rivaling Fanny Brice and
maybe even, in a couple of phrasings at least, Lady Day:

> Oh, my man, I love him so
> He'll never know
> All my life is just despair
> But I don't care
> When he takes me in his arms
> The world is bright
> All right
> What's the difference if I say
> I'll go away . . .

The lady lingered while the players hung over every note.
For whatever my man is . . . we were transported in a way I didn't
know bumpkins like us were capable of. Mrs. Farnsworth finished, or rather subsided, and this time the Grange Association knew how to respond. We stood and applauded like a real
Broadway audience. I was shaken to pure sinew and then Velma,
the only body still in her seat, stood up at our table. She walked
toward me. She put one hand on my shoulder and ran the other
up the back of my neck. She pulled my head downward so she
could look me in the eye.

"Olaf, you understand, right?" She dug her fingers into my
shoulder to get through.

She said, "Dame Leon, honey."

My brain ticked like a grandfather clock, lining up what it
knew, and suddenly, yes, I understood. Tears filled my eyes and

I sat down to obscure them but still watched Velma stride to the stage. She stepped up to Mrs. Farnsworth. The widow looked suddenly tall and broad-shouldered next to tiny Velma. The crowd quieted. Velma stood on her tiptoes to plant a kiss right on the widow's tastefully painted lips. And then Mrs. Farnsworth reached up to remove her hat, and then her wig, and shook out his own tumbling hair. And now he was our own unbelievable but familiar Leon Wheelwright.

It was as if Mrs. Farnsworth had been eliminated by a magic wand. She vanished completely even though Leon stood there before us in her now-absurd gown and makeup. In my first moments of comprehension I feared a sudden mob of angry country dupes rushing the stage to tear Leon's limbs from his frame, but the transition was so complete, his antics so local and warm-hearted that everyone went crazy again. Applauding. Laughing. Mimicking.

I sat overwhelmed, for the first time since Clara died fully taken by the magnitude of my loneliness. I sat and hung my head, too ashamed even to stand and exit. I could not staunch my own tears and they certainly did not diminish when Friedrich Lenz wrapped his hand around my stringy arm. He leaned down and muttered, "Let's get you home, Olaf." He put his own hat on my head. He nearly lifted me to my feet. He pushed my arms into my jacket.

"Carlie!" he called sharp, and the boy instantly materialized. We all walked out to the foyer and then out under the harsh spring stars.

"Take off one of the team," Mr. Lenz said to his son. "Ride home with Mr. Olaf. Make sure he's settled in and then head home. We'll follow soon."

Carlie was a good boy, hardworking and pragmatic, not prone to any strain of poetic dissatisfaction. He lived in a world that tended to make sense, and so he had no conception at all of what this task was about. He simply obeyed his father, coming up quickly, bareback. We brought my pony out of the barn, painfully small against the Percheron. Carlie rode all the way out to my place with me, silent and polite. He swung off the big horse once we reached my place.

"I'll see you in, Mr. Larson. Do you have a fire made?"

I didn't, but the boy set one for me and said, "How about I take your pony on home to our barn for the night? I'll make sure he's warm and fed. You can come by for dinner soon and pick him up."

Everyone knew I fed my horses the way I fed myself. Nearly nothing. I was ashamed.

"Please. Take him. I'll be in to see your folks tomorrow or the day after."

The boy closed the door quietly behind him. I stood to the window, watched him grab the strap and leap onto the Percheron's warm back. My pony followed meek, without a rope. A few days later I went by to pick him up. Mrs. Lenz made me a hearty sandwich, rare beef and thick yellow cheese on rye. German mustard. She packed the remaining loaf and a bottle of homemade huckleberry schnapps in a flour sack for me to take home.

Just as I was going out, Mr. Lenz opened the door to come in. There I was, face to face with the man I had hoped to avoid for a few more weeks at least. I'd wanted to give him time to forget that, upon the last occasion he saw me, I was crying over a man dressed in female clothing. Mr. Lenz did not look delighted to see me now. I opened my mouth to mutter apology and slink by, but he put a hand on my shoulder. He opened his mouth to speak and then did not. He searched my features as if they might convey something.

Mr. Lenz brought his hand back down to his side.

"Good afternoon, Olaf," he said, polite as he ever was.

"Good afternoon, Mr. Lenz. Thank you for your kindness the other night."

He reached out to shake my hand, which seemed overmuch for the occasion but I took it, and I think he said, "I guess the grass is itself a child."

Everyone spoke of Leon's marvelous stunt, repeating the details and reliving the whole egregious act. The story circulated for years, gradually devolving into the tale of queer old Olaf Larson instead of clever Leon Wheelwright. Word got around that I could not be dissuaded that Mrs. Farnsworth was real, despite the public dismantling of the illusion. The tale went that I wrote a love poem and mailed it to the Grange Association in Boise. After a while it all strained the most precious reason I had for staying in Idaho—my friendship with two of the most remarkable people I ever met in my life. Leon and Velma both expressed how sorry they were that it had fallen on me in this way. It was never Leon's intention. They were my true friends, loyal and never ashamed of me. But something broke in me that night, beyond those mortifying public tears.

My waning sense of community did help me locate the courage to confront my father's legacy. First his reams of beautiful botanical drawings which I unpacked after years of enclosure in cellar crates. I salvaged the best of the undamaged notebooks, intricate and idiosyncratic, and put them on the freight train to the university in Moscow.

That part was fairly easy, but there was the matter of everything else. My father's zeal for "science" collapsed into a burning intimate insanity long before I could identify it as such. We need our parents to be capable, something to emulate, and so I disavowed as long as I could. But his drive to collect and taxonomize, catalog and connect, shot well beyond the boundaries of curatorial reason. There was just too much, finally, to be named and settled into an order that's rampant delusion to start with. Papa was rational enough to realize that the task might grow exponentially bigger. He understood that there were too many things in the cosmos to be cleanly named. But his insanity bloomed in the conviction that he could accomplish his little part: Only But All Things, say, of Fremont County, Idaho. My father went mad over small infinities.

He pictured a little museum in Squirrel like some people fix their minds on heaven. A neat building of glass and cases, display shelves, catalogued and labeled specimens. I guess that was no crazier than dreaming up an airstrip and golf course, or taking a stab at dinner theater, or believing you can turn twelve kids into an orchestra, for God's sake, at the Drummond school. But my father crossed the fine line between dreamer and lunatic and kept going. At fifteen I deliberately stopped attending to his "collections," and when he died I stuck with my good instincts and stacked his crates and boxes where I didn't have to acknowledge them.

Now, however, I could not simply abandon them to the busybodies and so I spent the final weeks of my Idaho citizenship confronting my father's material chaos. I thought briefly to save the most rare and beautiful of his acquisitions, but after the first revelations I proceeded with systematic demolition.

A Ute war shirt, complete with shells and scalps.

Eggs, blown and preserved, from every bird I could name in Idaho from hummingbird to eagle. A stray ostrich egg, ordered from some catalog or bartered on one of my father's rambling acquisitive journeys.

A cigar box filled with human teeth. Another with the fangs and molars of animals. Spearheads and arrowheads, a box of flint chips. Eagle feathers. Blackfoot riding gloves, beaded and fringed, so beautiful—but they were not where they belonged.

Two human skulls and an assortment of human bones. A skeletal hand, wired together.

Documents, blueprints, sawdust. A dead porcupine, mummified, but actually I think it had simply wandered in and got lost. Wooden shoes. A chest of women's intimates. Corset bone.

Fragments of harness and tack, seven saddles beyond repair. Forks and spoons, a crystal ball, a Chinese teapot. Flower seeds, gourds, seats from an outhouse.

A wooden crate lay beneath them all, bracketed shut. I opened it warily, but not warily enough: six clear jars with human fetuses swimming in formaldehyde.

Labeled in a careful clinical hand: Month Three, Four, Five, Six, Seven, Eight.

I knew my father. He wanted One, Two, and Nine. One and Two would have been fundamentally impossible in that time, but that would not have occurred to a mad collector. The missing specimens must have kept him conniving in his sleep. I did not want to guess where he'd searched or begged or bargained, trying to complete the collection. I don't know how he acquired even these. Who would have sold them to him, under what kind of persuasion?

The bodies were wrong but utterly exquisite. Wrong, I mean, in that they should not have been in those jars, naked and perfect. I could not look. I could not look away. Fingers and little nails. Fine lips, sculpted shoulders. Eyes closed. After Month Four, semblances of race and family. Not one looked to be malformed, at least in my understanding of development, not even the larger ones. Despite myself I pondered the jars and each origin. I made up little stories against my will. I considered their mothers, and then forced myself to stop it. I considered burying them intact but I knew they would call to me forever, pounding their miniature fists on the glass.

I thought of Clara's respect for the elegance of change and decay. I was relieved to know she'd had no inkling of this crime of preservation, right here on our own property. It occurred to me that these silent floating creatures had been the very cause of our resounding and endless loss. These, suspended, calling to ours in vengeance.

Suddenly they seemed explanation for every terrible thing

that had ever happened to us. I knew I had to appease them.

I wrapped the jars, small to large, in Clara's disintegrating coverlets and packed them securely back in the wooden crate. I hitched pony to cart and drove east toward the mountains, back into the old landscape where the quakies and pines stood dense and fragrant. A fading sheep road drew me deeper in, well south of Horseshoe Lake. I tied the pony, picked up the crate, and walked in a half mile where the trail waned into latticing deer paths. I set the crate down and tied a kerchief to a slender aspen trunk just to make sure I could find it again. I walked back for my pick and shovel with a nervous eye for bears, but moved my pony to new grass and returned to the box without encounter.

I sat down and stared at the box, gathering my nerve. Because my mind was made after my father's, I noted how my own child would have filled a crucial blank in the collection. Month Nine. Not disintegrating into dust with its mother but here, floating and timeless among its little fellows. As perfect as any of these. A certain hideous appeal. A boy. I could not say it even to myself until that moment. I had not allowed myself to think about its sex, because that would have led to a name, and then an image of what he would have become at two, then five, then ten and twenty, a son for whom I would have done anything, given all.

"Clara," I murmured. I pictured the casket that held my wife, and our baby son in her arms, and pitied these suspended here in glass.

I shuddered. Reclaimed the saner portion of my mind. I tried to open the jars but they were sealed tight with something like epoxy. I laid them down side by side in the grassy shade in reverse order of gestation. I gave each one a quick rap with a sharp stone. The stench of formaldehyde and the sudden, shocking nakedness of the tiny rubbery bodies among the shards opened something strange in my mind. A run of black colors. Gravitational shift, vertigo. I stifled a scream and turned my face into the bushes to vomit. I sat a few minutes. The sun opened through the trees. Wind swayed the high tops. It gave me courage to stand up and lift the babies to fresh grass. Fingers and tiny toes. Three boys. Two girls. The tiniest, smaller than a peanut, was to me indeterminate.

I rewrapped each infant in another of Clara's weakening embroidered fabrics. I pressed the shovel to outline a rectangle of sod with its grass and moss and dots of wildflowers, then pulled it up carefully like a segment of carpet. I dug a trench deep as my shoulders, beating back roots, excavating stones.

Surfacing, I drew each parcel to the edge, one at a time, muttering an inchoate blessing over each. Three. Four. Five. Six. Seven. Eight. I choked each time I caught another whiff of the formaldehyde sinking into the soil. I hoped the chemicals would gradually seep from the tissue and intricate cartilage, freeing them to disintegrate. To come up again as wild Idaho grass.

I buried them right, then relaid the sod so the site would become indistinguishable. I repacked the broken jars in the crate and carried it a little further to an obscure pond. I filled the crate with stones. Weighted my gloves and put them in, too, then dropped it all deep into the dark water, sorry to foul it.

I scooped up hands full of pond dirt and gravel to scrub my hands. Rinsed, and did it all again, but I imagined my hands emitted the sickening scent of formaldehyde for another month. Sometimes, years later, I thought I could smell it in my own sweat.

I trudged in silence purely numb, back past the mass grave. The pony had been happy to graze. I remounted the cart. Picnickers passed me on the way back in and a few familiar woodsmen. We all waved, alive in the sunlight, and I went home to finish disposing of my father's insanity.

I burned books. I smashed eggs and ground them into the garden soil. I threw feathers into the Fall River churn from a high lava ledge. I buried the war shirt and hung a Cheyenne cradleboard in the spruces to dissipate. Dismantled box after crate after gunnysack. Every so often I'd pause, doubting myself, thinking that my father wasn't really so mad. Just an eccentric collector. And then I'd remember my boyhood hours, standing, waiting, invisible to him but for an extra set of arms to load. All those nights, rummaging and sorting, muttering to himself, shaking me awake to hold this, just here, put your finger on it, boy, keep it steady now! Don't let it slip! And Clara's voice would reassure me: set it free. Summon your faith in future forms.

I went back into the house, last of all, and gathered every figurine from the shelves and the painted dishes from the old country. I took them all outside, laid them out in the grass, and took to them with a sledgehammer until they were reduced to fine dust.

Ned Hess

It is possible I was the last Ashton friend to see him alive. My wife and I were on a bus bound to see her sister in California. We had traveled most of the way when the bus stopped at a crossing to let passengers off. About four seats in front of us Olaf Larson got up and left. I said to my wife, "That's Olaf Larson. Let's get off and visit," but by the time we reached the door the car was in motion and we saw Olaf through the window walking along the sidewalk, going wherever a man like him would be like to go.

Louisa, Carlie and Ellen's Youngest Daughter

Carlie had developed an early interest and love for cattle. Growing hay and grain on the dry farm in Squirrel supported and balanced the purebred Hereford business. His children's early shopping trips to Rexburg and Idaho Falls, as well as their early opportunities for travel to other Mountain West locations, coincided with bull sales and stock shows. His grand champion, Cedar Domino, graced the business stationery with the phrase "Lenz Quality Herefords" for years. He served as president of the Six-Point Hereford Association and was pleased to be named Fremont County Grassman of the Year, these positions reflecting his competence and reputation in his chosen work.

Allen Ginsberg

America when will you be angelic?
When will you take off your clothes?
When will you look at yourself through the grave?
. . . .
America after all it is you and I who are perfect not
    the next world.
Your machinery is too much for me.
You made me want to be a saint.

AGAIN WITH IGNATIUS

No, really, I've got this.

Choose.

Come on. I've been thinking about this one since I was a child. My father loved his uncle, Steven Porter—no one else would speak of him, except in the breathy tones of hushing a terrible tale. Dad said Steve was his favorite relative—charismatic and irreverent, made his solemn mother and sisters laugh despite themselves. Taught him to fish.

You have considered emulation. Do not approach this portal alone.

He was a man, back when the world belonged—even more than now—to men. He lived a life I couldn't begin to comprehend. Finished it in a way I couldn't possibly consider, let alone accomplish. Don't worry. I'm hearkening after the women he abandoned. His mother. His sisters. His wife. But none of them will take me there.

One of the little sons, then.

They don't know us. Don't want to. They owe me nothing.

Light a candle by an open window. Leave an offering. Set your boundaries to ink and paper or they will not depart, even once you want it finished. These lives, even gone, are turbulent and compelling.

I hesitate, but now the saint commands: *You've brought me here. This is not the end. Now set the scene.*

What's to set? We're back in Fremont County, Idaho, this time on the Mormon side. The old Lutherans are over there to the east, unobtrusive in this rendition. Also, we're in Essex, England, way back when it was a hotbed of religious mayhem in the name of Henry VIII. We're in New Zealand, between. And still some Arizona, where my grandparents Clyde and Connie are engrossed in raising small children. Remember? We've been driving through this territory for a very long time.

The Porters are my father's people—his mother's folks. Steven can tell the backstory, once you let me get in there. The Porters came from Essex via New Zealand, not convicts but certainly not the displaced royals they invented themselves to be. I trooped out to see their old "family" castle that day I left my husband to True Art in London. The swan pond. Remember?

I'm not accountable for your story. I stick with scripture. Remember? Your preoccupations border on travesty.

Just walk me to the gate and I'll point them out: Fred and Stella Porter, my poor but overelegant great-grandparents. Their oldest daughter is my grandma Connie, a sort of conduit of personal nostalgia. Her youngest sibling is Steven, really just a few years older than my father—a sort of big-brother figure to him in a season I now understand as a brink for them both. Steven married a woman who made a living by reading palms, prophesying through a crystal ball. He didn't survive.

Have you read up on the history of Essex since you so blithely wandered through in your twenties? This is not the stuff of casual tourism.

Yeah. Sure. Anne Boleyn's home ground. Country resort for the wealthy and dangerous. Richard Rich. I know. That castle I hiked to—his place. One of his places, anyway. The guy cashed in on his own program to suppress the monasteries of England, built his pretty vacation home on top of the razed priory. Killed his neighbors for fun and profit.

Slaughter.

Do you think that stuff stays in us, even sideways? Even after forgetting?

What say you?

Is it chemistry, or is it memory set irrevocable, one generation into the next?

What say you.

How is it the family body, itself, remembers?

DEVIL'S GATE

Ruth Loveday Porter

The first time I saw the man I married I was with my girlfriends, all of us at the Chief. The main feature was *Forbidden Valley*, about a cowboy who's never seen a woman before. Steve thought it was good right up till the end, he told me later, and we argued about it on and off for years beyond. I don't know why his firm opinion got me so steamed up. I didn't generally care one way or another how a movie found its finish. As my life went on I got so accustomed to my mystical talents, I could give just about anyone a glance and preview their mortal destiny. I could spot folks headed for years of dull old age. I knew by proximity who went home to secret family hells. I could survey a crowded room and sense flames lapping at souls pitched toward violent ends. But I couldn't predict the end of a movie to save my fanny.

I was awful young. Just eighteen but by then I'd been living on my own for more than a year. Daddy had gone on to other towns and I had no more need to follow. Mama was dead. Not that she'd been particularly alive in the past decade but now truly dead and cremated. My brother had jumped a boxcar to pursue his own story. Maybe we didn't seem too cozy over the years but we clung to each other. In the end it was clear my boys were Lovedays, even though their name was Porter.

Destinies are crazy cards. Every draw. Prediction is a gift, not a function of smarts and it never does add up to a complete picture. Movie lives are contrived, propped up in a logic too clean to follow. I never did think in regular ways, so movies to me were nothing but spectacle, no reading nor prophecy required. I liked the dark theater and the breathing close-packed crowd. The Chief made our minds collective, mesmerized by the pretty moving light. Out on the street though, in the low clamor of the milling crowd loaded on popcorn and Coca-Cola, I heard the snap of flames behind me. It was a chilly night, early April but I felt the tingling sparks of a soul approaching white heat.

Compelled, I let go of Colleen's and Laura's hands. I swiveled into the crowd. As it was Friday night and right here was the party, nobody was anxious to disperse. Flasks rose and dipped from hidden pockets. Clots of friends and hopefuls dotted the scene. I nudged my way among bodies and then got a clear eye full of the burning man, engulfed in searing blue. For a second he plain blinded me. I shut the eyes of my eyes, tamped my tingling skin and brought myself back to the mundane dimension. When he felt my gaze his head made a quarter turn. His hazel eyes were clear and focused. Stance like a resting athlete's. Nobody who didn't have the gift would guess that Steven Porter was bent on annihilation.

I grew up in railroad towns. My daddy was a section man. He risked personal harm if not his life every time he went to work. I did not need mystical powers to spot a Union Pacific employee, young or old. Men who backboned the rail towns were almost a genetic type: stained by soot and strain, a hard faraway look like they couldn't wait to leave us behind to take another ride. Men like that were made of knots and wire. They lived for the whistle. The man on fire—still a boy himself, not yet twenty-one—stood among an insolent crowd of wipers and hostlers, switch-engineers and brakers, laughing and ribbing as if he'd been born among them.

I knew different. Everything that man conveyed was a calculation. He was no joker, although when he laughed, the sound of his voice was pure abandon. His head reared back and his supple figure relaxed in the moment. Nor was he some happy-go-lucky Huck Finn although he was made from big country. He was neither coarse nor rough despite his efforts to convey it. And he sure didn't come from no rail tribe. Steven Porter was a Mormon farm boy and it showed through no matter how hard he worked to hide it. His features were clean and firm, sweet in proportion and peachy coloration. His hair dropped back to neatness despite the practiced tousling. His shoulders were wide and his back straight. His hips were slender and legs long, all of which made him seem taller than he was.

I caught his eye and made a point to swagger a little bit. His fascination with female audacity drew him to me. I laid my girlish hand on his hard biceps.

"You ain't no real railman. Although it does appear you're performing the job all right."

He didn't look surprised. And his answer was smart: "How do you define what's real and what isn't?"

"Well, one thing, you don't say ain't."

"Maybe I had a ferocious second grade teacher."

"Maybe you had folks made you resay sentences till you got them right."

That threw him.

I pressed it. "Maybe you had folks taught you to e-nonce-ee-ate."

He held his warm lips in a closed line, deciding what to reveal. He revealed his white teeth. "Sisters, actually. Pack of schoolmarms."

I said, "Let me look at your hand," and he held it out. I turned it upward and said, "You got a brother, too."

He raised an eyebrow. "Hey, you some kind of palm reader?"

"Some kind? The real kind, schoolboy."

"Tell me again now, how you decide what's real and what ain't."

* * *

Spirits and visions came to me from my first memories, and mine start earlier than most. I recall lying in my cradle, such an infant that I could not yet sit of my own strength. Flat on my back, arms and legs flailing with uncontrol, gazing for any face that might appear above me for no reason I could anticipate. Pissing and excreting as my body wished to purge, no sense of significance. I can bring it all back. The rough grasp of my mother's hands. The abrupt obligations of maternal care. I was a quiet creature content to lie. I received exactly the degree of nurturing my occasional cries required but nothing more. If it were not so already, my family's habits of negligence turned my mind inward to open perceptions beyond the immediate scene.

One morning—I can picture the sun's angle through the east window, warming toward solstice—I lay in my cradle. I felt a hand wave over my tiny form, chilling the atmosphere. The cradle rocked gently but fully side to side. As it tipped in either direction I caught sight of a throng: human figures altered, marred or cloaked, some smokelike, some stunted and opaque. The air was blue-green, undulating with transparent black. I was enclosed yet transported. Redimensioned. I never saw the figure that waved the hand or rocked the cradle but I perceived her proportions, sensing the control she held over her own boundless power. In my infant fashion I understood that this was my true mother, my authentic family in solemn congregation all around me.

That was my first lesson in discerning what's real and what ain't.

The movie crowd was dissipating. My girlfriends saw my opportunity and called goodbye. Steve waved off his buddies and leaned in to talk to me. He took my arm like a real gentleman and we walked through the gas-lit streets. I tried to keep my focus on the flaming darkness I sensed in him but his voice was animated, and he was a good storyteller so I kept getting distracted. The world for a few hours in the summer night was all there was, and we were lighted by our own sensations of each other. The stars shone down, cut crystal, moonless.

Even that first night, Steve stirred a hope in me for things I'd taught myself not to want. Until I met him I figured I'd find some hardworking but unambitious yard worker, hoped he'd share his pay, drink only sometimes and not lay a hard hand on me or our children. I'd already had a beau who liked to slam a girl around. He lost his hitting arm on a coupling shift—a clean slice—and disappeared into history. I did not cause it. I don't have that kind of power. Nobody does, but people read stories backward and look for portents and that's how women like me get sent up on the rails. So I had kept my mouth shut about it.

My main impression of Steve? The man lived for locomotives. He spent his boyhood watching trains go by. He fixed his heart on answering the whistle and he never unfixed it. He told me he was working the switchyard, didn't mind the hard dirty labor so long as it set him on the path to the long routes.

"My father's always tearing into me about sloth," he said. "I'm not lazy. He knows that. I like working so hard my brains swell up, no room for thinking. But I need work that moves. What I hate about farming is that it's stuck in one place. I don't like living inside a fence."

I said, "Well, people can't fly. Everybody's mostly stuck in the place they're in. Everywhere my daddy ever settled us turned into awful stillness and we weren't farmers."

"That's right, but the thing is everybody tells me I'm supposed to thrive on that. Stake your claim. Restlessness is a vice. Guess I'm full of sin, because once I get feeling like I can't escape a place my whole body starts to feel strange. I go crazy."

We walked a little further. I said, "My street's here," and we turned left.

"I don't mean a little bit," he said. "I mean my mind overheats.

How is it I live on a whole planet but I'm stuck in a damn box? Or acre? It makes my brain argue with itself. Like that story in the Bible. A legion of devils. If it goes too far something awful overtakes me and I can't come out of it."

"Can't you just take a walk? Calm yourself?"

"Sure I can. I can do lots of things, but . . ."

I witnessed a surge of panic blast through him from his thighs on upward, ending in a starry explosion in his skull. Maybe I should have been frightened but I searched and sensed no malice. I felt truly sorry for him. I was young enough to believe I could save him.

"Here's my place," I said.

He stood, wide-eyed, as if he had no idea where he was on the whole planet.

"Steven, do you want me to read your hand? It might help you understand some of your strange thoughts."

He snorted like a pony. "I don't put stock in that voodoo stuff."

"What do you mean? Are you afraid of it?"

"No, of course not. I mean no offense. I just don't purchase that brand of superstition."

I hated when people said that to me. All superior and rational. I had in mind to walk away but this man was something.

He stood in the chill, vivid under the springtime zodiac. Solid and warm as if mortality were the permanent truth.

I thought, hard. And I chose desire.

"Well, then want to come up for a drink?"

Good Mormon that he was, even raised with all those sisters of his, he feared to enter a woman's room.

"I'll go up and get a blanket," I said. "We can sit here on the steps."

I ran up and yanked my top quilt off the bed. I touched my fingers to the star crystal on the shelf as I ran past, and back down I went. We wrapped up and sipped our flasks and I said, "The cook here at this place, Mrs. Sanchez, she knows a lot more than me. About soothsaying I mean. I'm learning from her. I'm still practicing but I'm getting better."

Steve stretched his neck away from me, craning his head so he could show me one eyebrow lifted high. "Didn't I just tell you I don't believe in that stuff?"

"If you don't believe it, how does it hurt you to listen?"

He pulled close again.

"Oh, all right. Maybe I do believe a little. My cousins and I used to tell ghost stories up at Island Park, all of us around the campfire. They scared the pants right off of me. We'd have to whisper or else somebody's father would come out to frighten us even more. They told us that thinking about spirits would bring them into our midst. They said talking about evil was a direct invitation to Satan's minions."

"Well, maybe that's true. Speaking in certain ways can align the elements. Or tangle them up for a time. Stories. Spells. Riddles."

"Well, I can get the devil in me without even asking. Why would I want to summon him?"

"There's good and bad spirits, just like good and bad people. Some of them hover around us whether or not we invite them. Can't get rid of them if we try. Guardian angels, for example."

"Well, that's one thing I know for sure. I do not have a guardian angel."

"Everybody's got a guardian angel. There's one assigned to each of us. Maybe more than one, for hard cases like you."

He laughed. "Assigned? Who's up there assigning?"

"God, I guess. Or maybe it's just the great pattern of life. Dead people who have reason to care about you. Souls waiting for reincarnation. Maybe some kind of cosmic affinity. Probably there's certain kinds of angels drawn to train workers—maybe people who liked ships in another life. Wanderers. Animals that loved you once, or someone like you."

Steve thought about this. His breathing quieted, his ribcage expanding and receding against my own. "I must have an angry one, then."

"Angry at you? That's not a guardian."

"Just angry. Got something for me, got something against me. Can you read that in a palm?"

"Tarot, maybe." I considered. "Or a story. Mrs. Sanchez says that stories are the most powerful form of revelation. I don't have her skills of interpretation but she says if you ponder a story long and deep, it will draw you in and become real. You can walk around in it and talk to the people. You can think yourself right into another dimension and learn from it. The tricky part is, you have to discern which revelations are true and which are wiles. Sometimes it takes a lifetime."

"That sounds as complicated as pondering the life right in front of you."

We sipped in the dark of Pocatello, listening to the distant clanging and banging and whistling of trains coming and going.

"Nevertheless," I said. "Do you got a story to ponder?"

Steven Porter

Like lots of people whose parents needed solace from the hard American dirt, I was raised with a family legend of a castle, in this case Essex, England, where my grandfather was born. It was a tragic but bracing story of primogeniture, excess sons cast out so as to preserve the grand family estate, turrets and candy chimneys and all the trappings. Like me, English Gramps was the youngest son. His name was Arthur, like his oldest son, my illustrious uncle who couldn't shed the nobility delusion once he planted himself in Rexburg, the most self-important town in Idaho. My father was his meek younger brother, a small-time scratch-it-out farmer in Buttfuck Egypt a little farther north. Grandpa Arthur—not Uncle—made his way to Australia on a bit of family money as a young man. The story gets vague at the embarrassing spots but the gist was, being gentry and all, Grandpa wasn't packing a lot of practical skills. He had some princely habits though. He promptly squandered his legacy on impractical gifts for friends he mistook for vassals.

I mean impractical for my grandmother, Augusta Koebbel. I'll bet the vassals were appreciative. Augusta was the daughter of a prosperous but damned-harsh family of Austrian immigrants. It took me a long time to make sense of my sisters' distinction as they retold this story to me: Austrian, not Australian. When I was a little kid I could not figure out why they kept handing me the same word. I take it Austrians used to move to Australia for the same reasons as the Brits, at least the ones who hadn't been sent there in leg irons: they had no place in their own country. Therefore my grandmother was the daughter of an angry Austrian hillbilly looking to set himself up as a great man with a respectable estate. Maybe Augusta married Prince Arthur to boost her children's pedigree, but she was stung off that fantasy early on. Like my own mother she imagined marrying a Porter was marrying into nobility, but what she got was a guy who couldn't comprehend that *Little Lord Fauntleroy* was nothing but a trash novel. Grandpa wore his incompetence like a knighthood. He was thirty-five when he proposed to Augusta, who was seventeen. Augusta's father said, "I'm going to kill him," and when Arthur got wind of that blessing he said, "Fine, but he'll have to travel," and took his girl-wife to New Zealand.

In New Zealand my grandfather spawned a passel of kids, including Uncle Arthur and my father Frederick with their fine fancy names. He entertained and bestowed from a position of sheer penury. He moved every year to a new town to further starve his growing brood. One year he took in the Mormon missionaries and got himself worked up to be baptized. Augusta said no, no, no to the heretical religion until the last second, then picked up and went to the font to be dunked with her man. My sister Connie lavished this part of the tale with angels and heavenly affirmations, but my guess is the old man sought share of a new kingdom in Deseret.

Just about the point they really were on the brink of ruination a great miracle occurred: Grandpa's father died back in England. Money came. A thousand pounds, enough to buy passage to America for his family and two toady clans and some stray orphans to boot. They took a long trip in a steamship called *Lurline* and crossed the desert from California by rail. The train spit them out in Brigham City, Utah, where they resumed their regal lives in the town hovel.

Once he grew up, Uncle Arthur stepped forward to personify the fairy tale. I guess I have to admire him for it. Served his sentence as a missionary like all good Mormon boys. Connected himself there with sons of Utah patriarchs. Transformed himself into a man of letters at the agricultural college. Then he moved to Idaho and established a printing house in the ball-shriveling cold of Rexburg and proceeded to be Added Upon.

That's how the story goes.

My daddy Fred summoned the nerve to follow his brother to Idaho. Dad kept books for a lumber mill in Island Park and sent for his new wife once he could support her. Soon came old man Arthur and Grandma Augusta, and with my folks they staked a homestead in a nowhere spot at the eastern edge of Idaho's own Sahara, the Saint Anthony Sand Dunes. It was pretty country there on a long arc of Henry's Fork, but due to the sand blowing over it was a lousy site for farming. But what did they know? The settlers called it Ora and so created a town. I guess that made them burghers. That landscape ushered me into the world on a March night so bitter it might as well have been dead January.

The family name should have unraveled Grandpa Arthur's royalty yarn even before it got spun. Porter. Doorman. My folks were no dukes. No kind of earls. A long time ago they opened the front door for Richard Rich, the sycophant who sent Thomas More and a lot of helplessly proximate bystanders to the stake.

Or beheadsman. That part of the story evoked some stammers but we groomed the phrasing. Rich owned a country castle in Essex, built over the top of an old priory he'd purged in the name of Henry. Fronting the castle was a gatehouse embellished by a pond with swans—the very pond my grandpa, a fundamentally incapable boy, nearly drowned in when he was five.

I heard this story so many times, dressed up in the language of high heritage, I couldn't exorcise it for the life of me. Always came back to the same bullshit paternal maxim: "Always remember, son. Always remember who you are and what you stand for."

My wife Ruth, who could read your life in the lines of your hand, would tend to say a guy like Richard Rich had it coming. But then she'd counter that destiny is not so clean as all that. Rich was granted a good long life to torture and kill for fun, protected by a malevolent star. He left his sons with ample means to remember who they were and what they stood for. But eventually, like all families good and bad the Riches dwindled, their estates distributed to obscurer lords, and the Porters had no one left to open the door for. They became tenant farmers. Pretty fancy ones. Stayed in the house, the de facto inheritors of Leigh's Priory where the curdled spirit of Richard Rich sucked itself around the old brick chimneys, through the carriage arch that once sheltered the villain and his livery.

And so this whole squatter's tale got compressed into generalities loaded with words like "castle" and "estate," "primogeniture" and "inheritance," all very noble-sounding. We Porter kids bought the implication that we were cast-off dukes and duchesses. It was comforting as we hoed creeping Charlie in July or froze in a smoky November schoolroom. The story kept my father neat and elegant, my mother disappointed and remote in her long church gloves and city hats, and it kept my sisters embellishing fairy tales up in the bedrooms. We knew we were deep-down better than the folks who scratched in the same Ora sand. We reminded each other to be gracious to the townfolk.

Ruth Loveday Porter

Those hypocritical Mormons. Here they were all about angels and seers, visitations and magic books yet I know his family called me a delusional nut. They believed same as me that this world is a rushing conduit of revelation. The continent is one great seer stone. But Mormons shun affinity. They think they're the One and Only.

Electricity exceeds the grid, you know. It's a natural force and there's no sole proprietor.

Joe Smith, that man the Porters worshipped as God's own prophet, played at all the arts I practiced. How could they lord themselves over me? They were all here in America because some half-cooked seer said he could translate Egyptian signs into Mormon visions. Sure Smith was onto something but he thought it was all true simply by virtue of it falling from his blessed mouth. Here's something I learned early: people are constructed to make stories. We can't help ourselves. But stories are mostly just fancy lies the mind stirs up to make itself feel at home in strange circumstance. If you're in the business of perceiving truth, it comes in limited rays and cryptic clues. You have to sort between your brain's natural fabrications and what those fabrications are made of. You have to loosen the fitted parts.

That's what Mrs. Sanchez told me, but Joe Smith never took the time to do that. He'd grab a smidgen of this, pinch of that, sprinkle it into old stories everybody already thought were true. He ran with old Mrs. Morgan's rummed-up snippets of Masonry. He snatched the easy parts of the old grimoires, waved that dowsing stick and appointed himself prophet, seer, and revelator of the Latter Days. If he'd written dime novels he would have made a fortune instead of getting shot in jail.

A little self-doubt transforms a gifted man into a human being but Smith had no interest in that. Too busy picturing himself as god of a whole new universe. Of course doubt is also a devastating force, always snapping its teeth at the nape of the neck. My husband never found a reason he should have been made in the first place. Toward the end it was only the promise of death kept him with us, a little longer.

Steven Porter

By the time I put a bullet through my head, 1960, I'd had plenty of time to ponder the great blessings of being special and therefore, I guess, more aggrieved by the banality of getting on year after year, day after day. Hour by hour tending to the estate. Finally I just didn't have it in me. Forty-one years were enough.

Connie Porter Anderson

We all read the signs, or should have. Steven was born with a built-in thundercloud. Cutest little boy, but even small his brow was a perpetual knot. My mother was confounded by this. Didn't understand why he wasn't Billy Sunshine. She was convinced he had been sent to us for a heavenly reason, five full years behind Gladys who had always been called Baby. Mother searched her soul, and examined his as if there were some vital thing misplaced. And yet she never found it.

We all adored Steve. We dressed him up darling and brought him gifts. We read him stories and saved him prizes and treats. He lived in a world of doting big sisters. Vernon was too old to bother. He teased his much-younger brother and tossed him up on his shoulder every so often, but that was all. At first Steve hungered after Vernon but the brother bond never took. Vernon was away as a missionary for three years of Steve's childhood, and came back a stranger to him. Steve seemed determined to mark his own route. Ran away at seventeen, came back, left home for good at twenty, enamored of the rough motion of a railroad city.

I doubt he and Vernon saw each other more than a few times once Steve married that crazy woman and settled in Pocatello. The rest of us tried to stay in touch, some seasons less or more than others.

Steve might have been diagnosed with something, given a word to help make sense of his tumult had he been born a few decades later. Maybe a prescription could have eased his darker days. I don't know. Can't rewrite what's done. Can't change how we're born. I myself battled that internal darkness. Some awful bleak stretches but I was lucky to have it lift often and long enough to see my way through them. Mostly. I saw it prowl my children and several grandchildren too. The retreat behind the eyes, opaque. The drawbridge shutting everything out. Or in.

My folks in their generation had no ledger to account for such things. My sister Mae, maybe in perspective a deeper loss, at least came with an explanation. At eight years old she was nearly consumed by fever. Meningitis didn't take her life but it took its due. The quick curiosity of the little girl diminished to a handful of primal fixations, only tempered in her thirties as part of a larger disintegration. Her early love of exotic words and quaint phrasing dulled to echolalia. As sisters we learned to hold our patter beyond her earshot unless we wanted to hear our best banter waved about for hours, like a dead snake. We became accustomed to the person who took the place of the original, and we loved her. But Steven never knew her otherwise. Mae's tangled instincts, once designed as maternal, swarmed like honeybees toward Steven's rosy figure. We drew her off when it looked to overwhelm him but we couldn't always be vigilant. Restraining Mae was like admonishing the weather.

Stella Jeppson Porter

I sit in the white car with a little girl. We're sitting on hot blue seats and we're waiting for Connie. I do not know where Connie went.

"Where has Connie gone?" I ask the little girl.

"She's in the store. They're getting groceries."

"What do you mean, they? Is Erma with her?"

"No. Aunt Elaine."

The little girl's face is pink in the heat. She sits on the seat next to me, staring out the open window. Her yellow hair is wet with sweat.

We have been waiting in this car. I think it is a long time but maybe we've just arrived.

"When is Connie coming back?" I ask the little girl. I am not acquainted with this irritating child. To whom does she belong?

"I don't know," she answers. "Pretty soon I hope. It's really hot."

I sit in the car. It is hot and I look out the window and see the large building.

"R-E-A-M-S," I say. "Can you read? What does R-E-A-M-S say? Sound it out."

"Grandma, I'm nine. I can read. It says Ream's. It's the grocery store. That's where Grandma went. I mean Connie."

"Connie! Connie's in there? How do you know Connie?"

This is the kind of little girl who thinks she knows everything. I don't know why I'm sitting in the car waiting for Connie with a little know-it-all. The know-it-all shifts away from the window to take a look at me. She says, "Connie is my grandma. We're waiting out here while she gets groceries."

None of this makes sense. Connie is my own daughter. I intend to put a stop to this foolishness. This child needs a lesson.

"You're not making any sense. I'm going in there to get Connie."

I reach for the door handle. The door is locked. I raise my hand to the lock knob. My hands seem strange. The little girl springs into motion.

"Great-grandma, no! Don't do that!" She reaches across me to put her small hand over the knob. "Connie's coming back in a minute. Don't get out of the car. It's hot out there."

"It's hot in here," I tell her and rap my knuckles on her insolent head. She retreats to her side, sullen, and I see a truck pulling up beside us. A tall man and his daughters get out and go into the Ream's.

I gaze out the open window, following their progress.

"There's Papa," I tell the little girl. "Papa and the twins."

"Well, maybe he'll tell Connie to hurry," the little girl bleats.

"Don't you get smart. Children have no business advising their elders."

The little girl stares out the window of the hot car into the terrible heat.

We sit in the terrible heat.

"I've never seen it so hot in Idaho," I say.

"This isn't Idaho. It's Utah."

"I ought to give you a spanking."

The child is impassive. We wait in the car, in the hot, hot car. I wonder where my daughter went.

"I need to get home to Idaho then," I say mostly to myself. It seems to me I've left something undone.

I ask the little girl, "Where is Connie?"

Ruth Loveday Porter

My education had come to an end about the time we removed from Green River to Montpelier. I was approaching eleven. I was no scholar and there was no need to exert myself in that direction. I helped my mama take in laundry but she tended to drift off. I darned socks and tended other people's children for a nickel or so when I had opportunity, but that was all just about getting food on the table. I knew women who got by as whores and I had enough in common with them I must have understood it was a possibility. No girl from my station had the luxury to grow up innocent but something in me enshrined a dream of matrimony. I had in mind to avoid the brothels unless it just came at me.

When I was thirteen we removed for a few months to the godforsaken region of Bill, Wyoming. Bill's not a real town—just a place where railroaders stop and sleep according to the regulations, set down by the almighty Union Pacific. The line rode up that way in a northern arm not for any civic destination but to fetch coal. Shawnee was close as it came to a town out there, at least one we could walk to and one morning I came in with my daddy to pick up supplies, check his next shifts, kill some time among other breathing humans. Mama had declined to accompany us, content to sit out the hours of her life in a thickening trance. My brother by then had lit out so I might as well have been the only child.

It was a wonder I was remembered or noticed at all, and I was grateful that day to walk alongside my daddy and to feel a sense of purpose. Just short of Shawnee we passed a ragtag family of Indians, some of them half-breeds. They were camped in a little quakie draw and even though they were destitute the scene looked rather idyllic. A few hours later as Daddy and I set out for return the group seemed hardly to have moved. They were all in the very same poses, as if for a painting. We passed them by but just as I was about to forget them I heard a voice, doubtless within the confines of my own body yet clear and unmistakable. It was neither man's nor woman's that I could discern but when I was turned around I saw a lean, ageless woman not more than ten feet behind us. It was apparent she expected a response from me.

Her hair was long and braided. Her dress was not unlike my mother's or my own. The Great Depression had made us all indistinguishable. Yet the woman was in my mind exotic as if she had sprung directly from a time before white people had even dreamed of this place. It wasn't that she was Indian—her light-brown hair betrayed the interventions of trappers and soldiers, fortune hunters and traders in her making. The strange quality came from something else, and part of it was that she communicated in a language I understood more perfectly than the one I had been taught to speak. Her lips never moved. Yet I answered her even as my father clutched my arm beneath the shoulder and called out in audible English: "You leave us alone! She's got nothing to do with you. Get on back to your own."

Neither I nor the woman answered him. I could hear his muffled stream of protest in the background as I was captivated by her truer language. And then I was yanked about like a toy top, forcefully redirected toward hearth and home and my father's harangue took up the space between my ears. The woman's communion came to a close.

What she told me was my business then and forever, but I'll say this: some people are lucky to have a calling in life. That was the day I heard mine.

Steven Porter

My family never tired of reminding me how fortunate I was to be born last, once the farm was all bought and settled, once we had cars and a two-story house, once Vernon and Connie and Erma had done all the real work. By the time I showed up everything was easy pie. Every photograph of me as a kid demonstrates of the life of cream and privilege my parents and siblings provided for me.

Me and my little red wagon.

Me and Ralphie the noble sheepdog.

Me in the sissy Fauntleroy suit Connie made for me in her home economics class, down at the agricultural college in Utah.

"What a pretty little girl!" Vernon says, striding through the yard forever on his way to perform some important task.

"Pretty little girl!" Mae guffaws. I know I'm going to hear that one all day long. *Stevie! Stevie! Pretty little girl! Pretty girl!*

Me squinting in the sun, foregrounding my flapper sisters. I did love them. Sometimes my life was a beautiful dream of sun and lawn, hollyhocks and pea vines in the garden, swishy sisters in dresses and hats. My father's strong hand gentle on my shoulder, tousling my hair. Where was my mother in all this? Gladys said we lost her when we lost Mae, which means I never really had her.

Mother was tall and elegant. She was graceful and preoccupied in the kitchen, stately in our cramped parlor. Thanks to her our home was the only one I'd seen that wasn't decorated with deer heads. Credit where credit's due. Mother woke on Sundays well before sunrise, enclosing herself in her room and emerging just in time to leave for church, coiffed and done up regal as a queen. She wore elbow-length kid gloves and elaborate wide-brimmed hats while all the other women arrived at Sunday school in practical frocks shipped from Sears and Roebuck. My mother was beautiful and sometimes deeply conversational, quick-witted and warm. She was convinced of the rightness of her doctrines, but beyond generational philosophies of physical discipline she was not unkind. She just wasn't motherish. She was a remote but generally nice lady who lived in our house.

Connie was much more the mother figure and when she grew up to her own life I lost something crucial, even though Erma stayed nearby after she married Eugene. Gladys looked after me, drove me places. Once Gladys got married, sometimes I'd go down to Idaho Falls and stay weekends with her and Glade. Mae of course never embarked.

All that spoiled-baby privilege came crashing down in '29. The Great Depression is news to no one and there's no reason to go on about it, except that it put a wrench in my family's portrayal of themselves as the makers of little Stevie's fairy tale. I had just turned ten at the crash. Connie was the only one who managed a real income. The government paid her to teach at the Ammon School but not in actual money. She was issued monthly vouchers, an indefinite postponement. But she could trade them like cash, at least for diminished value, and bring home small change. We'd assemble our ration pieces and I'd watch her sit with Erma and Daddy to lay out a weekly budget, squeezing out the last half cent of value. They put aside a share for Vernon's sustenance as a missionary out there in the Southern states for three whole years. He became a specter to me, a minor character, the actual fellow long gone yet still a gap in the food allowance.

I gathered eggs each morning, trudging about the barnyard with a basket, jamming my hand into sticky straw like some recurring bacterial Easter. I learned to help my father butcher and pack a hog each year. Often a steer as well. In summer I woke up before light to milk the cow, tend the garden, chasten alfalfa and potatoes. Worked all day and into the darkness. The rest of the seasons in Fremont County were fundamentally winter, but unless the snow trapped us inside we went out to work.

October, November, December, January, February, and most of March I skied to school with Gladys. One time we came to an edge of the moonlit draw in time to witness a crowd of coyotes milling around the half-eaten carcass of a doe. We stood more awestruck than frightened. It didn't occur to us to turn back toward home. Our mother would have about-faced us before we got through the door, probably thumping our heads for good measure. So we stood and watched the demon dogs snarl and eat. They eyed us too. Finally one of the big ones took a leg in his jaws and backed away, dragging the carcass along. Once we were certain they'd made distance we continued on our way, skiing right over the blood-soaked path.

My own boys, Ronnie and Richard, would come to groan each time I launched another rendition of this woeful tale and I don't blame them. Ruth always said on cue, "You had a place for them cows and chickens, now didn't you?" I wasn't looking for sympathy. It's just the kind of thing that comes up. It's the stuff of lives. What else is there finally to talk about, to fill the awkward ticking hours among the strangers we long to know and love?

Ruth Loveday Porter

I set up a little table and altar in the room I rented. Landlord said I could put up a small sign: "Miss Ruth's Mystery Room: Palm and Tarot." Palms came easy. I had a talent for reading people's hands, even between the lines. But I had also made a study of it. The universe lent me a hand so to speak by delivering further knowledge as I required it. I had a book called *Chiromancy, or the Science of Reading Palms* on my shelf, mainly to boost customer confidence. But the book itself was magic. It had come to me in Soda Springs when I was fifteen. The communion with that woman in Bill had been haunting me, and I had been beseeching whatever force had touched me in the cradle. One day, dead winter, high wind and sideways snow at the cracked glass of the front window where my mother gazed, a sudden knock startled even her. My mother roused and relapsed into her oblivion, wrapping the blanket more tightly around her shoulders. I was about to call through the door, afraid of some awful news about my father somewhere out there along the tracks. I feared it was some wandering hobo, or maybe the police or landlord. But then I saw straight through the solid pine door. There stood a man with bright red hair and a matching beard. He wore shirtsleeves and trousers as if it were June outside. He held a parcel and when he opened his mouth to speak to me, it was my mother's voice coming from the chair that made his words audible.

"Delivery for Miss Ruth Loveday," the red-haired man and my mother said in unison. I turned to confirm it. She sat, ramrod straight.

"Open the door and take it."

I obeyed. Warmth flooded in as if I had stoked a fire. The man beamed and held out the parcel. I could see now it was wrapped in oilcloth but the surface wasn't wet in the least.

"How did you get here?" I asked.

"On the train, just like everybody. I have two of these. Thought you might need the extra."

"To keep?"

"It's all yours," he said and turned back into the wind. For him the snow might as well have been tropical rays.

I called after him. "Do you know my daddy?"

"He's fine," the man called back without turning his head, and then he was gone into the blizzard.

My mother was dead within a month of that encounter. After the quick funeral I had nothing to do but sit out the winter. I opened the book's pages sometimes. I read parts of it nights I couldn't sleep. I studied its diagrams and worked to memorize crucial principles. But I never liked to read. After a while the letters seemed to move around the page. Words became scrambled. The time I spent on those pages became unbearable after twenty minutes. Still I wanted to learn and my efforts paid off in a way I did not anticipate. The first year I lived in Pocatello—the last remove in which I was willing to follow my father—I was sixteen. He rented a place on Custer Street. I saw him less and less, and when the landlord came to evict us I just packed my valise and walked out. I found a sparsely furnished room along with work at the boardinghouse and with that I was all grown up. First room I cleaned was after a tenant who had moved on, so it was empty but for crumpled sheets, not too dirty, and a newspaper in the trash can. And there on the table was a polished stone the size of an egg. I thought for a moment it had been carved of wood. It was patterned like polished oak but when I picked it up there was no question it was mineral. It felt good in my hand, heavy, and although I considered for a moment turning it in to the front desk, the thought atomized. I knew the stone was mine. It told me so.

After work I put it on the table in my room. The place took on a cheerful aspect as if the window had stretched larger. I felt energized even after the long shift to put things to order, and over the next few weeks I bought secondhand embellishments. A cloth for the table. A candelabra. A cheap but sturdy bookshelf, and I enshrined *Chiromancy, or the Science of Reading Palms* right up there at eye level. I set a long-necked bottle of Florida Water on a doily on one side of the book, a crystal star ornament on the other. I spoke to the landlord and placed my little sign. From the very first customer I realized the stone was guiding me, delivering to my mind the contents of the book. The pages and pictures sprang up as I required them and the letters stayed put, illuminating themselves to prompt my understanding.

I liked the boardinghouse. It was there I learned the skills my mother never knew or at least never passed on to me. I dusted and polished, beat rugs and swept the floors spotless. Sometimes I washed dishes. I watched the Basque woman who made dinners and I was learning to cook. Mrs. Sanchez took me under her protection and taught me powerful mysteries. Her husband Ignacio, the maintenance man, was a wizard. They were the ones introduced me to mystical contemplation of true stories. She helped me refine my tarot. Not that I couldn't read the cards. I could. But I had to practice finding words to convey a language not human. The stone gave me a certain clarity of mind as my sensitivities refined.

Connie Porter Anderson

I was living in Safford, a small Arizona town near the Mexico border with my husband and three little children when Steve and Ruth first courted. Clyde went farm to farm testing well water and soils, making recommendations for farmers and local industry. He knew a lot about alkali. Sometimes they called him over to Morenci to analyze the tailings. It all fascinated him but I never really understood it.

By then all of us older siblings were married but Mae. The Depression was letting up but arguably for something worse.

Although he was twenty-one, Steve seemed to us too young to marry. But he was plenty old enough to get somebody pregnant whether or not we cared to view him that way. He was wild as a mustang. Pocatello was rife with prostitutes and conniving women, designing on boys like Steve, so probably he was not so inexperienced as we tried to believe. When we met Ruth, all of us in a staggered formation over the months of 1939, we murmured that it could have been worse. She was coarse, but polite and pretty in her way. The thing I had against her right off was that she came from poor folks. We struggled for money of course, especially during the Depression but we owned land. We came from education and steady professions. I didn't have anything personally against poor people. People can overcome their upbringing but it appears to be a difficult thing to accomplish. As they say, poor people have poor ways.

Still we harbored hope that Ruth would help Steve settle and grow up for good, but from the start they were stormy and private. None of us ever gained access to the weave of their private lives, because for all their contention they were tight-lipped and loyal even as their turmoil sprawled like a shadow play.

I believed I had more wisdom for them than I actually did. We all clung to the notion that we had only to impart correct principles at the right opportunity, and somehow beyond all prior evidence Steve's life would fall into rhythm. We thought Ruth's superstitions would diminish under right influence.

I was young and relatively untouched by fate myself, although real grief was impending. Memory is a paradox: to remember a time before I remembered a dead baby makes no sense. But in that summer I did not know I would soon deliver a baby girl, strange and deformed, unable to sustain herself beyond the womb for more than a few dire moments. Her fingers and toes were webbed. Thick folds of skin gathered between her chin and tiny breastbone. Her features were discernible but cauled as if her face were covered by muslin. Although I know everything is a part of a greater plan I could not help but wonder what this did, and meant. I dreamed about that baby for the rest of my life. Sometimes she simply nestled in my quivering arms, placid and asleep. Sometimes she opened her eyes and spoke from beneath that veil but I always awakened myself, too frightened to pursue the revelation.

Nor can I reconstruct a time in which I did not know I would be a young widow. One more dead and four more living children onward, after I thought we were established on a little family farm in Utah, my husband Clyde set out for a government job in Egypt. He made it safely to New York. Then London. And then Rome, but the jet exploded halfway over the sea to Cairo.

I guess that kind of disaster reminds anyone who's spared another day that we're not in control of much at all. But people shed unsettling knowledge as fast as they can. I lost count of the helpful folks who told me afterward that they'd foreseen the catastrophe. The jet blew because America harbors Communists. It exploded because the Millennium was nigh; I'd be greeting Clyde coming up out of the grave so soon it was hardly worth putting him in the ground. The jet crashed because Heavenly Father did not intend for human beings to fly, else He would have given them wings. Because Muhammed was a false prophet and Clyde was traveling to aid and abet the Arabs. My husband was killed because I had a college degree, which makes a woman prideful.

I loaded the younger children in the car and followed the train that carried the coffin, containing whatever it was the government had identified as Clyde, from Salt Lake to Idaho Falls. Mary and Tommy came in their own ways and met us at the depot; a hearse was waiting to carry the remains out to Ammon where Clyde grew up. At the funeral I stopped hearing the condolences. I was saturated with shallow wisdom. I greeted the well-wishers, mechanically thanking each indistinguishable face for whatever gobbledygook came out of it. And then suddenly Steve stood before me like a pure angel. My handsome baby brother. I saw how much my own sons resembled him. I had neither seen nor spoken with Steven for at least a couple of years, largely due to his wish to avoid us all but I confess as well because of my own recalcitrance. But now here he was and I collapsed into sobs and his powerful arms. I soaked his clean shirt and the woolen tie he'd probably retrieved from an army box. He held me tight to shield me from the unbearable multitude.

Finally I drew back, sniffling like a second grader. Steve unknotted his tie, drew it from his collar, and wiped my nose with it. He bunched it up and put it in my hand.

"You know I hate wearing this. Do us all a favor and clean yourself up."

I laughed a little and then perceived the doughy moon of his wife's face just beyond Steve's shoulder. Her dark hair was already graying. She looked twenty years older than him. I felt a surge of resentment at her mistrustful countenance. We all suspected she kept Steve in a froth against us.

At my best I recalled that my parents thought I had also married beneath myself. Clyde came from sheep men, a hard count against him where I came from further north. His family bore a history of apostasy and divorce and no recent generational uprightness could efface it. The Andersons were many, a few with obscure paternities. They were, all of them, hot-tempered and clannish. Several Andersons now stood about, none mixing beyond each other. And here my husband's remains lay in a sealed government casket, our children milling about in static incomprehension. Despite myself, when I saw Ruth I wished to believe she could impart an authentic cosmic insight. I wanted her to account for a convoluted universe that had swallowed the forty-two-year-old father of eight children.

Ruth stared at me with that baleful expression that always made me think she was about to bleat like a goat. But she was the only person that day who offered no prophecy of any kind, not even a facile prediction that all would be well.

"Such a terrible thing, Connie. Such an awful thing as this just don't make sense at all. I'm so sorry misfortune's come to you and your babies."

It would be easy to say I knew in advance that Steve was also in a death fall. But none of us really knows anything until it happens. In the meantime we merely watch, mistaking fear for prophecy.

Ruth Loveday Porter

First time Steve took me home to his family should have taught me better. We'd been getting along grandly in Pocatello. He'd be gone a week, sometimes two on a rail run. I'd get on with my own work, save my money, take extra shifts. I'd put on makeup and a scarf in the evenings to beckon wanderers in for a reading. When the train brought him home we spent every free hour and penny on pleasure. We saw all the movies. We danced at the saloons until we collapsed. Steve could drink longer than anyone but once he'd crossed the line he went down harder. One time his chums pushed him home in a wheelbarrow.

As spring came on we packed picnics—fat sandwiches, sweet carrots and pickled beets, boiled eggs and jack cheese curds. Strawberries. Sometimes chocolate. We'd hike into the hills along the Portneuf River savoring the afternoon warmth. He told me about his folks. I revealed a few things about mine.

"Your people don't sound so bad, you know," I told him one afternoon. "I imagine they miss you."

"I'm not saying they don't. But they can't help themselves. They won't stop going on about The Right Religion. Nothing I do is good enough for them. Only thing that's going to make me a good man in their minds is to go on a mission. Then? Find a nice Mormon girl. Marry her in the temple. Make babies. Squat right there in that arctic town, remember who I am and what I stand for, milk the cows, cut hay, pull spuds. Wear a tie and quote scripture. I won't do it, Ruth. I love the trains. I like strong whiskey. I'm happy to work but I'm never, ever going to farm. I'm going to be a fireman."

He grinned and grabbed my arm, pulling me close.

"I love my girl," he said and it was the first time he'd really confessed it. A thrill ran across my collarbones and on down my spine. But also I was dismayed.

"You don't want none of that?" I asked.

"None of it!"

"Not even babies? Are you set against getting married?"

"Oh, I don't mind getting married. Maybe even a kid or two. But the religion's staying out of it."

Well, that was fine with me, although at that point I'd never had enough religion put in me to resent it. All I had against churching was the snobbery, the conviction that some people was somehow better than others because they belonged to the Jesus club. Steven, though, was constructed to resist and all he saw was regulation. I took him to be a free spirit, easy to love and easy to manage so long as I didn't try to cage him.

I was right about that in a way. In his right mind he was a peregrine, made for wide motion but anchored by love of nest and family. In his right mind he was the kind of man who followed his true heart home. But in his dark mind he was monstrous and indiscernible. He was a fissure in the universe, a vault of guilt and revulsion, and nobody could release him from it. I did not understand. How could I? Folks in my world fought to survive, not to die. People I grew up with struggled to be seen, not to disappear. That kind of misery made sense.

Steve longed for hell. Not the fire and brimstone variety. What he hankered after was Mormon perdition—a silent, unassailable, endless reduction. The cave-black solitude of Outer Darkness. It was sheer horror to me once I perceived it. I tried to shut the door. But once it's opened it's open, and the more times a body passes through, the wider it swings.

* * *

Ora, Idaho, was such a pretty place it's hard to imagine in summer at least how that kind of darkness can seep into anybody raised there. Spend a January and it's not inconceivable but that's true of the whole northern trackway of the Union Pacific. Try Bill, Wyoming.

Now it was May in Ashton, not February in Bill and it looked like the whole world was blooming to life. Steve had not been home to see his folks since August, after a fit of family conflict nobody could quite explain. His daddy had driven down to Pocatello a couple times. It wasn't too far. Tried to coax his son back home. I guess there had been telephone talk and some telegrams. Far as I could see everything was lined up for reconciliation and maybe Steve thought so too, because he was buoyant as we boarded the train. Everyone at the yard knew Steve. Men hailed him from every quarter. They all treated me like a queen which nobody ever did for my mama, wife of a section man.

The Yellowstone Special was packed with fancy tourists from Boston and Europe and the like, all done up in brand new expedition costumes.

"Bear bait," Steve smirked and a few mamas reached for their children, reassessing their delectability. The train whistled and pulled out smooth, and it wasn't long before he was restless and took my hand and we made our way back to the caboose deck to watch the great state of Idaho go by. In May 1939 it was an awful pretty sight. We glided north up the rolling valley, bright green of its own accord as if bison and Shoshone still roamed wild upon it. We passed encampments and agency shacks as we funneled through Blackfoot. The train took on a few locals and leaned on toward Idaho Falls. We breathed the scent of the blue Snake River and its cascades. We waved at children, wives, teachers, and cowboys.

Tiny towns in a chain and then it was Rexburg. Steve pointed out the sites, a little boastful even in his disdain for the Mormon town and its high-falutin' pretense of culture. The grand Porter Printing warehouse. Yes, his Uncle Arthur was founder and proprietor, a man of letters in a town so stuffy it was hard to imagine what was worth putting to print. I met the illustrious uncle later on at our limpid wedding party at the Ashton ward house, and once again at the dismal wake for my dead husband at Rexburg's Porter Park. I met the royal cousins at family events along the way but I couldn't name a one of them now.

After Rexburg we crossed the river again, toward the Catholic town of Saint Anthony. The eastern hills gave way to a clear view of the Grand Tetons as if they just rose up that moment. Whoever once saw them as titties must have known witches because for one thing there are three of them, and for another—my God. No woman would stretch her imagination in that direction is all I have to say. If you can get that farfetched picture out of your mind then the sight of the Tetons is a mighty worthwhile view, and we gazed for several miles before Steve took my elbow and turned me in the opposite direction.

"Don't want you to miss the grand entry," he said. "You blink you miss it."

By now we were engulfed in farmland: green rows of sprouting potatoes, wide swaths of alfalfa and not-yet-amber waves of grain. White frame farmhouses stood amidst ample barns and granaries, dotted with sheep and chickens. Some of the landscape suggested cattle. Steve said it was the Lutherans, further east in Lamont and Squirrel, kept the big spreads.

"Those people out there groom their old homesteads with rattail combs," he said. "They spit-shine the dirt. And they keep to themselves. Those Kraut kids still talk with accents, even though they were born in America."

I'd been to Ashton before. We'd done plenty of riding place to place when I was a child. And anybody who ever went anywhere on the railroad had been to Ashton for the Dog Derby. I had intended to include this in our conversation but Steve was caught up in personal nostalgia.

"If you look real carefully now, you can see my family's place," he was saying. We moved to the west side of the deck, and just as we passed a narrow dirt track that curved its way toward the river we couldn't quite see, he said, "Look now!" and the two-story house rose narrow among neatly planted trees. I made out a couple of sheds and a small barn and then the ground swelled to obscure them. We made our way back to our berth a few cars up and the train slowed into the Ashton station.

A woman still in her seat took my arm as we passed her. The husband snored at the window and a couple of sweaty tykes stared up in a daze.

"We were assured that the bears were tame in Yellowstone. Isn't that true?"

"Don't worry," I said. "The bears live in little gingerbread houses. Some of them ride bicycles. Your children will have the time of their lives."

Steve giggled and drew me onward. I was thinking how clever I was but out on the platform I felt a fine cold chain drawing me backward. I turned to perceive a dark form, draped and cauled, wings flapping a bit against a nonexistent breeze behind the pale peering passengers. I shuddered and shut the eyes of my eyes and turned my head around to the world in the moment, because here were Mr. and Mrs. Porter dressed as if they were about to embark on the Titanic, first class. Thursday afternoon in the heart of homestead country and these people looked like they'd been lifted up out of—I don't know—Tarzan's English estate by some gigantic hand and dropped here in Spud Town.

I felt a tidal wave of anxiety, churned up from an old resentment for the kind of people I actually had never mixed with. I didn't know a thing about the life of hardworking settled farmers, let alone the hoity toity kind of people the Porters aspired to be. I don't think they did either. In America we all learned about fancy airs from books and moving pictures, didn't we? What set me off was that Steve's folks had the gall to think they were seeing themselves in a mirror when they took in that stuff. Never once occurred to me, watching a movie full of classy rich people, that I might be looking at an image of myself.

Funny I knew how to read other people's conflicting sensations but rarely my own. I read other folks forward, fortified with threads of the past. Only could ever read myself, and dimly, in rueful hindsight. Naturally, Steve harbored one view of himself as something special, and really what's the sin in that? Ain't that the whole story of America? Part of him longed to believe he was immune to the vicissitudes of fate. He wished to live assured that his destiny, as he had always been told, was manifest and golden. I can see now that I wanted to couple up and also be carried along that river of dreams. No one had ever expected a thing of me but to stay placid and only eat a small share. That was a good girl in my father's estimation. But with the Porters I came to understand I could only ever hover at the edges holding my hand out, illegible palm turned upward. These people only saw themselves as bestowing, not receiving.

Here on the platform, Mr. Porter had been taking me in as shrewd as I'd been him. He spoke gently, warm like he might be greeting somebody to church but I did not misunderstand the hard boundary. He spoke to his son but kept his eyes on me.

"Why, Steven," Mr. Porter said. "You didn't tell us you were bringing along a friend. Had we known we would have made the guest room ready."

I reached up to clutch my moon pendant. Reflex. Mrs. Porter stood like a statue but her eyes assessed her son in every detail. I could see she was overwhelmed with emotion but that was one woman not going to let loose her feelings.

Steve grinned at his parents. "Guest room? Since when do we have a guest room?"

Mrs. Porter pursed her lips and wrenched her gaze over to

me. Her eyes traveled down to my feet, and upward to the crown of my head adorned with last year's turban. She angled her gaze down again from her surprising height to meet my eyes. First I looked sideways and down, then considered it might seem devious so I forced myself to lift my face to meet her eyes.

"I'm very pleased to meet you, Mrs. Porter," I said, meek and polite as I knew how. "My name is Ruth."

"Steven," the woman said. "Don't you know how to introduce a lady when you bring her to meet your parents?"

"Oh, Mama, I'm sorry. Daddy. I forgot myself. This beautiful woman is my fiancée, Miss Ruth Loveday."

None of us knew how to respond to that. I'd assumed at least that Steve had told them I was coming. And I guess we were expecting to get married, but he hadn't asked me formal. I was too flummoxed to understand that he meant the introduction to shock his mother and father. It's the first time I experienced his capacity for meanness. We all stood stiff while Steve retrieved his better self. He took a deep breath. He wrapped his arm around my waist. He pulled me close.

"Right, Ruth?" he said. "We haven't quite come to a full understanding on this but I think she loves me, and I sure do love her. I brought her home to meet you all, because I hope she'll want to become part of this family."

By now the train had loaded its clutch of new passengers. We all started when the whistle blew. Black smoke engulfed us, giving Mr. Porter a reason to gesture, take his wife's arm, and lead us toward the brand-new Roadmaster. The Buick greeted us with its silver grille and round mechanical eyes.

"Where's Mae?" Steve asked as he opened my door for me. Nobody answered until we were all seated and shut in, and then Mrs. Porter said, "She's spent the afternoon with Erma. We'll pick her up on the way home."

Steve said, "I'll sleep in the barn. I like it out there. Ruth can have my room."

"Miss Loveday may sleep in the girls' room," his mother said.

Mr. Porter rolled down his window. Steve did the same and then leaned over to my side to crank mine.

Mrs. Porter did not make a move but she said, "Mae's been restless again. We've put the day bed in with us. Otherwise she wanders. A few nights ago she opened the front door and walked right out. We woke to the breeze coming in. Your father found her out past the gate, conversing just as if someone was standing out there at the road with her. We still don't know whether she was sleeping or awake."

All of them tightened their lips and looked out their windows, recalling incidents I had no access to. Steve broke the family reverie. "Well, maybe she was having herself a vision."

"Steve!" his father rebuked, and his mother said, "Don't be irreverent," and Steve said, "Anyhow, let's go get her. I've missed her the most of all of you."

This caused Mrs. Porter to twist around and give him a look. Mr. Porter reached for his tie—I thought maybe to loosen it in the warm air of the car but he actually cinched it up.

"Besides," Steve said. "I want to say hello to Erma."

I reached over, touched his knee to reassure myself, but he flinched like I'd stuck a blade in it. I pulled my hands to my lap.

For a guy who knotted his tie so tight, Mr. Frederick Porter drove that Buick like a cowboy on a steer. It wasn't just that one time. Something came out in him behind the wheel of his own automobile. It got wilder the older he got. Today he hit the main highway at fifty, rammed it up to seventy-five by the time he swung us off of it, taking a hard right turn after barely easing his foot off the accelerator. He careened side to side along the oiled dirt road, scattering a flock of crows like they were union agitators, and skidded into the driveway of a neat little house, connected to the larger spread among the tall box elders. Neither Steve nor his mother seemed alarmed by the carnival ride.

All Steve said was, "This is my sister Erma's place. Her husband Eugene is one of the Hesses who own this farm."

"They're a fine family," Mrs. Porter stated.

"I know it," Steve said. "I'm happy for Erma."

I took in my breath and reached to pull the door lift but Steve whispered, "Wait, Ruth," and I remembered to sit tight until he walked around to open me out. I didn't get one foot on the ground before I heard a raucous female voice shout, "Stevie!" first from a distance and then somehow already between Steve and me.

"Stevie Weevie! Little Steven! Stevie! Weevie! Stevie! Weevie!" and it didn't look to stop soon. Steve squeezed my hand and then let go, easing himself and his strange sister Mae away from the car so I could let myself out. Mae paid no mind to me at all. "Where have you been Stevie Weevie? I missed you so! Stevie! Where have you been all this time?"

I felt a gentle hand on my arm and I turned to face a very pretty young woman, smiling at me in query. If Steve was a girl he would have looked just like her.

"Hello there. What's your name? I'm Steve's sister Erma."

"I can tell. It's very nice to meet you. I'm Ruth."

Erma held her smile but waited expectant.

I said, "I mean, my name is Ruth Loveday."

"Steve didn't tell us he was bringing a guest. Are you Steve's girl? You're very pretty. I can't imagine you're anything but."

I felt my face go stupid and slack. It's a habit I learned from my mother I suppose. "Don't give no information to nobody," was her only real maternal advice. I forgot for a moment I wasn't a child anymore and didn't have to fade into scenery. And since Steve had already informed his parents that we were getting married, I gathered myself as I spouted words. I said, "Well, sure. I'm his girlfriend."

Then, "I mean I'm his fiancée."

Erma's eyes opened wide but she did not abandon her poise. "My goodness!" she said. "You're engaged to my brother! I'll take him to task for not giving us better notice. We should have been better prepared to welcome you."

I glanced toward Steve, who had moved a way off down the front ditch with Mae, who was still hollering. Their parents stood uncertainly between us and them, choosing in favor of Steve's general earshot.

"Are you from Pocatello?" Erma asked. "Is that where you met Steve?"

"I'm from all over the place. My daddy was a section man." I stopped because I understood what kind of impression I was making. I wasn't stupid. But I reminded myself I wasn't ashamed of my hardworking father. I took another breath and said, "I lived all over because of it. Even in Ashton for a spell. Idaho, Wyoming, Montana. Ogden for a year."

"What does a section man do?" Erma inquired.

"Well, all kinds of things. A section crew is in charge of maintaining a section. A distance of track. They watch for trouble. They replace ties and spikes. They look for bent rails. They make sure the cinder is stable and groomed. You've seen them, I'm sure. Got those tracks right across the highway there."

She looked at me closely. "That must be hard work. Did you ever want to settle down, like reg—I mean, I don't know, town people and the like?"

"Most section families do," I said. "Most of them live wherever the mother's family lives, send their men out. But my mama really didn't have settled family either, and she wasn't right in the head all the time."

We glanced toward the racket on down the ditch and Erma said, "Of course. I understand. For heaven's sake. I have no business standing here soliciting your life story. What in the world am I thinking? And there's Mae going on. She had a terrible fever when she was small. Steve must have told you."

Erma stood in her green calico dress and cooking apron, suddenly very bewildered. Both of us settled our eyes on Steve, laughing and hooting like a kid with his loony sister. Mae was cute. If you didn't hear her talk you'd think she was a college girl like her sisters. Her hair was dark and wildly curly. Her wire-framed glasses brought her eyes forward like a little owl's. Or like the Buick's. Her smile was adorable even vacant like that. I opened up my deeper senses and was startled to feel the same heat in her as I had in Steve, first time I sensed him in the street outside the Chief. But then it came to me I was perceiving fever. Past, not present nor future. Beyond that firewall was a cool mountain lake, blue descending into liquid black. But you wouldn't know that in the present ruckus. Erma took my hand and we went to join Steve and Mae, collecting the parents along the way.

"Mae!" Erma said, and abruptly the odd girl swiveled toward her sister's voice. But she froze like Lot's wife when she saw me.

Mae's eyes widened behind the wire frames and her jaw dropped open.

"Who're you?"

Steve said, "Mae, silly, I've been trying to tell you. Meet my girl Ruth, here. I brought her home to meet you."

Mae was as silent now as she had been loud a minute before.

"She's a nice friend for you," Erma said. "She's pretty, don't you think?"

Mae's eyes did not leave my face. She didn't look me up or down, just face to face. Finally she said, "Are you going to marry my brother Stevie?"

Nobody answered her. They all waited for me to confirm it.

I told her yes, but not by speaking.

Mae took it in.

"You're my new sister then," she said out loud.

And Mrs. Porter said, "Well, not yet," and Steve's father said, "Come on Mae, let's take you home. Old Buster's lonely without you."

"My cat is Buster," Mae said to me toneless, and we walked back to the car and piled in, Mae in front between her parents, Steve and me in the back seat. Erma waved from outside the window. Mr. Porter spun gravel behind us, Mae turned and fixed her owl eyes on me, and soon we were skidding to a stop in front of a storybook house with a trellis and picket fence.

I felt Steve heat, harden, and cool like magma, although his tone pitched exuberant. "Come on Ruth. Let's walk out to the river. I'll catch you a fishy-wishy."

"Fishy-wishy!" echoed Mae. "Daddy, Steve said fishy-wishy!"

"He sure did. And tonight we'll thank him for that."

Steven Porter

Turns out Ruth and my sister Mae had a special chemistry. I had feared that the proximity might ignite a certain chaos but what did I know? Mae's inability to let me be anything but a teddy bear in her tangled memory was gradually upstaged by her preoccupation with Ruth. I don't understand what added up to make it so. Ruth didn't ever have much to say to my weird sister. Stuff Ruth liked to talk about once she warmed up had no meaning at all to Mae. Ruth understood and didn't attempt it. But Mae quieted down around her and followed like a kitten. Played like one too, fascinated by bright objects and abstract motions. Slept in a ball, on and off, more like an animal than a human being. She never did settle again into day and night, exhausting my parents more every year they looked after a daughter who was forever a child.

I admit I sometimes regarded Ruth with a degree of suspicion. I watched for subtle gestures played out in Mae's direction. I wondered at the flashy pendants Ruth always wore, moons and stars and spirals that might be used to manipulate an otherworldly simple girl. But mostly I enjoyed the relief of peace and quiet Ruth caused when she was near Mae. Nobody said anything about it, at least for years after we married. I know my folks were relieved in the same way, overall, so none of us attended too closely to our suspicions.

Ruth could plumb a soul for deep character—at least for hidden malice or lack of it. She could sense a particular darkness or unusual light, and as the years went on she learned to discern qualities embedded in flesh-and-bone contours. On the other hand, I was limited to the plain discernments of the five human senses. Eventually we come to realize that's not much to go by. Sure, like any reasonably smart person I learned by trial and sometimes bitter error to spot an outright liar. I recognized a shifty bastard as well as the next guy, but if somebody makes a point to be deceitful there's no surefire way to know it.

Words explain entire worlds, not one of them reliably true: Ruth was an earnest fraud. Ruth was a witch who picked us out, malevolent, driving us to sorrow for sins we didn't commit. Ruth could see a few things darkly in the cosmic glass that other people could not. Just like she said. The fact is, all I could really know of her was what she told me and what I saw. We have to take the people we love as they say they are, or the world explodes into sparks and we burn out alone.

I learned all this too late. Something about Ruth, despite my confidence in her extra sight, elicited dark suspicion as I ventured deeper into her ways. And it started that night I walked her home that first time in Pocatello, when she told me how to ponder a story until it became real. Later when I met Mrs. Sanchez, the woman was a little surprised by our account. She seemed urgent to reiterate the principles of this magic: meditate to discern the good messages from evil. Many visions appear to be holy but deceive. Search your heart and attend with compassion. Try to find your likeness in even the most frightening or repugnant personage. Strain to hear the whole message offered you.

"Do you understand me, young man?" Mrs. Sanchez demanded. She took my chin in her fingers as if I were a child. "You entered a potent story. This is no trifling thing. It can petition darkness you have yet to comprehend."

Darkness was no stranger to me. Night-black spells overwhelmed me as a child and my family had become accustomed to the weeks, even months, I was so drawn into myself I could not be reached. But even so those intervals had been only a formless blanket thrown over my senses, a room within a room and yet within a room, muffling sound and obscuring vision. Everything I put in my mouth would taste like cotton. No fragrance filtered through—not roses, not mud, not cow dung, not my own mother's familiar array of colognes and perfumes. In a way it was comforting, or at least inert, but after that night with Ruth and Mrs. Sanchez my dark spells acquired contour. Characters and histories and half-exhumed memories. Conversations, encounters, grisly images and hideous crimes. I could never assemble a larger meaning. I could not discern one message from another. Sometimes it seemed the only explanation was that Ruth herself was the bad messenger, hellbent to destroy me. But there's no good reason for it. I believe she loved me. Why single me out that way?

Maybe she was evil, pure and simple. Evil requires no reason. Like sorrow, evil just is.

I knew that as well as Ruth. As a child I asked my father, "But why does Satan want to hurt me?"

"He's jealous. He sees your beauty and your goodness. He sees your opportunities. He's angry that he can't have them."

"Why can't he have them?"

"It's too late."

"Can't he say he's sorry?"

"No, son. Some things can't be forgiven."

"But in Primary Sister Forrester said we can repent and come to Jesus."

"Well, that's true if we were born to this earth. Those of us who earned mortality were among the righteous army in the

pre-earth life. We may have evil inclinations and we're all sus-
ceptible to temptation, but we can improve ourselves. That's why
we're here. But Satan and his army were denied mortal bodies
because they fought against Heavenly Father from their inception. They've been too evil for too long to redeem themselves.
They don't even want to."

"What if one of them changes his mind?"

"True evil does not change its mind, son."

"But, why? What if—"

"Steven! That's enough. Devils are all around us. They are
always listening. They want to penetrate your mind, to find the
evil in you and nurture it like a bad tree. Best not to talk or think
too much about these questions. Turn your heart to goodness.
Gladly obey God's will and you have nothing to fear."

Ruth looked like nothing to fear as we set out across the pasture and new-green fields. My heeler Ralphie trotted alongside
us, rolling every few steps in happy wonder over my return. I
held my fishing rod in my left hand, Ruth's hand in my right.
Her cheeks were rosy and round in the slanted sun, her hand
warm and dainty in my calloused paw. We could smell the fishy
froth of the river before we cleared the bank. I grew up along that
river. Henry's Fork, high branch of the Snake. Our farm dipped
toward the west, dropping lower toward the bottoms. After
that it wasn't far on out to the grassy oxbow. In some places the
ground tapered to the water but mostly it ledged off as vertical
rock. I guided Ruth to my favorite fishing seat. Five feet below
us the water flowed deep and still. We dangled our legs over the
edge while I baited and dropped the line. The float bobbed down
the current and disappeared just as I knew it would, thirty feet
out near a high jutting stone. Always a new taker out there. Some
mouth that hadn't yet felt the hook.

I yanked the rod just as I felt the strike. Up came the fish in a
beautiful silver arc. Every single time I caught one, I savored that

thrill of plenitude: how many men on this planet have traced those same motions? How many fish have risen, first to the bait and then to the alien sunlight beyond?

Ruth cried, "Oh! Look at it!" and I teased it in, a fine sixteen-inch rainbow. We admired its jeweled curve as I drew it into the still water beneath us. I should have walked down with the net to retrieve it but it looked solid. I flipped the fish right out of the water, over our heads and on to the grass behind us. If it hadn't been already, now the hook was caught deep, sunk through the roof of its mouth and curving back out again just below the eye. The trout pitched a terrific fight as I worked to release it from the line. I felt my good spirits deflate. I worked the barb. The fish writhed in my hand and the hook jabbed deep into my thumb, even while it held fast in the fish's mouth.

Ruth said, "Careful," and I snapped, "You teaching me how to fish?"

"No, I just . . ."

This hook wasn't about to come loose. I always enjoyed that moment of holding a beauty, de-hooked and sleek in my hands, alive but relaxed that last moment before I had to finish it off. Once a fish is dead it's a mere object and I liked to postpone it. I suppressed a flare of anger but even so I took the whole fish at the girth and slammed its head against the rock, much harder than I needed to. Ruth and I both recoiled at the little sickening crack.

Ruth said, "Well, now you got it."

I shot her a glare. All of a sudden she looked dumpy and ludicrous sitting there, hair falling and limp against her doughy cheeks and receding chin, color oddly drained in the orange light. Her breasts hung over her stomach like a limp cat. I felt time rush forward to a day I would sit killing hour by hour in a shabby parlor with an aging frump. Ruth was the only unnatural thing in the whole scene, except maybe the fish now dead and dull on the grass, deformed by the whack.

I unsheathed my knife. I picked the thing up and slit the

throat. I released the gills, then slid the sharp knife clean down the white belly to the shit hole. I put the knife on the grass and jammed my finger into the cut under the fish's jaw. I pulled the guts out clean and threw the mess out into the river where the cannibals rose to devour. I walked down the little path to the water's edge, rinsed the hollowed fish to a shine, and came back up to hook it on my tackle chain.

Ruth witnessed in silence.

"What's the matter?" I said. "Haven't you ever cleaned a fish?"

"Of course I have. Some days we wouldn't've had anything to eat if we didn't know how to fish."

"That's such a sad story."

I could see she felt the sting. Color came back to her face along with a new expression I couldn't read.

"What do you know about it? You ever skin a carp?"

I didn't hide my disgust. "You eat carp?"

She didn't respond.

And then she did.

"People swallow what they got to, Steve."

It occurred to me as I regarded Ruth that my mother and father had some swallowing to do, and that cheered me up a little. I did intend to keep my folks in a state of distress. I knew they were murmuring back at the house between themselves even now. *Railroad trash. Gentile. Prostitute.*

I felt heavy at the joints. The muscles in my thighs were tight and I felt a chill at the small of my back creeping upward. My ears rang even over the sound of the river. I heard a distinct but indiscernible murmur of voices at the bottom of my constricting brain as if there were an urgent meeting of some kind. Something opened my mouth.

"Witch," said my voice as if it had made a discovery. "You're a witch. Aren't you."

Ruth spun around and pitched up toward the road in a

single gliding motion, as if she were assisted. Once established on the rise she turned back toward me. I was down a few yards, still on the bank. She was a good way off and yet I heard her voice fill my head as if she were speaking between my ears. It wasn't a shrieking sound yet the drums stretched tight against the unnatural pitch.

Don't you ever call me that again! Do not use that word, especially here in this place. Do not utter that word to your grand family of alfalfa dukes. Do you understand?

I went down like a sledgehammer had slammed me in the head.

You think your family did wrong by you? They'd burn me at the stake if they had their say. You want to make them sorry for loving you? Sorry for thinking they're some royal family? Sorry for making you hoe dirt for your dinner?

My head spun with colors. Streamers of blue and green and purple. Strange letters and signals blinked like neon.

You want something to make them sorry for? Make them sorry they'd help a woman to the rack! Make them sorry they'd stand and watch while their friends and neighbors step up to the gallows!

I could hear the river, chuckling and familiar. Blackbirds called across the water and the earthy little quacking of mallards animated the reeds. I smelled home soil and emerging hay. Wafting scent of manure. But gradually my sensations were overcome by the texture of thick fabric, layered and draped, up close and smothering as I fell through dense folds.

Make them sorry for opening the door. And more sorry for shutting it!

Then I was a small boy in my family's kitchen, eyes just clearing the china bureau. My mother's voice from the back room.

You put those forks in neatly, Steven, in that uncanny way from her invisible place.

An echoing rendition of her favorite lament: *My papa, only forty-one years old! The doctor too ignorant to diagnose. Papa dead in the night, no reason but incompetence. Eleven children! Mama with a nursing infant!*

The scene changed and I sat on a hard stool trying not to fidget, fighting the oppression of hovering animus. My father's voice. *Prophets see ahead. They warn us of harrowing dangers the adversary has placed or will yet place in our path. Do you understand me, son? Prophets also foresee the grand possibilities and privileges awaiting those who listen with intent to obey. The somber reality is that there are servants of Satan embedded throughout society. So be very careful about whose counsel you follow.*

And now Ruth was shouting from the road above me in her natural voice from her own mouth loud and angry but at least it was here and now.

"What is it that's so terrible about all this?" She lifted her arms and gestured toward the river. The farm. Back toward the house. "Really Steve, what's the hopeless misery? Everyone got folks drive them mad, ain't that right? At least yours know the difference between you here and you gone. At least they give a damn. And it probably was lousy for your mama to get stuck with a dead handsome daddy and a pack of hungry brothers and sisters. That's a sad story! Have you got no human sympathy?"

I clamped my jaw because I had nothing to argue with. And besides, I was buried under a stinking pile of shit. No. A hell of a strange hallucination. I shook myself like a wet dog. I rubbed my ears and face, stomping as if my feet were cold and I turned toward the sun setting over the river. Birds in flight. The scent of water. One goddamned glorious all-American scene it was and me the shimmering son of Idaho. Yet I could only perceive the spinning morass behind the grand illusion, spiraling inward from the corners. I heard a guttural masculine voice expounding and accusing. I could neither understand nor stifle it. Black spots dissolved the veneer of orange light like acid. Times my mind slid like this I could hear the ageless leagues of Death intoning the condemned at Hangman's approach.

"Ruth. I know it. I've got nothing to cry about. I love my folks. Here I come back to the best place on earth, and it's Armageddon."

She stood, arms folded across her chest. The sunlight was full upon her on the hill. I implored the golden idol.

"Ruth! What's the matter with me?"

Ruth Loveday Porter

He was on his knees below me, distraught on the bank. He was as strong a man as I ever met—all that milk and honey transported to the rail yards to gain a nice polish of dirt and definition. Steve was still approaching prime. He was twenty-one on a rising course that had only begun to peak the year or two before he died, and that with years of bingeing on bad liquor, backbreaking miles at the boiler. If he hadn't killed himself probably nothing would have ever killed Steven Porter.

"I have no idea what's wrong with you," I called as he stood and staggered toward me. "No one can plumb the one mystery of a human heart. That's a secret ever unrevealed, even to the heart it concerns."

"What kind of talk is this?" he asked. I could not tell whether he was mocking and so I didn't answer.

He kept it up. "You knew I wasn't a real railman the first night you met me. You knew I had a brother. I want to think all that voodoo stuff you play at is just a sideshow but you've got some way with Mae that no one does. What's your mystery, Ruth?"

"I got no mystery. Dirt-poor girl from a train tribe. You know all there is to know."

"Where'd you learn all this sinister wisdom then?"

"Live among Gypsies and Indians, cross enough Chinatowns, you'll pick up a different education than the homestead girls. It ain't necessarily sinister. And you know Mrs. Sanchez."

He blinked. His cheeks went flush. He struggled to bring himself back but every time he opened his mouth he upped the ante. "You don't really believe in this hocus-pocus, do you? I'll grant that it's alluring."

He wasn't really asking. I knew that tone. The voice that comes out of folks who know deep down that they are the only True People. I was heating up as he clawed against the black pit of his afflicted mind. I could see him drop, plank by plank with every new effort to speak. I took pity.

"Steve," I said. "Come back to me, sweetheart."

But he only went deeper. I tried to command him in another manner. I put my hand on his forehead. I said low but audible, "Trust is needed. It's what we must see. Make Steven trust me. So must it be."

He opened his eyes clear and innocent as sky. He gave me a warm smile. I thought I had done the job but he was falling to a power stronger than my simple chant. I needed candles and paper, quiet time for a more elaborate spell. I quailed as his eyes narrowed.

"There's something you're not telling me," he said.

"There's plenty I haven't told you. We've only known each other for a few weeks. But I'm not hoarding some dark secret."

We stood face to face, drawn together and kept apart by an imperative that held us for two more decades.

I said, "You brought me here just to spite your parents."

"That's not true. I brought you here because—"

"Sure it is. It doesn't take a mystic to see it. We have fun and all in Pocatello but it's got nothing to do with coming here. You got a chip on your shoulder and you wanted to bring up some railroad tramp to set them off. I ain't no farm-boy plaything you know."

"Ruth—"

"I'm not a tramp. You know I ain't. I've been the one had to push you off."

His eyes were nearly black. His jaw went slack. He leered like a drunk.

"No," he said. "You're not a tramp. But you are a witch."

Steven Porter

The woman went berserk.

Don't you ever! . . . you stupid, arrogant . . . I got no powers to conjure . . . just because I can see something, doesn't mean . . . it ain't like your old Joe Smith, see . . . thinks he's some kind of . . . people who go around accusing people of . . .

The echo of her voice faded in my head with each new phrase. Something broke way back in the murk at the base of my mind and I fell down and down, striking hard ground in another place. It sure wasn't Idaho in 1939. That sensation of fabric returned to me. Tapestry, incomplete. Folded and torn, rumpled and ridged, sometimes threadbare and sometimes thicker than velvet. As I sank through like water the impressions were so intense that I inhabited form after form. I was everyone on a crowded platform, a holding pen, a forest and field—child and man and woman, accused and accuser, a sermon like a ponderous bell.

And then I stood at an ancient well.

I saw green fields and dense trees from a brick tower.

An emerald pond broken by the glide of swans.

The scene vanished, not so much a fading as an overcoming, blackness so dense I could taste it in my throat down my chest, filling my lungs.

I gasped for air but I drew in oil.

A woman's hand clenched my arm with sharp nails. I tore it away. My mind cleared enough to perceive the undulant deep-eyed woman I had brought home to my parents' farm. Her hair had fallen long and wild. Her teeth were large and ragged. I could smell her breath, or maybe it was her scent, human and clean on the high edge but rank and rot beneath. I heaved. I stood up and threw her like a puppet. She flew and for a moment I was myself and sorry but when I reached to help her up she leaped back, scrambled to her feet, and fled from me.

Connie Porter Anderson

Erma told me in a letter that she heard the dogs barking out in the yard. She looked out to see a woman striding past her house toward the highway. Strong legs and a mighty determination. For a moment she looked unearthly, like a skinwalker, and then Erma realized who it was and ran out in her bare feet to call out.

"Ruth!"

The woman kept right on moving.

"Ruth! It's Erma! Steven's sister, remember? Please stop! Can I take you somewhere?"

Ruth halted but she did not turn around. She stood stock still in the dark, face toward the highway until Erma caught up to her.

"Ruth, my goodness. Where are you going this time of night?"

Ruth swiveled her head like a tin toy and answered in a gravelly voice. "Night train. Pocatello."

"Do the folks know you've gone? Didn't anyone offer you a ride?"

"Didn't tell nobody."

"Can't you come back to my place for a minute? Gene's still awake. We'll drive you into town."

"I don't got a ticket," Ruth said, and she started to cry. She let Erma take her arm and they walked back toward the house, but Ruth wouldn't enter. She stood frozen at the doorway muttering little sentences under her breath. Eugene buttoned his shirt and found the keys to the truck.

Eugene attempted a few pleasantries the first half mile, but dried up as it became clear that Ruth was in no state of mind to answer. He pulled left onto the highway, gunning to speed while Ruth stared into the night beyond the headlights, fixated on the town ahead.

"Ruth, did my brother hurt you?" Erma found nerve to ask.

"No," Ruth said. "I just don't belong with you people. It's time to go home."

You people.

"That was a long walk from the home place," Gene said.

"I've walked further'n that."

"Train won't come in for more than an hour. Why don't we take you back to our place and get you something to eat?"

"Not hungry. I don't mind the depot."

Eugene pulled into the station yard. He glanced at Erma and said, "Why don't you two sit tight while I arrange for a ticket? Go ahead and keep the heater on."

Ruth sat still and Erma didn't pursue conversation. In a few minutes Gene came back, opened Ruth's door, and offered his arm. Ruth gripped it hard and heaved herself out like a sack of potatoes. Once she got going though she picked up that stride again. Gene had to trot to keep up. Erma regained her sense of decency. She clambered out of the truck and ran to catch up.

"Ruth, let us sit here with you until the train comes."

"No!" Ruth swung her face toward my sister, lips curled back. Erma swore Ruth's eyes reflected the streetlight just like a coyote's.

"Leave me here. I can fend."

Gene opened the door of the depot, ushering Steve's girlfriend into the lit-up room. Ruth spoke no words of departure.

"So," Erma wrote, "I guess that's the end of that."

Ruth Loveday Porter

Of course I knew he was back in Pocatello but I did my best to ignore it. What Steve loved most was trains anyway and I knew he was working continual shifts down at the roundhouse. He was determined to show the U.P. he was ready to advance. He was waiting for the next opening, any line but he wanted Portland. He'd been cozying up to the crew. He longed for the hills and valleys, tunnels and bridges, prairie to mountain to ocean. For now it was the tedious back and forth of the switchyard.

If that man was ever safe from his own hazards it was in the vicinity of a steam engine. And so he recovered for a while from his dark spell by shoveling coal like Casey Jones in the switch engine, waiting out his opportunity to join a proper crew. One day he realized the pall had lifted. His mind cleared like a strong wind had blown through. Sky turned blue again. It occurred to him he'd like to take a long bath and from that followed a hot barbershop shave. He found himself refreshed but powerfully hungry. It was end of June and good weather for picnics and one afternoon I came out the back alley behind the boardinghouse and there he was, a basket all packed, a blue flax bouquet in his hand.

He was so damned beautiful to me. I'd never thought I could make a man like that love me but here he was grinning like a kid, all clean and sweet-smelling. He looked as innocent as the flowers. But I'd been rehearsing this possibility in my mind over the past few weeks and I was ready. I had fortified my heart as best I could.

"You just get on out of here, Steven Porter."

He set down the basket. Held out the flowers.

"Ruth. I'm here to tell you how sorry I am. Please forgive me."

That took me by surprise. Wasn't on my practiced script so I was unprepared. No man had ever apologized to me, not in my entire life. They just came back after a while, expecting I'd feel lucky for it.

I stood there in my dirty apron. I sure didn't smell like flowers. I put my hand to my cheek, then checked my hair, pushing it about to find the pins.

253

"I'm in no condition for a picnic."

"You look beautiful."

"I've been working since before sunrise. I'm a mess."

"Let me walk you to your room. I'll wait outside while you freshen up."

Steve took a step toward me. I recoiled even as I also wanted to throw myself into his arms. He stopped in his tracks.

"Ruth. I know you're afraid. I can't account for what happened up there on the river. I don't understand what happens to me. Please believe what I say. Something takes over my mind. I can't help it but I'm trying hard to do better for you. I'm not asking anything right now but for you to let me walk you to your place, wait as long as it takes for you to feel ready, and then walk on up the hillside and enjoy a picnic."

He held out the flowers again. He pointed to the basket and picked it up.

"You hurt me, Steve. You don't know your own strength."

At that moment he looked helpless, and miniscule, against what rushed into my understanding as the infinite cosmos.

"Ruth. Truly, in my own self, I'd never in the world raise an arm to you. I'm not that kind of man."

"Well, it seems that sometimes you are."

"Can you make yourself stronger than me, in those times?"

"You mean, magic?"

"Yes."

"I don't know. Maybe if we don't tax it too hard."

"Tax what?"

"The power. Powers. Strength we don't exactly understand. Ours but not ours."

"Well, if I ever get close again to hurting you, I want that strength to kill me."

"It's going to kill us all, at some point."

"I'm not sure it's worth the wait."

"Steve," I cried, but some spirit shut me up, dropped a curtain on whatever it was I had thought to express.

"Ruth. Let's just have a picnic today. In this good sunlight."

"That's all?" I asked.

"Right now that's all. I promise. But I can't say I don't want more. I want you to give me another chance. Let this afternoon help you make a decision, how about?"

I wanted to sound casual. I tried to simply say, "Well, all right then," and walk in his direction all impersonal, but instead I fell into tears. He stepped forward and I let him wrap me in his arms.

That picnic got me pregnant. I'm not sorry about that now but at the time it seemed like the end of the world. Once I comprehended I wasn't just one, two, three . . . four weeks late on the blood it was close to August. Pocatello was hot as a boiler and the trains magnified it as they blew steam and coal pitch into the stifling air. Steve had pleaded his cause to the Portland staff. Young Horatio Alger pitching his grit and gumption. He'd got persuasive enough to be assigned as relief crew. He rode Butte and Lincoln when they needed him. Mostly he was called up as fireman but sometimes they needed him for other jobs and he didn't care so long as he rode the train.

He was gone for a week and I was keeping myself busy. Until it hailed me down I had held the intimation of pregnancy entirely away from my mind. But one particularly hot morning mid-shift, I swooned with nausea. I collapsed on a chair and nearly passed out. Once I collected strength to take in breath again I gulped air and called out to Colleen. She came running. Promising that she and Laura would double up and finish my work, Colleen persuaded Mr. Sanchez to let me go to my room. To my surprise he offered his arm and escorted me to the bottom of the stairs, solicitous.

"You'll be all right getting up there?" he asked. I said yes and made my way. The room was a suffocating cell. I opened the window. I rubbed my arms and neck with lavender. I locked the door and took off most of my clothing, and fell to the bed wondering what in the world could be wrong with me.

And then I understood.

Connie Porter Anderson

First lines of Erma's letter were, "Well, that wasn't the end of it after all. Steve's gotten that Ruth Loveday pregnant. We're going to have a new sister-in-law, and by golly, she's a keeper. She grew up on the train tracks. No family to speak of, although Steve says her daddy's coming in from the far edge of the known world sometime to bless the happy couple. And here's the best part: the girl's a fortune-teller. We have a Gypsy in the family!"

I didn't know what to make of that. I knew she wasn't a real Gypsy but everything that word brought to mind was disturbing to me—more so than I could account for. That night I told Clyde that Steve was getting married. I even told him the girl was pregnant and that she was one of those Pocatello types, but I didn't show him Erma's letter or mention the voodoo. I'm not sure why it was so hard to say it. Clyde would have made a joke and put it out of his mind. Even so I didn't want the words to come out of my mouth.

I feared if I said, "She reads palms for extra cash," or, "Steve says Ruth can read your life in a deck of cards," I'd make something come true that I was not prepared to contend with. I didn't believe in any of that Maid of Mystery tripe. And yet again, I knew there were supernatural presences, both good and evil, all around us. I knew that servants of Satan watch for any opportunity to enter our minds and convince us that their logic is our own. The devil's helpers are eager to answer when we call. Using the wrong authority to address spirits in the world beyond, even if they might seem benign, is asking for trouble. Steve of all people didn't need any of that. Furthermore, it was his responsibility as husband to control the spiritual communications within his household. The Melchizedek Priesthood is a man's sacred inheritance to be used as a blessing to his wife and children. To invert that sacred family order could bring down disaster.

I lay uneasy all night fearing that even Erma's letter had attracted the attentions of evil spirits. In the morning I carried it out to the bin and burned it.

Ruth Loveday Porter

In September I carefully folded and packed the dress my girlfriends and I had chosen for the grand occasion. It wasn't white of course. It wasn't even a wedding gown but it was pretty and demure. I looked respectable in it. Sky blue with a neat collar. Buttoned down the front but draping above the waist so I could wear it without calling attention to my widening girth.

I got some sleep after work but set my alarm clock for midnight. Steve waited outside. He took the valise from my hand and we walked on up to the depot, rode quiet, and left the sleeping tourists in the cars as we stepped onto the Ashton platform in dead dark. The train pulled away. Crickets chirped unnaturally loud. The grain and spud elevators stood like disapproving titans above us. There was not a human being in sight. Even the office was locked. A single-bulb lamp on a post emitted the only light but starlight.

We stood. The weather was turning and the slight wind made me shiver. Steve stood behind me to press his warmth against my back, bringing his hands around to shield the incomprehensible thing inside me.

"Don't worry, Ruth. It's all going to be grand. You and me and little Bambino. We'll take on the world. You'll see."

The sound of a lone vehicle on the highway filled in for conversation.

"Hope that's them," I said. We left the suitcases and walked out a way to see around the silos. We watched the headlights approach for a mile. The vehicle slowed at the Main Street turn, signaling right and the beams came around.

"It's not the Buick," Steve said, and in a minute we could make it out as a pickup truck. Suddenly we were all illuminated, stars of our own show. The horn made a little toot and a woman's hand waved from the shotgun side.

"It's Gene and Erma," Steve said, but he was wrong. The truck stopped and Erma spilled out from the driver's seat. Another woman hopped down from the other door.

"Steve!" they both cried and Steve said, "Oh! It's Erma and Gladys! What in the world are you two doing up this time of night?"

"What do you think?" said Gladys. "We're coming for the prodigal brother, and—" she took a gander at me, "—and the prodigal's fiancée! Hello, Ruth. I'm Gladys."

"Pleased to meet you."

Gladys was the prettiest of them all. Long curly hair. Wide shoulders and a slender waist. Her eyes were animated even in this darkness.

"I'll bet you're very tired," Erma said. "Pile in. Let's get you to a nice warm bed."

"Who sits on Steve's lap? Me, or Ruth?"

"You can ride in the back, big boy," Erma said. "In you go, Ruth. You can sit between Gladys and me. We won't bite."

"Didn't you bring any luggage?"

"On the platform."

"Here we go."

Steve leaped out to grab the valises as Erma pulled up to the depot. He tossed them in among the bales of straw, settled himself against the cab, and rapped on the window. Erma eased into gear and let out the clutch. I expected her to blaze out of the lot in the same fashion as her father, but she was decisive and deliberate.

"I've never rode in a car with a woman driver," I said.

"Didn't anyone ever teach you to drive?"

"We never had a car."

Steve's sisters considered this.

"It's probably a necessity of farming," Gladys offered. "Girls learn to drive tractors just like the boys around here. And somebody's got to run errands into town, isn't that right? Most of our mothers don't drive but girls our age do. Mostly."

"Connie's never quite gotten the knack of it," Erma said, and they both giggled.

Erma slowed to turn toward Ora and the Porter farm. The blinker sounded urgent in this early dark hour. "Ruth," she said. "Do you mind—I mean, for our parents' sake, we've arranged to have you stay at Gene's folks' place. They're awfully nice people. It's a lovely room, upstairs and quiet. You can sleep late if you like and get all refreshed and ready for the festivities."

"That's fine," I said. "I don't want to trouble anyone. Not your parents or nobody else."

Neither one of them answered until we pulled up to the house. As the truck came to a stop Gladys said, "It's all going to be all right, you know. We just have to get through tomorrow. Or today—whatever it is this time of night."

I glanced toward the darkened house. The porch light shone harsh in the velvet air. Steve jumped out. He came around to Gladys's door and opened it.

"Where's everyone sleeping?"

"I'm sleeping here," said Gladys. "And you are, too."

"Glade come with you?"

"No, he's haying."

Steve looked dubious about that but he said, "Can Ruth sleep with you, then?"

"She's coming with me," Erma said. "Gene's folks have a nice room all ready."

Steve flexed his jaw. He looked about to argue or go in and

confront his parents, but instead he said, "Well, that sure is nice of everyone to have it all arranged like that. Ruth, I'll come find you in the morning."

"No you won't," Erma said. "I'll take care of her. Groom can't see the bride until the wedding. It's bad luck."

"Oh, for hell's sake, Erma. Ruth and I have seen pretty much every inch of each other before the wedding. Everybody knows this is a shotgun affair. Now all of a sudden you're a bunch of busybodies."

I know I blushed, but it was dark. Gladys and Erma made a little disapproving gasp together. I didn't have the least idea what to say so I kept quiet, but Erma said, "Steven, Ruth is about to become your wife. She's going to be the mother of your children. Show some respect for her wedding day."

Steve made an odd sound at the back of his throat.

"You're right. I'm sorry. Goodnight, Ruth. I love you, honey. I'll see you tomorrow at the courthouse. You'll be the prettiest girl in town."

He turned and walked under the leafy silhouette of the gateway trellis. Gladys followed him into the house and the door closed. Although we strained to emanate camaraderie, Erma drove back to the Hess place in silence. She walked me into the house and settled me in the room. It was clean and quiet. I locked the door and sank in under the quilts but it took a long time to fall asleep.

I awoke to a light knocking and the sisters' voices, saying my name.

I opened the door and they came in like water.

"What time is it?"

"Nearly noon."

They stood back to assess. I imagine I didn't look too attractive.

"Let's get you dolled up," one of them said and they went to work.

I knew that a family lived here but either they were very quiet or they had gone out. The house seemed empty but for small clanks and quiet steps wherever the kitchen was. Erma escorted me to the bath, drew warm water, handed me clean towels. I would have enjoyed the luxury but everything was awkward. My skin tingled with anxiety. I felt like a rank intruder.

I came out of the water and made a long consideration of my stomach, swelling but not so much as to transform me. I had been grateful to feel no real sickness, which had probably helped me forget for hours at a time that I was pregnant. Now I thought about the tiny human inside of me. I pictured a white larva, a featureless wasp, which is silly to me now so many years beyond. Ronnie was bright and sensitive, no sting in him at all.

I raised both my palms to eye level. The children lines suggested many offspring. Six or maybe seven. I could hardly picture that. But only two were distinct. Flames shot through my line of sight. Behind them a dark wall. Beyond that—something else. I forced a wave of hard refusal backward through my skull. *Best not to try to read your own destiny*, the woman in Bill had told me, conveyed through the closeness of our minds. *Your gift is for others.*

Not that they'll appreciate it, I came to understand. Everyone wants a telling. But nobody hardly ever is willing to accept what's told. We spend our lives arguing with our own tales. Doesn't matter if we're reading them forward or back.

Stella Jeppson Porter

Now I recognize the little girl. I believe it's Gladys. She looks strange to me but it's hot in this car and my mind is unsettled. How could I not recognize my own daughter?

"Your hair's gone straight in this heat."

She looks at me, quizzical.

"I almost didn't recognize you," I prompt and she says, peevish, "It's all right."

"Your father couldn't bring himself to come. He'll compose himself for the get-together."

The child bites her lip.

"Fred has to consider his standing in the bishopric. How can he counsel other people about their children when his own are disobedient?"

Gladys here seems too young for this kind of talk. I nudge the parts toward congruence.

"Are you ready to go in?"

I had intended to see my last child sealed in the temple to a faithful wife. But here he is with that Gypsy. "I don't understand. I had a dream. It wasn't supposed to turn out this way."

The dream returns when I call it to mind, bright and identical. I have come home to Cache Valley to see my mother. I stand at the fold where the valley floor bends abruptly into mountainside. I can't tell whether it's winter or summer. The landscape is blue and white like December yet the grain rises up from the snow, a warm butter hue. I admire a herd of elk, regal and enclosed in their animal perceptions. A Shoshone encampment curls thin smoke in the distance but they neither frighten nor take notice of me.

I am home to my mother, and I am child again yet wife and mother and because I am a child, my father may be here. Immediately it is so. He's been here all along, just above me on the slope, looking in the same direction and directing my thoughts. He is tall and bearded just as I recall him. He has been guiding me and he says, "Look!"

I don't need to turn my head to see where he points. My sight follows his south through peak and pass toward Devil's Gate. The route is obscured but I know it well. I follow my father's spiritual sight. Together we watch a young man stride the mountain pathway. Swift and sure he comes our way, gaining distance like a traveling angel. He revels in the gliding motion of this journey.

At the high mouth of our valley he stops, sensing my beloved papa and me dead and living, vital and decaying, here and already gone. The young man smiles, luminous, and hails us with a call and waving arm.

My father cries out, "Forty-one. Too soon! I was only forty-one!"

Instantly the young man is with us, transported across the valley at celestial speed.

I explain. "It was appendicitis. No one understood until it was too late. The doctor went home to sleep. This man is my father."

My father says, "This man is your son."

"But I already have a son."

"Surely that's not all."

I awaken. I awaken my husband. Fred sits up abrupt and very surprised.

He answers, believing.

He comes.

Steven Porter

We stood in the foyer. Just Ruth and me. Ruth in her blue dress. My sisters had done her hair up pretty but it made her unlike herself. Besides, she looked tired and a little haggard which made me feel guilty for putting a child in her. Women live completely different lives from men. Coupling brings us together and then holds us forever apart.

Old Mrs. Hertig tap-tap-tapped on her typewriter, pretending that the room wasn't a pressure chamber. The telephone rang. Mrs. Hertig picked it up, chipper. "City hall."

The voice on the other end said something to make the old

lady glance in our direction, then quickly take up a pencil, feigning insignificance.

"Well, alrighty . . . of course. I understand. I'll tell Judge Harrigfeld. No, he's got nothing to press him. He'll be here . . . Okay, we'll be watching for you." She carefully put down the earpiece. Mrs. Hertig composed herself, enjoyed a smug moment, and then spoke to us.

"Steve, honey, that was Erma. She says they're on their way. Leaving the house in just a few minutes. Seems there's been a delay."

I took Ruth's hand and led her to the foyer bench. I knew the old biddy was pleased. I knew that everyone in the whole town was picturing, one angle or another, Steven Porter and some Pocatello chippy out in the long summer grass, sowing wild seed. Taking what solely belongs to the grim-lipped Puritans in their restricted rooms.

We listened to the ticking regulator on the wall. Mrs. Hertig went tap, tap, tap. Tap.

We heard tires on gravel. I left Ruth on the bench and stepped out to see Erma and Gladys. In Eugene's truck. They got out lipless and picked their way toward me in their fancy shoes. Neither acknowledged me until they were up the steps. Gladys pushed stray hair back into her hat. Erma dropped her bottom lip and glared at me as if to quell my question before I could ask it, and then she answered it anyway.

"Daddy and Mother aren't coming."

Several cars went by before I said, "What's that again?"

"Steve, let's just get this done and make the best of it."

"My own parents won't come to my wedding?"

"Steve, please. You know it's too much for them."

"What's this about respect for my wife on her wedding day?"

Gladys said, "Well, that's why we're here. I know it's dismal but we came, didn't we?"

We all stood wooden, restraining our sharp Porter tongues. I held my breath while I walked out to the asphalt shoulder. I stared out toward the Tetons, struggling to control my mind. I forced back the burning edges. I knew Ruth was sitting pale and still on the foyer bench. My sisters hovered on the porch. Eventually Erma pushed herself in through the doorway to greet her impending sister-in-law.

I walked back toward the building. My head was filled with helium.

Gladys said, "Oh. My goodness! Look!"

The Buick, coming our way. Everyone on Main Street turned to watch its grinding progress, painfully slow, overpowered in second gear.

If we all wanted to avoid a public spectacle, this was no dice.

"Is that Mother?"

"Mmm-hmm, I believe so."

Our mother cranked the wheel to her left, crossing the lane and mostly navigating the driveway. The front wheel caught the curb but she sustained speed enough to clear it, crushing a lovely patch of city hall marigolds. The Roadmaster kept right on coming at us and then killed all of a sudden, rocking on its chassis. Mother wasn't exactly in a parking stall, but she was definitely in the lot.

We stood dumbfounded.

Erma pushed open the door. Ruth and Mrs. Hertig peered over her shoulders. Citizens leered from the sidewalks and storefronts. None of us said a word as Mother, still inside the car, adjusted her hat and gloves. She checked her hair in the rearview mirror and shot the city hall an apprehensive glare.

"Go, Steve," Erma said, and I snapped out of the community trance. I loped down to open the door, bent downward and craned my neck to face her as I offered my arm.

"Mother! What in the world are you doing?"

She took my arm and stepped out, doggedly sedate.

"What do you think? I'm attending my son's wedding."

I walked her up the stairs, meeting my sisters' rounded eyes with my own and then Ruth's tight-jawed wonderment. Mrs. Hertig exclaimed over Mother, and now all of us as if we were showing up for a jovial church dinner. She hurried down the hallway to find old Harrigfeld. He came out in his white shirt and tie, pushing his arms through his suit coat, caressing it downward with his palms as if it were going to lengthen.

"Fred on his way?" the JP asked, and when nobody answered he swallowed a couple of times, throat protruding. "Well, alrighty then, should we get this affair ironed out?"

Harrigfeld took stock of my mother and sisters, then turned to examine me as if I were a used car. I'm sure we were both recalling an earlier appearance I'd made back when I was fifteen, a swimming-while-truant incident. I may have been inebriated. Possibly buck naked. Back then I mean. But Harrigfeld judged me now as salvageable I suppose, because he said, "Steve? You ready? How about you introduce me to the little lady here?"

Ruth blushed. She held her hand out, limp. I said, "This is Miss Ruth Loveday, my fiancée. About to be my wife."

Harrigfeld gave her a quick distasteful appraisal.

"Who's doing the witnessing today?"

Gladys stepped forward. "I am."

Mrs. Hertig said, "Well, we need two witnesses as per the law of the State of Idaho."

I looked toward Erma but it was my mother who said, "And so am I."

The man made short work of us and we were married. Gladys signed her name all pretty on the certificate. Mother's hand shook as she took the pen, but she wrote out her whole name in oldtime Spencerian hand: Stella Marie Jeppson Porter. She gained resolve as she went, finishing with a flourish and a haughty frown for

Harrigfeld. Once he'd finished the dirty work the man got jovial and confidential, sending us out the door with, "You understand of course, real marriage is only in the eyes of the Lord under heavenly authority. Not these mere legal pretensions. I look forward to seeing the two of you in the temple in a year or so. Miss Ruth, I'll be the first to congratulate you."

"Mrs.," said my wife. "Mrs. Steven J. Porter, if you please."

I took her hand. Erma seated herself in the truck and Gladys put herself behind the wheel of the Buick. I set Mother in on the other side. Ruth and I stepped into our borrowed coupe and we all drove home in caravan.

My noble father, probably exhausted by sole care of Mae for the last two hours, opened the front door for her the minute we pulled in. She tumbled out with her usual sideways gait. "Stevie Weevie! Steeeevie!"

But she stopped at the trellis when she saw Ruth. Mae threw her arms high, waving them like seaweed. "Here comes the bride! Here comes the bride! The bride is here! Did you get married Stevie? Is Ruth your wife now?"

"Yes, of course she is! Say hello to your new sister-in-law," I suggested extra loud so my father would hear. I looked toward the house. The doorway was open but empty. My father had fled to the barn.

Ruth Loveday Porter

"When I'm in the same room as your father I feel this powerful sensation of choking," I told Steve. I don't know the first time I said it. Maybe after the baby came.

"No joke? So do I."

"No, I don't mean it that way. I'm talking about something that's actually in him. Something conveying itself."

"You know, we took a Boy Scout trip up to Table Rock when

I was nine or ten. He and my uncle Arthur wore white shirts and ties. Only thing different from Sunday was they carried boots in the car. Changed into them for the hike. Back into the polished church ones when we got back down. My dad can't go beyond the farm without the gentleman costume."

"Maybe that's some of it. But I think there's more."

"I'm certain there's more. I just don't want to know what it is."

Fred Porter

Once when they brought the boys up to visit, Steve's wife told me she felt a choking sensation in me. I replied, "Ruth, I make no purchase in magic. I want to respect you for what you believe but I'm going to have to ask you to keep me apart from it. I don't solicit opinions from others about what I feel."

She blinked her ewe-ish eyes at me. I turned away to sort tackle on the kitchen table. "Come over here, boys," I called to Ronnie and Richard and they hovered in, pointing toward their favorite lures, examining unfamiliar flies. They were appealing boys, polite and wide-eyed as if they entered a wonderland every time they came to the farm. Ronnie came to us under sinful circumstance but there was no arguing he was a good thing that came of all that.

I felt his mother's eyes at my back, burning between my shoulder blades. I fought the urge to reach for my collar but could not stop myself. I checked the button and resisted a small convulsion at the base of my throat.

I glanced toward Richie, freckled and disheveled. He was missing his two top teeth. My mother would have pointed out his resemblance to me at the same age.

Their father—my son Steven—was in the upstairs room. I heard him stirring on occasion but he had not come down since their arrival last night. I could tell things weren't right with him, which was probably the real reason they had come here. But

I lacked the courage or even simple vitality to climb the steep stairway to admonish him.

Mae was in the bedroom with her mother, not asleep but lately in a strange new condition of torpor. Agitated when left alone, blank and disengaged among people who cared for her, Mae—or I should say, Mae's condition—was depleting us. If not for the presence of the boys I suspect we would have fallen into a collective trance and never awakened.

I surprised myself and startled the boys in a sudden compulsion to speak.

"Richie, did I ever tell you about the time I nearly hanged myself in the fork of a tree when I was a boy? I was just about your size when it happened."

Both boys leaned in.

"No, Grandpa. Was it the tree out there in the backyard?"

"Was it down by the river?"

"No. When I was Richie's age my family lived in New Zealand, on the other side of the world. It was a beautiful place but we were very poor. My father was away for weeks at a time working at jobs that paid barely enough to feed a family of mice. The house we lived in was so decrepit our mother thought it might blow away with each new storm, and boy could that wind rattle the place. The floor was made of flat stones from the river. We brought a few more of them home to her every time we went out to play."

I knew the boys were picturing Henry's Fork but I was myself drawn back through the mouth of time. The river of my childhood was shallow and warm. It ran green and yellow like a wet road paved through the forest. Trees grew thick and the ground was furred with tendrilled moss. Arthur and I and eventually our younger brother Tom spent entire days playing at the water, something to while away the hours while we waited out hunger. I felt sorry for the girls, who were kept closer to home. I don't know what they did all day but we played cannibals. We played

Excalibur and Napoleon and we beat back the bushmen. Even in New Zealand, we played cowboys and Indians. We climbed trees and swung from hanging vines.

One afternoon during a game of hide-and-seek, I climbed a slender red beech. I could see a nice little seat of branches up there, covered by foliage from almost every angle. I shimmied up the trunk until I could grab the lowest branches. Then I pulled myself higher, foot by foot toward my intended perch. I reached up and gripped each side of a forking branch, then bent my right leg high to anchor myself on a thin shoot. I pulled up with my arms and pushed down with my foot. The supple tree bent toward my weight.

I clung like a monkey, but my head had just cleared the fork when my foot slipped. Next thing I knew I was hanging there, caught helpless by my jaws and chin more than a man's height above the forest floor. I could not call for help. My legs were heavy and limp, my arms soft rubber. My eyes looked up through the leafy forest roof and into cloudless sky. Maybe I struggled, but soon I fell into a complacent trance well to the other side of fear. Numb anticipation. My mind was clear enough to hope it would not be my mother who found me, hanging dead from this natural gallows like the little criminal I was. I partly wished it would be my father, coming home from this week's precarious and unpromising job. I took some pleasure in the image of him falling to his knees, gnashing his teeth in repentance for his perpetual absence, his pittance of a wage, his stupidity for leaving the grand castle in England where my brothers and I were convinced we could have become knights with long swords and fair ladies.

I don't know how long I dangled there. I must have blacked out because I cannot recall the sound of my brother Arthur's voice, nor of the bigger boys who came running, probably for the spectacle most of all. But Arthur said Jack Larson was up in the tree quick as an adder. Afraid it would break and drop us both,

Jack stood upright on the branch, carefully bending the supple limb with his inching weight. He eased outward to push the fork and its prisoner toward the ground, until Sam and Kilgore could grasp the lower branches and hold it low enough for Arthur to wrap his arms around my hips. We fell together to the green stony floor. Arthur took a hard scrape to the elbow, which he held against me for weeks after we had all made an outlaws' oath to keep quiet.

But our mother shook it out of us the minute we arrived home. Arthur's arm was covered with blood. My neck and jaws were already swollen and blue. Mother was so frightened she took a switch to us both and Tom for good measure. Father didn't come home for three more days. In the nights between we heard her, long after she thought we were sleeping, sobbing quietly in the kitchen. I woke every night for a fortnight gasping for breath against my swollen throat.

At the kitchen table in Ora, sorting tackle, Ronnie and Richard had locked their dark eyes upon me. Their mouths hung open. Little fish in a bowl. I came back to myself. I told the boys to go out and call the dog and I'd be there in a jiffy. Out they went and I sat for another moment to collect myself. I felt the old tingling burn like a rash around the skin of my neck. I brought my hand to my throat, and then I remembered Ruth and turned to face her.

The woman had been perching there the whole time, unmoving and silent. Her eyes were oddly dilated in the bright windowlight. She still said nothing. Nor did I. I swept hooks and floats and sinkers into the tackle box and fled outdoors.

Unnerved, I walked toward the river with my grandsons, clearing my head as we progressed. The new Ralphie yapped at the kids, herding them along like baby goats. The sun was vivid and warm. Green hay and blue water perfumed the air. I thought of my brother Arthur and me playing along the banks of a river halfway around the globe.

I thought about the endlessness of guilt and hunger.

I dwelt upon my youngest son languishing in the gabled room of his boyhood, obscured in a twilight I could not plumb. I considered my daughter Mae, spared for us in shards, a perpetual child waning.

I walked behind two boys already too much acquainted with sorrow. And yet, I thought, who wasn't? Fairy tales consist of the awful things children know and fear. Right now, however, they frolicked along, exploding with little shouts and melodic retorts. I wondered whether any of this—a fertile field, a glittering path, an afternoon on the lapping banks of a blue river—were enough. I asked myself whether all that was lost was too great a cost for what was had.

I saw the future, at least a slender glimpse. These boys rising and falling, ashes to ashes. Another generation beyond, quick joys amidst long sorrow. I lived my life in faith that the valiant children of the Latter Days would survive the moon's transit in blood, the reign of Lucifer upon the land, and that they would rise triumphant to live on this very earth cleansed in the full knowledge of heaven. No more mysteries. All questions fulfilled. But on that afternoon I could not convince myself of this end. It all seemed forever only this rising and falling, perpetually askew. For a hideous moment I entered the mind of my son, hovering like a prisoner in the upstairs room.

We reached the river. The breeze blew toward us from the water's surface, saturated in the scent of what moved beneath. I had no knowledge of how deep it was, or what was in it beyond what rose to our lures. A sudden image of my tragic aunt in New Zealand surfaced in my mind. Her children stayed with us for months at a time as insanity consumed her in increments. In the end it took real effort, I imagine, to drown herself in the community watering trough. She must have sat on the edge and let herself fall backward. When we found her, Arthur and me and our cousin Clement in a wild pack of running boys, we could make no sense of what we saw. The trough stood high as my eye level. The tall spigot ran and water overflowed. A woman's stockinged knees were hooked over the rim, the legs below them flailing as if kicking of their own accord.

We drew nearer, five or six of us. We stepped up to peer into the tub. The body rose and sank in a bobbing rhythm, face obscured by the bubbling force of the spigot's stream. But we knew who she was and what she'd done. We leaped back wailing and fled. Clement kept on running, deep into the forest. No one found him until morning and even then he fought rescue.

To me the worst of my aunt's death was her discovery by a pack of curious boys. The final mortification of public retrieval. The whole town heard within minutes and gathered to watch as the men hoisted Martha's body out of the water and carted it to the coroner's. Dropping into Henry's Fork struck me as a far more private proposition, and I was so engrossed in the comparison I actually leaned over the ledge as if to prove it.

"Grandpa," Ronnie said, and I straightened and came back to the moment. I ruffled his hair with my fingers. I filled my lungs with air as I should and showed him again how to tie a fishing knot. Richie ran after grasshoppers, filling a paper bag with the jumping creatures. We laughed when he opened the neck; locusts burst out like popcorn.

My mind fell calm.

We caught several trout and even an errant sturgeon, heavy on the rod and too fierce for an old man and his grandsons. I cut the monster loose the moment I saw its fearsome form break the surface.

I showed the boys how to gut the trout. We made a little fire and cooked three of them right there on the bank. When we returned, Ruth and Steve stood together on the porch waiting to greet us. In the peculiar light they looked older than Stella and me, and more weary.

Steven Porter

Ruth got fat pretty quick after she gave birth to Richie. It didn't affect my attractions either way. She was beautiful in her easy sensuality, which was most likely the simplest reason my kind were afraid of her. She lived in her own body as a natural fact; she stirred me when she was a girl and equally so as an ample woman, so long as I wasn't lost in mental affliction. But it did seem as though she were living in passing time while I remained youthful, almost as if there were some temporal boundary I was forbidden to cross.

Each succeeding spell of melancholia slammed us like a wrecking ball. It got so I could sense it coming a few days ahead of full impact, and for me the anticipation became more awful than the pit itself. Once infused I felt almost nothing at all, and this was relief after the clawing tumble into an abyss so deep I lost myself but for the smallest stirrings. It was quiet there. Sounds from the world above were muted, distorted as if I were bobbing along the bottom of Henry's Fork. Light reached my perceptions only in undulations and broken rays. It was cold I suppose, but like a fish I felt no contrast between my own body and the deep still current. Small communications presented themselves, tantalizing in their promise of new coherence. But I had no will to answer.

Is it so now, beyond the day I forfeited my capacity to return? Do I reside beyond the pistol in the peace of nullification? I will not reveal this mystery to you. I did not ask you to summon me.

But came a time, the only clear thing to live for was the next rail run. Always before embarking, the night of anticipation when the hours drew in quiet, I could not stay asleep but had no reason yet to get up. I would lie in bed with Ruth, a woman who knew how to sleep—her breathing steady, her body evacuated.

Who knows where her soul went at night? Once she settled there was no moving her; I contoured myself to the available space. Sometimes I could hear the boys upstairs, shifting and snoring, uttering conversations within their own night worlds.

I loved my sons but they frightened me. I feared unnatural chemistries assembling in them. I never met Ruth's mother but I sensed a disturbing affinity. I reacted too forcefully when I saw portents in Richard or Ronnie. I would not allow them to sit. If I caught one of them gazing out the window or too deeply engrossed in a radio episode—or merely lying on the summer grass in reverie—I shook him into action. I doled out useless tasks, ordering them to mow the ragged lawn or run to the corner market for butter.

Ruth said, "Steve, leave them be. They've done their chores," but I couldn't abide my fear for them. I'd take out the fireman's manual and set them to calculations. I'd copy poems my sister Connie taught me and make them put the lines to memory:

> . . . And my father sold me while yet my tongue
> Could scarcely cry "weep!" "weep!" "weep!" "weep!"
> So your chimneys I sweep and in soot I sleep.

It got so my sons would slip out of the house every time they saw me coming. They'd beeline for the corners where the delinquents gathered for marbles or cards, coughing attempts at cigarettes. I didn't mind their mischief. I only feared their languor. I'd guess the three of them—Ruth and the boys at once—breathed a sigh of relief every time they sent me off again.

It's not that I didn't love or long for them. It's not even that I loved the train so much, but the boiler consumed my body and mind completely. No leeway for strange thoughts. Adrenaline conserved, sustained, and spent in the delirious miles between Granger and Portland kept my nerves aligned, my heart pounding sublime.

But the return and sudden stillness were unbearable. I'd ride the passenger line back in from Granger enjoying that long curve from Kemmerer to Montpelier, summer or winter. It always fooled me into a certain pleasant anticipation. Looking back toward Bear Lake, ultramarine, infused me with a distinctive joy I believed would follow me home. The rails followed the southern crease of the high valley through hills that looked almost Mediterranean. Soda Springs with its curious junipers made me think of Ruth, because she experienced a miracle there. It was a sweet thing to envision it. The ride wasn't long after that. A cliffy descent into the Portneuf valley, a hard swing north, quick stop in the narrow neck of Inkom and then the multiplying tracks as the Pocatello yards opened wide.

It was only after I'd slung my duffel bag over my shoulder, euphoric with exhaustion, that time ground to its regular pace. The fatigue hit as if I'd just then encountered the truth of gravity. Dead weight forced my shoulders down. My arms ached and my ears rang and I would walk home spent. Sometimes I could rally to greet my boys, kiss their mother, and sit down for dinner. Sometimes I could sleep and recuperate and go out with a ball and bat to hit a few with the kids. But the exhaustion was not a thing to simply sleep away. The truth of it was that old fight, a slipping grasp on the endeavor of living.

I began to postpone my returns to the house. I'd come off shift and go straight to the bar. Spoke to no one, not even my pals in the yard or tavern. They learned to leave me alone. One night I came home late and drunk. I opened the door, took one step into the kitchen, said something surly and cruel to Ruth right there in front of my sons and dropped like a shot mule. My mind plain lost its will to hold my body up.

Ruth said, "Ronnie. Go get Mr. Sanchez," and both boys bolted.

* * *

Next thing I knew I was flat on my back in my bed. Ronnie and Richard sat solemn on either side of me, legs crossed, shoeless feet. Sabine Sanchez stood opposite Ruth, one at each of my shoulders. When they saw I had opened my eyes they leaned down together to read my expression. I swatted, weak. I meant to sit up but it was as if I was restrained, so I lay prone as Sabine's husband Ignacio entered the room. I knew him, a good neighbor. He and his wife were protective of Ruth in my absences. Ruth had always insisted that Sabine's mystical powers went beyond her own but neither had mentioned to me that Ignacio was a sort of magical priest.

"*Sorgin*," Ruth said now.

"*Sorginak*," Sabine replied. She put her hand on my chest, leaned in close to speak very quietly as if she didn't want the boys to hear. "Brother. Steven. My husband and I are here to help you. Do you wish to be helped?"

I disliked the sensation of her hand on me. I struggled beneath it, or thought I did but I was held fast, and suddenly I relaxed as if I had been shot with morphine. Heat emanated from her flat palm to the far reaches of my nervous system. My toes and fingers kneaded the sheets. The tight muscles in my neck went soft and I felt the knots in my back and shoulders dissolve.

"Help me?" I asked, but what I meant was, *What do you mean by this?*

She took it as assent. She signaled Ignacio, who walked first to the foot of the bed where Ronnie and Richard sat mesmerized.

"Good boys," said Ignacio Sanchez. He placed his large hands on the backs of their necks, gentle, caressing upward into their hair. They rounded their eyes in surprise, turning toward me. I felt a reach of love and power. My sons relaxed in unison. Ruth and Sabine each picked a boy, tender, and carried him out to bed.

The women returned wearing veils. They seated themselves on stools on each side of me. Ignacio stood at the foot of the bed.

"You must understand, Steven, we are not real *sorginak*."

Ruth and Sabine said together: "We are not. We are indeed."

"The ancient ways are lost to us. Like all mortals we contain our past in fragments. The old magic is powerful only as it weaves and binds with other strains. My power can carry you over the brambles, under the clouds but only into your own mind and its own ways."

"What the hell are you talking about?"

"Do not speak of hell in this room on this night," Sabine commanded, gentle but unanswerable. My lips clamped themselves together.

"Hell may come, or shades of it, without your invitation," Ignacio said. "You must not give it strong welcome."

Ruth said, "Every word we speak from this moment forth until morning will bind itself to the immortal dimension, and in one way or another become real. Every word is a spell. Speak with care."

I opened then shut my mouth. All I could do was lie on my back and stare up at faces that hovered like nurses. Or inquisitors.

"Are we ready?"

"We are not. We are indeed."

Ignacio's voice sounded like several: "Steven J. Porter, by the power of the ancient *sorginak*; by the force that empowered Laveau; through the sorrows of the cross and its many martyrs; through the sacred imagery of the Blackfoot; by the lineage of your father's Melchizedek priesthood and the heartfelt mysteries of your mother's dreams, we anoint and bless you."

The scent of clean grass and citrus, rain-wet stone and bleached sand. I inhaled deeply, twice and again and my heart slowed, every stroke efficient. The figures above me lost definition. I could hear their voices but their forms were osmotic. Ignacio put his hand on my forehead and I was comforted. Formless but for the insistence of my own pulse.

* * *

I stood up.

I knew I was in a hideous place.

Stone walls, sweat, human sounds I did not wish to interpret.

I turned to Ignacio, who stood with me. "I can't do this. I know where I am but I have never been here."

"You know enough. This is a stage for your own meditation. The gaps will fill themselves."

"What the hell am I supposed to meditate upon?"

"Do not summon more evil than this room already contains!"

I felt a constriction. I reached for my throat. "I'm sorry. Help me. I do not know my part."

"You have created this place. Attune your senses. What do you see?"

"A woman. Prone."

I groped for likeness. "In my position."

"Then begin with her. Speak to bring her forward."

I stared down at the bed. No, not a bed. I did not want to perceive.

For the moment she lay relaxed. No. Unconscious. I was loath to rouse her.

"It is a story, Steven," Ignacio said. "She is not here, and yet she is indeed."

I spoke against my will, and more roughly than I intended. "Who are you? What will you tell me?"

The woman awoke. She was small and fierce, with the pinched features of a lifetime fanatic. She was undressed to the final layer. Sweat and contortion revealed her, grotesque. Arms and legs splayed. I tried to prevent my eyes from following her limbs to the truth of her position, and now I am ashamed to admit I was grateful she was tightly bound. Somehow I knew that her release would obliterate my every memory, all recognition. Often I wished to go forward to dissolution, but never to have been made at all? I don't know why that was different, but it was and I felt something savage rise up in me. I wanted to tear the woman apart.

"My God! Who are you?!"

She answered, helpless, wrenched, unrelenting. "You know me, Porter. I am Askew!"

A man's voice, behind but also in me, intersecting. Giddy. "Only woman ever tortured in the tower. Once you're standing in my position you can see why. It's not so hard to understand now, is it?"

I turned away from Askew. But I could not step away, as if I was restrained in a transparent column.

"Release yourself," Ignacio said.

The column shattered and I stood free to move about. I leaped away from a pig-eyed gloating man at my face. The smell of him was overwhelming. It wasn't just the stench of his heavy clothing or the unwashed folds of skin beneath. It was the palpable scent of a man in high stimulation.

"Speak to him."

"Who are you, then?"

"You know me, you fool."

"I do not know you! I have no commerce with you!"

"Surely we have something in common? Did not my house infuse your own?"

He touched his hand to his throat. "I am Rich, of course."

"We did not come from you. We were servants. Peasants put to use by you and your kind."

"Did you not open the door? Was it not your grandfathers who stood so elegant there, welcoming the architects of mayhem?"

"What does that have to do with me and my life? I was a dirt-poor kid from a place you never heard of, you sick bastard. I was never rich like you."

And yet together the man and I turned to gaze upon the

woman on the rack. She looked to open her eyes again and speak to us. I averted my eyes. Anything to keep her still.

"All that hard work!" Rich said. "Such fine upstanding people. Your folks were sober and obedient. Answered as they should to the right authority, at least in my time. Produced their share of reprobates over the generations but they learned how to salvage their name and status. Wore the colors, deepened their voices, took my house by staying put and marrying up. Rose from costumed monkeys to country squires. A fine family project, wrought upon the legacy of Henry's most loyal henchman. Why do you think your folks survived to tell the tale, out there in—what do you call it? Oh yes. Buttfuck Egypt."

He smiled, paternal. "I am not from your time but I do grasp your meaning."

He reached to pat my head. I spun away but he stepped right over to follow, narrating the scene at my ear. His dead breath blew my hair as he spoke.

"See this woman? She looks helpless as a kitten but why do you think she requires such brutal restraint? She threatens the right order of things, so carefully maintained by a king put here by God himself to reign. A hag of her kind can dip her fingers in the waters of power and siphon it to drought. She floods the wrong fields. She saturates desert sand."

The monster wrapped around me from behind. A subtle thrust. He rested his chin on my shoulder. He took a long lick across my jawline, put his tongue in my ear. I shuddered but had no strength to extricate myself from his embrace. I said to him, in my mind without having to open my mouth and enunciate, *The earth blooms where it's watered.*

"It verily does, young man. And for that reason we must control the channels."

There's no reason one field should yield harvest, any more than another.

"We say alike."

I could not see my guide but I hoped he was still in the room. "Ignacio, may I please speak with someone else?"

Rich took it upon himself to answer. "Speak to whom you wish. But I have one more thing to impart. You are a man, and a lucky man at that. A kingdom has been cleared for you—so various, so beautiful, and still in your American dreams so new. Do not hesitate to claim what has been so grandly bestowed. The fun is in the taking. Do you covet the rack? Do you have a woman's heart? How does this become the golden son of opportunists?"

I summoned my father's teaching, and raised my right arm to the square. "Get thee behind me, Rich," I commanded, and stepped out of the awful room, right through the thick stone walls. I strode through wet grass toward a red tower. I copped a low hill to see a green pond dotted with white swans. A small boy stood at the bank, hoping I guess to catch a glimpse of the swimming fish.

"Arthur!" I called, sharp the same way I called to my boys when they leaned too far over the Portneuf riverbank. "Step back! You're about to fall!"

Sure enough, in he went. I trotted over, waded in, and yanked him out.

"Get on home to your mama," I said. "And buck up and take care of your children."

Arthur squinted up at me, a runty kid, water-eyed and devoid of common sense. But he answered me in a grown man's voice—my grandfather's, to be exact.

"Lord, keep me poor, that I may keep the faith."

I'd heard that one, too many times, and so I dove into the pond myself. I came up from a wide river but it sure wasn't Henry's Fork. It appeared I was in a jungle. No longer a body, only an accompanying presence, I ran with a crowd of ragged boys through the trees, hopping along river stones and emerging among fences and cultivated fields. Something moved rhythmic and unnatural at the trough. I regained my height and stature as we approached. I arrived tall enough to look down into the water. A woman's form, caught at the rim by the knees. The body bobbed up and down at the head, always about to surface but plunging back under with the pulsing force of the well stream. The motion was graceful, hypnotic.

Suddenly she opened her eyes and spoke from drowned lungs, bubbling but distinct.

"Steven Porter! Look to the many women who love and guard you!"

I did not stay to see her retrieved. Instead I crossed the sea on a steamship, rode the train from San Francisco, stepped out in Salt Lake City and took a rambling scenic walk. Wasatch peaks rose sharp against the yellow sky. Deep canyons beckoned but I turned at the sound of frantic tapping from inside a closed window. A white car.

I didn't recognize the make. I looked it over. Dodge Dart.

I leaned down in the blazing summer heat to see my mother behind the glass, beseeching. "Take me home," she pleaded. "This bad child won't let me out. Take me back to Idaho."

"Well, come on, then. We have to walk fast. Are you strong enough?" I opened the door for her. I took her hand. "Who's the kid?"

"I have no idea. An insolent little girl. Connie will come for her."

We glided north, heading home.

"Take your opportunity," Ignacio prompted. "Converse with her."

But my mother was already speaking. "Devil's Gate," she said, pointing along the rising hills. "This is the way you came."

"All right then. Let's go that way."

The day softened. The heat dropped as the altitude rose. We passed Shoshone encampments, oblivious to us and busy in their ways. We walked right through a trappers' rendezvous. We threaded our way among hungry Mormons and nudged long-horned cattle aside. We emerged upon Cache Valley, green and gold, veined with blue streams. My mother said, "I dreamed you here. Tell me the reason for it."

"Mother. The mystery of a human heart is not a thing to be revealed."

My mother blinked in the sunlight, tears held back. She drew herself up and asked me hard and cold, "Did that wife of yours tell you that?"

"It doesn't matter, Mother. You know it's the truth."

We stood on the fossil shoreline, steep mountain slopes rising behind us.

"My father should arrive," she said.

Woman, Jesus is long since dead.

"What in the world do you mean by that?"

I had no reply. "But here's the train," I said. "I know the conductor."

Ignacio stepped out to us. He held out his hand to my mother and gestured grandly.

The Pullman held only us—my mother and Ignacio, and me. It felt as if the train stood still while the scenery moved by at its own strange pace—sometimes very slowly, sometimes so rushed it was as if we were falling through space. Planets rushed by but when the train slowed it was pulling into the regular old Ashton station. Mother adjusted her hat and gloves. She took my hand and we stepped off.

Mae was there to greet us.

"Want to go straight home?" she inquired. "You've been gone a long while. Do you want me to show you all the changes?"

She spun the key ring like an outlaw's pistol. Incomprehensibly she wore trousers and a man's shirt. She reached toward her neck to loosen a soft silk tie. Mother seemed uninclined to answer, and since we were in my story I said, "No. Let's go home. I want to go fishing."

Mae drove us home clean and smart. I stepped out of the polished Buick. My father, neat and formal, opened the front door to hand me my rod and tackle. As I passed through he said, "Son, remember who you are and what you stand for," and I walked right on out the back door, strode through the barnyard, eased myself between the taut lines of barbed wire, and found myself transported through the greening fields to the river.

My Ruth sat on the hanging rock, untrammeled by the stunted and perplexing life I'd put her through. She smiled and held out her hand. I settled beside her. We took off our shoes and hung our legs off the ledge, savoring the cool air that rose from the blue water.

I required no prompt from Ignacio.

"Ruth," I said.

"Steven. I'm here."

"Help me make sense of this story."

"I can't. It is not mine to decipher."

"I just need a little guidance. Am I only here because my mother dreamed me coming?"

"Might that be reason enough?"

"I don't know. Please tell me. Please."

"Must there be only one reason?"

"I don't know."

"Must there be any reason at all?"

"What is there to give to my children, if I have no reason?"

You must answer your own question.

I looked to the water. I could see right through the blue, into the whole underwater terrain with its depths and features, eddies and schools. I saw how far it was to the bed, even out there beyond the jutting rock. The trout that mustered in its shelter, hiding at lee to take my bait, were but small representation of the multitude that swam beneath us. Silver fingerlings intercepted the sunlight, their shadows stippling the stones and waving plants below. Gold motes spiraled behind the fan-tailed fish, galaxies and cosmic dust. Engrossed in the wordless beauty I nearly forgot I was rockbound above it. Ruth sat beside me, caught up in her own visions but attuned.

I saw a long shadow, sinister and very deep, submerged in a chasm of bedrock a hundred feet down. The shadow rose, and as it emerged from its low lair I shielded my eyes from the iridescent scales. I quailed at the muscular strength, its languorous gesture. The forked head rose, tentacled and swiveling on the sinuous neck. Somehow the creature gave me consolation in its grotesque but exceeding beauty. I knew it had no name. As it rose toward the sunlight it appeared to have many eyes, like a peacock's tail, but I knew they were not eyes. They were not, and yet they were indeed.

I stood on air, rapt. I leaned back against the force of the creature's draw. I rolled and banked as if swimming in light water. The sun floated far above and I could see infinite night, Bear Lake blue, beyond.

"Ruth!" I cried. "Do you see it?"

I do not. And yet I do indeed.

Connie Porter Anderson

It seemed those last years that Steve was settling into the man he was intended to be. He kept up regular work, combatting the cycling returns enough to redeem his reputation with the Union Pacific. Firemen were becoming an oldtime breed as steam power gave way to diesel; we all thought he'd become an engineer, maybe even advance to conductor. He loved to describe the intricacies of the cross-country routes. He knew every bend in the tracks, the angles of the mountain passes, the pitches of twisting valleys and the precise distances between each consecutive range. When we gathered in Ora he'd come in an easy mood with Ruth and their sons. He'd chaperone a herd of kids out to the river to fish and come back laughing and tumbling among them. My son Tommy was enamored of his uncle Steve, mimicking his jokes and gestures and looking after Ronnie and Richie as if they were his younger brothers. I feared Steven's wild heart in Tommy and watched my son for signs of that darkness. But as Steve's boys grew toward manhood I came to believe, at least, that the worst was behind them.

As for Ruth, I never felt like I was fully acquainted but we learned to sit on the back porch and enjoy light conversation. She bristled like a porcupine at the slightest whiff of religion, and so we veered off of that when all of us were together. Such suppression made for long silences. My family's faith infused us and we did not know how to unthread it from our casual talk. It must have seemed we were withholding ourselves from her.

We weren't, but then again we were. Can we be blamed for that? Ruth wished to be included among us yet would not abide the saving truths that bound us. Heaven must not be forfeited no matter how we might long for the lost. Never in her presence could we express our sorrow that she had drawn our brother from us, that by her influence our family was rent.

But in the mortal meantime the men frolicked and fished, and we women cooked and gossiped and washed the dishes. They seemed so timeless, those summer afternoons we all sat together. Eternity dropped like a curtain, preserving the scene more sharply as memory than it ever was in the moment.

Steven Porter

The peacock serpent, or whatever that thing was, gave me solace precisely in this way: I knew it would wait. It would always be there. Sometimes I walked out to the river just to sense it beneath the water, to draw strength for another bout of living on. And I knew it would rise from the chasm when I called it.

You want to know the tipping point?

It arrived, that's all. The strength of my mother's dream ran out, cinders beneath the boiler. I was left to my own composition, and I simply wasn't made to cohere.

The revelation was right there all along: I was dropped onto the planet, I took joy in the glittering beauty of a purposeless world, and then it was time to leave it to the poor players still willing to strut and fret their parts upon the stage. I'm sorry for my boys but I had no more to give them living than I did stone dead. I took too much from my wife Ruth, both in life and death. That's my one true regret.

I drove my pickup out to Ruby Valley, across the Nevada line. No reason but I'd been through it a few times. I was drawn to it as somewhere and absolutely nowhere at once. It was serene and remote, one of those sweeping desert stretches that conveys the only good meaning of eternity. I enjoyed the long drive, turning south again just shy of Elko and bumping along a dirt road at the base of tilted slopes until I felt the urge to stop.

I parked along the marsh line. I left my rod and tackle in the cab and waded through shallow water. I walked a few miles east toward the merging of sage and sky, savoring the muted colors. I whistled little tunes to myself. I recited a couple of Connie's beloved verses.

Little Lamb, who made thee?

The gun came smooth from the holster. A single motion and I was done. So sweet. So simple and right.

Stella Jeppson Porter

I see him approach as he strides in from the fields. He is young and strong, lit up by the sun just as I dreamed him. He bursts through the back door as if doors were a personal affront. His boot heels pound across the pine plank floor. He leans toward the basin, fills and drinks a tall glass of water in four gulps. He fills the glass again and drains it like he's made of sand.

His hair falls over one eye.

His high cheeks glow peach and rose.

He wipes his forehead with his hand, and then his hand on his trousers.

He gives Mae a little punch on the shoulder.

"Bye, Pillbug."

Her eyes follow him, bedazzled. He yanks open the door, steps out, heads for the outhouse. We hear the door bang shut. We hear the door fling open. He whistles and the dog rockets toward him. I catch a few notes of a wordless tune floating back on the autumn breeze.

And he is gone again, already.

IGNATIUS

My God. Maybe I've had enough. Let me go home to my own descendants. Maybe my grandmother was right: why dwell on such tragic tales?

You're in too deep. Sudden withdrawal will harm you, distorting all that you dream.

What, like meth?

I do not understand your meaning.

I do not understand my meaning, either. How do I return?

Return is eternal. There is nothing but return.

I'm not yet ready to believe that's true. Derrida says the real future is the one we have never seen. I take that to mean our children may still have a few surprising options.

Who the fuck is Derrida?

Never mind. Send me one last guide. Someone to help me find my mother's lost people. Please. I want to bring them to her while I can. So many early deaths—no one to preserve the stories. Her mother's whole family vanished, so young, so many consecutive generations. So many well-meaning replacements insisting on their erasure. How can you tell a four-year-old to quit crying for the sudden disappearance of all she understands? She sure did learn to stop the tears. Taught us to do the same. Do we even exist—did we ever exist—if the stories, even the imperfect ones, even the fragments, dissipate with the tellers?

My leg hurts.

Mine too. So I want a guide on this one. Rational, undramatic, sympathetic. Like my mother.

Woman, all you have to guide you through this last mystery is the internet. You've run the well of revelation dry. I'm very old, and I'm tired. You purport to be a scholar, do you not? Find her people within the Babel of that lighted box. They do trace themselves in her; you will recognize them as they speak unto your mind.

Give me a head start. How far back before we find something familiar? An origin—not just a genealogy?

Not so far, in my reckoning. A long time in yours. Begin in Providence, say, 1800. They are, already, five generations made by this perplexing and violent New World. You will be among fellow Americans.

Okay.

Two brothers, Silas and Festus Sprague, seven years apart.

Twin sisters, Barbara Ann and Millicent Lindenberger.

The brothers are first cousins to the sisters.

Now a multi-family removal to the Ohio frontier. A ricochet of marriages and a sensible family's capitulation to a story of American angels. A trek to a landscape alien as a moon.

My mother wants me to disentangle an administrative forgetting: "The record says that Barbara Ann is married to *either* Silas Sprague, or Festus Sprague. Which is it? We need to get it right."

Her urgency is different from mine: she wants to put those old lives in order. She wants to send correct information to Salt Lake City, so the Mormon Church can make the long-ago union eternally official.

I wish to deconstruct.

But we're both leaning over the same diorama. So I'll do the homework, and then I'll walk her in. I will be my mother's guide.

INVOCATION: TOOELE VALLEY THRENODY

Barbara

B y the time my dust went to dust in Utah's waning summer heat, I had left a dark astronomy of gravestones behind me that spanned nearly a century and a continent. It was my husband Festus who spent his life trying to make sense of it all, straining toward pattern and transcendence. I put up with this because—well, we have to think about something in our short season of daylight, and Festus had good reason to seek. But it was me, finally, who rose up babbling prophecies.

My father was a toolmaker in Rhode Island, come out of Boston. Lindenberger was a successful name, made more so during the Revolution when loyal Americans boycotted English goods. Even so, a craftsman's wealth set poorly with my mother's family, Providence Spragues, enamored of letters and politics, prone to admire the flourish of their own signatures. Our Sprague cousins up in Cayuga met with awful fortune in 1810. Uncle Stephen and his wife and two of five boys died in a month, all of the brain fever. Silas, that year sixteen, and Rhoda, just younger, sold everything they could not carry in a light wagon. They made their way to Providence, cajoling two younger brothers and carrying the little girl, four hundred miles under hard circumstance. For a season they lived among us, Festus and Alpheus and baby

Millicent. We called her, simply, "Baby" because my twin sister, too, was Millicent. Patterns of names, generation by family by generation. Silas and Rhoda stayed nearby with other kin. I admired them but was always a bit afraid, partly for the natural awe a child feels for older cousins, but also because they seemed another breed from us. That journey had made them preternaturally capable, but immune to the warmer tones of human reach.

My father offered him an apprenticeship, but Silas wanted what was left of them to live together again. He spoke to our uncles and to my father as if he were already a man, and in truth there was no boy left in him. His mother had come from the Ohio territory, and Silas had a deep conviction that the western frontier was the place to start anew.

Our brother Christopher, enamored of Silas, said at supper, "I'm going with them."

Father said, "You picture yourself the young Meriwether Lewis, is that what?"

Christopher said, "*Mijn vader*, just imagine it. There's land out there just for the claiming. We could all go. I can help Silas and Rhoda carry the little ones out there safe. You can settle your affairs here and we could all move on."

"That country is a powder keg. Tecumseh eager to take the scalp off a yellow-haired upstart like you."

Christopher said, "I can't live afraid of Shawnee. And we already whipped the English," and Papa said, "Go on then, fool," but it was not precisely permission because Christopher was already alight.

My twin sister and I were of the age to dream of strong men and brave adventure. Early stirrings open a child to formative impressions. Our hearts fixed on Silas. He was by now seventeen, same as our impassioned brother, and we thought him very handsome. His dark tumbling hair thick and casual. His deep eyes were guarded and opaque, yet sharp and alert, the color of August foliage. His faceted shoulders lean. Millicent and I played with Festus, sweeter and at the time more like a girl than either of us. Long lashes, frail resonant voice like three small boys speaking in unison. He was born the same year as my sister and me, first year of the new century. In his company we were solicitous and maternal. His gray eyes opened wide when he talked, earnest in the expression of our childish games. It always seemed he was about to cry, whether from the joy or tragedy of any fantastical moment. In his every gesture the bewilderment of an orphaned child. We made him baby, little brother, lost kit. Nary man, nor husband.

After they departed, Millicent and I both yearned after Silas. At least I believe she did. It was so long ago I don't rightly recall what belongs to me and what to her.

Our cousin and brother came back two years later, bringing word of family, telling stories of war and Wyandots, green forests and newly cleared fields. My mother cried in Christopher's arms, her son a man, and then again when he told her he was married to Rhoda with a baby coming. Father sent them off with merely a wave.

But another two years and suddenly our father caught the Ohio spirit. Perhaps he had been putting his careful mind to the matter since the first departure. The war was over. His son's wife bearing children. Papa put notice in the papers, set our mother to provisioning, sold the bellows and forge and released the apprentice. He took a bad cut to his arm helping lift a barrel but paid it little mind. When Silas and Christopher came to guide us out, Festus was with them. He was more slender than his brother had been, still seeming frail but only due to his manner. Festus was made by backwoods New York, and now rough Ohio. He was tall and pretty, very strong, but Millicent and I had always made him a little brother. He stared around himself as if he had chanced upon Athens of antiquity. Wide-eyed, surprised by the crowded streets, the grand walls of the churches and smooth university lawns. Festus blushed and turned away when

Providence girls tried to capture his gaze, while Christopher and Silas strode through the city as if returning heroes.

All was rush and preparation. Once his forge was disposed of, excess tack and tools carried away, Father was almost drunk with anticipation. Then he caught ill, his arm swollen and red. He was hale all his life, but after three or four days it was clear to him and all of us that he was finished. Another week and we stood around the dead man, our mother uncomprehending, the rest of us amazed, straining to know what it meant. And it meant, of course, that there was nothing to keep us. We were going to Ohio.

Millicent

When I try to rise it is from beneath, or behind, the frigid hold of fever. Secret ice rising from the black swamp draining. The steaming summer green.

Even so I am filtered through the waning bones of Barbara Ann, who was my own body and not. Our distanced deaths finally only one, as was our birth. In Barbara my image extending, flesh, womb, muscle, bone, our long brown hair graying on her aging head, her long years depleting our youthful height.

I was the prettier one. Folks remarked how perfectly we were twinned, but in truth and to our separate grief, the men who courted us began with her. Stronger features, or a stronger soul behind them. I was bashful. She attracted them first, but then the young bachelors turned to me, soothing their impetuous inclinations. Something about my sister—her frank replies, her gaze forthright like a man's—made even Silas fearful, and so the shift, a turn of eye and heart to softer me.

I married Silas Sprague on the Ohio frontier in the same season we arrived to join his family, who were also ours. I was almost eighteen and he twenty-four. Barbara stood as maid, never allowing an emotion.

I would speak something for Silas but as wife and husband

we were too brief. I was in a state of becoming, too new to know myself. In Ohio country in 1818, a young woman might die by bear or cougar or wild hog. She could be taken by miscarriage, heavy weather, even Indian attack, although by now this was old fear more than likelihood. Vapors rose up from the ancient swamps as the men dug drainage. Cold fever stalked the settlements, and although Olive Green was set high and known for healthy air, still the malady could find its way. It courted those of courting age, stalked young parents in their prime, left the little ones and old folks bereft. It seized us in summertime, set us to melancholy and emanations of horror. Cold fever blued the skin, seeped inward to the vitals, freezing us in the midsummer heat.

Barbara

I mourned the loss of my sister twice and in quick succession, the second time so awful that recalling the wedding became a source of comfort. Silas vanished into the uncleared groves and worked himself to insensibility. Our mother descended into a long twilight of half-remembrance, a middle place between living and living dissolution. In Mama's mind, Millicent had never disappeared because the copy stood before her daily. She called me Barbara Ann, or "Melisaint," or even the names of her four sisters, dead one by one in Providence, each by fifteen. To my mother until she died, I was the bodily sign of never-occurred. Never-twisted, never-frail, never-grimaced, never-phantasmic.

Silas swore he was marrying me, not some resurrected sister, on our wedding day. Our families had been commingling for so many generations it was inevitable. The family temperaments were compatible, a web of support and relation. Yet I had been taken for so many others, and I had recalled so often that Silas had chosen my sister first, that I made my vow in a disposition something like resigned, something like hopeful. Silas looked older than he was but it became him, and my mother murmured,

"Praise the Father hallelujah." Christopher slapped him heartily on the back, and my sweet cousin Festus, now brother-in-law, kissed my cheek in congratulation. My sister Mary and her fat husband Pompey Mason, notorious for never confessing Christ, hosted the celebration and by the late night it truly was an occasion of joy and restoration.

By May I was heavy and due to deliver. Rhoda and my sisters sat with me while Mama rocked in her own personal night, although it was broad day. Silas seemed nearly joyful, although restrained, and late afternoon he went out for the midwife. He took his gun for the sake of habit, slinging the long barrel over his shoulder. I heard his black horse pivot in the hard dirt and sensed the first low rolling of thunder. Mary stood at the door and told us the storm was a good way off. We waited, and night fell, and we waited yet, but the storm and the baby did not. Mama came to good enough sense when Rhoda took her by the arm and showed her the crowning, told her to warm linens. I called for Silas and my daughter came, but not the midwife, and never again my husband.

Festus

She was beautiful, the one I loved, strong and ready for the long life ahead. The little girl was bright and fierce. When I found the courage to ask Barbara to marry me she said, "Festus, we've been easy between the two of us since we were children. I imagine we can make a good life together."

The wife I had always longed for. At the cost of my brother, her husband.

Rosamond

I called him Pa, never queried after the other, but for one day. When I was twelve years old, I asked, "Can't you tell me something to make him true to me?"

And Festus said, "Come on then."

He reached to the hook, took a straw hat, put it on my head. "He was plenty real. This was his. Now it's yours. Let's walk."

We set out beyond the road into the forest, dark and dappled and down a path he said was once open and bright as it led to the old midwife's place. In my later life I might forget for months about that day with my almost father—my father's brother—walking the overgrown path under the summer-straw hat of Silas Sprague. But then, even until my old age, the scene would come back very sudden, as if I were a thin girl again returned to a vanished world. We walked up a small rise to an open spot, just big enough to be a meadow. Festus strode to the center. Turned around and watched me come to him. "There you are, walking his same road. He never reached the midwife, so we know he was coming this direction."

I approached, stood with him where my father was struck. I said, "I keep trying to make some meaning of it."

"We all do. None of us can stop ourselves. When we found him the ground surrounding him was written on, like an Indian picture. The very same marks down his back and leg. Folks call them lightning flowers. It's the natural work of electricity but even so I'm overcome by a sense of significance. Like signs in a language I can't read. How could it mean nothing at all, to be electrified the very day his first child is coming?"

We stood in the meadow, the light perfectly transparent. Air blue and yellow together. That sweet true note of the redwings. Pound of a peckerwood. If Festus hadn't stood there and told me, the meadow would never have revealed a thing, no matter how long I stood, no matter how many times I walked along my father's path. The meadow lay shining, as if everything could only ever mean itself. Nothing else.

Festus said, "His horse was still standing there. Looked the same, but turned out he was addled. Couldn't recall how to chew grass or drink water. Didn't run, but didn't know us, either. Couple days later we understood and put him down."

Silas

Never learned whether son or daughter, quick or still. As I rode I spoke to myself, a hard talking-to. Shouted out loud that I had to come back to the human race. I was young, not old. I was about to be a father; I truly hoped a gentler one than mine, a stalwart man and unyielding. I shouted out to myself over the thickening atmosphere, the pounding hooves, "This is your child coming! Your wife in throes you caused! Rise up and return to life and season!"

An answering strike. And now, the emphatic dark.

Festus

I knew the Mormons were working Delaware County. They came down from Kirtland as often as other itinerants, but in our county they had scant congregation to hear them. The Methodist pastor and the Moravians and even the Blacktown preacher set their people to vigilance. Each community appeared quiet when the elders arrived, all of us instructed to act as if nothing were irregular. That is precisely what I had done until 1840: obeyed the preacher and deacons, turned my back to the Mormon missionaries. My people the kind to mind their own faith, leaving others to theirs. Old man, bearded, and always a younger companion, sometimes clean-shaven and always bright-countenanced. I saw my daughters Lucinda and Eveline, too young for flirtations, lift their eyes under their lashes toward the earnest young man.

That year I had lost an almost hopeful conviction that I would make sudden purchase like my brother Silas, or even like our parents and brothers. By then if I ever understood a sign it was that God intended to deplete my days in steady increments. But I did not comprehend what he meant for me to make of them. Why he took Silas, the better brother, and set me in his tracks.

The house in Olive Green was filled with children. They came up like trees. The chores of each day laid Barbara and me down so tired at evening we hardly spoke. Every night I lay awake just long enough to sense old haunts recurring.

Barbara

Somehow the Mormons caught him on the right day. I was on my knees, not praying but pulling weeds from the kitchen garden, when I saw them approach. I smiled to myself, knowing Festus would tip his hat and turn his back, but something the older man said caught his attention and my husband started as if he'd been struck from above. He leaned in listening. He gestured with his right hand toward the sky, bringing it down, pointing there, there, and there at the ground around his feet, redrawing the jagged lines. I had never seen nor heard him tell that story but I knew exactly what he was portraying, line by line. I shuddered and went in with my dirty hands.

Of course I had not seen Silas fallen in the meadow. The hard truth of that view belongs to his brother, who went to retrieve the body as I nursed my baby daughter in her conception bed. That night my own image of Silas was seared immutable upon my mind: timeless, transfigured by a blinding bolt to gleaming glass. Vertical and naked: smooth hard suspension over the wreckage of mortal flesh. In my diminishing dreams, even now, I reach to caress.

Festus came in the door with the Mormons speaking of signs and translations, the whole American continent the burgeoning Celestial Kingdom, the ground shining up like crystal, one great Urim and Thummim. Festus was a good man but in his manner timid. Silas the better lover, Festus likely the kinder father. Festus intelligent and esteemed but inconfident in his personal wisdom.

But on this day he stood with his brother's stature and a burning conviction. Our last child rolled inside me eager to arrive. And everything changed for us.

Rosamond

I was seventeen and strong-willed and I wanted nothing to do with the grand immersion. I had appointed myself defender of the old order, speaker for the lost. I fancied that somehow I was not only the child of the electric man but also the daughter of my mother's twin sister, dramatically young and obscured in the emerald secrets of the old wilderness. I sat on the bank of Sugar Creek to watch the usurpers go under the water and rise up Mormon, filled with the Holy Ghost and ready to hold forth in prophecy. I may have wished in some deep portion of my mind that the Latter-Day Spirit would release the tongues of my wet people, that my parents could speak some fiery truth in the voices of the dead who haunted them, but the one revelation of the day was my mother's condition; when she came up, the water showed her contours.

I watched my sisters Lucinda and Eveline lifted from the symbolic grave, silly and shrieking although Lucinda acquired an air of almighty importance soon enough. Little Fess went down and came up calm and decided, harbinger of the man he intended to be. Edwin hated the water after nearly drowning as a tyke, but he would not be outdone by William. They went under together and came up gasping the same way they were born, in quick succession. The littlest girls, Emily and Dorcas, played near me on the bank in the Indian summer light until our mother was dry and put together. I maintained a stone countenance but I soon realized I was in no temper to align myself with the townfolk, either.

People in Olive Green were stunned and censorious. Any time we came nigh, familiar faces smoothed themselves to taut inscrutability. Neighbors and old friends and even family patronized my mother as if she had lost her wits. Aunt Mary and Uncle Pompey affected an ironic little air of toleration and townsmen stopped conversing when Festus approached. They would greet him and feign camaraderie but yield no personal or communal confidence. One local wit behind me at the mercantile said, "Your ma's plenty enough for one man to handle, ain't she? What's got into that Festus Sprague? That old man got the stamina to be Mormon?" and everyone laughed but Willard Green, recently come down from Chenango and just then stepped in from the street. Willard so big he looked like a brown bear had ambled in, and he said to me, "Lady, you need me to knock the stamina clean out of this jackass?"

Festus

An uncontrollable mechanism of my mind clicked into a perpetual circuit the day I took my brother's daughter to the meadow. Afterward I went back to that place again and again, like a dog returning for a stolen bone. I went back like a drunkard to a hidden cache, looking over my shoulder to slip away quiet, hoping none would witness my compulsions. After we joined the Mormons, I thought I would find peace but I instead redoubled. I believed if I prayed fervent, banishing doubt I might be granted the key to understanding. But I did not believe well enough. The Prophet Joseph went to the woods to pray in perfect faith, nothing wavering. Satan took his mind and body but just as the boy thought all was lost, God the Father and his son Jesus came to him in a pillar of light, bright as the noonday sun.

I asked for nothing of that magnitude. I could descend into mental darkness without the help of Satan, and I simply hoped for some key to legibility. I never understood my calling. Silas was destined to be a great man, cut out to be the patriarch of a grand family, a godly city, apostle of the Restoration. Yet he was cut short, his destiny installed in me, the wrong brother, the absolutely wrong man. I feared I saw it in Barbara's face in the late nights of our privacy. I sensed Rosamond suppressing her indignation though she never spoke an ungrateful word to me. I felt it every time I wrote my name in my brother's stead, agent for his property, laying out roads with my wife's brother Christopher, my brother's bosom friend.

I remembered the figures in the meadow all my life, every line and angle. I could project the whole scene before me like a magic lantern, sometimes at will and sometimes against it: Silas fallen like an ancient warrior, face to the sky and wet in the diminishing rain. Intermittent moonlight. The tall black gelding. The lightning's writing in rays like hieroglyphs, visible for months even beneath the summer flora that rose to obscure it.

The Prophet Joseph could set a seer stone in the crown of his hat and summon scripture, the mysteries of the universe laid bare, the ear of his ear attuned to the language of heaven. Joseph could read the marks on gold plates and ancient papyrus with the clarity of Adam's pure language. *If any of ye lack wisdom, let him ask of God, who giveth to all men liberally, and upbraideth not, and it shall be given him.* And yet God was not liberal in this way with me. I went to the meadow in daylight. I went in the dark night. I strode out in a thunderstorm, pleading for a strike. A key. A stone. A breastplate. An angel. A spirit.

God gave me half a gift. A message, but never, in all my days, illumination to read it.

Rosamond

My mother feared it was unwomanly the way I clung to independence. Willard Green the only man who didn't see it so. I kept him waiting until I was twenty-five before forfeiting the schoolroom and my own pay. Willard, an orphan since ten, had fled a cruel apprenticeship at thirteen. He had grown to enjoy the ways of solitude. And so we made a queer and happy pair, liking but not for many years needing each other's propinquity. We headed for Iowa soon after our sons Silas and Emerson were born. Once I had some distance, my heart frankly softened to the Mormon cause—if not to the precepts then at least my family's unity of conviction. Willard said it made as much sense as any other nonsense, and he didn't dislike the idea of moving further west. Mormon immigrants flowed continuously through Iowa and sometimes we helped them outfit. My mother sent letters with friends and friendly strangers. In 1850 my sister and brother passed through. Lucinda was married to James Bay, the company captain. My young brother Fess was tall and growing a beard. His eyes were green and deep-set. His voice was warm and resonant. He told us the twins were nearly as grown as he was, the little girls noisy, and I said, "If the folks ever go out, we'll come on with them."

Lucinda, important now as the wife of a grand pioneer, said, "Best not delay your salvation. Every knee must bend, every tongue confess the only true and living gospel," which caused me to delay my salvation quite a while longer and caused Willard to say, "Well, it might just be easier to let someone do it for us after we're dead. I believe that's my favorite doctrine of your religion."

Lucinda sniffed. James Bay looked stern and intoned, "The doctrine of vicarious endowment is not designed to be a short-cut to exaltation, sir."

Willard said, "Guess I'll take the extremely long route, then."

Fess grinned, ducked his head, and went out.

Barbara

It was five long years in Ohio I didn't see Lucinda or Fess and hardly Rosamond. By then we had a small but tight-knit Mormon congregation. We met in the Sunbury schoolhouse, scheduling hours around the Methodists. Our neighbors had mostly got used to the fact of our peculiar faith but we endured a barrier, a mistrust never fully eased even though Spragues and Lindenbergers had laid out this township in the first place. We came from strong family, educated in fine universities. We were hardworking and judicious people, long accustomed to the esteem of our fellows. Mostly I could dismiss the social encasement but it wore on us. Finally I said, "Festus, we enlisted with a new tribe. Olive Green's showed us all the hospitality it intends. Why don't you walk on out to that meadow and ask God or Silas or whoever you think will answer whether we shouldn't dwell in the mountains and desert with the people we've chosen."

Festus gave me that little-boy stare of his. He went out, and came back much later and said, "Well, nothing told me to go. Nothing told me to stay."

"Then let me be the voice of inspiration. Let's pack up and go."

Millicent

Did the bright air above my slow silent night alter when they left me here? Did a part of me pursue, or was it just the old image of myself in my sister, remembered and forgotten in the dimming of our family mind? I can't say. Too long gone.

Silas

To whom will ye liken me, and make me equal, and compare me, that we may be like?

Barbara

Truth is, I wished to leave my sister to her impenetrable business. And Silas too. And by now my dead mother. Olive Green, Ohio, belonged to them, not us.

Festus

So many have told embellished tales of their journey from the soft green of the East to the hard blue West. Immigrants to Utah clung to tales of hardship to make themselves heroes and visionaries. Believed they were owed something for it. All I have to say is, America is a broad continent and we were grateful to witness a long stretch before the railroad changed it forever. Barbara and I were fifty-seven and fifty-six, too old for such adventure but the trail was established. Our children were grown and strong and made it mostly easy for us. Barbara seemed relieved to depart, uncannily young and light in her legs and shoulders. She was joyful to find Rosamond and Willard and their tall boys in Iowa, loaded to accompany us. Barbara loved the nights under the stars and did not fear the sound of wolves in the darkness. She became a woman I had not known nor ever imagined in such a way. After the plains and then the Rockies I believed that the very sensation of Ohio, humid and mulched and rolling in the hue of trees, had been beaten clean out of me. But we do not step so easy from the landscapes of memory. After the first season of adjusting, I dreamed each night in Olive Green, then woke each day to the blinding blanch of the Great Salt Lake.

Barbara

Young Fess rode his horse to Red Butte the evening of our last encampment. I could hardly take the vision in, my beloved son, easy stance in the arid sunset. A white penumbra shone about his head and shoulders from the unearthly backglow of the inland sea, which did not resemble water so much as a sheet of immense and burning glass.

Festus

He looked like the angel I had been seeking all my life. He came up the trail light in the saddle, a natural cowboy. This was no Sprague my Providence grandfathers would discern. His smile brightened the shade under his wide hat brim. My son, the image of my brother in the new dispensation, dismounted and reached first for my hand in a manly shake, and then a strong pull to embrace me.

We sat long around the campfire, every one of us together there in the desert twilight: each of our children, grown, and our grandchildren growing, alive and vivid, laughing and swapping stories and still more coming. The city below lay visible in entirety like an unfurled map.

We settled in to sleep, one more night in transit under the Big Bear and the Pleiades and Milky Way.

My old mind returned, and I murmured, "Why isn't it Silas here?"

Barbara rolled, a bit laborious, and turned her face toward mine.

"Festus, don't you ever ask me that question again. Don't ask God that question again. Don't ask the prophet, don't ask the scriptures, don't even ask the devil. Here we are surrounded by our children. Rosamond's as much yours as she is your brother's. More. He never spent an hour with her.

"Everyone that matters is here surrounding us. I don't care what anybody says about the coming order. I've seen nothing of it. All I've seen is vanishment. This is you here, not your brother. This is myself, not my sister. If Silas and Millicent wanted this, they should not have gone and got themselves dead. We are Festus and Barbara, warm and breathing right now under this celestial night, shored up by all the significance we have a right to ask for."

Barbara

Next morning we awoke and descended with the rising sun behind us. The long shadow of the mountains pulled off the flat valley bed like a lavender coverlet.

Young Fess had a little cabin nearly built for us in the Tooele Valley, forty miles farther west in a new settlement with an unsettled name, but the year was troubled by the federal march and Indian anger and so the whole town, once Twenty Wells, then Willow Creek, now trying out its new name Grantsville, was evacuated. We waited several weeks in temporary quarters in Salt Lake with Fess and his wife Lydia before traveling a short day west. On that day we followed the arc of the salt-aproned waterline and then took a sharp turn southward to our new home. For a while it was small and rustic living, more like bivouac than habitation, but I confess I was almost regretful that the conditions improved. Something cleansing in my mind about making do.

The more I acclimated, however, the more I found myself trying to convey this strange yet strangely familiar landscape to my dead sister, buried deep in the fertile soil of Olive Green. I worked continuous words in my mind, straining to describe to her the granite fortress of Deseret Peak, its upper walls so sheer the snow could not cling. I had long told Festus to stop dwelling over the dead, but in this distant place Millicent became less and yet more a part of me. Speaking to her was a way of talking myself into clearer states of mind. I tried to explain how the west mountains contoured the bottom edge of sky at sunset, high evergreen forests packed in angular canyons and lining the northward slopes. I described the sheer blue barrier that rose between us and the Salt Lake Valley, cutting into the shifting pools of uncertain shoreline. There was no means to depict, to an unmade girl lost in the deciduous hues of old Ohio, the glittering sheets of shoreline salt, the unrippled mirror of the famous brine lake evaporating in the desert sun, the barren geometry of islands inverted in the depthless mercury.

Had it not been for Millicent I may have gradually forgotten to note the strange light and its endless variations, because the days rose quickly to the old surprises of mortality. In the long view death is such a mundane story it seems we would become inured to the shock of it. But never so. Our Emily married and bore two little sons, but then lost her husband in a throw from an unbroke horse. Young Fess and Lydia had three little girls, one named for Lydia's dead parents, the next for me, and the last named Lydia in memory of her mother, who died delivering her. Lucky all their lives to live among parents and siblings and now their own offspring, my children reeled at the losses, but like we all do learned to get on in an altered state.

My husband Festus was aging and as far as I know he had ceased his secret habit of pleading. Sure he said the right words in Sunday meetings, and he blessed the food and laid his hands on the heads of those in need of Melchizedek power. But the man had stopped his old beseeching, whether from despair or satisfaction or complacency I do not know. Once on a warm spring day we all walked out to see the Indian writing on the peninsula. My husband gazed and scratched his head, tracing the lines with his bent fingers. Little goats and antlered deer. Horned warriors. Suns and wavy lines and something like rivers, and stars or planets. Lightning. I put my hand to my forehead and braced for a relapse of sign-seeking but Festus said, almost absently, "Aren't they pretty," and turned back to the bread and cheese, apples and air and boisterous grandchildren.

My husband took a particular heart to those motherless little girls. They stayed with us in the daytime while their father rode herd. Grandpa took them on picnics. He let them ride the gentle pony he'd bought to pull our provision cart. He set them in the wagon and drove them to the shore, bringing them home with their bare feet sunburned and limbs powdered in salt. Young Fess remarried, a girl named Mary, seventeen years younger than him. She had an older way about her and made a good home, and bore him a son. I thought we'd reached an untroubled spell but then Lydia, six, died of the whooping cough.

This one we could not philosophize.

My son disappeared into the foothills every day, cattle his alibi, leaving his wife in care of the darkened household. My husband sat in the tall wooden chair on the back porch and stared toward the Oquirrh Mountains, or maybe through them to Ohio. Finally I said, "Festus, get up. Your son needs your good example," and he stood and shook himself like a wet hound. He walked across the field and over the stile to stand in wait for our son. When Fess came in late, I saw them both in full moonlight confrontation, the old man pointing his finger and pushing a bit at the chest and shoulders of the younger. Far as I could see, there was no effect. Young Fess took it standing still and then walked stiff and stricken into his low-lit house.

But next morning he came out with the two girls frolicking and giggling and little Orlando in his arms. Mary stood on the porch and then sank to her knees overcome, and Fess turned back, took her by the hand, and they walked together toward our place.

My husband kept up a show of good spirit on into winter, but one morning no different from any other that I could tell, he put on his long overcoat, laid his rowboat over the wagon, and said he was going out to think in solitude. Although Great Salt Lake water is too saline to freeze, it can churn and cap and overturn a boat in bad weather. But on this day the wind was low and the sun quite warm. I said, "Festus, I'm worried you'll get yourself all worked up out there, pleading for some kind of revelation," and he answered, "You know I'm through with that."

I sent him out with milk and bread and a pocket of dried pears. I waved goodbye and told him to come back safely, and for the second time I waited a vain and endless night for a husband's return. After the funeral Rosamond whispered, "A man's got to work hard to drown in the Great Salt Lake."

But no one beyond that asked me what were his intentions, and in truth I do not know. I never had any gift of prophecy or discernment beyond the common wisdom to know there was no foreseeing the hand of death. It comes when it wants, and no spell of grief or joy or peace or fear before it provides a sign. Maybe this knowledge was my sister's gift to me, and our brief husband's, but I can't see how any person can live long in this world without acquiring it.

But for all that I must have been grieving too deeply to maintain my good sense the day the rest of the Tooele Valley got fevered up over the outlaw Albert Haws, come out of Nevada after killing a man for no clear reason but the thrill. It was known he was in the area. He had kin among the Taway type who lived in the foothills, and somebody had heard Haws swear he was happy to kill again if the law was crazy enough to pursue him. The marshal in Salt Lake had issued a warrant. A federal man named Storey went out, and sure enough the criminal shot him down.

Next day our own sheriff mustered a posse and my son Fess was the first to volunteer. Mary, five months with child, looked at him in sheer disbelief, and I felt an old seize of horror and said, "Fess, you have three little ones. They've all been through too much for you to take such a foolish risk."

But Fess was caught up in some vivifying sense of manly purpose. I went home and like a fool, burdened with too much recent sorrow, fell to my knees and prayed to God for assurance and I felt it strike me with a force I believed was undeniable. I felt a burning certainty that my son would be delivered. I stepped out and I prophesied to the knot of gathered family and friends that he would return unharmed, just like the stripling warriors in the Book of Mormon. I said, "Ye never have fought, yet you do not fear death. You have been taught by your mother, that if you do not doubt, God will deliver you!"

Our neighbors nodded in hope and recognition, and off he rode with the eager posse, disappearing into the sage and juniper foothills.

We all heard the shots. One hit my son, and seven the outlaw. The men said Fess volunteered to follow Haws's trail into the juniper blind of a deep ravine while the rest held back. All praised his courage but I cannot account for his foolhardiness. Maybe my certainty had assured him, or maybe he had lost a certain cling to love and life.

The posse carried my son home, shot through the chest but still breathing, and I bore witness to the gathered crowd that I knew it would all be well, that God had sealed the promise of mighty Helaman. I declared that his good wife and his little children would be blessed with the long life of my son Festus Sprague. The doctor stayed all night and so did I, taking turns with Mary sitting at the bedside. In the morning the doctor confirmed to the delegation outside that Fess had taken a good turn, that he'd be back among us in no time. "In a few months," the doctor told us, "it will simply be an exciting story to tell our descendants."

Fifteen minutes later my son sat up, eyes warm and golden green. He looked about to speak, but then he coughed blood, and seemed amazed, and was dead before he fell back.

Rain fell a full day and night. Everyone but me called it a blessing.

Lucinda justified my spiritual certainty this way: truly all was well as I had prophesied. Fess was in his heavenly home, reunited with his father, with Uncle Silas and Aunt Millicent, with his first wife and his beloved little daughter. He was preaching to the dead who had not yet heard the gospel, preparing them for vicarious baptism. He was staking a heavenly homestead for our exalted reunification.

Rosamond explained it like this: only so much a human heart can stand. Then the mind finds ways to trick us into risking yet another mortal day.

Rosamond

After Fess went down the family scattered. We left him buried beside his father and his two Lydias. The twins went south and Edwin, who always hated water, kept right on to Arizona. Lucinda and James Bay held family council and proposed to Emily together, the first and last in our family to practice plural marriage. We all thought it was just as well. Emily's heart for any semblance of florid romance was gone, and this contract returned her to the skein of legal relations. By then Lucinda was to me unreadable. She was a hardworking woman, gone nearly rigid in her devotion to the purifying cause of the Latter-Day Saints. Her children spoke in the pompous and didactic tones of their father, who despite his high public righteousness was also a good man after his best lights. And so I chose to admire their enfolding gesture, even though it also heightened Bay's esteem in the visible ranks of the Kingdom and probably broke Lucinda's waning delusions of perpetual bridehood. All the Bays took their children in this new configuration to the southward red rock country.

Our sister Miranda, born the year of Mormon immersion, was called up with her husband to settle Round Valley, up in the high cold country on the lower tip of Bear Lake: fresh blue snowmelt water, deep and full of fish and some said a monster in it. Mother said, "Of course there is," and departed with them.

My son Emerson married the young widow of my brother Festus. She was only a few years older than he. They finished raising my brother's children, and they made their own, and many of us now lie still in Yellowstone country, in an abandoned spot called Farnum after my middle name, after a road in New

England somehow significant to my mother. But I've forgotten why, because memory seeps into the swallowing land.

Fess Sprague

In my twentieth year I left my home in Olive Green, Ohio, and traveled with my older sister and her husband in the Sixth Handcart Company to the Great Salt Lake Valley. Doubtless the journey was tedious and exhausting, and possibly more dangerous than I perceived even while my brother-in-law felt compelled to intone over every single white grave we passed along the trail. But I was young and strong. I had neither wife nor children. The events that would define my brief legacy were incipient shades. I rode the fine horse my parents had purchased for me. I carried my rifle and scouted into the country well beyond the trail to bring back game for the women and children and family men. I gained some sense of the magnitude of America, its forests and rivers and prairies, and its native peoples whom the Prophet Joseph had revealed to be a branch of mighty Israel.

At the time I could not know that the span of my life was already at its apex. The world was beautiful and I moved easy in it. I perceived the truth of grief and time and slipping away but only secondhand; to me it was all the more evidence that the earth bore me, here and alive, an especial goodwill.

One night in Wyoming after we corralled the animals and turned to our fires and songs, after the smallest children were asleep and the parents about to settle in their wagons, I stepped away to check my horse. It would be my turn to watch before morning but I felt enlivened and alert and I even considered staying awake to read a while by the full moon, which was so bright it cast my shadow crisp on the ground as I walked. When we passed her home in Iowa my sister Rosamond had tucked a pamphlet in my coat pocket, a long poem by Ralph Waldo

Emerson. I was working to memorize it as I rode the long prairie miles:

> The eager fate which carried thee
> Took the largest part of me:
> For this losing is true dying;
> This is lordly man's down-lying,
> This his slow but sum reclining,
> Star by star his world resigning.

As I said, I was young and thought none of this applied to me, so I was in fine condition to savor the beautiful human tragedy of it all. The heartbreaking verses of a grieving New England father struck thrilling chords in my romantic heart. And then just as I reached the corral I heard a woman in the encampment cry, "Look up!"

I turned and lifted my face to see a star falling from the east, brighter than the full moon, streaking across the sky in a long shower of sparks. The geometric landscape lit up like a brief day, revealing its distant contours. Shadows swiveled left to right as the meteor blazed and sank and vanished at the western horizon. The scriptures say that one day on Kolob is a thousand years of our own; that night, until I forgot again, I sensed temporality as God comprehends it.

My parents always sought for the meaning of signs, hoping to discern the heavenly language of things. Maybe the shooting star that night really was a message, but if so I figured it was aimed toward someone else. I was lucky to stand and admire. And in my whole life, it was the most beautiful vision I ever had fortune to see.

GOODNIGHT, SAINT

M y mother has fallen and cracked her vertebrae. She is in great pain.
    My son is in a hospital, far from me, flailing among hallucinations.

His siblings stand bewildered.

The mountains of my home state are burning uncontained.

America, the beloved country, rent beyond retrieval.

I wish I could explain to my father, dead a mere twelve years.

(Ah, love, let us be true to one another!)

ABOUT THE AUTHOR

Karin Anderson is a gardener, writer, mother, wanderer, heretic, and English professor at Utah Valley University. She hails from the Great Basin of Utah.

TORREY HOUSE PRESS

Voices for the Land

The economy is a wholly owned subsidiary of the environment, not the other way around.
—Senator Gaylord Nelson, founder of Earth Day

Torrey House Press is an independent nonprofit publisher promoting environmental conservation through literature. We believe that culture is changed through conversation and that lively, contemporary literature is the cutting edge of social change. We strive to identify exceptional writers, nurture their work, and engage the widest possible audience; to publish diverse voices with transformative stories that illuminate important facets of our ever-changing planet; to develop literary resources for the conservation movement, educating and entertaining readers, inspiring action.

Visit www.torreyhouse.org for reading group discussion guides, author interviews, and more.

As a 501(c)(3) nonprofit publisher, our work is made possible by the generous donations of readers like you. Join the Torrey House Press family and give today at www.torreyhouse.org/give.

This book was made possible with grants from Utah Humanities, Utah Division of Arts & Museums, Jeffrey S. and Helen H. Cardon Foundation, Barker Foundation, and Salt Lake County Zoo, Arts & Parks; donations from ATL Technology, Wasatch Advisors, BookBar, The King's English Bookshop, Jeff and Heather Adams, Robert and Camille Bailey Aagard, Curt and Nora Nichols, and Paula and Gary Evershed; generous donations from valued individual donors and subscribers; and support from the Torrey House Press board of directors.

Thank you for supporting Torrey House Press.